GOLD $_2$ DUST

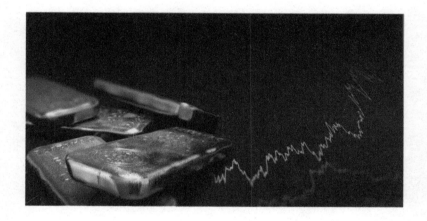

GOLD ₂ DUST

Jīnfěn   金粉

THE SEQUEL TO DARK POOLS

** TWO YEARS LATER **

BRIAN TERRY

AUTHORS NOTE

Gold 2 Dust is the second work in the Dark Pools series. It takes many of the characters lives forward two years when, yet again, another financial crisis looms on the near horizon. The world's gold markets are in turmoil and economic catastrophe seems only moments away…it's time to get the band back together again.

ACKNOWLEDGEMENTS:

A very special thank you is due to my dear friend Alasdair Macleod, whose incisive economic commentaries and thought provoking articles on the gold market were the inspiration for this book. All technical errors are, of course, the authors!

GRATEFUL THANKS:

Several people deserve special mention for reading and commenting upon early drafts: Mary, Alasdair, Lewis, John, Beth, Desiree, Lucy.

List of Principal Characters

Major Lyn Andrews	US Army Delta Force
Lieutenant Hazel Opie ("H")	US Army Communications Expert
Oakes and Walker	US Army Staff Sergeants
Ramos	MD ChinKo Inc, Panama
Charles Sheer	UK Prime Minister
Amanda Price	UK Chancellor of the Exchequer
Sir John d'Abo	Past Chairman of d'Abo's Merchant Bank
Lady Isobel d'Abo	Widow of Sir John d'Abo
Sebastian Fortes	Board Member of d'Abo's Merchant Bank
Dr Alex Cadbury	SQT
Lewis Moyns	Chairman, US Federal Reserve Bank, New York
Professor Dominic Carrington	Chairman, London Bullion Market Association
Sir David V Stone	Governor, Bank of England
General James Sanford	Head of Strategic Air Command, Europe
Pietro Zucca	Captain of the Jin-Ton
Captain Graham Rogers	HMAS Darwin
The Butler	Triad boss, Shanghai
Lieutenant Qiang Li	China Station Manager tracking the JinTon
General Xiao Fan	Head of the Chinese Army
Vice-Admiral John Oliver	Australian Chief of Defence Staff
Chen Liu	Deputy Governor, China Central Bank
Carter Meggs	Director, CIA
Robert Simpson	Disgraced ex-Chief Constable
Naylor	CIA operative
Sapphire	CIA operative
Reed	CIA, Hong Kong desk
Lord Harvey McMullan	Chairman, Barclays Bank
Emma Clarke	Head of MI5
Bill Coultard	US Ambassador to China

Abbreviations

The Fed	Federal Reserve Bank of New York
B of E	Bank of England, London
PBOC	People's Bank of China, Beijing
LBMA	London Bullion Market Association
COMEX	Commodities Exchange, New York
SQT	Saturn Quantum Trading, hedge fund, Connecticut
IMF	International Monetary Fund
CIA	Central Intelligence Agency, Langley (or the Company)
GCHQ	UK Government Communications Headquarters
SAC	Strategic Air Command
POTUS	President of the United States
MIA	Missing in Action
AWOL	Absent Without Leave
BIS	Bank for International Settlements

CHAPTER 1

Southern Somalia

The sniper's bullet travelled the 4,000 feet across the desolate landscape in a matter of milliseconds, viciously smashing into the man's chest, ending his life in the blink of an eye. The phenomenally destructive power of the second high-velocity projectile instantaneously decapitated the leader of the group; while the final four shots, all originating from the undercover Special Forces squad, rapidly took out the remaining members of the al-Shabaab insurgents. It was all over in a matter of moments, but had taken many months of covert preparation to accomplish. An eerie tranquillity returned to the surrounding shrub land.

The eight man reconnaissance team, led by Major Lyn Andrews, had been surreptitiously dropped into the country by helicopter, courtesy of the Australian navy, some five months earlier. With 'Phase One' of their mission now satisfactorily accomplished, they quickly commenced their withdrawal. The group had previously established a makeshift base-camp deep within Somalia's Lag Badana-Bushbush National Park, one hundred miles to the south, to which they now returned in high spirits. A mission-completed 'SitRep' was immediately dispatched to their commanding officer in Fort Bragg detailing the day's outcome and requesting instructions for the next part of their assignment.

The elite troop of US soldiers, attached to Delta Force, had been secretly tracking a rag-tag assortment of rebel terrorist cells, various militias of every hue, and innumerable tribal warlords for weeks. Their military objective was to feed back information about the seemingly endless catalogue of narcotics traders who were using the deep water port of Kismaayo to smuggle arms, explosives, contraband and drugs into nearby Kenya. It had taken Major Andrews, a highly experienced counter-insurgency specialist, many months to identify the real ring leaders; but their painstaking efforts, in combination with the invaluable intelligence information fed to them daily from CIA headquarters in Langley, had at last borne fruit. Once their targets had been successfully identified, it was only a matter of time before they were located and eliminated.

While the capital of Somalia, Mogadishu, located to the north of their current position, was the piracy and hijacking hub of the war-torn country; the city of Kismaayo was the Indian Ocean gateway to the whole of southern Africa, through which every form of illicit trade now flowed. There was, of course, a never ending stream of new recruits ready and willing to fill the shoes of those left for dead; but, temporarily at least, following the elimination of their leaders, the drugs cartels would be forced to curtail their activities and the torrent of hard currency flowing into rebel hands would hopefully dry up... for now. A more permanent solution to these problems would have to be left to the diplomats and politicians; soldiers could only do so much.

Within a few hours the detachment had driven back to their temporary home deep within the rain forest and received the enthusiastic congratulations of their colleagues who had been left behind to guard the camp. The National Park, while providing excellent cover, was teeming with gun-toting rebels of every persuasion – constant, round the clock, vigilance was needed to remain concealed. Pretty soon after they had settled back into the routine of their improvised camp, new intelligence traffic started to flow into them with increasing urgency.

Lieutenant Hazel Opie, affectionately known to everyone as "H", ran the highly-sophisticated communications equipment for the group. It was her role to decode and pass on the unencrypted reports to Major Andrews.

"Ma'am, Fort Bragg has identified a major shipment of what they presume to be narcotics, heroin or cocaine – they are not sure which – and apparently it's heading our way. They estimate that it's due into port within a couple of days' time and has been traced for delivery to the al-Shabaab operatives you and the guys have just taken out."

Andrews picked up the transcripts and read them to the troops who were seated within ear-shot.

"It says here that the CIA satellite surveillance team has been tracing the suspect ship for months, but it has taken a very circuitous route indeed to get to Somalia. Odd that, don't you think, H? Apparently, the usual Afghan conduit for drugs shipments is nowhere to be seen, so the spooks reckon it must be carrying something out of the ordinary. In the opinion of the Agency staffers who've been assigned to monitor the case, they want us to make a detailed inspection of whatever is on board."

"I'd have thought that was going to present more than a few problems for us ma'am", said Opie.

"It sure the hell is, Lieutenant; as John Wayne may well have said."

"There is more encrypted Intel just coming through Major. The updated report says that the suspect ship had docked in endless obscure locations on its journey from Europe, via Africa, and is heading to Dandong in China, of all places."

"Where the hell is Dandong, H?"

"Apparently, it's on the Yalu River, ma'am, immediately opposite the North Korean border with China. Curiously, it also says here that one or two of the smaller containers have been periodically taken off the ship, held in storage for a day or so, and then put back in the hold. The CIA briefing says that they desperately need to know what cargo has been left on board after the drop and, more importantly, where the containers suspicious contents have originated from. They say, if it's not drugs, then it could be a major arms caché destined for al-Qaeda and therefore deem it a priority target to be intercepted and evaluated."

"Thanks H, anymore to add?"

"Only your new orders ma'am."

"Let me take a look, thanks." After a moment or two skim-reading her updated instructions Andrews said: "OK guys; gather round. We are immediately tasked to devise a plan to hijack the inbound freighter and, God help us all, sail it to an as-yet-to-be confirmed port. They are suggesting the Emirates, or possibly Mombasa, or Dar es Salaam, where the cargo can be very carefully analysed by a forensics team they are planning to fly in."

Andrews paused for a split second: "Do any of you reprobates have the vaguest idea of how to actually captain and navigate a ship?" Heads were shaken in unison.

"No, thought not: we're totally screwed! H, can you let the guys in head office know that we have a skill shortage here and kindly figure out what the hell we are supposed to do?"

Within moment of transmitting this request, they received a reply telling them to expect the imminent arrival by helicopter drop of four officers from the Australian frigate, HMAS Darwin, which fortuitously was conducting a routine counter-terrorism operation nearby in the southern-quadrant of the Arabian Sea.

"Listen up group", said Andrews, "the predicament we have to solve is how to get twelve people into the dock area undetected, somehow purloin the vessel from under the very noses of its crew and sundry gun-toting, drug-fuelled, mad-as-hell rebels; then blithely take it back out to sea with its precious contents still intact. No brainer really! Thank Christ for the Aussie navy, their arrival will at least give us a fighting chance here."

She was extremely well aware that under normal circumstances, the agreed UN protocol was for the ship to be seized in international waters, whatever contraband was found would be thrown overboard, its junior crew set free and, in all likelihood, the vessel sunk for gunnery target practice. However, the CIA, sensing something out of the ordinary with this particular cargo, wanted the ship available to them in one piece.

Opie, listening intently on the satellite radio interjected, "Ma'am, Langley says the freighter is apparently scheduled to dock in two days' time."

Given the organisational chaos within the port, everyone knew this was a very vague estimate at best. The corrupt port authorities routinely demanded large dollar-denominated bribes for a precious "clearance to off-load" certificate. In this case, however, the intended recipients of the cargo were all dead. Their organisation had been temporarily rendered dysfunctional; and the 'normal' procedures for transferring the containers into the warehouses suspended -- until such time as someone emerged from the void to 'pay the piper'. In all likelihood therefore, the ship would anchor out at sea for a few days until the docking formalities had been completed and considerable amounts of hard cash had changed hands.

This delay was an absolute godsend for Lyn Andrews, giving her army and navy teams' precious time with which to plan an assault on the ship. Despite the ramifications of an ongoing civil war, it would be standard practice when offloading contraband for the vessel's captain to come to a stop; say a mile or two out at sea, weigh anchor and commence negotiations with the harbour master to dock. Once the formalities were completed, the crew would gratefully receive their not-inconsiderable payment for the safe delivery of whatever smuggled goods they had deposited in the warehouses, after which temporary shore-leave would be granted to everyone. Following which, drink, drugs and wild women would then occupy the crew until their ill-gotten gains were utterly spent and their bodies wrecked; at which point they would set sail for the next port on their itinerary.

Earlier in the day, the local CIA informant, at much risk to his own life, had furtively managed to obtain a copy of the ship's manifest and its highly dubious bill of lading. In the opinion of the spooks back at Langley, the latter was a complete work of fiction; describing the cargo as grain, medicines and sundry humanitarian supplies.

Following the interception of earlier ship-to-shore communications, the nature of the shipment became even more mystifying. It transpired that the captain intended to off-load a dozen-or-so containers from the freighter and then continue the journey to Dandong with only two more left in the hold. This paltry cargo was bizarre in the extreme as the ship would be continuing to China more-or-less empty.

In a direct conversation with Andrews, the CIA analysts running the case, conjectured: "Perhaps Major, the mystery of this vessel's true purpose is to be found in the two containers that remain? It's vital that you and your team get to the bottom of this, pronto. If our suspicions here at Langley are correct, we may well have an international incident on our hands here."

Chapter 2

Downing Street

The solid oak door to the Cabinet Room, located on the ground floor of Number 10 Downing Street, was violently slammed shut as the prime minister entered, rattling the door-frame and disturbing the carefully hung pictures on the nearby walls. The force of the ensuing draught was sufficiently strong to scatter the papers of those in closest proximity across the cabinet table. The thump of the door was immediately followed from inside the room by an explosive, 'Jesus Christ! What was that?' The poor soul responsible for the expletive quickly lowered his head and averted everyone's gaze, praying that no one had seen who was guilty of making such a career-terminating remark. Utterly out of character, the PM stormed into the room conspicuously tie-less, unshaven and clearly spitting blood.

"Bastards, absolute bloody bastards!"

Anticipating nothing more than an early morning, very inconsequential, update on the latest opinion polls, the assembled inner-circle of advisers abruptly sat bolt-upright, instantly put down their mobile phones and wondered which one of them would be the recipient of the PM's wrath.

All those present would have readily concurred that it had been a very tricky couple of years since his elevation from chancellor. The economy was on a fairly even keel, that was true, but relentless backbench pressures on a seemingly endless stream of other issues were creating concerns for the

Government's stability and, by inference, his future. The last thing anyone wanted was another crisis.

Charles Sheer could unquestionably roll with the punches: he had already demonstrated the tenacity of an ox over negotiations with the European Union and, at times like now, established beyond all doubt that just beneath the surface he possessed the vindictiveness and malice of a crazed mafia boss.

Someone was going to pay for whatever had upset him this morning and nothing, simply nothing, was going to stand in his way. The next general election may well be on the horizon, but he had absolutely no intention of relinquishing his position as First Lord of the Treasury to anyone.

As the most senior member of the cabinet in attendance, the PM focussed his ire directly upon the home secretary. "Do we know who is responsible for this scurrilous, utterly unacceptable piece of garbage in today's Sun? I want his balls and still-beating heart delivered before the end of the day. Do I make myself abundantly clear – especially if it's the bloody limp-wristed leader of the opposition?"

The lurid front-page headline, trumpeted in the newspaper's typically strident tones, posed the alliterative and provocative question:

'Is PM behind d'Abo Dodgy Deal?'

The opening paragraph went on to suggest that there was something extremely duplicitous, and quite possibly criminal, being intentionally hidden from the newspaper's loyal readers. The editor promised a grateful nation that it would pursue the story with its customary vigour; proof would be found; the guilty named.

In carefully measured tones, befitting his self-perceived dignity and status, the home secretary cautiously replied: "We are endeavouring to establish who is behind the article Prime

Minister; and with the greatest of respect, I'll leave others to collect his dismembered body parts for you."

The home secretary's horn-rimmed glasses, having momentarily slipped down his nose, were pushed languidly back into place: he had somehow managed to deflect the PM's implied censure, at least for the time being.

"I've already asked the metropolitan police commissioner to look into it. I will, of course, immediately report back the moment I get some definitive information."

Highly defamatory, unsubstantiated and infuriatingly 'non-contributory' stories seemed to be appearing with increasing frequency in the press over the past couple of months; almost all of which had very tenuous and, in the PM's view, wildly conjectural and entirely spurious links back to the death two years earlier of the prominent city banker, Sir John d'Abo. It was increasingly clear to him and his close colleagues that there was a slow, but very discernible, head of steam being built up in the media for an official investigation into his conduct during the latter part of his time as chancellor.

Charles Sheer had no difficulty whatsoever in blocking out each and every unpleasant truth that crossed his path: it went with the territory. After all, he was the only one who knew what really happened to d'Abo on that fateful evening in August. Normally, he effortlessly managed to convince himself that the press articles were simply a case of out-and-out jealousy, perpetrated by his political enemies, of which there were many. However, some of those present around the cabinet table may well have concluded that, on this occasion, he was becoming increasingly delusional and paranoid.

The PM knew full well that, eventually, there was bound to be a negative reaction to the innumerable plaudits he received on the world stage for his role in the dollar scandal with China. The praise, however, had only served to feed his narcissism and inflate an already outsized ego. He had mentally prepared himself for some sort of diplomatic backlash in Asia, but today's poison was far too personal to have been the equivalent of the normal political 'tit-for-tat'. After all, he knew full well that MI6 had enough dirt and scuttlebutt on the Chinese Premier to ensure he didn't last into next week as head of state, after 'the boys' had carefully choreographed its disclosure.

Logic dictated to him that the Chinese could not be responsible for the story: but who the hell was?

Whilst outwardly debonair and, in public at least, always apparently calm, today the PM was demonstrably tense and agitated. Speaking to no one in particular, he slammed both hands on the cabinet table and said:

"Well, if that's what they damn well want, then they will get both barrels in return."

No sooner had he sat down than he immediately sprang to his feet and started to leave the room, brooding silently to himself: 'If the source of this article comes from within the cabinet, well they had better watch their backs. I've had endless experience dealing firmly with unsavoury people who stand in my way: John d'Abo for one.'

A collective sigh of blessed relief was palpable after he had left.

Despite the exceptional care he had taken to cover his tracks, Charlie Sheer knew that the root cause of his current problem would inevitably be uncovered; by someone, some day. Hopefully, he prayed, that time would be well into the distant horizon. There were simply too many people involved, especially within senior banking circles; but he felt confident, despite his evident paranoia, that the document trail leading straight to his door had been comprehensively destroyed. Added to which, the security services had, at his explicit request, diligently and forcefully put 'the frighteners' on all those who were involved.

Nonetheless, the newspapers were clearly hinting at the

possibility that the UK Treasury had inexplicably loaned a considerable sum of money to d'Abo just before his death. However, after years in politics, the PM was supremely confident that a mere hint could easily be swatted away, dismissed at a press conference as tittle-tattle, or better still, just ignored... providing it went away...and very soon.

When his equilibrium was eventually restored and sartorial elegance regained, the PM sat down in his private office and started to go diligently through his daily mountain of Red Boxes containing briefing memos from civil servants and cabinet members. After an hour or so, he came across a paper provocatively entitled 'Naked Shorts', which immediately caught his attention amidst the otherwise utterly dreary contents. The Bank of England rarely featured in his boxes, but here was a briefing memo suggesting that he should urgently focus his attention on, of all things, the world's gold market and asking him to consider why China was increasingly acquiring vault-loads of physical gold.

He had always known, of course, that the people of Asia – and indeed their central banks – had a limitless penchant for gold; almost it seemed in preference to their own, or indeed anyone else's, paper money. But the motives and the exceptional tonnage of gold being hoarded in China was starting to worry those monitoring the situation at the Bank. Could this, the briefing paper conjectured, be a prelude to yet another highly unstable development in the financial markets – this year's Black Swan event – which inevitably would attract the more dodgy hedge funds, casino bankers and speculators in droves?

There were an increasing number of London-based international banks and bullion dealers, the Bank's report said, who – to use the technical term running throughout their report – were 'Naked Shorts'. They were holding highly speculative positions in the gold market which were not supported, in any shape or form, by physical gold. While this was perfectly legal and, under normal circumstances, an everyday occurrence of speculating whether the price of gold would go up or down, the numbers were growing alarmingly. If, for whatever reason, these companies were eventually forced, heaven forbid, to produce the actual gold bars and unwind their exposure, there was simply no way it could be done. The paper went on to comment:

> *The latest People's Bank of China official report, published last week, states that 'the country holds just short of 2,800 metric tonnes of gold' – an admission that we at the Bank of England find exceptionally hard to believe. US intelligence sources confirm that over the past twenty years China has secretly imported over 20,000 tonnes of gold, while its citizens are believed to hold 13,000 tonnes. Where it has all gone, we simply do not know? This very much larger unofficial figure, which we have every reason to believe is correct, and indeed may be an underestimate, means that China now holds more gold than all the other central banks of the world put together. We deem this to be thought-provoking at the least…and a matter of grave concern at the worst.*

The PM, whose attention was focussed on other highly-personal problems closer to hand, hastily scribbled a note in the margin to his chancellor, Amanda Price:

'We need to discuss this – can you get to Chequers at the weekend?'

CHAPTER 3

Chequers

It had become a regular occurrence for Amanda Price, the UK's enormously talented financial supremo, to spend her entire weekends conscientiously working on Treasury matters, often late into the night. After all, she rationalised in those rare moments of navel-gazing, she was single and utterly dedicated to her work; besides which, she much preferred the grandeur of Chequers to her official residence at Dorneywood.

After graduating, she had spent five very successful years with JPMorgan in its Bond Origination Department, rising quickly and effortlessly through the ranks. However, after much deliberation, while endlessly navigating the dubious delights of Canary Wharf, Amanda Price concluded that despite being an avid capitalist, she had had quite enough of banking, thank you, and was now going to enter politics. Her potential was recognised immediately by her local Conservative Association Chairman, and with the candidate nomination secured at the hustings, she went on to gain an unprecedented 38,000 majority in a fortuitously timed by-election. In one fell swoop, and not yet thirty three, she had secured the safest seat in the House as the Honourable Member for Esher and Walton.

While this was an enviable accomplishment for any aspiring politician, her mind never strayed very far from her eventual elevation to the highest office in the land. Such was her confidence in this outcome, that she was already making surreptitious plans to change the stuffy and pretentious decor at Chequers when she eventually became the beneficiary of this most enviable of prime ministerial trinkets. The frequency of the visits did, however, cause a few jealous whispers amongst her colleagues that she and Charlie Sheer were getting 'increasingly close', as the euphemism goes.

There was, of course, absolutely no truth in the rumour. Far from it, she very discreetly preferred girls on the rare moments these days when she was not in the limelight. Her appreciation of the beauty and delicacy of the naked female body was confirmed beyond all doubt at life-classes while studying fine art at The Ruskin, in Oxford. She only failed to keep her peccadilloes under strict wraps once when, after an exceptionally liquid reception at the Italian Ambassador's palatial mansion in Rome, she none too cautiously slipped upstairs with a particularly accommodating secretary from the adjacent Swedish Embassy. Thankfully, it was in the era of the infamous bunga-bunga parties, so no one batted a proverbial eye-lid and discretion prevailed. However, as on many previous occasions when such gossip surfaced about her relationship with the prime minister, she quite deliberately decided to let the speculation run without correction, calculating that one day it may prove useful in her never-ending lust for power.

Arriving just before lunch, the UK's first female chancellor was the epitome of elegance in her blue Armani trouser suit and pink shirt. On several formal occasions recently she had increasingly been known to wear extremely flamboyant ties, which made many of her more stuffy male colleagues feel very ill-at-ease indeed. Behind very tightly closed doors, they were often to be found whispering conspiratorially that she was either going barking mad as a direct result of the pressure, or even more dangerously, she was symbolically making a brazen and ballsy bid to usurp the PM's authority. Others sarcastically believed she increasingly reminded them of Mrs Thatcher's deeply unflattering caricature in Spitting Images. It was, however, openly acknowledged by virtually everyone, that – despite her tender years – she had more brains and cunning than the rest of the cabinet combined. Her jealous colleagues knew full well that she could effortlessly manipulate the PM whenever she wanted to get her way. She was equally as adept at charming and beguiling the electorate. Quite frankly there was no one to stop her reaching the top, but herself.

Over the smoked salmon canapés, the chancellor was the first to broach the subject of the Bank's paper.

"Charlie, earlier in the week I received a second very detailed background note on some issues in the gold market from the Governor. I skim read it but formed the initial conclusion that it was a curiosity and nothing more. However, it's very clear from the tone of their remarks that a great deal of head scratching is going on at the Bank, based on trying to understand the motives for why vast quantities of the world's gold is being hoovered up by the Chinese."

"I totally agree it's very odd Amanda, but it's just not a priority for me at the moment. In any event I find it utterly incomprehensible to fathom China's possible motives and objectives for more or less everything. Bloody Confucius has a lot to answer for."

"In all likelihood it's a symptom of their deeply felt insecurity, Charlie. Our Ambassador in Beijing tells me that they still continue to feel utterly humiliated following the 'Dark Pools' debacle. As you know only too well, the disastrous consequences for their currency which immediately followed has been profoundly embarrassing and economically painful for them. However, on the upside, at least the IMF has gradually been rehabilitating China back onto the top table. Now that they have embarked upon a course to liberalise their economy, it won't be long before they rejoin the world's elite reserve currencies; and regain 'face'."

"I still don't trust them as far as I could throw them, Amanda: once bitten, and all that."

"From my viewpoint at the Treasury, some sort of harmony between us, however artificially induced, has been thankfully restored. It's to everyone's benefit that a more stable future is opening up again for China."

"I take your point, so do we both conclude that the Bank of England is being typically over-cautious?"

With a collective nod of the head, the topic simply drifted into the ether. The PM flippantly adding as an afterthought, "Perhaps they are getting married in droves over there and need the gold for the rings, or their fillings."

Over a very leisurely two-hour lunch in the mahogany-panelled private dining room and with that topic off the agenda, they returned to the more pressing matter of the source of the press leaks and what – if anything – could or should be done about it.

On previous occasions, when something politically unsavoury had somehow made its way onto the front pages, the PM would simply invite the paper's proprietor over for a quiet, but firm, word. Today, however, he instinctively felt that this course of action would simply draw uncalled-for attention to the problem. Perhaps it was time for MI6 to revisit some of those who were present at the time and not so politely remind them of their vow of silence; especially if they valued their kneecaps. The PM certainly knew how to put the fear of God into any opponent. Amanda Price, in contrast, quietly and calmly managed to convince him that no one in the cabinet had the audacity, or the balls, to confront him, even by stealth. They would have to search elsewhere for the culprit.

At the end of what they both concluded was a very convivial, if largely inconsequential, get-together, Amanda was escorted to her ministerial car by Charlie Sheer. Casually lowering the window to say goodbye, she nonchalantly dropped into the parting conversation:

"Didn't your dear friend John d'Abo live close by here in Buckinghamshire, Charlie? The village of Haddenham wasn't it? I wonder where he and his dark secrets are buried. We must go and pay our respects sometime soon."

Charles Sheer merely gave her a withering and sarcastic smile: "No point raking over those very old coals Amanda. Best for us all that he is left in peace."

CHAPTER 4

d'Abo's Merchant Bank, London

The intense dramas which unfolded at d'Abo's Merchant Bank following the untimely death of its chairman were now a distant, but still painful, memory for everyone who worked there. City adulation and seemingly limitless praise and honours for those involved were mixed with managerial turmoil. The febrile atmosphere within these particular corridors of power was exacerbated by there being no succession plans whatsoever. The bank's late chairman and owner was deemed by his colleagues to be practically immortal, with all concerned anticipating years of robust good health ahead of him.

A seemingly unbridgeable vacuum had been left at the top of the organisation which would be hard, if not impossible, to fill. His natural successor, Sebastian Fortes CBE, had chosen to take an eighteen month sabbatical to assist his friend CJ after he had won the Hong Kong elections. Seb had only very recently returned home to the UK and his new role and position in the merchant bank was as yet unclear. He had been elevated to the title of Board Director, but had little instruction as to what he was supposed to be directing. Many of his associates who were still working there speculated that he may well leave soon for pastures new. His heart didn't seem to be in it anymore.

This oversight, by the weakened and rudderless board of directors, had not gone unnoticed by the many city predators who stalked the corporate jungle looking for vulnerable prey.

d'Abo's Bank was definitely 'in play', as the saying goes, and would have inevitably fallen into the willing clutches of a competitor, had its ownership not been in the sole possession of one person. However, this did not stop months of board room distractions, instability and uncertainty. Transactions almost ground to a halt, highly valued staff were leaving, and tempers were decidedly frayed. The bank had become rudderless and was sliding inexorably down the Olympian slopes it had once effortlessly commanded.

Sir John's widow, Lady Isobel, after much deliberation and soul-searching, had at long last made a decisive decision not to sell the family bank, despite many entreaties from an endless stream of larger institutions willing to buy it. With that now settled and grasping the nettle firmly by the hand, she unceremoniously dumped her Argentinian playboy lover and caught the next flight out of South America.

On her return to London, and with her customary penchant for self-publicity, she arranged a press conference at the bank's Berkeley Square offices and flamboyantly declared to the assembled hacks: "It is my avowed intention to steer this business into a safe harbour and make d'Abo's great again."

With absolutely zero demonstrable talent in the field of banking or commerce, this – many of those present felt – would surely end in tears.

Completely contrary to all expectations and dire warnings of doom and disaster from every quarter, she effortlessly charmed and captivated the joint chairmen of the enormously successful US hedge-fund, Saturn Quantum Trading. They readily agreed to immediately make a significant equity investment into the organisation. The newly re-capitalised merchant bank now had access to the simply enormous financial clout of SQT and the deals started to roll in through the door like the old days. The fickle UK press, of course, loved it and rapidly hailed it as the triumph they had always expected.

SQT, which had worked closely with d'Abo's during the currency crisis, were as always brimful of cash and could see nothing but good news coming out of such a corporate hook-up. They had tried on several occasions in the recent past to get the bank's chief deal-maker, Sebastian Fortes, to jump ship and join their organisation. Nevertheless, out of loyalty to d'Abo's and his mentor Sir John, he had forsaken their monetary blandishments and flattering offer of a supremely valuable multi-million dollar partnership. Now, however, they were to be on the same team again. The possibilities were endless and the champagne trolley would surely re-make its customary rounds on Fridays to thank the staff for all their hard work.

Two years previously Sebastian had taken the highly unusual and for many a very quirky decision, to return immediately to Hong Kong, despite being fêted on every occasion by the media for his brilliance. The unexpected death of his colleague had hit him very hard indeed. As a result, he increasingly felt such public praise to be hollow, unwarranted and meaningless. Reluctantly, however, he eventually concluded that he needed time to reflect on the tumultuous events he had been through and engross himself in an entirely new challenge. The metamorphosis of Hong Kong under CJ's leadership into a reinvigorated, increasingly capitalist, business hub was undoubtedly due, in large measure, to his personal contribution and foresight. China had recently announced its 'thirteenth' five-year plan, the publication of which had convinced him that now was the appropriate time to pass the mantle of Financial Secretary to a fresh candidate and seek pastures new.

When he had initially arrived back in the UK with his simply gorgeous girlfriend, Lyn Andrews, what now seemed an age ago, Charlie Sheer had explained to them that the untimely death of John d'Abo was a toxic mixture of exceptional stress and an undiagnosed genetic heart condition. As if this was not bad enough, Lyn was almost immediately re-assigned once again to the Middle East, on some covert operation that, quite naturally, she was not at liberty to disclose to him. The upshot was that they had not seen each other for over a year now. Despite many attempts to establish where she was and if she was OK, even his old friend and colleague, General James Sanford, was deeply reluctant to elaborate upon her whereabouts. He readily agreed to pass messages back and forth between them, when time and circumstances allowed, but no more. Sanford's only comment to Sebastian, through gritted teeth was: 'Every additional hour I sit behind this goddamned desk, I wish I was back on operational duty with her and the team'.

Life continued, but much of its sparkle had gone. He needed to fully absorb himself in a new project and soon. The prime minister had, of course, tried his very best to smooth Sebastian's re-entry back into the City and the upper circles of the 'Establishment'. Largely this was in deference to the esteem in which he was held and, on behalf of a grateful nation, for his past contribution in keeping the UK economy out of harm's way. However everything the PM suggested found no resonance whatsoever. The present financial environment was benign – arguably dull in the extreme – and no place for the exercise of his unique problem-solving skills. He reluctantly realised that he had become addicted to adrenalin-surges, crisis and adventure, whereas the PM was offering him ambassadorships to Washington or Paris, the chairmanship of endless Quangos and, God help him, a choice of mind-numbingly tedious roles at the IMF or the World Bank. Although one door had shut – admittedly of his own volition – there was precious little sign of a new one opening up which caught his fancy. And patience was not his strong suit.

Sebastian was fast approaching the dreaded forty, with the world in theory at his feet, but he could not shake off the overwhelming feeling of emptiness. It was only by the strangest of distractions, to an otherwise tedious day, that Rebecca, his long suffering secretary, entered his office with that day's post.

"Nothing terribly interesting Sir; just a couple of internal announcements and a draft information memorandum from a company seeking a financial adviser."

Such glossy brochures passed through his hands almost on a daily basis at the bank, but this one in particular caught his attention, because the company concerned was trying to raise money to prospect for gold, not far from where he used to visit with his beloved VW Camper Van, 'back in the day'.

"Ah, my misspent youth Becks: camping on Polzeath Beach, hours spent surfing, drinking beer all night and chasing the girls at every opportunity. Wow, this takes me back to my teenage years. Have you ever been to Rock?"

"I went to Torquay once as a kid; is that nearby?"

"Close enough. Sod it Becks, I'm going crazy with the boredom: it's time to re-live my adolescence. Find out where I can hire a wet suit, would you? I'm going to take the week off. Assuming I stay sober, I'll go and check out the mining company's new facilities."

The rest of the afternoon was spent staring aimlessly out of the window in dreamland and on the phone to rent a Camper Van. Having read the information memorandum, Sebastian's natural curiosity caused him to delve further into the rationale for re-starting a defunct Roman mine after a thousand plus years. It didn't take him long to look up the charts for recent gold prices and see that the trend was only one way; inexorably upwards.

He called one of the junior analysts in the bank.

"Jimbo, have you anything on a company called Polvere Doré Mines; it goes by the initials PDM apparently? I'm going to have a browse around their new facility this weekend. Can you email me a briefing note on the gold market, there's a good chap?"

"Not the slightest problem, Mr. Fortes; I'll email our most recent research note immediately. We track the gold market assiduously down here in the dungeon; and the boys upstairs in the posh seats trade the stuff in zillions. When you study the numbers I'm sure you'll reach the same conclusion as we do: something very strange is going on!"

CHAPTER 5

Bank of England & the London Bullion Market

The vast quantities of physical gold flowing overtly and – far more disturbingly – via surreptitious means into China, had not escaped the eagle-eyed attention of the chairman of the London Bullion Market Association.

Professor Dominic Carrington had been at the helm of the organisation for over ten years and was regarded by all and sundry as the world's foremost authority on gold. A distinguished scientist by background, he divided his time between Imperial College, where he was head of the chemistry faculty, and holding the prestigious chairmanship of the Bullion Market.

Despite his acknowledged scientific expertise, he was regarded as somewhat of a left-wing radical by his colleagues at the university; someone who didn't quite fit comfortably into the senior common room. He didn't care one jot. However, whenever he left the corridors of academia to be amongst his chums at the Bullion Market, his alter ego rose to the fore: his reputation for caustic wit and a delight of fine wine could not have been in sharper contrast to his white coated, deeply serious, demeanour in the laboratories.

He revelled in the contrasting careers he had carved out for himself, but readily acknowledged that his political views were out of step with the government of the day and as a result he often missed out on lucrative research grants. Frankly, he didn't have much respect for politicians, and the feeling was mutual: he was inevitably *persona non grata* in Downing Street. However, it was entirely predictable that the Bank of England staff should seek his cooperation as part of their background research into the paper they had been preparing for the PM, despite knowing full well that it was a risky strategy having him as the co-author.

"Dominic, my dear friend, do come in; very nice to see you again. How are you?"

The Governor of the Bank, the highly distinguished Sir David V. Stone, effortlessly engendered in his staff the impression of being everyone's favourite avuncular grandfather. He could always be relied upon to be full of bonhomie, unexpected acts of kindness and a 'hail-fellow-well-met' heartiness. His easy-going manner prompted respect and admiration in equal measure. The only time anyone had seen him even mildly agitated was when the then Prime Minister, Gordon Brown, decided in 2001 to sell vast quantities of the country's gold reserves: for a pittance. He was too early into his tenure at the Bank to have his reservations taken seriously by senior management, but he never forgot that moment.

In his youth Sir David had been a celebrated long distance runner, but the passing years had taken their toll on his waistband and knee joints, so that now he preferred nothing more strenuous than croquet and a glass or three of Sauvignon Blanc. While his command of macro-economics was legendary, many colleagues felt his eccentric personality was a deliberately cultivated party ploy, developed over the years, to counterbalance his encyclopaedic knowledge of the UK tax code.

"Prof, I've asked you over to agree a strategy on this gold business and ensure the PM supports our position. I gather he is more than a little indifferent to the conclusions we have reached which, frankly speaking, is quite unsettling."

"Bloody typical of the man", replied Carrington in a very disparaging tone of voice. "All he is interested in is the next election and his self-aggrandisement on the world stage. If he doesn't pull his finger out on this one, he could find himself out of office very quickly indeed. Hopefully with egg all over his face. I should say that nothing would give me more pleasure, but the consequences of his failure to act could be profound in the extreme."

"Best keep those views under wraps for a little while longer then Dominic, we've a job to do. I take it you'll have seen the latest paper from the World Gold Council? This year's statistics for China's holdings of physical gold are, quite honestly, utterly unbelievable: it's just a pack of lies, if you will excuse the expression."

Carrington nodded in complete agreement, before the governor continued.

"I presume like me, you are also getting a steady flow of briefing papers from the Joint Intelligence Committee? There seems to be a never-ending stream of clandestine shipments of gold into Asia. Apparently they have traced the recipients to various organisations and locations which, without a shadow of a doubt, have direct, incontrovertible connections to the Communist Party in China. Very senior people within their Army seem to have got in on the act to: why such organisations needed vast quantities of gold defies common sense. The deeply-held conviction of the security services is that the smuggled gold was simply being transferred by the lorry-load directly to the vaults of the central bank."

Dominic Carrington raised his eyebrows in a weary gesture of total agreement.

"It's very difficult to fathom out, Governor. Despite my very best endeavours, a normally functioning market place seems to be a thing of the past. Professional speculators are relentlessly piling in as the gold price rises daily. It's all very destabilising, I have to say. I've decided to arrange an emergency meeting of the fourteen member banks in the bullion market to see if they can somehow put a lid on it. As you well know, they hold literally billions of dollars' worth of futures contracts which simply add to the speculative feeding frenzy. I'm concerned that the market is being rigged by the less scrupulous banks, for which read probably all of them, using increasingly sophisticated financial instruments. I'd be very grateful if your technical chaps could take a serious second-look at this, please. Another opinion would be most welcome."

In addition to presiding over this increasingly complex marketplace, Professor Carrington had felt a growing unease throughout his tenure that his organisation was being gradually and inexorably usurped by the Shanghai Gold Exchange, which had been established in 2002. In a relentless flurry of publicity and appeal to national pride, the Exchange had encouraged the Chinese public to buy gold, which they had responded to with great enthusiasm. The local politicians continuously heaped praise upon their patriotic efforts and pulled every lever available to them, via the state-owned banking system, in order to provide loans to its population so they could keep on buying. The result was a foregone conclusion: the price of gold inevitably rose as demand far outstretched supply. Its citizens were delighted as their holdings grew in size and value. With every price rise, the clamour for yet more gold grew exponentially.

To add momentum to the whirlwind, China's state-owned gold mines and refining facilities were acknowledged by everyone in the business to be working round the clock to accommodate any demand which had not been fulfilled from overseas sources. Vast quantities of the country's financial and engineering resources were being poured into gold mining and its manufacture into ingots.

"Governor, I've been around the block often enough to recognise that China, deliberately and blatantly, is seemingly hell bent on cornering the world's gold market. The only thing I cannot figure out is why? They have even started converting the standard 400 ounce bars which we have all over Europe and America into the new one kilo bars which the Chinese want to adopt as the new world standard. Again, I ask myself why?"

He continued, adopting his usual professorial tone.

"If they truly do have the intention to corner the world's physical gold market, then their actions must have another purpose, as history is strewn with the dead bodies of those who had tried and failed similar things. You will readily recall that Bunker Hunt and his Texan brother famously tried to do the same in the 1970's with silver; frankly, they fell flat on their faces and lost billions. At the time, the US government regulators felt they had no option but to intervene when they felt the market was being manipulated. They temporarily suspended the rules of the game, thereby instantly causing the price to crash through the floor. We may need to adopt similar tactics, I fear, but the consequences could be unimaginable. China, for one, would be seriously pissed off with us!"

"Indeed, Dominic. I'm sure you will also recall the trader at Japan's Sumitomo Bank – in the 1990's I believe – who tried to do the same thing with copper. He very nearly succeeded before the marketplace turned against him, prices collapsed virtually overnight, and the bank was left nursing horrendous losses. Our own banking system is weak enough as it is, the euro may well implode at any moment and, frankly speaking, I am not so sure we could cope with another crisis of that sort."

"Well, Governor, someone is most definitely endeavouring to manipulate the gold market. My fear is that it could backfire very quickly indeed with devastating effects. However, as you know only too well, no one appreciates words of caution, no matter how well intentioned, when the price of something is rising. Regrettably history always shows us that a boom is almost inevitably followed by a stupendous crash."

The room fell into silence as the two men absorbed the consequences of what both instinctively felt was an impending, but deeply perplexing, crisis. Sir David, pulling their joint report to the PM out of his desk drawer, was the first to speak.

"I'm particularly taken by this comment you added to the submission, Dominic. If I can quote you: *'The very significant escalation of China's gold holdings since the Dark Pools affair may be entirely coincidental, but it is too statistically significant to overlook'*. That's just got to be true."

This thought resonated exactly with the Bank's own experts who hinted that history may be about to repeat itself as China's economy was rapidly turning around and enviable growth rates were being re-established. In their view, a steady stream of testosterone-fuelled proclamations once again seemed to be rampant in the Great Hall of the People. Everyone at the Bank of England who read his contribution to the report vigorously underlined the statement made by Professor Carrington that:

> *'From the days of Sun Yat-sen, the early 20th century founder of the Republic of China, every modern leader has harboured the dream of restoring the country to its rightful place as the most powerful nation on earth'.*

It was more than conceivable, the Bank's unpublished analysis concluded, that today's more senior members of the Politburo intended to achieve this objective but via the gold market.

The meeting drew to a frustrating close with an agreement to write a joint follow-up letter to the PM politely asking him to think again. Despite his unquestioned leadership two years previously, it was just conceivable that history was about to repeat itself. Beijing was continuing to make great progress economically, but no one could fail to notice that it continued with the declared aim of replacing the US dollar with their own currency, the Chinese renminbi. Now something decidedly suspicious was taking place in the gold market.

It was deeply disappointing to them both that neither the chancellor nor the prime minister responded to their entreaties to take this matter extremely seriously. They had requested that the PM set up a task force to enquire more thoroughly into this subject, but it had fallen on deaf ears. In the pecking order of domestic political problems, their concerns had simply failed to register.

On his way back to the university, Carrington scribbled his bullet-point notes of the meeting on his laptop. As far as he was concerned, it was indisputable that the Shanghai Gold Exchange was now becoming the world's most important physical gold market. Worryingly, their senior directors had made it crystal clear in recent press coverage that, very shortly, they intended to re-price their gold in renminbi. By unilaterally dropping the US dollar as the world peg for gold pricing, utterly catastrophic global consequences would surely follow. He decided that they must respectfully beseech the prime minister to revisit the subject, urgently.

Dominic Carrington was not normally a man to overly worry, but the more he thought about the implication of what he and the governor had discussed, the more it became clear to him that an unstoppable sea-shift in the balance of political and economic power was now under way. At its core was the gold market over which he presided. The West could very easily be held to ransom by the Chinese, unless some action was immediately taken to put a break on these events. Carrington reluctantly drew the obvious conclusion that, without question, his organisation and its members were now under mortal threat and, if they were, then so to was the country.

Under normal circumstances he would have simply arranged a drink at the club with his 'favourite City guru', the late Sir John d'Abo. He could always be relied upon to provided wise counsel and advice when things got a tad tricky.

Despite his professorial title and undisputed intellect, what he urgently needed was a dispassionate sounding board to provide some much-needed guidance; someone with whom he could openly air his increasing number of concerns.

He searched for his phone lurking deep within his briefcase and rang d'Abo's Bank. The receptionist responded after the second ring: "Sorry professor but Mr. Fortes is away for the weekend, but you will undoubtedly be able to catch him on his mobile."

★ ★ ★

Sebastian Fortes was behind the wheel of his newly hired VW Camper Van, smiling broadly in a 'I just couldn't-care-less' frame of mind. Although he was missing his hippy beard and torn tee-shirt of yesteryear, nothing was going to stop him reliving his misspent youth as he nonchalantly drove along the A303 heading to one of his old haunts, the surfing town of Rock, in Cornwall.

The passage of time had not improved his singing, which he would readily acknowledge was undeniably boisterous and without question tuneless, but when the Beach Boys 'Good Vibrations' was playing at full volume, frankly, who gave a damn.

The incessant ringing of his mobile phone gradually crept into Sebastian's consciousness, drowning out the music and crushing the mood completely.

"Carrington here, London Bullion Market; is that you Fortes? I need to speak to you in confidence on a matter of grave importance."

The impact of the word 'grave' immediately jerked Sebastian back to reality, as the urgency of Carrington's tone sunk in.

A, "yes it is", was reluctantly replied as he turned the CD off, "but I'm driving. Is it important, professor? Didn't we meet a few years back in Hong Kong with my chairman?"

"We did indeed; you'd just closed some airline deal or other and were intent on partying the night away at the Peninsula. If my memory of the evening serves me well, the Kobe-beef was exquisite and saké sublime. Deeply unhappy not to be able to chat with my old friend Johnny-boy, so thought I'd call you instead. It's absolutely imperative we meet as soon as possible; not a moment to lose. I'm completely convinced the Chinese are up to their old tricks again. So too is the Bank's Governor."

It was as if a bolt of lightning had immediately shot through Sebastian's entire body: the hair on his arms rose as the adrenalin surged through his veins, his mind racing. The torpor of recent weeks and months just fell away. "Tricks, what tricks?"

"I think they are deliberately trying to rig the gold market and if my hunch is correct, then we have a very serious problem on our hands. When are you back in London?"

"I'm in Cornwall surfing this weekend…it's a long story… so shall I see you on Monday morning? Would Claridge's for breakfast suit you Professor Carrington? I'll organise a table for nine sharp."

CHAPTER 6

Off-shore Kismaayo, Somalia

The ageing rust bucket, masquerading as a seaworthy freighter, had eventually come to a complete stop directly outside of the port of Kismaayo and was bobbing gently in a moderate swell. The iridescent blue-green of the ocean was a delight to behold as the ship's complement lined up on deck to stare longingly at the city, a mile or so away.

Captain Pietro Zucca was to be found in his usual place, pacing the bridge and checking the increasingly useless instrument console. Of Italian descent and having a decidedly fiery temperament, he could not remember when he was last on home soil: ten years, twenty years, it was all a blur. His skin was bronzed, weather-beaten and tough as a rhino's hide, while his fists carried the scars of many an encounter with unruly subordinates who would not bend to his will. He brusquely issued the orders to shut down the engines, drop anchor and, having satisfied himself that everything was in good order, joined his crew on deck in the blazing sunshine. They had been at sea for seven or eight weeks now and the incessant, monotonous, boring daily routines were taking their toll on everyone on board. Despite the all too apparent scars of the civil war on the nearby buildings, no one cared. The illicit pleasures of shore-leave for the captain and crew were only hours away. The silence was idyllic; the anticipation immense.

Zucca returned to the bridge in order to place his routine

radio call to the harbour master and, assuming it was safe to do so, make arrangements to dock later that evening.

"Sorry to be the bearer of bad news, Captain. Your consignment will have to stay on board until such time as the appropriate fees are paid."

In this part of the world, baksheesh and bribes were an essential part of doing business, any business. Simply everyone, especially those running the highly lucrative port facilities, demanded their pound of flesh. Until money changed hands their precious cargo stood zero chance of being off-loaded.

This disastrous news spread quickly throughout the entire ship's company, dampening their spirits and engendering mutinous thoughts. Rebellion could only be a matter of a couple of hours away if this was not resolved very quickly.

The captain was faced with little choice but to disobey the strict rules of his contractual engagement. Over what seemed like a never-ending stream of faxes and phone calls prior to the voyage, he had painstakingly agreed that there should be absolutely no communications whatsoever with his clients once they were underway. Zucca now reasoned that he had no viable option other than to try to get hold of the people who had chartered the ship under his command and explain the predicament he now faced. If they didn't find a way to 'pay-up' then he would have to go ashore and, one way or another, negotiate some sort of deal himself, or leave without unloading the cargo. His big pay-off came at the end of the voyage; these irritating intermediate stops en route to Dandong were a means to an end. No more, no less; somewhere the crew could let off much needed steam.

It would be true to say that Captain Zucca was not someone who took the filing of important papers terribly seriously. His cabin was strewn with empty bottles, cigarette ends, salacious magazines and detritus of every sort. In consequence it took him several hours to find the appropriate contract documents and the relevant name and phone number of the shipping agent in Panama. No sooner had he started to contact the person whose signature was on the crumpled piece of paper, than the CIA surveillance team in the United States were immediately tracing the number and listening intently to what was about to be discussed.

"Zucca, Captain of the Jin-Ton, here; I need to speak with Ramos urgently."

To say the recipient of the call was utterly furious at being contacted would be an understatement writ large.

"What the hell do you want Zucca? You know the rules, no contact whatsoever."

"Don't get shirty with me, Ramos. I'm at anchor offshore Kismaayo. Why has no one paid for the bloody cargo to go ashore?"

"How the fuck do I know? It's your problem, you fix it."

"That's fine, we will just dump whatever crap we are carrying into the sea and be on our merry way."

After what felt like an endless pause, Ramos burst into a tirade of Spanish oaths and curses directed towards anyone and everyone involved in his organisation for their ineptitude and utter incompetence. He was about to close the office early and spend the evening carousing with one of his many mistresses; the last thing he wanted was to have to work through the night sorting this mess out.

"I don't give a damn for your problems Ramos. Get these matters fixed or we depart tomorrow; *Comprendez*?"

"OK, and for Christ's sake Zucca, calm down. Go ashore now, schmooze the harbour master, assess the situation and report back this time tomorrow. I'll try to find a way to trace the whereabouts of the clients who were expecting your delivery and get them to resolve this immediately."

"You owe me for this, Ramos. It's not my job to clear up your dirty work."

The captain had no idea – how possibly could he – that the shipping agency that habitually employed his services at vast cost was, in fact, a very convenient front for both North Korean and Chinese interests. The shipping agency, known as ChinKo Inc., was a highly discreet conduit through which millions of laundered US dollars flowed annually. To him it was just one more voyage amongst many, all involving a never-ending stream of dubious deliveries and collections: cash on the barrel head, no questions asked. It was not his role to query the motives and objectives of his clients. Frankly, he couldn't care less about them.

The two countries, brothers-in-arms since the Korean War in the 1950's, had used this opaque corporate structure as a mutually convenient way to conceal the movement of goods and arms around the world for years. Any sanctions that had been periodically imposed upon either of them were thereby rendered totally ineffective. International regulators, banking supervisors and a long list of security agencies were left to try and unpick this clandestine operation as best they could, often to no avail. If they ever felt they were coming close to disclosure, those running the secret organisation would simply shut the current business down and immediately start another one. There was a symbiosis of objectives linking all the participants in this complex chain of events; a mutually beneficial relationship between both countries that hid innumerable sins and where all involved profited very handsomely indeed.

★ ★ ★

"If you think you can intimidate me, Captain", sneered the harbour master from behind his desk, his contempt apparent for all to see, "I have to tell you that you're dealing with the wrong man. I can have twenty guys, all armed to the teeth, in here within thirty seconds and your bullet-riddled body will shortly be floating face down in the water outside. So pay up, or go: there is absolutely no chance of you unloading those containers."

"You know full bloody well that I don't have access to that level of cash on board. Don't you have any idea who the bloody goods are destined for and how to make contact with them?"

"That's your problem, my Italian friend. Now get out of my office and don't come back until you have the money."

★ ★ ★

Later that day Zucca begrudgingly made a second radio call to the shipping agent in Panama City. To say it was undertaken in a foul temper would be a severe understatement; he was livid. "Ramos, you son-of-a-bitch, my patience has run out, the crew are threatening to jump ship, so I want this mess sorting out pronto, or we leave back for Europe on tonight's tide."

"Jesus, chill out, will you. Go tell those sons-of-whores that I've made arrangements to get the required funds to them in two to three days' time, so just stay close by the communications room and await instructions. You leave Kismaayo and I swear you will die: *lei capisce*?"

Zucca would have killed him with his bare hands had they been in the same room, but that pleasure would have to wait. Reluctantly he ordered the re-launch of the ship's tender and went once more to visit the harbour master who, on seeing him enter the office, raised a jaundiced eyebrow when told about the news of the further delays.

"The big bosses here have said that until you resolve this matter, your crew will not being granted permission to go ashore. They suggest you take the opportunity to visit one of the nearby liquor stores, stock up on the local hooch, and somehow keep them amused until such time as this matter is amicably resolved, in our favour, naturally."

It was just a matter of pure good fortune that the harbour master's chief clerk, sitting almost unnoticed in a darker corner of the office, happened to overhear the magnanimous suggestion being made to Captain Zucca.

This snippet of information was quickly and discretely relayed to his CIA handlers. The news of the delay and, however trivial, the three or four cases of highly dubious whisky now being transported back to the freighter, was immediately passed through to Major Lyn Andrews. A short window of opportunity had gratefully now opened up for her team, which she felt must be seized at all costs.

She assembled the two platoon sergeants, Oakes and Walker, and ran through the options open to them:

"If we attempt a direct amphibious assault on the ship then it seems inevitable that there will be a full-on gun fight. I'm rejecting this course of action as being too dangerous. Agreed? So we need another approach." Both men nodded.

"Oaksey, could you give us all a quick assessment of the intelligence you've previously gathered on the harbour and its facilities?"

"Yes indeed, ma'am. They do have low grade security systems in place, but these work sporadically at best and often not at all, due to constant electricity blackouts. It's possible that we may meet some resistance from the local militias but this is very difficult to gauge: they seem to be permanently distracted fighting each other. If we could somehow get into the harbour undetected, then Plan A would be to appropriate a motorised dinghy or two, if they are available, and use them to get to the ship."

"I'm willing to bet," Andrews interjected, "that the crew of the Jin-Ton will be exceptionally disappointed not to be out partying in the local bars tonight. They'll probably drink themselves into oblivion this evening once they've got a taste for the newly arrived whisky. If we make an attempt to board them, say around midnight, then with any luck the ship's crew and its captain would all be in a drunken stupor, fast asleep, or incapable of resistance."

She continued, "OK, decision made. We immediately make preparations to abandon our camp, head for Kismaayo this evening and take the ship one way or another tonight. If we time our arrival for, say, 2300 hours, it should provide the maximum amount of surprise and the greatest possibility of having minimal or no armed confrontation with those on board. It also has the benefit of a drive there in the dark and the best hope that the harbour patrols, such as they are, may have stopped earlier and gone home to bed."

Andrews promptly radioed her plan through to Delta Command's headquarters in the States. In short order it was approved with the directive that, once they had secured the freighter, they were to immediately head north to Dubai. Normally, that would be a very dangerous seven or eight day journey across nearly 1,700 miles of very hostile seas, especially for a ship that normally plied its trade in coastal waters. However, in this case arrangements had been made to place them under the protection of the Australian and then the US navy, once they had made it to the international sea lanes.

They arrived at the outskirts of the city around 2100 hours thankfully without incident. It had been decided that a three man squad, led by Sergeant Oakes and two of the navy team, would initially reconnoitre the harbour and make a search for a suitable vessel to transport them to the freighter.

They moved slowly and silently through the empty streets on foot, armed with only hand pistols and a flashlight, until they came to the waterfront. The wharf area was eerily deserted and thankfully poorly lit; the quayside empty of larger craft. However, there was a preponderance of small fishing smacks bobbing gently in the harbour, but no dinghies. Oakes quickly concluded these were too slow for their purposes. However, what did catch his eye was the Maritime Pilot's boat. It was fast, highly manoeuvrable and undoubtedly sturdy enough for their purposes. Given the absence of any security patrols, he felt it would be possible to surreptitiously get everyone on board without detection and, with any luck, get the boat out of the harbour. It was a calculated risk, but in the circumstances, an acceptable one.

When the team got back to Major Andrews and the others, Oakes reported his assessment of the situation.

"Ma'am, we believe our best option is the pilot's boat. We reason that, to the casual observer, it would seem a perfectly normal occurrence for this to be taken out to sea, despite the hour. Walker and I figure that a covert undocking of a ship, especially under cover of darkness, is an everyday occurrence in this part of the world. Plus, if by any chance there is a lookout on the freighter, then he may well consider such an unscheduled visit from the Pilot somewhat irregular, but nothing more."

Walker continued, "As you are only too well aware, ma'am, in this part of the world, nothing whatsoever is conventional. We believe that the same reasoning will apply equally to any careless soldier-of-fortune who just happened to be located within the confines of the harbour itself. Our previous experience around here suggests that most people preferred to look the other way, not get involved, and mind their own business. Who the hell cares about another routine journey out to sea in the dead of night? Our Aussie chums also tell me that the cloud cover, onshore wind, modest current and tides are in our favour; and it would appear that there are no physical obstacles to clearing the port without mishap."

Quickly concluding that there were few other options available to them and that the risk assessment seemed acceptable, Lyn concurred.

"Right, that's a go; H, could you jam all mobile phones in the area: that should improve the odds in our favour."

The troops collected their night vision equipment and heavy weaponry from the back of their vehicles, which they then immobilised and abandoned. It was a still, humid night as they crept through the empty streets, making their clothing damp and their pistol hand decidedly sticky. Keeping to the shadows, they stealthily made their way to the harbour area, half a mile or so away. They could hear sporadic gunfire and the distant burst of a machine gun, but this seemed to be an altercation well away from their objective. The shooting of guns and the odd explosion were a nightly occurrence in Kismaayo and an inevitable consequence of living almost anywhere in Somalia. Oakes led the way through the outer ring of the harbour and quickly clambered aboard the ship.

Leaning over the railings he whispered to the team waiting patiently alongside the ship, "The pilot's vessel is unmanned and apparently seaworthy ma'am."

The Australian navy contingent quickly followed and immediately released the four mooring lines and two back springs attaching the vessel to the quay, while making preparations to depart. A quick review of the charts indicated a reasonably event-free route to the freighter which was at anchor only a couple of miles offshore.

The engines started without any drama and, undetected, they quickly guided the pilot boat out of the unlit marina for the short trip to their objective. Within what seemed like only a matter of moments they had reached the Jin-Ton, which seemed devoid of life.

Half a dozen of the men, led this time by Major Andrews, scrambled onto the vessel, suitably armed and expecting trouble. Instead they were met with the sight of a crew which had either passed out on deck, or were being violently sick as a result of God knows what poison – masquerading as whisky – they had all been drinking. In short order they had satisfactorily secured the boat, rounded up the captain and crew, locked

41

them in their quarters to sober up, and started the engines. They left the pilot's boat bobbing at anchor and proceeded on a north-easterly course to link up with the Australians, some one hundred odd miles out to sea.

"ETA with HMAS Darwin in approximately eight hours hence, ma'am", said one of the navy contingent now captaining the freighter.

Satisfied that the ship and its cargo were secure, Major Andrews contacted her commanding officer, followed quickly thereafter by the captain of the Australian frigate. Both congratulated her for gaining control of the vessel without bloodshed and confirmed that a US warship would liaise with the Jin-Ton later in the voyage in order to escort them back to Dubai, where a proper forensic analysis could take place. Meanwhile, the CIA had requested that the team make a preliminary inventory of the contents of the containers, as well as forwarding any documentation which they deemed worthy of more detailed scrutiny through to Langley.

"H, turn off the transponders, we'll make our run to the Darwin without ship-to-ship identification; and let's cut the navigation lights. Spread the word: black-out conditions. Oaksey, take a team below. Methodically and painstakingly make your way through the captain's filing cabinets trying to find any paperwork which could possibly help us identify the group or groups behind this enterprise."

Despite their diligent efforts there was precious little which caught their eye in the captains' quarters, beyond the name and a telephone number in Panama which, once forwarded to the States, was already well known to the analysts. Having concluded that this was a largely futile activity, they turned their attention to the twelve containers.

It wasn't proving difficult to open those kept on deck. The problem was the very confined space of those held in the hold which meant they were obliged to work in exceptionally warm and very cramped conditions indeed. As they suspected, the contents were the expected mixture of guns, ammunition, explosives and unlabeled drugs of various kinds. Nothing struck them as especially noteworthy or, given the circumstances, out of the ordinary.

The team were conscientiously making progress towards the back of the hold, systematically recording the contents as best they could, when they eventually made it to the final two containers. These were clearly marked as being destined for the port of Dandong, although there were no details on the outside of whom the intended recipient was. Oakes had become quite practiced at this point in opening each container and peering inside, notebook and flashlight in hand. It was difficult, if not impossible, to see to the very back of each container and unrealistic to actually get inside any of them given the very restricted area they were working in. It was perfectly feasible, therefore, that the first ten containers did indeed hold items which were extremely interesting to the CIA, but whatever it was must be hidden at the unseen ends of each steel unit.

On breaking the seals of the exceptionally well-protected double doors of the eleventh, much smaller container, Oakes exclaimed:

"Holy shit, get Major Andrews here immediately; you are simply not going to believe what I have just found! Come and take a look at this, guys. It's like Tutankhamun's tomb in here; the place is full of bloody gold bars!"

CHAPTER 7

Panama and Beijing

The absence of an 'update' message from Zucca didn't unduly worry Ramos; after all, the radio system onboard the Jin-Ton was notoriously unreliable and very erratic even on a good day. No doubt Zucca would give him the courtesy of a call when they had unloaded the cargo and departed for China, until then he could resort to his default position: 'to hell with it'.

When he was in this frame of mind he rarely bothered going to the office. Instead, his attention and whatever enthusiasm he could muster were consumed by the physical attributes of his favourite girlfriend, lying naked on the bed of his apartment enjoying the never ending stream of tequila shots they were sharing. He just automatically presumed that all was now back on schedule, that the bribes had arrived, the cargo safely stored in the warehouse and, presumably, all was well with the world.

His ultimate 'lords and masters' in Beijing however, were of a very different disposition. Within five minutes of the transponders being turned off they were alerted to the ship's apparent disappearance. The bank of screens they used to track all the vessels which the shipping agency had chartered no longer had a flashing identification dot from the Jin-Ton.

The manager responsible for the unit which monitored the various ships who were transporting cargo for the company immediately tried to establish whether their own satellite or computer systems were at fault. The technicians quickly reported back to him that they were all working satisfactorily. Next he consulted the Lloyd's Register of Shipping to double-check the precise specifications of the missing vessel. It reported that the freighter was over twenty years old and – although certified as currently seaworthy – it did flag it up as a 'high premium insurance risk' on the basis of its age and condition. Finally he requested a precise weather assessment for the area, which came back as 'sea swell moderate, visibility good at ten miles plus, no storm warnings'. Nothing untoward there, he thought.

Next he quickly checked with the accounts department that the slush money for the port officials' bribes had been transferred. He established that it had indeed arrived at the local bank but, as yet, no one had thus far been to collect it. Confused as to what to do after he had methodically gone through the check list of procedures and drawn a blank, he made a call to his supervisor.

"Boss, I don't know what has happened but the Jin-Ton, currently offshore Somalia, has just disappeared from our screens. It's just possible that it's somehow inexplicably sunk, but I very much doubt it. More likely it's a transmission failure from their side. Can you come and take a look please?"

Qiang Li eventually entered the room in a state of trepidation: once he received the call from the duty officer, he immediately knew that if the valuable cargo was lost, his prestigious role in the department was, in all likelihood, over. Failure was not expected, or tolerated, within the organisation he was proud to run. Military discipline and therefore military punishment were ever present. Serious mistakes such as this were invariably punished by summary executions or much worse, twenty years in some god-forsaken gulag being re-educated: his next trip may well be to the dreaded 'Laojiao' prison, where death was prayed for daily by those incarcerated there.

"Show me the last known position of the ship."

Pointing to the monitor in front of them, his colleague said: "It was here Sir, two miles off Kismaayo. It's been stationary for nearly 36 hours now. I'm told by the banking department that progress has probably been held up because the docking fees have only just been transferred. Other than that we have had no recent communication with the ship or our agent in Panama."

"Curious. Get me Ramos immediately. Also find out what resources we have on the ground in Somalia that can go to the port and establish what has happened."

"Will do Sir. I gather we have a couple of operatives in the city. Shall I try and contact them as well?"

★ ★ ★

In the throes of passion, Ramos didn't hear the mobile phone for quite some time. He would also have been the first to admit that he was drunk as a skunk and, given the gravity of the situation, in no position to take the call. Through slurred speech he garbled:

"Yes; what is it? I'm busy. Call me tomorrow."

"It's Qiang Li here, China desk. I take it from the tone of your voice that you're not exactly sober Ramos? What the hell has happened to the Jin-Ton, we've lost contact with it? Has the captain been in touch with you in the last twenty four hours?"

"Not a word. I'd assume they have left port by now."

"Not a word, eh? You've been neglecting your responsibilities Ramos. Pity."

Qiang Li calmly put the phone down and turned to his colleague, who by now was cowering in anticipation of his own fate.

"Arrange for him to be taken off the payroll, permanently! I'll leave you to try and make contact with the ship, plus you had better get our contacts in Somalia to the harbour with the cash without delay. Find the ship, or you will find yourself suffering the same misfortune. I'm going for a meeting with the chief."

★ ★ ★

The drive across Beijing was full of foreboding and apprehension for Qiang Li. Up until this point he felt reassured that his military career was being fast-tracked and his life-chances materially enhanced; now he was convinced it would all end in ruins. Fate, in the shape of a missing dot on a computer screen, had dealt him the ultimate 'dead hand'.

He dreaded visiting the August 1st Building, headquarters of the People's Liberation Army, as his presence there had only one purpose: to report serious trouble. His commanding officer and de facto head of the army, General Xiao Fan, was not a man to take bad news lightly. Both men knew that the possible loss of the extremely precious cargo – from which the general would benefit handsomely when his ten percent cut of the 'merchandise' was eventually deposited in his own very private vault located close to the North Korea border – far outweighed the life or career of one individual.

"So Qiang, I gather you have lost one of our beloved country's most valuable ships?" The general didn't even bother to raise his head from the papers he was studying, as the much junior officer stood rigidly to attention on the other side of his desk.

"Get it back, or face the consequences."

"We are trying to get a new satellite fix on it, Sir."

He slowly put his pen back into its holder on the desk and stared intently at the person in front of him.

"Don't bother Comrade Qiang, I have already received that information; it would appear to be heading towards an Australian naval ship. The Darwin, I understand. The captain of the Jin-Ton may well have been given a better offer by the capitalist lapdogs. I'll deal with him personally later. We currently don't have any navy assets of our own nearby, but they are studying whether it's feasible to somehow recapture our own ship and return the cargo to its rightful owners. Now get out and await my instructions."

General Xiao was now faced with what seemed like an intractable dilemma. Without question its resolution would require political input at the highest levels within the Politburo. He placed a call through to his counterpart on the Standing Committee.

"We have a problem on our hands minister, which needs your immediate consideration. It is quite possible that the master of the Jin-Ton, an Italian called Captain Zucca, has gone 'rogue' and deserted our cause. My initial guess is that he had inspected the cargo and decided he would help himself to its contents. Zucca has been completely reliable and trustworthy for the past ten years, but overnight he appears to have departed from his planned route back to Dandong, without dropping off the military supplies we have arranged for al-Shabaab. I have a team tracking the ship and they are currently working on a plan to recapture it."

"So, Xiao, what is the crisis?"

"It would appear minister that we have a political problem to deal with. It's just possible that Zucca could be heading towards a rendezvous with the Australian navy, who fortuitously just happen to have a warship stationed to the south of Mogadishu. It's therefore quite plausible that he had been persuaded to change sides and, if so, he may very well disclose the entire operation of ChinKo Inc. to his new allies."

"Well just close it down and re-open another company."

"That's already in hand minister. The political dimension is that, eventually, he is certain to admit that the ship had been chartered by China, so very soon the entire world will know that we are complicit in smuggling guns and contraband into

Somalia. By the same token they are going to have one hell of a surprise when they open the rest of the cargo. Even if you gave the command, we don't have any ships or submarines close by to sink it: an aircraft strike would almost certainly be immediately intercepted. So I think its damage limitation time minister, possibly with a pre-emptive denial in the world's media?"

"I want our gold recovered, is that clear?" He paused to check his diary.

"Good God Xiao, I've just realised, we have the Australian Prime Minister here on a State visit in three weeks' time. Find a way to intercept the damn ship before they get their hands on it. You are on my list as the first person to be hanged if this goes wrong. I'm afraid that this matter may have to be referred to the Premier, who, I have a feeling, will not be best pleased with your pathetic efforts."

CHAPTER 8

Claridge's & Downing Street

The exquisite art deco 'Foyer' restaurant at Claridge's was unusually busy for a Monday morning, but Sebastian Fortes was a frequent visitor and could always be guaranteed to get a table for breakfast, lunch or dinner. Over the years he had come to regard the hotel as the extremely expensive 'works canteen', given its proximity to the bank's offices in Berkeley Square.

The waiter was hovering attentively by their table, menus in hand, but both men had been here often enough to know it by heart. Carrington was the first to speak.

"Ah, good man: I'll have the scrambled eggs *'en brioche'* with caviar and a glass of champagne. You're still using the d'Aquitaine caviar I take it?"

"It is indeed Sir, and may I recommend the Pol Roger 2000, the Sir Winston Churchill, exquisite bouquet, perfect accompaniment for caviar? And for you Mr. Fortes, eggs Benedict as usual? And a large Bloody Mary?" Sebastian nodded his approval.

"Perfect way to start the day Sebastian; a healthy breakfast! Now, to the business in hand. The Governor of the Bank and my good self have recently submitted an urgent report to the government on the state of the gold market, which I will quickly attempt to summarise before our breakfast arrives."

He raised his glass and symbolically made a silent cheers gesture towards Seb.

"Firstly, there is a huge discrepancy between the amount of gold that China says it has in its vaults and the amount we believe it to really hold. And when I say huge, I mean stupendous. Secondly, over the past few years we have seen a very significant surge in bullion imports into their country, which just seem to disappear from the radar once it's got onshore. Thirdly, from our intelligence sources on the ground we have a good handle on the amount of gold which China mines each year, give or take a few tonnes; however for some reason only about two thirds of this gets recorded in the official statistics. Fourthly – and for the time being at least, in order to give me time to eat – the stockpile of physical gold held by the private sector seems unbelievably vast. We suspect it somehow finds its way into the country's vaults and is not being held by mom-and-pop under the bed. Now, what do you think of that."

"I'm only just getting to grips with this market Dominic, but that's an impressive list of curiosities to say the least. As you will recall, my recent involvement with China has concentrated exclusively on the shenanigans with its currency and the way they have tried to manipulate it in relation to the dollar. So it wouldn't surprise me in the slightest that they have moved their focus of attention onto another target. Having only recently returned from my stint in Hong Kong I know full well that China has never dropped its desire to have their currency rule world trade. By coincidence, on Friday I asked one of the analysts at d'Abo's for their client report on the gold market, which I managed to read through last night. They concluded that the futures market had become dangerously unstable recently. So, if you hadn't called for this meeting, I certainly was planning to do so."

"Good; we are on the same wavelength."

"The problem as I see it Dominic, is that China simply feels that over the past twenty years it has accumulated far too many dollars and therefore its reserves are overly concentrated in one asset class; US Treasuries: one point three or four trillion of them at the last count. It is quite easy to understand that at times they feel very vulnerable to America's manipulation of the dollar by the Federal Reserve, and they get it in the neck every time the US sneezes. I am willing to bet that they believe they have effectively lost control of their own currency, other than by the occasional tactical devaluation. My guess is that they will publically defend any surge of their gold bullion holding as being a simple expedient to diversify away from the dollar. No one will really blame them for that; and neither should we. Although I should add that I don't understand why they go to so much trouble to actually conceal their gold holdings from the rest of the world."

"I can't fault that logic Sebastian, but it leaves the Western banking system very dangerously exposed indeed."

"Why?"

"Because every major bank in the world has a bullion desk on their trading floors which speculates in gold for themselves and their clients. The Bank of England holds the view, as indeed do I, that the short positions now being taken by these banks have become as dangerous as the sub-prime mortgage scandal ten years ago. The trading in gold futures is simply vast – astonishingly so – measured in trillions of dollars; but the physical gold supporting this trading is, for the most part, now sitting in secret vaults in China. Our banks have precious little gold themselves, so this has all the hallmarks, if you will excuse the pun, of a massive speculative crisis: they can create short positions out of thin air all day long and presume nothing bad will ever happen to them. The banks think they are in control of this process for their own commercial benefit, whereas I think they are being suckered into an ambush."

"Jesus Prof, this calls for a couple more drinks! I think I'd better have a quiet word with our trading desk, pronto. Better make that a bottle."

★ ★ ★

"The Secretary of State for Defence is on the line Prime Minister."

"Put him through please Nadia."

"Charlie, I have just had a message in from my Aussie counterparts in Canberra. I gather that one of their navy ships, which is apparently stationed offshore Somalia on a routine anti-smuggling patrol, has linked up with a barely seaworthy rust bucket of some sort. Nothing especially odd in that you may say, except it has a compliment of US Special Forces on board who appear to have recently hijacked it. The report goes on to say that it is stuffed to the gunnels with arms and so forth, although what caught my eye was the statement that it also has two containers loaded with gold bars in the hold. Christ knows how valuable that is, but there seems to be tonnes of the bloody stuff. According to the latest transmission into the Ministry of Defence, the Americans are going to escort the freighter to Dubai for a detailed forensic analysis. Bizarrely, the bods in the MOD must have spent slightly too long in the bar today as they seem to think the ship is called the 'Gin and Tonic', would you believe. Anyway I digress; the killer piece of intelligence is that it's destined for Dandong which is located on the border of China and North Korea. If my supposition is correct, this directly and incontrovertibly links China with arms smuggling to al-Shabaab and quite possibly al-Qaeda."

Ignoring what the minister of defence clearly thought was the most important matter, the PM exclaimed: "Did you say gold?"

"Yes, it says here that there must be several tonnes of the stuff on board. When Langley inspected a photograph of one of the bars they told the Aussies that, given the markings on the ingots, it must have originated from a Swiss refinery. I know sod all about gold bars, but it's mighty odd, don't you think?"

"Extremely interesting indeed. Can you get a more detailed report sent through to Number 10, with a copy to the chancellor?"

"Not a problem Prime Minister. I'm also going to see what US Naval Intelligence is prepared to tell us about this; more specifically, why they have a crack Special Forces unit on board. I'm also checking with the First Sea Lord to establish if we have any vessels in the area which may be able to assist."

The call having ended, the PM's mind drifted back to the Bank of England's paper on China and the threats it implied to the UK financial system if it was true. He quickly picked up the phone to his secretary: "Nadia, can you get in touch with Amanda, the Bank Governor plus that odious fellow Dominic Carrington at Imperial College, and set up a meeting here for tomorrow?"

★ ★ ★

"So let me try and understand all this Prof", said Sebastian as their glasses were generously re-filled, "the banks in your organisation are probably all 'Naked Shorts', implying that they have insufficient gold to support their trading positions and are praying for a fall in the price of gold before these contracts mature. In that way they can profitably cash out ahead of the game. Last night I saw in my bank's strategy paper that it suggested that the four largest bullion traders have now written approximately 250,000 futures contracts which are net short. That's 25 million ounces of gold; or nearly 800 tonnes. Is that correct?"

"Absolutely spot on, Seb! And most of this exposure is not hedged by counterbalancing long contracts, which would be the obvious and prudent thing to do. Plus, of course, the price of gold continues to rise, not fall."

"As the regulator can't you or the Bank of England stop that happening? Isn't this market-rigging on a grand scale?"

"It could very easily be described that way Seb: as you well know, for every winner in this market, there is an equal and opposite loser. I guess it depends on which side of the fence you are sitting. For the losers there will be blood on the floor, that's for certain. However, I'm willing to bet that most of the traders involved think of themselves as just the dog's bollocks; financial geniuses. Or they simply revel in being plain old fashioned East End spivs worth millions when down the pub with their mates on a Friday night, bragging about how they have screwed whatever sucker bought one of these contracts."

As the bill for breakfast arrived, Carrington's phone went off rather too piercingly for the near silence of the dining room. He answered it straight away, if for no other reason than to put a stop to the contemptuous stares directed towards him from those on adjacent tables. His eyebrows instantly rose in surprise:

"Good heavens", he said rather too flamboyantly, "I'd better take this in the lobby Sebastian; it's Number 10."

CHAPTER 9

Indian Ocean

The rendezvous between the Jin-Ton and the Darwin occurred approximately one hundred and fifty miles east of Mogadishu in waters that demanded constant vigilance. The threat to shipping in the area had increased materially in recent months, with the number of piracy attacks escalating once more. The Australian navy warship was already on a heightened level of security given the volume of shipping traversing the coast of Somalia that month, all of which were highly susceptible to hijacking, bloodshed and extortionate ransom demands.

The imminent arrival of the Jin-Ton merely added to the navy's task-list of concerns. The week had already been exceptionally busy for them, as they escorted two very substantial oil tankers and an LPG carrier in convoy south through the Indian Ocean, thankfully without any drama.

Once the freighter was stationed alongside the warship, it enabled the Special Forces team under the command of Major Andrews to be transferred to the safety of the frigate and, temporarily at least, to be relieved of their duties for this mission. All they really wanted however was a square meal, clean uniforms and a long, hot shower.

The captain of the Darwin, Graham Rogers, was now being inundated with requests from a stream of intelligence agencies, asking for any information that could be extracted, preferably very quickly, on who the Jin-Ton's real paymasters were. As yet it was unclear whether her captain would co-operate and provide the details the CIA and others wanted. Perhaps they would have to wait for the American warship to arrive with their contingent of specialist interrogators.

Rogers called for a meeting with Lyn and her team to assess what to do next.

"Firstly, my congratulations on a brilliant job by all involved for getting the freighter here in one piece and with no casualties; apart from the self-inflicted hangovers some of these guys now have. I'm told there were a dozen, mixed nationality, crew members on board. They are currently being treated under armed guard in the sick bay for alcohol poisoning and severe dehydration, but they will all live I gather. At some point we will have to arrange a helicopter transfer of you to whatever US ship they send to link up with us. It's unclear as yet if the American authorities intend to take Captain Zucca and the crew into custody, no doubt they will let us know their intentions soon enough. I have a number of volunteers from the Darwin who will take the freighter up to Dubai. So enjoy our Aussie hospitality until the position becomes clearer. Oh, and Major Andrews, you have a request to call General Sanford when you get a moment; I believe he's presently in the UK, Strategic Air Command, European HQ. I'll see you all in the mess at 1900 with any updates we receive."

A couple of hours later and US-Australian relations were deemed by all present to be in excellent shape, as the group enjoyed the generous hospitality of the Darwin's wardroom. The sun was most definitely over the yard arm – to the delight of every man jack in the navy for generations past – and the celebrations were in full swing.

"Nothing binds people together more quickly Lyn, than a common cause, a shared purpose and a large drink: I raise a toast to our newly invigorated *entente cordiale*." Captain Rogers was eager to allow them as much respite as they needed in order to recover from the depravations and hardships they had endured while they were in camp.

"So ladies and gentlemen, what's it like being holed up in the jungle behind enemy lines for six months? I think the navy's equivalent is being in the engine room sweating blood for the entire trip, but without the bullets. Isn't that right Chief Engineer Barker?" The entire table roared in laughter as, once more, the port was passed to the left.

"Well Captain, it was more than a little testing at times," said Lyn, "but we are well trained for such things and our objective was always very clear. The only thing to come totally out of the blue was the request to capture the Jin-Ton. That posed a few technical challenges I have to say; and without your help it could have all ended in tears. Presumably you have had one of your staff inspect the cargo. We're all baffled as to why there is so much gold on board."

"Indeed. As yet no one has satisfactorily explained it to me either, Lyn. I gather Zucca didn't know what he had in the containers, but that seems to be quite common amongst these rogue ships; the cargo is never inspected. He is currently in the brig keeping shtum, exercising his right to silence and non co-operation. What is it the members of the Sicilian mafia say, *omertà*? Ten to a penny the CIA will request that we keelhaul him if he doesn't speak up very soon."

"Perhaps we can rustle up a horse's head from the galley, Captain?" interjected Oakes.

"I'll see if we have one on board!"

The mess orderly entered the room with two notes for Captain Rogers.

"Message from the interrogation team, Sir."

The captain quickly skimmed through the first item.

"Well there you go, tell the chef to cancel the horse's head. Just to contradict my previous statement Lyn, I gather Zucca – who's now sober by the way, but desperate for another drink

– has decided to be very helpful indeed. Remarkable what you can extract for a couple of bottles of vodka and that filthy stuff, what's-it-called; grappa? He's behaving like every mercenary since time immemorial; willing to work for whosoever looks after his own self-interests and naturally, he will line up behind those that pay the best. Your colleagues in Langley have very deep pockets apparently, which seems to have persuaded Zucca to retire to some villa in Tuscany."

"And this just in from Vice-Admiral John Oliver, Sir."

Rogers slowly and carefully read the second message in silence, before placing the paper face down on the table, his face a picture of puzzlement.

"I'll be damned Lyn, our Chief of Defence Staff in Canberra has issued me with quite extraordinary new orders. It also says that you will be receiving similar instructions from General Sanford apparently. I take it you haven't called him yet? You'd better do that as soon as possible, I suggest." Lyn nodded.

"We are to release the Jin-Ton back into the hands of Zucca, put a detachment of men on board and sail it to Dandong. It would appear the CIA now believes that, on balance, they will learn more by allowing the ship to continue its journey, minus the gold naturally, which they think has been purloined in Eastern Europe. Zucca is to be persuaded to say to the Chinese that he decided to leave Kismaayo without unloading, because he couldn't resolve the requirement for a bribe and couldn't reach Ramos, whoever he is."

"There is an element of plausibility in that I guess", said Lyn, "and if he can let the bad-guys know the transponder is playing up, then they may well believe him. Oh, and he should mention that the radio is only working intermittently."

Captain Rogers nodded.

"I think we need to expedite this immediately; the longer the two ships are alongside the more likely it is that we will be spotted by someone. Not sure it's going to be feasible to transfer the gold, but we do have a largish crane aft, so we'll have to see what we can achieve. I'll give orders to commence the transfer of everyone back to the Jin-Ton at first light and see if it's possible to move the gold."

"Excellent, then I will try and reach General Sanford now Sir. Do you think we should also accompany the ship to China?"

"Doesn't say here Lyn; I have been ordered to deploy half a dozen of my men. I have no objection to you adding to that number if you wish?"

"I'm more than willing to go, but maybe it makes more sense that only Staff Sergeant Oakes joins your team. It's not exactly a big vessel so it's going to get very crowded if we all go. Is that OK with you Oaksey, a serious boys' outing to China? You get the Presidential Suite."

"Fine by me, ma'am; just about got my sea legs by now! I take it the rum ration will be commensurate with my new responsibilities?"

By 0630 the following day, the navy had transferred the majority of the gold bullion onto the Darwin and relocated Zucca and some of his crew to the ship. Oakes and the Australian contingent had gone on board earlier that morning to supervise the movement of cargo and personnel which were gradually being moved back and forth. They were now safely ensconced on board the Jin-Ton undertaking last minute checks before they departed. It had been decided overnight that Captain Rogers would immediately head south, away from the freighter, and the Jin-Ton sail directly north-east, so as to quickly put as much distance as possible between them.

Overnight Lyn had an extensive conversation with her mentor and friend, General James Sanford, each briefing the other on their respective view of the current situation.

"Good to hear that all is well with you Lyn. Given your involvement in this mission and our past exploits in Asia, I've been delegated to act as mission controller from now on. A spot of active duty will be good for my soul. The first thing I want you to do is re-locate back to London. We are going to get you off the Darwin as soon as practical, probably drop you off at the Seychelles and fly you back from there. If you wish, I'll alert Fortes you are due in town, must be quite a while since you were last together. Has he given you a diamond ring yet?"

"That would be great General. How long will I be in the UK? Oh, and no he hasn't; you couldn't go and rough him up a little could you?"

"You got it. I suspect your trip to the UK will not last very long. Apparently there is something profound happening in the gold markets Lyn; involving our friends the Chinese again. I'll brief you on it when you get here and I have a clearer picture myself. Do you recall our old buddy at the Federal Reserve, Lewis Moyns? Well, he has asked me to try and re-assemble the Dark Pool team in a big hurry? Not entirely sure why. He is flying into the UK in a few days time; so you're on furlough till then. I'll see what can be done to pick you up after I've arranged your transfer back here, hopefully starting at dawn tomorrow."

"OK Sir, I'll just go and pack my non-existent wardrobe in a carrier bag, then have a final de-briefing with Captain Rogers and the team. We intend to put some distance between us and the Jin-Ton, but you are probably aware of that? And Zucca seems to be happy to lie through his teeth on our behalf, providing we extract him from Dandong with his balls intact and re-house him in some style. The interrogation guys tell me he's got his heart set on some place called Castello di Sismano in southern Umbria: they checked it out and lost count after 40 bedrooms, God knows how many acres; but it's a steal at 10 million dollars I gather."

"Zucca's a bloody reprobate; damn CIA has more money than sense. And don't forget Lyn; bring back a gold bar for analysis! See you soon Major."

"Yes, Sir! I can bring two if you promise me that no one will notice."

★ ★ ★

"If I may, I'll also have Sebastian Fortes join us?" Carrington paused momentarily awaiting confirmation from the Number 10 switchboard, "Jolly good, we'll both be there at 5pm tomorrow." He casually meandered back across the lobby at Claridge's where his new found companion was waiting. "Presumably you can make a meeting at Number 10 tomorrow at five sharp, Seb? The PM wants to discuss this gold business."

"Yes, that's not a problem, Dominic. It will also give me time to do some background reading and talk to my guys in the bank."

CHAPTER 10

Beijing

Five hours since they left the safety of the Darwin, Zucca was instructed by Sergeant Oakes to turn the ship's location beacon back on and place a call through to the shipping agency in Panama. The radio transmission was being constantly monitored not only by the American's but, more importantly, it was being instantly re-routed to the military unit tracking the vessels progress in Beijing.

The Chinese soldier whose task it was to spend endless hours patiently waiting for the illusive phone call, or radar ping, from the lost vessel shouted over to his colleague:

"Would you believe it's the captain of the Jin-Ton, Sir? They are back on the screen and he has just radioed Ramos and wants to speak with whoever is in charge."

"Put him through to my office; and let General Xiao know at once. Tell him I'll be in touch with him immediately I've finished this call."

"Lieutenant Qiang here, is that Captain Zucca of the Jin-Ton? Go ahead please."

"Who the hell are you and where's bloody Ramos? I hope you've killed him because it's the first thing I intend to do when I get off this godforsaken ship?"

"Ramos is, how do you say in English, permanently indisposed Captain and his duties have been transferred to my authority here in Beijing. Can you explain why you failed to deliver the cargo in Kismaayo and why you have been off the radar screens for the past day and a half?"

"Because the ship you have given me to command for this voyage is a pile of miserable, useless junk, where nothing works. The crew are idle bastards, the radio is hopeless, the engines need constant attention, and what do you mean we are off the radar?"

"You are not transmitting your location Captain. We have lost you on our satellite system. Have you interfered with your Automatic Identification System or the transponder?"

"Well just add that to the list of things that are buggered on this ship, will you."

Oakes and one of the Australian navy team were sitting next to Zucca in the confines of the small radio room listening intently to what was being said to ensure nothing untoward was revealed or implied. They both gave him an encouraging thumbs-up signal and whispered encouragement to keep up the exaggeration and bluster.

"And another thing Qiang, or whatever your goddamn name is, none of your guys turned up at the port to pay for delivery of the cargo. What was I expected to do, stay there and rot? The crew were ready to jump ship; they got crazy drunk on some rotgut whisky, woke up in a very ugly, mutinous mood; so I decided to head straight for Dandong before they all swam ashore."

"Understood. Do you still have the containers? All the containers?"

"Of course we do, you idiot; I've just told you I couldn't unload them."

"OK, I will report our conversation to a higher authority and then give you further instructions. I think your voyage is compromised Zucca: so for the moment do not head to Dandong, but steer for the port of Hambantota in Sri Lanka. We have secure port facilities there and can either escort you to China, or transfer the cargo to another ship."

"No way, Qiang! I don't trust you people with money

anymore; and we are not docking anywhere until I have bank confirmation that our contract is paid out in full. If not, then we will divert to Diego Garcia and surrender whatever it is we have in the hold to the British or the Americans. I'm sure they will be most interested in it."

An infuriated Qiang spat back, "I'll contact you again within the hour about the funds transfer; meanwhile, head for the secure port at Hambantota. The coordinates are 6.13 degrees north, 81.1 degrees east. I will have my people there to meet you; go to Quay number 8."

Oakes made a signal with a hand gesture across his throat to indicate that Zucca should cut the conversation.

"You'd better have crystal clear evidence that the money is in the account Qiang, otherwise our business together is through, permanently!" With that he switched off the radio transmitter and turned to Oakes who was smiling broadly.

"Well done Zucca; that performance deserves an Oscar. Most definitely calls for another bottle of vodka." He patted him firmly on the back and pulled out the charts to see where the hell Hambantota was. "We need time to think our options through here. I'm sure my boss would prefer it if we went to our original destination, but I'll check with her before we reconnect with Qiang."

★ ★ ★

"Could you put me through to Major Andrews, it's Sergeant Oakes here?"

The ultra-secure ship-to-ship communications link to HMAS Darwin was virtually instantaneous and crystal clear, "Oaksey here ma'am. The Chinese want us to divert to Sri Lanka, some place called Hambantota apparently, and unload all, I repeat all, the cargo. I gather they have a dedicated port facility there, but Zucca is stalling for time until we know what our response should be. He's using the ruse of wanting cash up-front before he releases any of the containers. We are expecting their response momentarily. Can you establish what our comeback should be please?"

"Got that; my initial reaction is to insist on heading to Dandong. I gather they have a substantial, but private, gold vault there which it would be good to have a closer look at, but I'll double check. My only concern is to get you and your navy chums out in one piece wherever you end up. Stand by, back shortly."

Lyn moved away from the microphone and for a fleeting moment Sebastian image came crashing back into her consciousness. She had managed to keep him out of her mind for all the time she was in Somalia, but her legendary self-control slipped momentarily and a tear of relief once more filled her eye. All she could think of was his re-capture in mainland China what seemed like an eternity ago and the fervent hope that history was not about to repeat itself with Oakes.

★ ★ ★

Within thirty minutes she was back on the radio.

"Oaksey, I've just finished a long conversation with General Sanford who is taking over command of this mission henceforth. He would like you to play very hardball indeed. The General has confirmed that Zucca should continue to insist upon immediate payment of all his fees, expenses, the crews' wages and a big bonus up-front, before any decision on which port to head for is confirmed. That way we can at least track where the funds originated from – the CIA are very keen indeed to establish whether its North Korea, or China, or both via some joint bank enterprise they are not aware of."

"No problem with that suggestion from this side ma'am; it's already been done."

"Great. Assuming Beijing buys that; then Zucca is to confirm to them that the Jin-Ton will indeed head to Sri Lanka. The General is very confident we can protect the team if you have to dock there, but his preferred outcome is to make it all the way to China, even though it's considerably riskier for you guys."

"I think we can do that ma'am."

"At some point in the voyage north we are going to have to fabricate a very good reason for you to bypass Sri Lanka and head to Dandong. But no one has come up with a suitably bright idea yet! If you get an order to go round in circles for a while Oaksey, you'll know its situation normal and we are still struggling for ideas."

Hating loose ends in the midst of a mission, Lyn decided to head for the sanctuary of her allocated bunk, sleep on it overnight and pray that a flash of inspiration would be forthcoming before her departure to the UK at dawn.

CHAPTER 11

New York, London and the Indian Ocean

Lewis Moyns stared intently out of the enormous floor-to-ceiling windows of his suite of executive offices on the upper floor of the Federal Reserve building, his feet resting languidly on the desk. The New York skyline was as spectacular as ever, with the morning sun glistening off the endless glass-fronted skyscrapers in the downtown business district. The reflections and quintessential imagery of the city below acted as a welcome distraction to his train of thought, while he patiently waited for his call to be placed through to the UK prime minister.

It had been almost two years since he and Charles Sheer had last spoken at a suitably extravagant White House reception in their honour, during which time they both had the good fortune to see their careers prosper spectacularly. As the newly appointed chairman of the Fed, following the retirement a year earlier of the indomitable Alison Fletcher, Lewis would have made his late mother very proud indeed. In his mind, however, he had not yet reached the pinnacle of his ambitions: to create the best thoroughbred stud in the country, based, naturally, in his beloved Texas.

To his everlasting regret the flamboyant cowboy boots and Stetson hat were, of enforced necessity, less in evidence these days. On innumerable formal occasions since his elevation to the hot-seat at the Fed, they had to be replaced by very sombre pin-striped suits befitting his new found status as head of the world's most important central bank. However, he had no intention whatsoever of abandoning his cherished heritage: once a cowboy, always a cowboy. Thankfully for the free world, his passion for crisis management was still very much intact and he could feel in his bones that a humdinger of a disaster was brewing.

"Charlie, its Lewis here. A very good morning to you Prime Minister from a sunny New York and a pleasure to chat again after so long. I hope you're still looking after the talented Miss Price for me; and that reprobate Fortes? Jeez, I miss those guys. Look, I'll be brief, I received a courtesy copy of the 'Naked Shorts' paper on the gold markets from the Governor of the Bank. I should tell you that its ramifications have been worrying me deeply ever since. I'm totally convinced that those bastards are at it again. So, if it's OK with you, I'd like to set up a meeting with the boys and girls from our 'Dark Pools' days to discuss the implication and see if we can figure out what's going on? I can be in London tomorrow for a group meeting and, if you don't mind, there are one or two things we need to discuss in the strictest of confidence, very much in private."

"OK, you've got my attention Lewis. By pure coincidence I have a meeting scheduled for this very topic tomorrow at five. I'll send you a list of the attendees. Should I defer it, or can you make that?"

The prime minister, who considered himself to be a seasoned exponent of the dark-arts of high-stakes politics, frowned as he let the phrase 'very much in confidence' roll around in his mind for a split second. Given the twenty-four hours a day demands of his office, he had not really given much thought to Lewis for a considerable time. Now that he was chairman of the Federal Reserve, perhaps he had better take him a little more seriously and put to one side his highly prejudiced view that he was a happy-go-luck, hard drinking, Texan. He didn't know it, but the feeling was mutual: shallow, self-obsessed and not really trustworthy would have been the chairman's very private 'file note' on the UK's prime minister.

"Not the slightest problem Charlie. See you at five, sharp."

The instant the phone was placed back on the receiver the bonhomie immediately drained from the face of Lewis as he pondered how much of the truth he dare tell the prime minister.

★ ★ ★

The radio transmitter on-board the Jin-Ton buzzed incessantly, echoing noisily throughout the bridge one deck above it. When it was eventually answered, Zucca and Oakes were summoned to the five square feet space that masqueraded as the communications room.

"Qiang here. Listen carefully Zucca; my bosses have confirmed that they want you to dock in our port facility in southern Sri Lanka. We will arrange for a replacement crew and passage home for you and your team. I'm also told from Beijing that your fees will be paid, but only when they see that the contents of the containers have not been tampered with and are intact."

"Well that's just not going to cut it Qiang. It's a daily drama here trying to stop all these bastards attempting to kill me. If they become convinced you are up to your old tricks, then they will mutiny for sure and take the ship Christ knows where. Besides which, many of them don't want to disembark in Sri Lanka. One of the guys tells me he's wanted for attempted murder there, a regrettable consequence of the last time they docked in that country. Plus, two of his crazy pals are accomplices. So that's damn near half the ship's crew who will refuse to go there."

Oakes gave a broad smile of admiration towards Zucca, whom he had grown to like enormously in the few days they had been shipmates. This guy's 'on-the-hoof' improvisation is really good, he silently concluded.

"This is not a negotiation Zucca, it's a command."

"Well you know where you can put that Qiang, as we say back home: *su per il culo*. See you in Dandong."

With that he leant over and deliberately shut the radio down before there could be a reply, thinking the best course of action now was to let them stew a while. Turning to Oakes, who was clearly perplexed at the Italian turn of phrase, he said in a matter of fact way: "I think it translates loosely to 'you can shove that idea up your ass', so let's hope they have a recording of that in Beijing."

"Well if that doesn't get us blown out of the water, nothing will. Let's hope the gold is worth more to them than the pleasure of torpedoing us. Care to join me in a glass or two of vodka Captain; we may need more of your courage, or foolhardiness, before this voyage is completed."

★ ★ ★

Professor Dominic Carrington thoroughly enjoyed the silence and sanctuary of the university laboratories, especially very late at night. It was his special place to retreat to and contemplate life's intractable problems, mercifully devoid of students to disturb the tranquillity. He needed a clear head in preparation for what he expected to be a difficult meeting tomorrow with the PM, who would undoubtedly make him a scapegoat for whatever problems were coming down the track if he was not very careful indeed. Earlier in the evening he had received a call to say that the chairman of the Federal Reserve, no less, would also be in attendance. Something rather more pressing must be afoot for such an august participant to join them.

Number 10 was delighted with the suggestion that he bring Sebastian Fortes with him, so his stock had temporarily risen, but quite naturally he didn't want it to crash spectacularly to the ground by being ill prepared. Perhaps this would be a suitable occasion to repair his fractured relationship with Charlie Sheer, but he doubted it. The man's still an idiot, even if I am invited over for tea and Downing Street biscuits. He would just have to work through the issues in his usual methodological way and re-read every file and article he possessed on cornering the commodities market.

Carrington sat in contemplative silence running through the meeting he was also planning to have with the bullion banks in a couple of days time and how best to use Fortes' talents to maximum advantage. Pacing the lab benches he kept repeating to himself, 'Just what the hell is China up to'; and equally importantly, 'was there anything he, they, we, any bugger, could do to stop them'? Especially if it was going to plunge his organisation and the gold market into mortal danger.

Although the equivalent of a tightly-held state secret, the statistics on China's gold holdings were more-or-less irrefutable, give or take a few hundred tonnes. He conjectured that the Fed may have a totally different opinion, of course; but he would soon be able to establish their position. If they were in accord, or worse, there was indeed a hell of a problem to deal with. He had often met Lewis Moyns predecessor, but not the man himself – let's hope he likes French wine and English hospitality!

CHAPTER 12

Downing Street

Sebastian Fortes awoke at six thirty to bright sunshine flooding through the blinds into his apartment overlooking the Thames. The familiar sight, many floors below, of the river at high tide was a source of continual joy to him. As usual, it was teeming with early morning activity: pleasure craft repositioning themselves for the day ahead and the ultra-keen rowers already expending far too much energy for such a beautiful summer's day. Fumbling over the endless complexity of his new coffee machine, while attempting to make his customary double espresso, he absentmindedly unplugged his phone from the charger on his desk and commenced checking the endless messages he had received overnight.

Since returning to London, Seb had, by his own admission, become a creature of sloth-like habits at this time in the morning. He somehow managed to function instinctively, as if by remote control, trying desperately to get his bearings for the day ahead without mishap in the kitchen or bathroom. He manfully tried to steer well clear of any sharp knives, boiling water and valuable objects he could easily knock over, if at all possible. When he eventually managed to find 'the bloody TV thing', which was inevitably lost under the pile of cushions on the sofa, he would flick on to the early morning business show to see what, if anything, had happened to the markets in Asia. His interest in the economic welfare of Hong Kong burned as bright as ever, despite the hour.

These days it seemed to take him a good ten minutes, or more, to regain consciousness: 'that's what happens when you approach forty' he thought. To his delight and utter amazement his in-tray didn't just contain the inevitable dreary emails from colleagues at the bank, but amidst the listing he had received one each from both Lewis Moyns and General Sanford. It was as if the world had been instantly turned back two years and could only mean one thing: trouble with a very large capital T.

He chose to read the one from his distinguished buddy at the Federal Reserve first as he was somewhat hesitant to open the mail from Sanford, fearing it may contain bad news:

Am on the red eye to London, Seb. See you at 5.00pm with Charlie Sheer for the 'Naked Shorts' gold meeting. Lots to discuss! All the best, Lewis. Oh and can we make time for a beer or two afterwards, get a table at Annabel's if it's still there, I have a little job for you. Free up your calendar for a while… what is it you Brits say? 'There's a good chap'…we need to saddle-up and re-assemble the team.

A shiver instantly ran down Sebastian's spine as he recalled meeting Lewis for the first time at the Treasury what seemed like a million years ago and the life changing consequences that ensued. They had often talked by phone during his tenure as the financial secretary in Hong Kong, but mostly it was inconsequential, technical chit-chat and friendly low-grade banter. It didn't take a genius to figure out that this latest email was a call-to-arms once more.

His finger then moved tentatively over the email from General Sanford, paused for what seemed like an eternity, before he bravely clicked the 'read' button.

Fortes, good news: Lyn will be in London the day after tomorrow, assuming no screw-ups in transit. Brief visit. Have scheduled a meeting at the American Embassy, 1900. Important you attend. Sanford.

No sooner had he managed to absorb this tremendously exciting news and the resultant warm glow of seeing Lyn again after so long, than Dominic Carrington called.

"Sebastian, sorry it's so ridiculously early, but I wanted to catch you before you got engrossed in something else. Just to confirm that you are formally invited to my meeting with the PM later today. Five o'clock, Number 10; I've cleared you with security. I'm assuming that won't present you with a problem? It would appear that we have got their attention at long last. It's a hell of a cast list; the chancellor is coming and even the governor is attending."

"Well Dominic, you can add the chairman of the Federal Reserve to that, who has also just told me I'm required to attend! I've had an email from him overnight. There must be a humdinger of a flap on somewhere or maybe the penny has finally dropped that we have a very unstable and highly volatile gold market to deal with?"

"Probably both, knowing that snake-in-the-grass Sheer; he's a past master of shifting the blame, so watch your back even though you have arrived late to this particular party!"

"Will do Dominic, see you at five."

★ ★ ★

"Do you know Seb that the '0' on the entrance door is displayed to the outside world in a very eccentric style indeed and is actually painted at a 37° angle anticlockwise? Curious don't you think?"

"Only you would know that prof; and I presume that the

1 isn't vertical either, or had the decorators been enjoying the hospitality of the Dog and Duck public house before they set to work?"

Sebastian Fortes and Dominic Carrington were chatting amiably in the entrance hall before they were eventually directed to the State Dining Room of Number 10 Downing Street, located on the first floor. One of the more obsequious senior flunkies instructed them, in a rather overly flamboyant gesture, to take quite specific places at the boardroom table and await the arrival of the others. Disdainful fingers were then pointed at the standard issue, civil service, refreshments at the back of the room and it was curtly suggested that they help themselves to lukewarm coffee and biscuits.

"The welcome is not exactly overwhelming is it Seb? I think Sheer is trying to tell me something; he has always been a vindictive bastard."

"You're the guy who wrote the paper, Dominic. He's probably just upset that you've forced it onto his agenda. I gather he controls this place with a rod of iron."

Dominic allowed a wry smile to cross his face, before replying, "Possibly. I always hate these moments before everyone deigns to turn up and grace us with their superior presence. There is something disingenuous about the whole process don't you think Seb? Far too much sycophantic bowing and scraping in this place! Well I, for one, am not kowtowing and grovelling to our utterly unworthy, hapless, politicos."

"That's the trouble with you left wing academic radicals; never happy unless you are on a protest march or occupying Senate House. One lump or two?"

The arrival of the Bank's governor, Sir David Stone, broke the train of anarchistic thoughts which bubbled remorselessly in the subconscious of Professor Carrington.

"Ah David, welcome. Do you know Seb Fortes? I've asked him to join our merry throng; well not just me, but the chairman of the Federal Reserve has requested his presence as well. Popular chap apparently."

"I'm not sure we have met Seb, but I have followed your career with considerable interest. You did a splendid job getting matters back onto a stable footing in Hong Kong; how is CJ by the way?"

"Thank you very much Governor. As he would undoubtedly say, we meet in interesting times, do we not? Let me see, the last occasion I saw CJ; yes, he was showing me around his latest boat, which is even bigger than the last one. So, if nothing else, hopefully that's keeping him out of trouble."

"I doubt it. By the way, on another subject altogether, we have a vacancy coming up on the Bank's Court of Directors at the end of the year; I'd like to talk with you about that a little nearer the time if that's OK with you? We could benefit from your international experience." Sebastian nodded. "I presume you have read our 'Naked Shorts' paper to the PM? Have you briefed him Dominic, we don't want to seem ill-prepared given the gravity of the situation?"

"Yes, he's up to speed and displaying a highly commendable 'Stared First' in curiosity."

"Excellent. Now where is everyone?"

It was the prime minister's practice to never arrive early for any meeting, including cabinet, if for no other reason than to deliberately wrong foot the other participants. 'Make 'em sweat a while' was always his default position. Today was no exception, on the very simple basis than he wanted to instantly exert his dominance over Dominic Carrington and ensure that his supreme authority prevailed.

The enmity between the two of them had its roots in a very public spat a couple of years ago when Carrington had made an after dinner speech, possibly somewhat worse for wear, or 'tired and emotional' as the more delicate phrase goes, berating the elevation of Charles Sheer to his current role. He had the temerity to question his fitness for office and his all too obvious lust for personal glory. To this day Carrington remained convinced that he had placed too much pressure on his friend John d'Abo, which led directly to his untimely death. From that moment on, the PM had Carrington at the top of his target list to get even with, no matter how long it took. After five more minutes wait, the PM and chancellor casually strolled silently into the room, both carrying large folders, and took their places at the head of the table. Lewis Moyns, one step behind, was first to speak.

"Seb, good to see you after so long." He nodded casually to the governor, "And a delight to meet you again Sir David. Ah, you must be Professor Carrington. I've heard a lot about you. Great paper."

The PM frowned pointedly at Lewis as if to say – 'I'm running this damn meeting, so I and I alone, will decide whether it's great or not, so be quiet and follow my lead' – before opening the discussion.

"I've summoned you all here to discuss the Bank's paper and to establish whether it's a figment of the Professor's all too vivid imagination or, however unlikely, we have a deep seated problem here. Under no circumstances will I allow this issue to escalate into any form of crisis. Sterling couldn't cope with the shock and the government may find itself in a very awkward position. So, in the words of my illustrious predecessor, 'I want solutions'.

The PM made a deliberate and highly provocative hand gesture towards Carrington, adding, "…and not tittle-tattle", as if to imply to everyone seated around the table that the meeting was a complete waste of his precious time.

"I've been persuaded by the Chancellor and others that this subject merits deeper investigation, so let us do just that. You've got my attention for forty-five minutes."

Although everyone present would willingly have plunged into the debate to air their opinions, undoubtedly in very forthright terms, they all deferred to Sir David and the gravitas implicit in his office. Given the tension in the room everyone, bar the PM, was grateful for his carefully calibrated views.

"We have formed the conclusion, Prime Minister, that the gold market has become dangerously unstable. We need to take immediate, corrective, action in both London and New York and rein in the activities of the bullion banks before it is too late. Our fear is that we have let the short positions held by licensed banks ramp up to such an extent that the bubble may burst very soon, with disastrous consequences for our economy and way of life. If that were to happen and pray to God that it doesn't, then the only winner would be China because of its enormous, undeclared, holdings of physical gold."

"Let's not bring the Almighty into this Governor. Just brief me on the technicalities and implications of this phrase, 'Naked Shorts', if you would be so kind."

"Perhaps I should endeavour to explain," interjected Dominic Carrington, to the visible irritation of the PM. Over the years Charles Sheer had developed a fine line in contemptuous sneers that shrieked: 'I don't care what you have to say, your advice is going straight into the dustbin'.

"We know that China has far more gold in their numerous vaults than they are prepared to admit to. I think we can all agree on that, even if we may disagree on the precise amounts involved. As we have stated many times in the paper, we don't know why they keep adding to their stockpile with such unrestrained abandon. The upshot is that they are sucking the market for physical gold completely bone dry; and that, potentially, is a major problem for us all."

"Yes, yes, yes. But what exactly is the problem? They can have the whole bloody lot if they wish." The PM's ire was directed once more at Carrington, as they stared at each other, not as members of a team trying to solve a predicament affecting them all, but like a cobra facing a mongoose.

The governor intervened once more, sensing the meeting was getting increasingly personal and tense. "Prime Minister, we need a substantial level of gold reserves in the UK in order to give credence to the strength of our currency. The Chinese cannot, as you put it, 'have the bloody lot'. If they did we would find ourselves living in a banana republic with a valueless currency equivalent to that in Zimbabwe. I'm sure that's not what you really meant to imply?"

Ignoring the governor completely, the PM continued, "Mr Carrington, could you kindly get to the point, assuming there is one?"

"It is Professor Carrington thank you; I ceased being a Mister twenty five years ago. The structural dilemma we have to address is how the gold market functions and how the world's central banks respond to it. I'm afraid to say that the market has become highly susceptible to manipulation and we have to address the matter with the utmost urgency." He took a sip of coffee before continuing, fearing that a long technical explanation would simply inflame the Prime Minister – who's short attention span was well known – even more.

"If I may, I would like to take a moment to describe how the banks, which control the London bullion market, actually operate. At its most basic their clients want to buy physical gold from them for cash; that much is straight forward. Crucially, however, the banks concerned almost invariably don't have this gold in their possession; they simply create an entry in their books which gives the appearance that they have the physical gold. Each bank pockets the money from its client and immediately creates a notional account saying it holds the gold for the customer, but in reality it has no such thing, it is pure fiction. By sleight of hand, they have created a liability to produce the physical gold some months or years into the future – should the client ever demand it."

As with every lecture he gave, Carrington paused

momentarily to gauge whether his students had grasped his words of wisdom.

"The problem arises for the banks when they are contractually required to fulfil that promise. In order to do so they would have to go out and buy whatever gold is needed in the market place. For every ounce they currently hold in physical gold they probably have at least twenty times that in uncovered obligations – which they will find very hard indeed to purchase, because China is in control of the physical gold market. That is the definition of being a 'Naked Short'. In the dreaded incomprehensible jargon of central bankers, this is called fractional reserve banking in gold. It's a trick worthy of Houdini. But there is an equally difficult problem that runs in parallel."

Carrington let that thought roll around for a moment before continuing. As he was about to restart his explanation of the second problem he looked across the table to see a mixture of utter contempt, disdain and glazed eyes from his nemesis Charles Sheer.

The PM violently slammed shut his folder and turned to Amanda Price sitting on his right, "You take this meeting Chancellor; I've got better things to do with my time. Fractional banking bollocks!"

As he stood up to leave, Lewis Moyns, who had patiently remained silent throughout, decided it was time to intervene.

"I'm sure Amanda will hold the fort admirably Prime Minister, but there is an awful lot more to discuss which needs your personal attention: if not today, then sometime very soon indeed. This really is far more serious than you seem to realise, as I'm sure Sir David would be only too pleased to elaborate upon. Plus I need a moment of your time in private at some point."

Turning to the PM, Amanda Price immediately interjected, "Let's not make this personal Charlie, you invited these good people here, the least you can do is listen to them."

The PM rolled his eyes heavenward and picked up the briefing folder.

"Well I remain completely unconvinced Amanda; but if you can be persuaded that we are truly in the mortal danger that Carrington is trying to encourage us to believe is the case, then I will revisit the subject. Till then, good day Governor; Mr. Moyns."

When the PM had left the room a shocked silence filled the vacuum left in his wake. Amanda decided nothing less than a fulsome explanation was warranted.

"Please accept my sincere apology for the way the meeting has gone, especially after your overnight journey Lewis. In confidence, the PM is unduly focused on the personal drubbing he is getting in the press regarding Seb's old boss, Sir John d'Abo. I'm afraid he is taking the allegations rather personally and it's affecting his ability to focus on anything else. He's only interested in the big picture these days and minutia – no matter how vital to the national interest – just don't get a look in."

Seb spoke for the first time in the meeting, "Do you think we should take a break Chancellor and perhaps reconvene tomorrow or possibly the day after, when the dust has settled? As Lewis indicated, we have only just scraped the surface of the problem. Sorry to be so blunt but the PM has got to find time to focus on this."

"OK Seb, probably wise to let him sleep on it. Is that acceptable to everyone else?" A half hearted series of nods followed, "Same time two days hence then, unless something unforeseen occurs. I'll have a word with the PM about rescheduling the meeting, but don't be surprised if he's a no-show."

Amanda Price left the room and immediately headed in contemplative silence through the labyrinthine of corridors connecting Number 10 to Number 11. To say she had a broad smile on her face as she entered her private office would be an understatement writ large. To the casual observer the chancellor would have appeared to be the cat that got the cream. She poured herself a very large whisky, sat down at her desk and rummaged deep into the bottom of her handbag to retrieve a very private mobile phone. She placed her 'Naked Shorts' folder into one of the drawers, straightened her skirt, and pressed re-dial. Within a matter of moment the call was answered.

"Well, well, well. It's been a quite while. I was beginning to think you'd changed your mind. Do we have a deal?"

The chancellor was equally curt in response, "Meet me at Imperial College at ten tomorrow morning."

CHAPTER 13

American Embassy, Nine Elms

The newly occupied American Embassy, now re-located south of the River Thames in Wandsworth, was considered by more or less everyone to be a stunning symbol of power, grandeur and a none-too-subtle reminder of the occupants unrivalled position as leader of the free world. There were other more regal opinions of course, where the phrase 'a carbuncle on the face of London' was frequently to be heard, but as a statement of imperial intent, frankly, it was without equal. Apart from GCHQ, it was also deemed the most secure building in the country and ideal for a crisis ladened *tête-à-tête*.

Sebastian Fortes enthusiastically changed for the upcoming meeting in his new dark-grey suit, matching pocket handkerchief and, unusually for him, an open-necked, white shirt. The anticipation of events to come had quickened the pulse and put a spring back into his step. Purpose had re-entered his life once again; he just hoped it didn't involve getting kidnapped and savagely beaten up this time around.

Not long after the meeting with the prime minister he had received a call from the ambassador's private secretary informing him that the get-together was now to be taken in two parts; with a request that he attend both. The more formal opening session was to be a technical briefing by Lewis Moyns and Sir David Stone on the positions being taken by the Federal Reserve and the Bank of England; while the second half of the meeting, at a time to be established, but probably the following day, was to be a discussion by General Sanford on the possible military ramifications of China's actions and a debate about the appropriate response from the USA and Britain.

The embassy staffer also mentioned, without any idea of the relationship between the two, that a Major Lyn Andrews would hopefully also be attending the latter presentation to update everyone on a modest, but highly significant, gold shipment discovered aboard a ship called the Jin-Ton. The secretary adding that the Major was due back in the UK from a tour of duty in East Africa later in the day and, after a military debriefing, hoped to be at the embassy the following day. With his testosterone levels on overload, Seb was torn between getting to the bottom of the issues in the gold market and somewhat over eager to get to a similar place with his newly returning girlfriend.

While he wasn't expected to make his own presentation, Seb was extremely keen to discuss the information he had garnered regarding the soon to be re-opened gold mine in Cornwall. He had unearthed an intriguing mystery as he began background checks on his newly acquired client, although he had no idea whether it was relevant or not. While he was out of the office yesterday, his assistant manager had been called to the bank's reception to meet, as she described it, "a person of distinctly Chinese origin", who had requested to see him privately.

"It was most odd Sebastian. I said you were out at a meeting, so he handed me his business card, asked you to call him at your earliest convenience. He then immediately turned tail, leaving a sealed document for your personal attention."

When Seb returned to the office later in the day he discovered that the envelope contained a formal request for an exclusive mandate to buy the mine. It was remarkable, unprecedented even, to have a cash buyer sniffing around so early in a project's life; especially as it had not become public knowledge that d'Abo's were involved in the fund raising. He deemed this oddity worthy of comment, if for no reason other than they seemed prepared to pay a substantial premium to the mines real value. He got his colleague to make the customary due diligence enquiries of the purchaser only to find a somewhat tenuous link back to a Panamanian company, after which the ownership trail ran dry. The 'Know Your Customer' requirements, which these days were imposed on all banks to prevent fraud and money laundering, could therefore not be met.

If he wished to follow up the Chinese enquiry, he would have to seek regulatory approval to take the matter further. What was clear to him however – once he had extended his enquiries to encompass other gold mines around the world in his attempt to gauge a comparative price level for 'his' mine – was the staggering number of gold mines and refining facilities which the Chinese had recently amassed. It seemed to be a global phenomenon; every time a mine or tract of land with geological possibilities became available for sale, it was immediately snapped up. If time and circumstances permitted, he would throw this titbit into the discussion tonight.

Seb took a ten minute taxi ride to the embassy, where a visitor's pass was already prepared for him. Within a matter of moments he was escorted to the private lift and descending four floors to the suite of briefing rooms.

"Welcome to 'The Chamber' Mr. Fortes, you know everyone I assume?"

"Yes, thank you Mister Ambassador."

"I can't stay for your meeting, so I will have to leave you in the capable hands of the Governor and the Chairman; small reception upstairs with the Russians which requires my attendance I'm afraid. Drinks will be available afterwards when you have concluded your business; you are all most welcome? See you later chaps, or should that be: *dasvidaniya comrades!*"

"Sit down here Seb," Lewis Moyns pointed at the empty chair and the series of folders directly in front of it. "We'll commence immediately. The Chamber is a fully secure room, so feel free to express your opinions. Would you care to begin, Sir David?"

A polite nod ensued as, in synchronisation, they all opened of the first folder which had the seal of the Bank of England on its cover. The governor sat back in his chair and adjusted his countenance from a smile to a frown.

"I want us to focus on just one thing tonight, namely what are the consequences of China buying vast quantities of gold – ostensibly quite legitimately – from the bullion banks, located both here and in the States, and countless other sources. It is a statement of the obvious that there is only a finite supply of gold in the world at any given point. Therefore, because China is reducing the physical liquidity in the market, consciously and no doubt deliberately; it is placing great strain on all the other market participants, including our good selves at the Bank and, more than likely, at the Fed as well."

Sir David paused for a sip of water before continuing. Beads of sweat started to form on his forehead.

"In order to balance their books and hedge their risks, the bullion banks under Professor Carrington's stewardship, have no option but to turn to the one secure source that has physical gold – to wit – the world's central banks. To try and minimise their exposure, they lease the gold from us and other central banks, on a medium term basis. We are normally very willing participants in this activity because we can earn a tidy sum in fees for doing so. Helps pay for the not inconsiderable costs of secure storage in our respective vaults."

So far, so good, he thought; now for the tricky bit.

"The whole market is chronically short of actual gold. These, how shall I put it, 'household-name banks', simply don't have access to the stuff they are merrily trading in such vast, eye watering, quantities. From my seat, as the country's Lender of Last Resort, this is very problematic and a prime example of a 'systemic-risk'. That is because gold traders and their clients borrow enormous sums to finance their speculative positions on the basis of very little collateral. They are, to use the technical term, highly geared." He paused for breath before continuing, "We all know what happened when the housing market was ramped up to provide 110 percent mortgages: it went, if you'll excuse my French, 'tits-up' very soon thereafter.'"

Sebastian intervened in an attempt for everyone to have a little time to absorb the details.

"Sir David, do I understand you correctly? The whole of the gold market operates on the basis of the bullion banks selling gold they don't have, to people who have borrowed enormous sums to enter into highly speculative gold contracts; all back-stopped by the world's central banks? Isn't that a recipe for another catastrophe? A very dangerous and highly destabilising Lehman Brothers, take-two?"

"That's a fairish summary Sebastian. The banks try and cover their position of course, but the speculators are always 'net long' and the banks always 'net short'. It ends up with everyone involved writing more and more contracts to cover the ones they already have. You could say it's a giant merry-go-round where everyone takes in each other's washing. At some point it will inevitably be forced to stop, and then all hell will break loose."

Professor Carrington, who thus far had not said a word, simply said, "Seb is quite correct. In fact, it could be said to be even worse than that. How much of the gold held in the Bank of England's vaults would you say is leased out to third parties, for which read the bullion banks, Governor? I'm guessing 3,000 tonnes, some of it the UK's official gold reserves, plus other significant amounts from central banks who store their reserves with you?"

"I can't confirm the exact figure Dominic, even amongst such august company, top secret and all that; but the last press release we issued is public knowledge and this put the total amount of gold held by us, that's ours and other countries, at approximately 5,000 tonnes. So an awful lot of it is being hocked to the gold market to enable it to function: it's the central bank equivalent of pawn broking."

Carrington continued, "Just so that you can put this into perspective Seb, even though the Governor is unable to formally comment, the UK's official gold reserves today are approximately 300 tonnes. You'll recall that idiot Brown sold off 390 tonnes between 1999 and 2002 at the bottom of the market; otherwise we would have had more. It is, however, a proverbial drop in the ocean compared to other central bank holdings. Again, Lewis will correct me in due course, but by contrast America has some 8,200 tonnes held at Fort Knox and yet more at the New York offices of the Federal Reserve. I should add that a significant amount of the Fed's holdings belong to other countries, who deposit it with them for safe keeping."

"So, if something were to go severely wrong with the market," interjected Sebastian, "the UK will be disproportionally harmed because we have virtually nothing left?"

The endless vigorous nodding of heads around the table had clearly hit a raw nerve. "Oh, and didn't I read somewhere that the estimate of the private holdings of gold by Chinese citizens alone is around 10,000 tonnes. And we have only 300 tonnes supporting our currency. I seem to recall that China mines more than that each year? If you'll excuse the phrase I think we are totally and utterly screwed!"

"Quite possibly", replied Sir David. "Official gold reserves are a rather tricky subject, which we try our damnedest to keep away from public gaze. By buying so much physical gold, China has forced the bullion banks to, in inverted commas, borrow gold from the official reserves of the central banks. This obviously leaves these critical institutions in a vulnerable position should the banks default for whatever reason."

The room filled with furrowed brows.

"When a customer wishes to actually take possession of the gold bars something quite complex happens. It's very rare that the gold actually moves from the vaults as that's impractical. Instead it becomes a ledger entry which shuffles around in the books of all the participants. It goes off the accounts of the central banks into the possession of the bullion banks and then into the possession of the customer. The central bank then has to hope that the bullion banks can eventually find the gold elsewhere to re-balance its own books. It moves from owning the gold to having an IOU from the banks. That's why these days the published accounts for central bank always show that they hold 'gold and gold receivable'. In other words, the whole system assumes that no one will default; otherwise it's the proverbial pack of cards tumbling in on itself."

Sebastian took a sharp intake of breath. "Bloody hell, Governor! This means that the entire edifice of the world's currency system is vulnerable to attack and possible implosion because the central banks have potentially lost control of the gold to implicitly support their currency? They have lent it to the speculators for a quick buck! If this were to become public knowledge then their credibility and, more importantly, our confidence in the US dollar, or the pound, would be in shreds. Is that correct?"

Somewhat too casually for Seb's liking, Sir David continued: "That is one way of looking at it, I suppose. Many commodity markets work in very similar ways of course, it's just that the gold market has, how shall I phrase it, well; it's gotten out of hand. More dramatically, China is now the de-facto driver of the gold market and it may well be out to crash the car."

With that, the governor dramatically closed his file. Amanda Price, the UK chancellor, who had been uncharacteristically quiet thus far, suggested they should break for coffee and a very large brandy, "before we all have", as she delicately put it, "a touch of the vapours!" She, for one, would not be voting to renew the appointment of Sir David V. Stone next year.

★ ★ ★

Although many regarded General Sanford as a cold-hearted, emotionless bastard who would kill an enemy without the slightest hesitation, on rare occasions – and only when the recipient thoroughly deserved it – he would fleetingly demonstrate a softer side, especially when it came to the welfare of his men. The first class window seat taking Lyn from the Seychelles to Heathrow, which he had thoughtfully arranged, was a welcome change from the very uncomfortable C-5 Galaxy US air force transporter planes she seemed to spend an inordinate amount of time on these days. At least she wouldn't have to parachute out this time.

Her new wardrobe for the trip had been acquired in great haste at the duty free shop and bore all the characteristics of play-time in the sun: flamboyant top, loose fitting skirt, both amazingly colourful and worn to best effect having drinks by the infinity pool in temperatures of 30 degrees. The army fatigues and combat boots were in the hold ready for whatever was going to be thrown at her when she got to London, or God knows where, next.

Sanford had also managed to provide her with a mobile phone, which had Sebastian's UK number already loaded, and a secure laptop. There was also a note saying *'sorry I couldn't get the CIA jet on this occasion'; and that, after much consideration, he had decided not to 'rough Seb up', at least for the time being, as he may come in useful as things progress'*. What things, she wondered, and would Seb still feel the same way towards her after so long apart?

★ ★ ★

When the meeting of the great and the good eventually resumed at the embassy, an air of calm had been restored but it was clear to everyone that minds were racing with the implications of what they had just heard and, heaven forbid, what they were now about to hear from the chairman of the Federal Reserve.

"Let me try and put your minds at rest", commenced Lewis Moyns in his avuncular Texan drawl, "we are not facing another South Sea Bubble here. This is not a re-run of 1720. We have far more sophisticated tools at our disposal to deal with this and bring the gold market back to reality. Be assured, the United States government will stand full-square behind the smooth operation of the market and ensure it functions to everyone's satisfaction." He could just as well have added, 'especially ours'.

A palpable sign of relief filled the room; only Sebastian sensed this was not entirely the truth, nor even close to it. Why was his friend from the Federal Reserve being so intentionally optimistic in defiance of the facts? Perhaps this is why Lewis wanted to meet him in private later that week; a sure sign, if ever there was one, that things were far more serious than anyone wanted to admit.

★ ★ ★

As the group said their goodbyes on the steps of the embassy, Amanda's mobile phone rang. The chancellor scrambled deep inside her bag to retrieve it while Lewis and Seb amiably debated where they were going to spend the rest of the evening carousing and catching up: probably a noisy pub by the river.

"Sorry guys, see you all tomorrow. I've got to take this, profound 'matters of the State' and all that."

She waited until they had all moved sufficiently far away, waving enthusiastically to her colleagues, before replying.

"Cressida, what a pleasant surprise."

"Amanda darling, remind me what time is our get together tomorrow?"

CHAPTER 14

The Cradle of Gold – Saudi Arabia

In a deliberately choreographed arrival, touching down just before dawn broke, the unmarked corporate jet landed without fanfare at one of the more obscure airfields to the west of the Saudi Arabian capital, Riyadh. The unassuming civilian airport was deserted apart from the early morning cleaning squads and a carefully selected group of senior officials ready to welcome their important guests. The arrival point and timing had been specifically chosen to avoid drawing unwarranted, indeed any, attention to the identity of the people on board. It also had the merit of being located well away from the endless military airfields which, these days, were habitually crawling with American or British personnel in their never-ending war against ISIS.

The top-level delegation from the central bank of China, headed by Chen Liu, the all-powerful, highly manipulative deputy governor, flew into the Kingdom completely determined that the world should never become aware of their presence. Hidden, incognito, amongst their company was General Xiao who, uncomfortably for him, was travelling out of uniform. To the outside world, however, he was utterly indistinguishable from the team of bankers he was accompanying. Only his fraught demeanour, which was quite at odds from his normal commanding presence, betrayed a nervous disposition.

For Xiao this was a mission of the utmost importance,

arranged at the eleventh hour and laying waste to a much anticipated weekend with his younger brothers discussing family business. Unless he somehow managed to redeem himself in the eyes of his superiors, it was a trip that could quite possibly destroy his career and maybe end his life. He didn't need reminding that this had become a prerequisite to his survival following the unfortunate incident with the freighter, the Jin-Ton.

Secrecy was uppermost in the minds of all concerned, as the two countries embarked upon what both hoped would be a major shift in economic cooperation between them and a re-balancing of power in a profoundly uncertain world. Naturally, the two nations routinely maintained and encouraged close diplomatic ties; but both regional superpowers had concluded that it was in their collective best interests to forge a new geo-political alliance. This issue had become increasingly critical for Saudi Arabia as relationships with America had become more and more strained following the decision by Congress to release secret papers on their alleged involvement in the 9/11 attacks. Not only was this vigorously denied at every opportunity; but it placed in jeopardy every dollar asset they possessed as litigation-hungry lawyers circled the billions of US treasuries held by Saudi Arabia, intent on taking them for every cent they possessed.

★ ★ ★

Before he departed from Beijing, the general had been summoned at very short notice to the premier's suite of offices. He assumed that he would be expected to provide a detailed update on the whereabouts of the Jin-Ton and when it was expected to be returned to Chinese control. Regrettably he had absolutely nothing new to report, which, prior experience told him, would not be well received. True to form, the diminutive chief secretary to the Politburo proceeded to harangue and humiliate him as if he were some new recruit on the parade ground who didn't know his left foot from his right. Worse still, there was an indirect, but pointed, reference to the never-ending purge of corrupt politicians and servants of the State who had chosen to enrich themselves. A warning, normally delivered tangentially and in opaque language, but on this occasion it was a quiver aimed straight at his heart. Before he could try to explain or preferably vent his anger in response, the subject matter instantly changed.

"Xiao, the Premier has instructed you to accompany Banker Chen Liu on a mission of the utmost importance. I'm sure you appreciate that we have an undreamed of opportunity to establish a new strategic union in the Middle East. The depressed price of crude has caused panic for the Saudi elite who cannot contemplate the end of their place at the top table. It is now clear to them that their never ending wealth, how do they put it, ah yes, 'beyond the dreams of avarice', may be lost forever. They are now reluctantly being forced to make a complete re-assessment of their status in the world. At long last they have realised that they must adopt a different strategy to suit the new economic world order. Even the possession of staggering oil reserves is no longer sufficient to guarantee the Kingdom's prosperity."

"Agreed and understood, Mr. Secretary."

In the never ending, deeply poisonous game of 'snakes and ladders' that was the *realpolitik* of the Chinese government: both men, in their arrogance and self-importance, perceived the other to be the weaker. Xiao knew full well however, that if he failed in this new mission, which was entirely out of his comfort zone, his entire way of life was in jeopardy; but if he succeeded, then this upstart scribbler would be crushed beneath his feet, like so many before him. It had been made abundantly clear in the earlier tirade of abuse directed at him, that his position was decidedly precarious. He had lost that precious resource, trust.

The failure to ensure the Jin-Ton was safe and indeed may have been captured by the enemy, could already have sealed his fate. Perhaps he was being deliberately set-up to fail and this trip would be his last. Despite his enormously powerful position, paranoia was forever present in the mind of Xiao; enemies were to be found everywhere, under every tarnished stone, in every corner of government and especially within the hearts of the mandarins who served it. He had concluded long ago that his limited number of friends were unreliable, untrustworthy and ephemeral. His colleagues were even worse. He had to somehow prevent his world from falling apart and, if he concluded it was, then he must somehow get a message through to his beloved brothers. One way or another he had to give them sufficient warning to protect the family and its wealth. His mind would not stop racing, planning, plotting. Was he the tethered goat being circled by the lion, or was this opportunity an unexpected pathway to glory and even more riches?

The secretary's eyes gave no clue, as he paused before continuing.

"The upper echelons of the Saudi government have at long last concluded that they are over dependent upon their links to America – which as you will hopefully be aware, plays to our global agenda. This revised position, when combined with the inescapable fact that their country's currency reserves are dwindling at an alarming rate, leaves them immensely vulnerable. They know full well that something has to be done and done quickly, if they are to rebalance the country's books. They are now obligated to take every step possible to move away from their total reliance on oil. We therefore have them exactly where we want them: over exposed to the US dollar; chronically short of funds because they are incapable of constraining government spending; and therefore prepared at last to run into our arms to do a deal. Just make sure, without fail, it is on our terms, Xiao."

On the plane over, the general had replayed this conversation a hundred times in silent deliberation. The battle ahead, if that is what it was, would regrettably be held on a field of combat which was not of his choosing; and one which he was singularly ill equipped. What the hell were 'our terms'; no one had had the courtesy to tell him.

As was his wont ahead of every mission, he war-gamed the various outcomes: none seemed to end well for him. It was also deeply unfortunate or, knowing the machinations of his superiors, quite possible deliberate, that the head of the delegation was none other than Chen Liu. He had spectacularly – and publically – fallen out with the central banker many times over army budgets and secret slush-funds; and lost on every occasion. Perhaps his disdain for more-or-less everyone in higher authority and his incendiary temper, would now be his undoing.

★ ★ ★

The phalanx of central bankers were swiftly ushered through airport security and discretely chauffeured away in a fleet of limousines destined for a series of meeting to be held in the isolated dessert region around Medina. The meticulous preparations by the hosts included the construction of a purpose-built tented village featuring sumptuous facilities befitting the visit of a president or a head of state. The proverbial red carpet was very much in evidence, although two days without alcohol may place great strain upon them all.

Holding a central bank briefing file on his knees, the group's administrative assistant spoke in very subdued and reverential tones befitting his level within the deeply hierarchical society he served. He was extremely afraid of General Xiao and for good reason; having previously seen one of his over-zealous military subordinates removed from a budget meeting, never to be seen again.

"General, just to recap. The central bank's agenda consists of only two items, each of equal importance, covering the future political relationship between our two countries and the new commercial links we now intend to forge."

"Of course, you idiot! Remember who you are talking to."

"My apologies, Sir. Our respective diplomats have now had four secret meetings in Switzerland, which were deemed to have gone very well. It is the central bank's belief that only the finest of fine details remained to be concluded before the agreement can be formally signed and initiated. It is strongly felt that the Saudis are fully committed to the outline deal."

"It better had be; or you're all dead men", growled the General, the bags under his eyes betraying the fitful sleeping patterns of the journey.

Visibly shaking, the assistant continued, "At the top of the Kingdom's agenda is the intention to sell state assets in order to maintain the levels of prosperity its rulers and population have become addicted to. Saudi-Aramco, their state oil company, heads the list of family silver which they intend to sell piece-by-piece to the highest bidder. We provide an ideal and, most importantly, a particularly discreet solution to their problems: we can be invisible to the outside world. Our involvement also had the merit of avoiding the sharks on Wall Street crawling all over the company's previously secret accounts."

Despite the limousine's air conditioning system making a valiant attempt to counterbalance the searing temperatures outside, beads of terror-induced perspiration were very present on the assistant's shirt. He coughed nervously before continuing.

"I'm sure you are aware, General, that Saudi-Aramco is without question one of the most strategically important companies in the world. It has a market valuation measured in many trillions of dollars. Our government, quite naturally, is more than delighted to accommodate such a purchase. The premier has made it abundantly clear that we are more than willing to invest $200 billion or even $500 billion, in order to buy a modest share stake in the company. Our instructions are to suggest we purchase, say, a holding of five percent of the equity and request a seat on the company board. From what was said in strictest confidence to our diplomatic mission during the meetings in Switzerland, they are ready to agree to this."

Chen Liu, who everyone assumed was sleeping, awoke from his apparent torpor and the effects of too much champagne on the flight over. Sitting bolt upright he quickly waded into the conversation.

"That's quite enough General," screamed Chen, "remember you are here only as an observer. Trading cheap insults with my junior staff will get you nowhere. This is not the army and you are not in charge here; the poor man is only trying to provide you with a background briefing. You ought to know damn well that this deal is a marriage made in heaven for our country. We have an unquenchable desire to secure oil supplies to support our ever expanding economy, so kindly don't rise above your station and say something you will regret and which I will have to report."

The limousine fell silent as the two men glared at each other, wondering who would be first to place a call to Beijing accusing the other of being an ignoramus. After what seemed like an eternity, Chen decided it would probably be best for them both if he outlined the second, equally vital, purpose of the meeting.

"General Xiao, in your capacity as head of the army, I believe it would be beneficial that you are made aware of our second objective: it will go some way to reducing the problems you have created with the missing freighter."

A shudder ran down Xiao's spine; how could he possibly know about that?

"In order to grease the wheels of the deal, the central bank had also gained permission from the Politburo to make a very substantial ten-year dollar loan to Saudi Arabia. We know they desperately need the money, so it will be like feeding cherries to a baby. Critical to this agreement however, will be our insistence that it will be repaid not in US dollars, but in renminbi. If they agree, which I am one hundred percent confident that they will, then this will be an unparalleled 'win-win' for China: an enormous political and economic coup. I, and I alone, will disclose it to the world when the time is deemed appropriate."

Chen extracted a cigarette from his case and slowly lit it, much to the annoyance of Xiao. The smoke seemed to be directed straight at him in what he instantly perceived as a gesture of dominance. Pausing only momentarily, he continued.

"For Saudi Arabia, this loan will instantly ease the pain of deflated oil prices; and at zero percent interest, it will be irresistible. In one simple move it will also enable China to reduce our own enormous pile of dollars. The master stroke is to get paid back in our own currency. This single event will become the first act in our express determination to dethrone America as the world's economic super power."

Xiao's mind was now in ferment; he had previously been caught off-guard by the disclosure about the Jin-Ton, but he could instantly recognise a good idea when it was so eloquently presented. Somehow he had to wrestle this remarkable, indeed inspirational, proposal from the hands of the bankers and into his own.

"I'm sure even you will readily appreciate General, that there has to be an exceptionally expensive *quid-pro-quo* extracted from Saudi Arabia: after all, our generosity and largesse could never be expected to extend beyond the boundaries of our own self-interest. Today that means only one thing: the acquisition of gold. In return for providing the loan and making the share purchase in Saudi-Aramco both of which, I think we all agree, are being made on highly beneficial terms, China wants exclusive access to the gold reserves at the 'Mahd adh Dhahab' mine."

He turned briefly to address his startled colleagues and added, "The mine is located not far from where we are currently meeting, in the area known as the Arabian-Nubian Shield."

Xiao was dumbfounded; none of this had been explained before the trip, which meant only one thing: he was here to be punished. He knew instantly that if the plan was to somehow fail, it would be leaked to the world's press, when he would be ritually and publically defenestrated. The powerful image of a tethered goat loomed large in his mind.

Long regarded as the mythical location for King Solomon's mines, 'Mahd adh Dhahab', when translated from Arabic, became known in the west as 'The Cradle of Gold'. It was believed by many to be the location for the biblical Garden of Eden and the provider of power and wealth over the ages for those who controlled its output. Undue sentimentality was not within the purview of Chinese central bankers; their sole objective was to secure the gold. Legends were for dreamers. Within their grasp was the largest mineral deposit in the Arabian Gulf, producing around 100,000 ounces of gold a year: China intended to be the recipient of every speck of gold the miners could extract.

Although the ensuing negotiations were protracted and detailed, the first two documents were ready to be approved by late afternoon. The agreements lay on the ceremonial table waiting to be signed and sealed in a ceremony within one of the sumptuous tents erected for the visitors. On conclusion of the formal procedures and the exchange of gifts, Chen stood to address the Saudi delegation and proposed a toast to their continuing prosperity.

"On behalf of a grateful Chinese nation we are delighted to have reached an accord on the loan facility and the share purchase. I would like to turn now to the very important matter of the gold reserves you extract from the 'Mahd adh Dhahab' mine. It would be our government's wish to acquire the entire output."

A loud gasp was audible in the room from the hosts, clearly taken by surprise by such a brazen suggestion. Chen pressed home his advantage.

"Naturally, we would be prepared to pay very handsomely indeed for this privilege and propose a 15 percent premium over the spot gold price, no matter where it went up to. For the next ten years your country would be paid for the gold ingots you supply to us, not in dollars, but in Chinese currency. This will help you build up funds to repay the loans you have now committed to. In my country, poets would describe this as the enduring balance of the Yin and the Yang; together we have engineered a perfect harmony. It is a deeply symbolic symmetry, you would be diversifying your reserves away from the dollar, which we understand is of paramount importance to you, and building them up in renminbi, which is of equal importance to us."

The gasps were now replaced by the vigorous nodding of heads as the logic of what was being proposed gradually dawned on those present. Indeed, the more senior functionaries amongst them considered this to be a master stroke; one which they would fight for the privilege to lay at their masters' feet later that evening.

"I hope our private discussions today have demonstrated to you beyond all doubt that it is our intention to eviscerate the dollar, eliminate its dominance in the world and replace it with our own currency. We trust that such an offer would find approval with the Saudi Arabian ministers who toil daily on behalf of the King?"

Advisors and civil servants scurried off into the night to brief their respective departments and recommend the newly presented proposal. By the end of the second day a formal agreement for the gold purchase had been signed off by both governments and a visit arranged to the mines in order to finalise the shipment details.

China would make plans for a consignment of gold to be collected monthly from the port of Jeddah, under the auspices of its Panamanian shipping company. Arrangements would also be made to deliberately conceal the gold transfer by bundling it up with other export and imports so as not to arouse suspicion. Both parties set a date for the first transfer to be made six weeks hence.

Delighted with their collective efforts, the Chinese banking delegation once more left in the middle of the following night, highly satisfied with their endeavours. There was even a tantalising hint that Saudi Arabia would be prepared to sell a considerable quantity of its own gold and silver reserves, should its economy suffer any further dramatic downturns.

Xiao, who had been deliberately sidelined at every gathering between the respective teams, was both furious and terrified for his future. During the entire series of meetings and social get-togethers, he had managed only snatched conversations with members of the Saudi delegation: most of which were met with highly suspicious looks from his colleagues. Moreover, Chen told him, in no uncertain terms, that his highly lucrative command over all the gold shipments and storage facilities would cease immediately and be transferred to someone of the government's choosing. Then, with nerves jangling, came the throw away comment that a car would be waiting for him at the airport. Ominously, Chen informed him that he was to be driven immediately to the ministry to receive further orders, which could mean only one thing: his time had come. The *coup de gras* was clearly only moments away and, if history was any judge, it was unlikely to be delivered with any form of mercy. He who steals from the King will always pay the penalty with his head, eventually.

Once inside the departure lounge and well away from the preying eyes and ears of his companions, Xiao made a desperate call to his brothers.

"Clear the private vault immediately and I do mean immediately. Is that understood? Get every man you can muster and move the special cases today, without fail. Put a decoy of heavy bricks into similar cases and move them to the warehouse. Then transfer the real cases to the barge ready for immediate departure. If I do not call you within 24 hours, set sail for Shanghai. Make contact with our friend, 'The Butler'; get his name and details from the safe. He will guide you, but do not fully trust him. Be on your guard and farewell brothers."

It would be a long and ulcer-inducing journey home.

Once they were safely onboard and secure within the privacy of their private jet, Chen went into the cockpit and placed a call through to the premier's private secretary, content in the thought that he had ensnared the Saudi's into a deception from which they might never escape.

"Immediately relay the following code to the Premier: 'The trap has been set'. Also tell him that, as requested, I have concluded that Xiao is unfit for office; in my judgement he is a megalomaniac and a psychopath with a highly inflated view of his own self importance. He has become corrupt, greedy for power and wealth; and is therefore expendable. Plus you are to alert Captain Zucca and his crew to head to Jeddah and prepare for another voyage. Double their pay. I will present the signed documents to the Premier immediately on my arrival into Beijing."

With that simple message – which was instantly intercepted, unscrambled and logged in the CIA headquarters at Langley – the fate of all on board was sealed.

CHAPTER 15

Imperial College and Number 10

The ministerial car pulled up at the very discrete rear entrance to Downing Street at 9.00am sharp, engine still running. Tom Earle, one of the more senior drivers on duty that morning, had been summoned to the exit of Number 11 at short notice with the highly unusual hand written instructions:

'No bodyguard needed today and don't bring the ministerial Jaguar. Use one of the Land Rovers with the blacked-out windows: destination to be given when in the car'.

He cast his mind around to when, and if, this had ever happened before in his twenty-five years of service; but he drew a complete blank. Strict protocol, endlessly rehearsed security rules and plain common sense seemed to have gone out of the window: no senior politician travelled without armed police protection these days. He wondered if this trip had actually been formally authorised, whether it had been logged in the duty roster, and whether he should radio the dispatch office for clarification. But before he could do so the door quickly opened and the chancellor stepped briskly out.

To say Tom was jaw-droppingly flabbergasted would be the understatement of the year, if not the century. Flustered, he leapt out of the car to open the rear door and take what seemed like an overnight bag from her outstretched hand. He quickly ushered Amanda Price into the rear compartment of the car where it would be impossible for the paparazzi, or indeed any casual onlooker, to see who was on board. The ever elegant, highly coiffured image was nowhere to be seen. Instead she had her hair in a ponytail, was wearing jeans and what could only be described as a sloppy-joe jumper, all topped off with the biggest pair of sunglasses he had ever seen. The words 'utterly bizarre' stayed with him for hours.

"Imperial College please Tom. I will be there no more than half an hour so park the car somewhere inconspicuous and I'll call you when I need to be taken on to Dorneywood."

It had been a week since she had met the prime minister to first discuss the 'Naked Shorts' paper during which time she had formed the inevitable conclusion that he was putting the economic security of the nation in great peril. Her initial opinion – that this was yet another scare story filled with the usual hot air of a civil service briefing memo – had changed to one of deep concern. To make matters worse, and despite her protestations in private, the PM refused point blank to focus on the dire ramifications to the country; the banking system, the pound, her position as chancellor and God knows what else. She had come to the reluctant conclusion that she must act; and must act decisively.

She walked briskly and purposefully into the college entrance and asked one of the staff at reception where the junior common room was. Within a couple of minutes she had found it and went straight into the adjacent coffee shop as agreed. She immediately recognised her co-conspirator, who was positioned very discretely towards the back of the busy space now full of students chatting animatedly while having breakfast.

"Ah, there you are. Bloody odd place to meet Amanda! Anyone would have thought you'd brought me here for a quickie in the student dorms."

The infamous, venomous and deeply malicious female editor of the country's leading tabloid newspaper was, as instructed, equally casually dressed. Her reputation as a kingmaker was indisputable and her nose for a story was second to none. She was a past master of the euphemism, 'undercover' journalism – she would unhesitatingly sleep with anyone for a scoop. This wasn't the first time she had met the chancellor in odd locations: she was always delighted to be fed highly defamatory information on her cabinet colleagues. She would just go with the flow and see who the indomitable Miss Price was going to knife in the back today.

While unusual, a bustling university early on a Saturday morning was a perfectly chosen setting for a political assassination she thought. Two mature students casually drinking coffee and chewing the cud; what could be odd about that? Given the somewhat eccentric location for their meeting, whatever was about to be disclosed would undoubted by highly toxic and front page news by tomorrow.

"I don't want to be here long but it is very important that you mention Imperial College in your piece. You picked up the story here. Is that agreed?"

Cressida Armstrong pulled out her note book and pen, readying herself for whatever was to be disclosed; but Amanda delicately placed her hand over hers and whispered, "Strictly off the record, no notes, undisclosed source; the usual newspaper baloney if you don't mind."

"If that's how you want it Amanda, fine. Fire away."

She slid an envelope across the table.

"Don't open it here Cressida. It's the original, unredacted, autopsy on the death of Sir John d'Abo. I won't dwell on it right now, but you will see that it differs materially from that which was disclosed at the time. It was either suicide, which is quite plausible given the circumstances, or in my humble opinion, it was State sponsored murder. I'll leave you to form a suitably damaging headline. I'm pretty confident that this is one of, if not the only copy left un-shredded. I have tried tracing the doctor who performed it, but he is now nowhere to be found.

What is certain, however, is that d'Abo didn't die of a heart attack as was stated in all the official reports at the time. The unpublished report states he died of gunshot wounds; note, please, the plural. Suicides don't often shoot themselves three times. The key question, obviously, is who ordered it? I'm sure you will conclude it must have been Charlie Sheer."

"Curiouser and curiouser, cried Alice." Scenting a truly sensational story, the newspaper hacks pulse began to race.

"Are you saying that there was a conspiracy of some kind going on? And if so, our current PM was the one pulling the strings? I will have to find a water-tight way to corroborate this somehow; otherwise I can't print this on the front page without all hell breaking loose? Any ideas how?"

"That's your problem Cressida, but for now I'd be grateful if you could point the accusing finger in the most appropriate direction. Shake him up a little. Rattle the cage. Blood on his hands, that sort of thing. He'll obviously come back fighting like a banshee, so I don't need to tell you to tread very carefully indeed."

"Well Amanda, you never cease to amaze. How come someone who studied fine art at Uni can be such a scheming bastard? And what, pray tell, do you personally want out of this?"

"We'll discuss that topic at the appropriate time. Meanwhile, I stress again, you must mention, however tangentially, that you got the information here. It will throw the blood hounds off the scent!"

The most powerful woman in the media leaned over and delicately caressed the chancellor's hand.

"It's a deal. And nice top by the way!"

As they were simultaneously picking up their paraphernalia from the floor, Cressida carefully placed the intriguing envelope into her handbag and smiled contentedly.

"My choice of location next time Amanda darling; perhaps the Italian embassy? They love a spot of *la dolce vita,* which could perhaps do us both some good in these troubled times."

★ ★ ★

Earlier in the day, the head of the Federal Reserve paced the reception room of Number 10 impatiently waiting to have his very private audience with the prime minister. On his absolute insistence there was to be no other political advisors, cabinet colleagues or civil servants present and no tape recording or notes were to be taken by either side; what Lewis Moyns impolitely called the 'Tony Blair Sofa Protocol'. This was not an occasion to share with those of a delicate constitution.

At his express request the meeting was to be held at 6.45 in the morning, well before the Downing Street offices became very busy and the paparazzi turned up for their daily shift to peruse the ceaseless comings and goings. He had made it abundantly clear to the PM: only the two principals, otherwise he could not reveal his message. He had even taken the precaution of emphatically stating that his appointment was not to be officially recorded in any visitor's book or government papers: too much was at stake.

Lewis was rarely, if ever, anxious or phased by momentous events; but today was an unusually humid summers morning and he was already perspiring beneath his grey pinstriped suit. He knew full well that, very soon, he would have to disclose one of the most closely held secrets in the United States; something he only became aware of, via the head of the CIA, when he assumed the responsibilities of the chairmanship of the Federal Reserve. He wondered how the news would be taken and equally importantly whether Charlie Sheer could be trusted not to use the information for his own political purposes. Although he respected his position as prime minister, complete confidence in his colleague was distinctly lacking.

He had carefully weighed up the probabilities and concluded he must be forthright, succinct and, as the saying goes, 'speak truth unto power'. Under all circumstances he must have the

PM on his side on this issue. The head of the world's most important and influential central bank strode purposefully and confidently into the PM's private office and spoke before Charles Sheer could utter a word.

"You're no doubt familiar with the doctrine of 'Deniable Plausibility', Charlie? Well this get-together may well test its limits. Good morning by the way."

"Unusually abrupt aren't we today Lewis? I always thought you cowboys only got up this early to rustle cattle?" The PM put down his cup of coffee and pointed his index finger to the table, "Help yourself, it's still warm, I think."

"Charlie I've been mulling over our regrettably brief meeting on the 'Naked Shorts' paper – which you should have take a lot more seriously if you want my professional advice – and think you should be brought into 'the circle of four': that's me, you, the CIA Director and the President. It used to be three, but I'm sure you get the picture."

"What in God's name are you talking about Lewis? What bloody circle? Dominic Carrington is just stirring up trouble and has wound you and the governor around his little finger."

"Wish it were that simple Charlie, but the situation is far worse than your worst nightmare. This is so profound a revelation that I'm sure you won't believe it for quite some time and, like me, you will take an age to figure out the ramifications. Now, where to start. When I took office I became privy to a few state secrets which just make your jaw drop in disbelief. I'm sure it was the same when you took over this job?"

"Just the odd 'eye-waterer' as the permanent secretary to the Cabinet Office eloquently described them; yes." The PM sat back wondering what was about to be revealed that was so secret it was only know to three people.

"Do you know – and this is truly remarkable Charlie – that the gold reserves of the United States have not been audited since 1953, and that was only a very cursory inspection at best:

odd that, don't you think? Sixty plus years of undisturbed peace and quiet, with not so much as an independently verifiable check on our nation's wealth. I'm sure you appreciate that this deliberate safeguard is a happy consequence of the Fed being a private company operating under the supervision of the US Treasury. Technically speaking, we function under the umbrella of the Gold Reserve Act of 1934, which has within it something referred to as the Exchange Stabilisation Fund. This little beauty enables the Treasury and the Fed to manage the dollar. What is even less widely known is that Congress has absolutely no legal right to see the gold accounts or question its officers. All very convenient for us, totally top secret and clandestine what?"

He cleared his throat and took a sip of lukewarm, weak coffee; almost spitting it back into the china cup it was so terrible.

"And do you recall back in 2013 when the German's asked us to repatriate all the gold we held on their behalf at the Fed offices and at Fort Knox. Some 350 metric tonnes, or 28,000 gold bars, give or take a couple. They were also agitating hard for an audit of their holdings but, surprise, surprise, they didn't get it. We made up some cock-and-bull story about having to re-cast their gold ingots into modern day bars with the appropriate weight. Anyway we eventually sent them a paltry 5 tonnes as a token gesture and promised the rest in due course. Privately we told them thirty years, which pissed them off I can tell you. Anyway, for the sake of keeping them on-side against the Ruskies, the President decided to secretly transport 300 tonnes a couple of years ago. From our special reserves."

"Yes, the first bit does ring a bell Lewis; but you kept the last bit quiet. I thought it was just a diplomatic spat: a way of them telling you to get your faltering economy in order and follow some German fiscal discipline and economic rectitude. A none-too-subtle slap on the wrists. It quickly dropped out of the headlines so I thought no more about it."

"You and endless others, thank God. Well here's the punch line Prime Minister, so brace yourself: we basically have no gold left; zip, nada, zilch. Or as you Brits like to say, 'Sweet FA'. All the stuff you see in the endless glittering photos in the vaults of the Fed offices, neatly stacked 80 feet below 33 Liberty Street, is for the most part counterfeit: gold plated tungsten. So for Christ's sake don't tell the Germans."

"You've seriously got to be kidding me Lewis. How come the governor of the Bank of England hasn't told me this?"

"I think you'll find he has somewhat of a similar, but slightly different predicament which he daren't tell you about. There is some bullion in both our vaults, certainly. But I don't need to remind you that every central bank in the world, except China, lends or sells their gold to other banks, companies, indeed anyone who will pay the piper. Been going on for years; I think I'm correct in saying your chaps in Threadneedle Street invented the idea during the Napoleonic wars. We have got to the stage where we've been through so many financial crises and economic shocks that selling the gold, and mindlessly printing trillions of dollars, has been the only way to keep America functioning. How do you think we managed to somehow get out of the mess of 2008? Had to sell tonnes of the bloody stuff to keep afloat. It's just trickled through my predecessors fingers, without a word being said. More importantly, no one knew about it."

"Flooding the world with dollars I understand, but you telling me that the United States has no gold… that's preposterous Lewis? I'm going to give Sir David Stone a total bollocking when I next see him. Does Dominic Carrington know about this?"

"I doubt it very much Prime Minister. Even the Governor is not on the US government's 'need to know' list. So, mum's the word, right Charlie!"

"You have my word that I'll keep this very disconcerting

matter to myself. I'm going to have to think long and hard about the implications of this Lewis. But what's all this got to do with the 'Naked Shorts' paper?"

"Ah, funny you should ask that, but don't take too long chewing it over as time is very definitely not on our side right now."

They both stared at each other, wondering who would speak next.

"Ever been to a rodeo Charlie and fancied your chances with the meanest bucking bronco you ever saw? Well we are about to have that experience but a hundred times worse. In fact, we are totally f…"

At that precise moment there was a knock on the door and a secretary's head popped around it. "Everyone is assembled for your next appointment Prime Minister."

"Get Amanda to urgently reconvene the meeting for as soon as possible, Lewis. I have a lot of thinking to do."

CHAPTER 16

Dandong, Beijing & The Lamb and Flag

The youngest brother of General Xiao put the phone down in a state of shock, fear and trepidation. Unquestionably that was quite possibly the last time they would speak. Without a moment's hesitation he set off for the gold warehouse and urgently assembled his brother's loyal followers. Once they had been briefed on the contents of the earlier call, they knew that the secret police would now immediately turn their full vengeance upon them and their families. No one would be spared; all knew their lives were now forfeit. Flight was their only option.

Because of his exalted position as head of the army, Xiao had effortlessly purloined over a hundred tonnes of gold into his private vault, making him one of the wealthiest men in the country, if not the world. A ten percent cut of each and every cargo was deemed perfectly acceptable and entirely appropriate, providing the residue of the smuggled gold found its way, no questions asked, into the central bank's vaults in Beijing.

Although this was tolerated under past regimes, the tide had abruptly turned recently and disaster loomed large for everyone involved in his operation, unless drastic action was now taken. If Xiao could be accused of anything, it was his inability to see this change coming and to seamlessly shift his allegiances to those now pulling the strings of power. The premier's eye was now focussed upon him and all his corrupt colleagues.

Without a moment's hesitation, preparations were underway to transfer the gold ingots to a barge and make the perilous journey to Shanghai. Smaller denomination bars were distributed to those loyal followers who could not travel with the precious cargo and instructions given to flee the city of Dandong that very night.

★ ★ ★

When the private jet containing China's central banking elite landed in Beijing, there on the tarmac, as promised, was a phalanx of limousines waiting to disburse the dignitaries to their respective offices and homes. Out of the corner of his eye, as he descended the steps of the jet, Xiao noticed one of the cars had army flags fluttering on the front wings of its bonnet. By the grace of God, or whatever deity he believed in, his luck and possibly his life's destiny now changed. The hapless functionaries charged with transporting Xiao to his fate, had sent his own staff car to pick him up and deliver him to his executioners. Stepping into the rear seat he closed the door, grateful that they had not placed a guard in the car. Slowly he lifted up the central console and retrieved the small pistol he always kept there.

As the line of cars moved seamlessly into the city, one by one they peeled off in different directions. Within a few minutes he was presented with the opportunity to escape as they pulled up at some traffic lights. Unhesitatingly he raised the pistol; without a flicker of emotion he instantly killed the driver. Getting out of the car, he retrieved his small case, casually stole the driver's wallet, and, with the car's engine still running, began to walk purposefully to the nearest underground station. He pondered how long it would be before the authorities realised he had escaped their clutches. Maybe he had an hour, maybe less? Thankfully he was wearing nondescript civilian clothes. It was still early morning as he descended the metro escalators and effortlessly blended in with the rush hour crowds. Revenge and retribution were his first priority; recovery of his fortune a close second.

* * *

Within seconds of the car failing to arrive as planned, the Beijing authorities initiated a search along the route. Having found the driver dead at the wheel and the head of the army missing, their immediate presumption was that Xiao was now on the run and, in all probability, would scurry home to his family in Dandong; a nine hour drive away. A well-practiced process of alerting the secret police and every branch of government was immediately put into place to find their missing fugitive: dead or alive.

It was simply taken for granted – by the entire country – that every senior member of the Politburo was complicit in what they euphuistically referred to as 'top slicing' anything of value that passed through their hands. Priority was always given – without a moment's hesitation or flicker of conscience – to their own pound of flesh over that rightfully belonging to the State. The hoard of gold under the control of Xiao was therefore a highly prized asset to be plundered upon his downfall. When a member of this elite group transgressed, their fortune would be immediately seized and, in all likelihood, find its way into the hands of one of their fellow conspirators. An unseemly scramble would shortly be underway to confiscate the bullion which they all knew was in the vaults in Dandong.

After due deliberation, especially from those amongst them possessing the more devious minds, the thought struck the inner circle that maybe Xiao had actually conspired in the disappearance of the Jin-Ton. Perhaps he knew they were watching him; perhaps his plan was to secretly deliver the entirety of the ships gold into his warehouse. It would not be too difficult to concoct a story that it had been somehow stolen by the Americans. If that was indeed the case, then it made great sense to somehow catch him red-handed. They could then make great political capital out of the entanglement with the Americans and redistribute the gold amongst the chosen few. It also rapidly occurred to the more politically astute amongst them that they could also blame the United States for smuggling the arms cache, which would be conveniently found on board the ship, into Somalia. If this sequence of events was indeed true, then it made sense to let Xiao make his way home without detection and let matters unfold under their close surveillance.

Qiang Li, the man in charge of the tracking the errant ship's progress, was immediately alerted and told to urgently contact the Jin-Ton with new instructions. He could not believe the highly confidential news that General Xiao was missing and that, on pain of death, he must report any contact with him immediately.

"Captain Zucca, its Qiang here, Beijing office."

"About bloody time! Have you transferred our money? I've just had to throw one of the crew overboard in order to prevent a mutiny. Believe me when I say, it's your turn next the moment I make it to Beijing."

"I've just been told by my superiors that all financial matters will be taken care of later today and that I should be able to confirm that to you by the end of the afternoon. On that basis, your destination reverts to Dandong. Make full steam, or whatever it is you say, and there will be a handsome bonus waiting for you."

Zucca stared at Sergeant Oakes in wide eyed wonder thinking, 'what the hell has happened here'. With a shrug of his shoulders, accompanied by a nod of the head from Oakes, he replied as nonchalantly as he could.

"OK, if I receive that confirmation, we shall sail for China as agreed. If I don't, then we head back to somewhere more welcoming."

"Good, I will be back to you within six hours."

★ ★ ★

The Lamb and Flag, in London's Covent Garden, is as incongruous a place to meet for lunch and discuss momentous world events as you could possibly conceive. A favoured haunt of Charles Dickens, the pub continues its well deserved reputation for being noisy, boisterous and quintessentially English. All that was missing was sawdust on the floor and the occasional bare-knuckled fight. In the opinion of Lewis Moyns, the maverick chairman of the US Federal Reserve, you could not wish to find a more appropriate venue to have a couple of beers with his old ally, Sebastian Fortes.

"Two pints of Pride and some pork scratching please." The barmaid was more than happy to oblige with a smile and a provocative flash of cleavage.

"Seb, let's grab a table and sit in the corner before it becomes chaotic. We need lots of background noise to talk about things. Here, have some lunch! Makes quite a contrast with my meeting with Charlie Sheer this morning. Do you trust him; the truth now?"

"Expense account running a bit over budget is it Lewis? First things first: cheers, your good health!" A sip of beer consumed, Seb continued. "Why do you ask such a pointed question? He's our prime minister. I've no reason not to trust him. I assume you've asked because, well, for some reason you don't?"

"Sixth sense Seb, something's decidedly wrong. I've had to disclose a very hush-hush secret to him this morning. It hardly caught his attention. OK, he's agreed that we are going to have another shindig with Amanda and the others, but this is so serious a matter that he should be focused solely on resolving the looming crisis."

"He's getting unmitigated grief in the press these days, maybe that's the issue? Anyway, why the pub lunch and what's the big secret, assuming you are willing to tell me?"

"There's a lot to tell Seb, but I can only open the window a little today. The most important thing is to have a better grasp of the problem. We now have two directly competing forces in the gold market: the West wants the gold price to remain low because we – and I'm speaking here now about the United States – don't want the dollar to lose its prominence as the world's currency. No one truly backs their currency with gold these days; it's just supported by everyone having unshakeable faith that the dollar will always rule the world. If we lose that trust, and say the people feel safer with a currency backed by gold – like in the olden days – then we, and everyone else are utterly screwed. That's why the East, and especially China, wants the price of gold to rise."

He cast his eyes around the pub to ensure they were not being overheard, before continuing.

"Given their enormous undisclosed reserves, at some point they will put the screws on the bullion banks and demand they make-good their gazillions of forward gold contracts and produce physical gold....which we all know they don't have. The banks are then forced into an unseemly scramble to buy gold to fulfil their contractual obligations, the price rises inexorably because there is no one selling – China having all the bloody gold – and hey presto in rapid order, every major bank you can name becomes insolvent. The dollar goes down the gurgler and the renminbi emerges triumphant from the ashes. That, as we say at the Fed, is the ultimate nightmare scenario."

"No wonder its pork scratching for lunch! But how is all of this going to be triggered Lewis?"

"Another pint first. Chips?"

Seb was left at the table to contemplate what, if anything, could be done to prevent Armageddon and, far more importantly, what he was going to be asked to do.

"They are called crisps here, Lewis", who shrugged his shoulders in a 'whatever' gesture, before continuing.

"We have another meeting at the embassy tonight when General Sanford will fill you in on the military dimension to all this, which became incredibly intriguing overnight when China's top military man went AWOL."

"What? No way! Is this connected to what we are talking about? He's probably just bounced off for the weekend accompanied by some 'tart-with-a-heart' on his arm, as you would, undoubtedly, so elegantly put it."

"Wish that were so, but it's a tad more serious than that Seb. I'll leave that topic to the General. The serious point I'm endeavouring to make here is that someone, presumably China, through an endless stream of clandestine intermediaries, shell companies, bogus individuals, opaque agencies...I could go on and on...has built up a staggering long position in gold futures with the western banking community. It's taken quite a while to fully appreciate that these folks were possibly connected, but after a bit of sleuthing a disturbing picture is emerging. China has unquestionably cornered the physical gold market and my sources tell me it has built up an unbelievable strangle-hold on the gold futures market. The question is: what do they intend to do about it, and more importantly, when?"

Seb took a very large sip of beer, if for no other reason than to give himself time to think. Lewis looked him squarely in the eyes:

"That, my dear friend, is why Uncle Sam needs your help."

CHAPTER 17

American Embassy, London

General James Sanford and Major Lyn Andrews weaved effortlessly along the contours of the River Thames, some fifteen hundred feet below them, as the bright, late-afternoon sunshine cast its shadows over the city's famous landmarks.

"Fabulous views General. It's good to be back."

Sanford pulled smoothly back on the helicopter's cyclic stick and rapidly descended to touch down without drama at the Battersea heliport. After engine shutdown, the two of them marched in perfect synchrony towards the waiting car.

"Haven't done that in quite a while Lyn! Takes me back to Tripoli in 2011."

The journey to the US embassy would take no more than five minutes; and, as was to be expected, they were meticulously on time for their six o'clock meeting.

"Really delighted to have you back on the team, Lyn." He opened the car and gestured for her to get in. "You've had a tough year. My only concern is that it just may get tougher."

It would be the first occasion Lyn had seen Sebastian in many, many months. From her perspective she was convinced that she hadn't changed very much in the intervening period; OK, she had killed a few highly undesirable people, but that went with the territory. Inside she was sure that she was the same person as before, but wondered what had happened to Seb and whether their relationship had survived her absence?

121

Sanford was curiously non-committal when pressed on the subject.

"Lost a lot of his effervescence I'm sad to report Lyn; needs a strong woman by his side, take him in hand. In my opinion he could also do with being exposed to a spot of danger."

The past twenty four hours had been spent in a routine debriefing session with the CIA, sketching out the details of her six-month assignment in Somalia. All involved considered the mission to have been a resounding success. This was followed by a wide-ranging discussion of the curious gold shipment found aboard the Jin-Ton; which port it would eventually sail to; and the, as yet unpublicised, disappearance of China's most senior military commander.

Sanford marvelled at the contrast between Lyn's obvious femininity, when not in fatigues and camouflage face paint; and the steel-tipped military leader she had now become. He frequently commended Lyn during her report to the intelligence officers for the clarity of thought, decisiveness and courage she had displayed. There was little doubt that he saw great potential in her and, without directly saying as much, hoped – when he would ask later today – that she had one more overseas operation left in her. He instinctively knew the answer was yes.

Already assembled within the embassy's secure room, colloquially known as the 'Chamber', was a formidable team of gold experts and the world's foremost central banker; all complimented by the UK chancellor. By contrast Sebastian Fortes felt that, amongst such distinguished company, he was the proverbial, 'plus-one', and simply there to listen.

When Lyn entered the room and smiled at him, every emotion he had for her, every memory of their time together, were rekindled in an instant. He wondered whether it was wise to stand up. There was an overwhelming desire to embrace her, but given the circumstances, he knew that would be inappropriate. Hopefully, that was an event to be savoured later.

"Good evening General, good to see you again after so long. I hope all is well at Strategic Air Command?"

Sebastian shook his hand warmly, received a curt nod to suggest all was indeed well, and introduced him to those members of the group he did not know. He kissed Lyn gently on the cheek and whispered, "You're looking fabulous darling, as always."

Sanford sat at the head of the table and was, as Seb had seen on many such occasions while together in Hong Kong, all business.

"Gentlemen, Miss Price, I'd appreciate it if no one took any notes of tonight's proceedings and that we kept this conversation strictly between ourselves."

Everyone shook their heads in agreement, except Dominic Carrington, who enquired of no one in particular, "Why is the PM not here?"

Amanda Price interjected: "He's in the midst of some press flap or other, Dominic. If there is anything to report to him, I'll do it myself tomorrow."

"A dereliction of duty if you ask me, Chancellor."

Amanda smiled, but before this line of conversation could be taken any further Sanford intervened.

"Let's all focus on the issue at hand, please. Firstly, I've included Major Andrews and Mr Fortes in this meeting because I want them to more fully understand the background as to why we have to act urgently; and in concert."

He paused momentarily, as if for effect. "It also enables me to brief them on a task I wish them to undertake shortly."

Lyn and Seb looked at each other in mild bewilderment, but neither spoke.

"You may not readily appreciate that there is a significant military dimension to the events unfolding in the world's gold market. Contrary to our country's stated position, the USA, regrettably, is chronically short of gold."

A look of disbelief spread across the faces at the table.

"Mr. Moyns would undoubtedly confirm this to you – should he ever get the President's permission to do so, which he never will, of course. Sorry to embarrass you Lewis; but it's time we all stopped pretending things were peachy and faced up to the truth before it's too late. We are so short in fact, that we have had a long-standing and covert policy to plunder any gold we can, whenever we can, from whomsoever we can. When Libya was about to fail, a Special Forces team under my command went in to 'recover' their gold reserves."

There was an audible gasp in the room, before Sanford continued.

"Thankfully we were not detected, but should we have been, we would have spun a story that we didn't want it falling into rebel hands. By the same token, when it looked like Ukraine may be overrun by the Russians, we repeated the same process. Same reasoning. The Polish are still desperately looking for the train containing the Nazi gold from World War Two: waste of time, we have that to. I could go on, and on, and on...."

Sir David Stone sat open mouthed: "The history boys at the Bank have often wondered what happened to that train; we thought the Bolsheviks had snatched it. Our military chaps had heard unconfirmed rumours about Libya, but not Ukraine." He took a deep breath before continuing:

"In the spirit of Anglo-American camaraderie, I might as well issue a very British *mea maxima cupla*. Our actual gold reserves are much, much, less that the published figure. I've never had the opportunity to discuss this with Lewis, but we've often suspected that the Fed's figures must be – how best can I express this delicately – suspect. The Threadneedle Street vaults are full, but not much of it is ours anymore."

Before he could continue, Dominic Carrington intervened.

"Bloody hell, David! This is an unmitigated disaster. If the major central banks of the world can't continue to supply the bullion banks with gold to cover their short positions, then we are totally, and utterly, screwed."

Dominic Carrington wiped his brow before continuing, his mind racing with the consequences of what he had just heard.

"I took the opportunity overnight to have a reassessment of Russia's gold reserves with my chums at MI6. They reckon that they have stashed away 8,000 tonnes: much, much, more than the official figure. When you add that to China's enormous holdings, we are in one hell of a fix here. I'm officiating over an organisation that is a busted flush."

Sanford intervened, "The CIA believes that figure is an underestimate, Professor Carrington. We would go with 10,000 tonnes, or higher. If I understand the workings of the gold market correctly, we are all in one hell of a bind. The CIA uses its enormous 'black budget' to surreptitiously buy any physical gold it can; but this pushes up the price. This is not wanted politically, as it plays directly into the hands of the Chinese and Russians. That's why it's been decided we must covertly get our hands on as much gold bullion as we can; if for no other reason than to help us forestall any crisis by parading rows and rows of the stuff in front of the worlds, hopefully highly gullible, press."

The stillness in the room was palpable as everyone began silently reassessing their positions. Seb was the first to speak.

"So why am I here General? And what's this assignment you referred to earlier?"

"It hasn't hit the news-stands yet, but China's senior-most military chief has gone missing. We've been watching him like a hawk for the past few years because he has been in charge of all the covert operations to smuggle gold into China. We know he has a private vault in Dandong which contains one hell of a lot of the stuff which he has accumulated over the years. The CIA has been monitoring his organisation from the get-go, and is of the opinion that he is about to transport the entire contents to Shanghai by sea."

"Wow", that's the prize then?" interjected Seb.

"Indeed. We assume that the Chinese Premier has concluded he's over stepped the mark, taken corruption too far, and is now on their most wanted list. That's why I want Lyn to intercept the ship, or ships, and get whatever gold he has stolen back under our control. If you wish to go along for the ride, Seb, you'd be most welcome. We have heard intercepted conversations suggesting he has 100 to 150 tonnes in his private vault. It's a drop in the proverbial ocean, but it may cause a significant distraction amongst the apparatchiks in the Politburo, make them think twice and slow down the smuggling network. If we can somehow get our hands on General Xiao as well, then all the better."

"Do you mind if we take a five minute break," asked Sir David, "I just want to clear my head! Can I have a word Dominic?"

"Of course, Governor, over in the corner perhaps?"

Out of earshot of the others, Sir David said:

"All this daring-do is fine and dandy Dominic, but we have to figure out some way to minimise the banking crisis that will hit us, should the Chinese and the Russians act precipitously and demand physical gold. If that happens we are, not to put too fine a point on it, utterly buggered. I think we need Sebastian working on our problem, not getting – what is it the Americans say in those ludicrous gangster movies – 'tooled-up'. He's already had one of his nine lives, so let's not push his luck. I think we ought to dissuade Sanford and redirect Seb's endeavours to thinking about the troubles ahead for the bullion banks."

A sage nodding of heads was followed by a moment's hesitancy, before Dominic almost blurted out.

"I can't help but agree David, but the General is steeped in the military way of resolving anything, so that's his default *modus operandi*. Perhaps we could suggest that Sebastian could exert more influence in another unexpected direction. Suppose he were to persuade his own bank to unwind their futures contracts and see what happens in the market. See if the Chinese bite."

They stared at each other for what felt like an age, before the governor of the Bank of England chose to speak.

"Interesting, a kind of controlled deception. You and I need more time to think this through very carefully of course, as the gold price will, in all probability, become exceptionally volatile? We have to develop a contingency plan just in case we let the genie out of the bag, but it would almost certainly flush them out. We'll also need a hell of a lot of gold to close out the contracts. If Seb could somehow manage to make them think that he could be advantageous to their scheme, then he might be able to infiltrate whoever is behind this. Shall we share this idea with the others?"

"Let's be better prepared David. Best to just sow the seeds of doubt in Sanford's mind, why don't you ask for twenty four hours to consider all the revelations we have heard tonight, then make our proposal." They once again nodded in agreement.

"Then the floor's all yours, Governor."

The meeting broke up somewhat prematurely and, in several people eyes, highly unsatisfactorily. Sanford reluctantly agreed to defer any decision about Sebastian's involvement until the following day and, if necessary, confirming that he would go in his stead.

Everyone departed in different directions, with only Lyn and Seb, hand in hand, taking a taxi together.

CHAPTER 18

London

The UK chancellor, Amanda Price, got into the back of her ministerial car – inwardly grinning broadly – and immediately phoned the prime minister.

"Just finished the get-together at the US embassy, Charlie; inconclusive, as always. Strictly between the two of us, I think Dominic Carrington still bears a huge grudge against you for this d'Abo business. He was very rude about your absence, but, to give him his due, he is trying his very best to help. To the extent you want my advice, I'd say watch your back; there is a lot of bitterness and rancour just below the surface. I'm not sure, to purloin a well-worn phrase, that he's 'one of us'."

The PM just replied, "mmm....interesting."

She then sent a text message to her favourite newspaper editor, Cressida Armstrong:

> *'Made any progress with the story yet Cressida? If you can run it at the weekend that would be excellent timing. More salacious material to follow, if you're good to me! Imperial College remember!'*

Within a matter of moments she got a reply:

> *'I always try to be good Amanda, and when I'm not, I'm naughty. Still fact checking! Might have to run it next week. Keep close.'*

As she approached Downing Street in pensive silence, her mind was focused upon one thing and one thing only: when to administer the *coup de gras;* the release of the killer document still in her safe that would see Charlie Sheer thrown in jail for a very long time indeed. Ultimate power was now within her grasp; but would the gold crisis derail her entire plans, or merely accelerate it? She would bet all on the latter.

★ ★ ★

Lyn entered the penthouse apartment at St George Wharf and marvelled at the panorama of the Houses of Parliament spread out in front of her. Within a proverbial snap of a finger, Seb had proffered a glass of ice cold champagne as they flopped down close together on the sofa watching the last rays of sunshine.

"This looks very much like an unloved bachelor pad Seb, which, I have to say, pleases me greatly. I'll run a DNA trace for suspicious blond hairs later! Any stray findings and you'll be singing falsetto at the bank's next karaoke outing."

He roared with laughter, while placing a hand provocatively on her thigh.

"Just checking for knives…"

"You certainly know how to impress a girl. May I reciprocate and check if your weapon of choice is primed and ready for action?"

A long tender kiss followed as they slowly and sensuously re-explored each other's bodies.

"Seb honey, I have counted every second we have been apart. You do understand there has not been a moment in the last nine months when I have been allowed to be in contact with you: first lesson of being in the Special Forces I'm afraid. Total silence!"

"I do understand Lyn, although at times it's been very lonely here staring at the wall, while you've been gadding about having adventures on the high seas and eating creepy-crawlies on toast. Speaking of which, shall we go out to eat, or shall I cook one of my specials?"

She smiled and once more melted his heart.

"No, we'll stay here. You don't happen to have any whipped cream by any chance? I have one of two suggestions."

"I'll check; probably more likely to have a whip than cream! Let me top up your champagne? Did I understand Sanford correctly tonight; that you may be off to pastures new again very soon?"

"He has only said that I may have to go back to the ship we hijacked, the Jin-Ton, and take it to Shanghai, or Dandong, or Christ knows where. I've still got one of my team on board, so there is a clear line of responsibility back to me I'm afraid."

"Let's draw a halt in the shop talk tonight, Lyn. I have a big surprise for you."

"No, I'm not doing that again, Seb! My throat still hurts."

A wicked, impish, smile crossed his face. He raised a glass and mischievously clinked their glasses together.

"What's the phrase; ah yes, deeply sorry to have made such a gigantic culinary cock-up! You have my word that I will never put that many Habanero chillies in the salsa ever again. Follow me, Major, and brace yourself for something hotter."

★ ★ ★

Upon entered his hotel on Park Lane, the concierge handed Lewis a short message from Sir David Stone.

'Can we meet later? Dominic and I would like to bounce an idea off you?'

Within thirty minutes he was being dropped outside White's in St James's Street and wondering what they had to discuss at this time of night that was so important.

"Glad you could make it Lewis. Did John d'Abo ever bring

you here; he was a long standing member and the chap who introduced me to the club."

"No, afraid not Dominic! Large bourbon on the rocks, if you're buying?"

"Delighted, and for you Sir David? Shall we share a bottle of house claret?"

The governor of the Bank of England cleared his throat before starting to elaborate further.

"My dear Lewis, Dominic and I wanted your opinion on an idea we are in the process of formulating; I think you chaps call it 'blue sky's thinking'. I prefer to call it blundering around in the dark looking for answers. Now, suppose that the Chinese really are up to no good. Could we somehow get them to reveal their hand? What if we were to use Sebastian's bank as a stalking horse and see if we can draw them out? Discover who the real players are, what their motivations are, that sort of thing?"

"Interesting idea Governor, providing we can contain the consequences, whatever they may be. What do you have in mind?"

"Perhaps Dominic could explain."

"Delighted to David. I haven't checked, but I'm assuming d'Abo's Bank would be willing to assist our cause? Front the operation, so to speak. Especially if we both agree to – how shall I put this delicately – arrange to rig the gold price on the COMEX Exchange in New York so that it falls and back-stop their possible losses. They would then start selling forward contracts in big numbers which the Chinese, or whoever, would presumably be only too pleased to buy. Our intelligence agencies believe they surreptitiously buy gold whenever there is an unexpected dip in the price. If our theory is correct, then they would demand settlement in physical gold. We would then have the opportunity to identify who is the true threat here."

Lewis leaned forward to take his drink from the table.

"Well his bank does have a reputation for divergent thinking, although everyone will know they have taken a big loss."

"True Lewis, but it would be a one-off event to begin with. It's not as if their share price is going to take a dive, but Seb may feel his standing in the banking community would plummet?"

"He's big enough to take that if he knows we have his best interests at heart."

Lewis stared into space in quiet conjecture, and a smile crossed his face; the first one in a very long time. Dominic leaned forward,

"I know that look, Lewis; a light-bulb moment if ever I saw one!"

"Possibly. We would have to ensure that we have access to the level of bullion required. Plus there are one or two tricks the boys back home have – which I sincerely hope you don't know anything about – that will help us immeasurably. I know just the man...any chance of a top-up? We'll meet with Seb tomorrow to discuss the details."

★ ★ ★

Although the meeting had concluded several hours ago, Sanford was still restlessly pacing the US embassy rooms late into the evening: a product of too much coffee and a troubled mind. He was concerned by the lack of direction the technical discussions were going with his banking colleagues and his inability to move the game forward to a satisfactory conclusion. It was not his style to hesitate, but to act decisively: he hated loose ends, unfinished missions and, above all else, vacillation on the part of others. His train of thought was rudely interrupted when a message was handed to him from one of the military attaches.

Eyes Only, General Sanford, SAC Europe. Intercepted reports out of Beijing confirm that General Xiao is indeed missing, presumed on the run. Whereabouts currently unclear. CIA does not as yet consider him a candidate for defection; but closely monitoring situation should events change. Chinese authorities strongly believe he must be attempting to rendezvous with family members who, overnight, have completely emptied his personal bullion vault in Dandong. Assessment by Langley suggests the secret police have issued a 'no capture' instruction: thereby allowing him to travel freely and consequently enable them to recover the gold. Unclear if this is being transported to North Korea by road, or elsewhere, possibly by sea. If so, Shanghai or Hong Kong are the obvious destinations. Is it feasible that the freighter Jin-Ton could somehow intercept? ETA would be three/four days. More follows. Stop.

Although nearing midnight, he immediately picked up the phone to Lyn.

"Sanford here, Major. Can you get back to the embassy, now please?"

★ ★ ★

"Sorry Seb, duty calls; got to meet the boss immediately. Clearly a flap on somewhere which needs my urgent, undivided, attention. Do you have a spare key? I'll let myself back in. No need to salute, you can stand your friend to attention later."

★ ★ ★

The situation room at the US embassy was a breathtaking, truly awe-inspiring, visual spectacle seen by only a rarefied few who were lucky enough to have top secret clearance. Row after row of computers and wall-mounted screens filled the place with an iridescent blue light. Mission Control at NASA was amateur hour by contrast. Manned constantly, it had unrivalled technology and every conceivable form of eavesdropping equipment available on the planet. Each terminal was the recipient of privileged and highly classified information, satellite images, video streams and conversations being constantly monitored, scanned, analysed and logged into its data stores from a million locations.

It was unprecedented that the head of the Chinese military would go AWOL, so every effort was being made to establish why he had taken this action; to what end; which colleagues may be leaving with him; and whether these exceptional circumstances could somehow be exploited.

Sanford escorted Lyn into the 'Holy of Holies' and they sat together in front of a communications station, whose operative was poised to do his masters bidding.

"Get me – what's the name of your guy on the Jin-Ton, Lyn?"

"Oakes, Sir"

"Get me Oakes."

★ ★ ★

Aboard the Jin-Ton, Staff Sergeant Oakes and Captain Zucca were playing an endless game of poker, drinking copiously and, as was their wont, talking gibberish about football and women. The heat was becoming oppressive and the idea of anyone wearing a uniform was deemed utterly laughable: beer stained tee-shirts and ripped shorts were the preferred dress for dinner. They had only recently passed Sarawak en route to their destination, which they both presumed would still be Dandong, when their revelry was rudely interrupted by the harsh tone of the secure radio transmitter.

"General Sanford and Major Andrews here Sergeant. Is the Captain around? I have new orders for you."

Oakes nearly fell from his chair and instinctively stood to attention and saluted.

"He's right next to me, Sir."

"Good, I want you to continue your present course to Dandong, but at the last possible moment be prepared to make a switch for Shanghai. I'm arranging for the two of us to be dropped on board the Jin-Ton, say in three or four days time. Details of how and where will follow, when I have figured it out. Just play along with the Chinese if you have to report in: situation normal, as far as they are concerned. They will only realise you're not going further north after the actions I'm contemplating have been concluded, by which time it will too late."

"Yes, Sir. I take it we keep the transponder on until directed otherwise?"

"Random changes; say a day on, then half a day off. Keep them on the back foot. If contacted just grumble about the rations, the crew, the weather, the lack of sports coverage, the usual BS."

CHAPTER 19

The Yellow Sea, China and London

The tramp steamer was slowly and ponderously navigating its way down the Yalu River from Dandong, transporting the stolen gold bullion. To the relief of all on board it had now reached the open waters of the Yellow Sea, which was mercifully calm. The port of Shanghai was still many days sailing away but everyone knew it would be a perilous journey, fraught with terror and requiring constant vigilance. They were leaderless and their plans ill-formed. If they were intercepted by the Chinese Navy, there would be no escape; punishment would be swift and terminal. Xiao's loyal brothers and close family were on permanent watch for any signs of danger, but they had no means to defend themselves, even if they felt so inclined. They were fleeing for their lives, with not the slightest possibility of ever returning. Their only hope in avoiding detection lay in being able to blend in with the countless, indistinguishable, similar ships plying the same route.

No further instructions had been received from their elder brother, so they had little option but to proceed in blind faith, as instructed, to an obscure port to the north of Shanghai, where they hoped the mysterious 'Butler' would be waiting. What they were then supposed to do remained a total mystery. Their only hope was that Xiao would somehow be there to meet them and take command, assuming they managed to get that far without capture.

The vast apparatus of the Chinese state had, as yet, not managed to establish where Xiao's co-conspirators had fled to. Those in the upper echelons of the military didn't need reminding that he had developed deep and long-standing contacts in North Korea which, in his role as head of the army, the Politburo had actively encouraged. Common sense suggested, therefore, that he would seek sanctuary there in return for foregoing some, or all, of the gold he possessed. Their gold!

Diplomats were already being urgently dispatched to Pyongyang to remind the North Korean leader who it was who held the dominant position of power in their increasingly fragile relationship. Should they acquiesce to Xiao's entreaties for protection and shelter, then aid of every description and vital political support could – and surely would – be withdrawn in the snap of a finger. They had no choice but to bend to China's will on this matter.

Xiao was not without friends on the mainland, whom he knew, without even asking, would be willing to assist him in return for a generous 'slice of the action'. The question at the forefront of his mind, as always, was: would they betray him; could they be trusted; what would they want in return for their help. More worryingly, would he instead be held as a very valuable hostage? The list of concerns seemed endless to him.

It was comparatively straight forward for him to make his way cautiously south from Beijing to Shanghai without detection. He was confident that he could rely on his numerous, long held, contacts in the underworld community to help. After all, he had often deliberately overlooked their criminal activities in return for a handsome share of the spoils. However, he had never had cause to test the hypothesis of whether there was indeed 'honour amongst thieves': he doubted it very much indeed.

When Xiao approached Nantong, on the northern outskirts of Shanghai, he was exhausted, hungry and in desperate need of sleep and fresh clothing. With what money he had left, stolen from his long-dead official driver, he checked into a modest road-side hotel, locked the door and slept for eighteen hours. On waking he felt refreshed and sufficiently reinvigorated to venture out for a new shirt and trousers and, rather appropriately he felt, decided it was time to make contact with the Butler.

The moment he turned on his mobile phone and began dialling, its exact location and recipient were immediately identified by the CIA and re-transmitted to General Sanford in London. The most sophisticated satellite tracking system in the world would now be able to follow his every move, his every call, his every mistake.

★ ★ ★

Zucca and Oakes were elated at the prospect of visiting the innumerable flesh-pots scattered around two of the greatest cities in Asia. They didn't give a damn where they docked, so long as it was soon. Oakes was open-mouthed when listening to the lurid stories of red-light districts across the globe which had been frequented by his degenerate friend. Frankly, he was amazed Zucca was still had a pulse and whether he was capable of captaining the ship, any ship. It had to be said, however, that they were less enamoured by the prospect of a two-star General casually 'dropping in', probably armed to the teeth, intent on mayhem. The arrival of such a senior figure could only mean one thing – serious trouble lay ahead.

The Jin-Ton thankfully contained endless weapons and ordnance, all of which were originally destined for the al-Shabaab insurgents. Oakes reflected that, given the circumstances, it would be wise to extract these from their containers and establish if any of them were in working order. An inventory was quickly completed and the most suitable side-arms distributed to the Australian navy contingent and those other members of the crew willing to, as he indelicately put it, 'play real soldiers'. As most of the original gang of reprobates, laughingly called the crew, were fugitives of one sort or other – and to a man permanently on the run from countless authorities – it went without saying that they would certainly be able to put up a decent fight, should it ever come to that.

★ ★ ★

Sanford and Lyn sat in silence studying the charts and listings of all the American naval craft capable of intercepting the Jin-Ton.

"It doesn't look good, Lyn; there are precious few ships at our disposal. Our aircraft carrier the USS Bataan is currently too far north to help and the logistics would be a nightmare. How many jumps have you had?"

"Probably a hundred plus General; mostly from altitude, not much low level experience really."

"OK, just to make it fun for you, we'll do a helicopter insertion. You can swim, right? Sorry, only kidding. I think I'll contact my counterparty in Brunei and ask if we can borrow one of their Apaches for a day or so. You game for that?"

"Certainly am Sir. I take it no sharks are involved?"

"That's the spirit. What could possibly go wrong? If I can get everything squared away, shall we plan to leave in say twenty four hours?"

Lyn nodded.

"Better go back to Fortes and, although it won't be easy given his wayward peccadilloes, try to get some rest! I'll arrange for new kit to be delivered and call you mid afternoon."

★ ★ ★

The Butler was the very embodiment of a taciturn man: very few words ever passed his lips, they didn't need to. His power was derived from an emotionless approach to death; other people's death. He commanded his hundred-strong *Sun Yee On* triad group with a rod of iron, both physically and metaphorically. All bore the scars of being in the pay of the most powerful man in Shanghai. His nickname had been gradually acquired over the years by virtue of his practice of sending severed body parts to the hapless widows of anyone who dared to cross his path, or challenge his authority. His minions were instructed to deliver them on a silver platter.

Xiao had met him on three or four previous occasions when narcotics were being transported and safe passage requested. They held a grudging respect for each other; they both knew they could trade favours, for a price.

"Xiao here. We need to meet. I have a private shipment to deal with in a few days time; I assume the usual financial terms will be acceptable? Your warehouse tonight, nine pm? I'll be alone and out of uniform."

The next problem he had to resolve was how to contact his brothers, presumably via a ship-to-shore radio. He felt pretty sure that it would be pointless trying to use his mobile phone as he didn't know where they, or their ship, presently were located. They would surely be out at sea by now, so it had to be via VHF when they got closer to port. Perhaps the Butler could help when he got to the wharf? Or perhaps he could just break into some random ship and use theirs? Then the big one: what in God's name to do with the gold? Store it somewhere till the heat was off; sell it to the triad at one hell of a discount; swap it for something, but for what? Endless questions, all needing resolution in very short order.

★ ★ ★

Lyn got into bed around 3am without disturbing Sebastian and was instantly asleep. It was eight-thirty the following morning before he woke to the wonderful surprise next to him. Slowly he leaned over to kiss her cheek and stroke her blond hair. A tiny purr emerged from her lips as he held her tightly and softly asked if she wanted any breakfast?

"I don't recommend my coffee, but the scrambled eggs are divine and the Tabasco in the Bloody Mary's will blow your socks off! Speaking of which..."

"Give me ten minutes tiger, we need to talk first."

"Not the 'Dear John' speech I trust?"

"Don't be silly: you're a keeper, providing you continue scoring straight tens between the sheets. Seriously thought Seb, I have to be ready for departure this evening to Asia. I have absolutely no idea how long I'll be away, so we have only a few hours together, so we had better make them count."

"Jesus, you've only just arrived. I'm going to make us a drink, to hell with the time."

"Well then better make mine a stiff one."

"Always happy to oblige."

★ ★ ★

Professor Dominic Carrington and Sir David Stone were having a breakfast get-together in the governor's private dining room at the Bank of England. Both men hated early morning meetings but if they were to persuade Lewis Moyns of their 'plan', they concluded that – whatever it was – it had better be water-tight and thoroughly thought through.

They had both previously agreed that the basic objective was to flush out China, or whoever was behind the attempt to corner the gold market, by making them reveal their hand. With any luck this process would also expose the 'how' and hopefully the 'why'.

After an hour they were sufficiently high on caffeine to have migrated from fruitlessly discussing the more mundane solutions, of which there were precious few, and into an exercise in lateral thinking. The more they talked, they more they convinced themselves that only the unconventional would work.

"Dominic, I believe it's true to say that both the Russians and the Chinese will buy physical gold on any dips in the price? They are in a constant frenzy to add to their stockpiles, so perhaps this is their Achilles heel? We therefore need to engineer a fall in the market with carefully orchestrated announcements to that effect by, say, a well respected US hedge fund."

The governor gestured for yet another pot of coffee.

"Well David, my suggestion would be to use d'Abo bank's owners, SQT in Connecticut, to start these rumours. They have helped us in the past with the Dark Pools matter, are amongst the biggest hedge fund in the world and have enormous clout in the market. If we can persuade SQT to set up a series of short sales, of say 5,000 futures contracts on COMEX, which at the standard 100 oz per contract, would be a highly visible 15 tonnes sale. By the immutable laws of supply and demand, if they initiate sufficient of these contracts the price will fall significantly."

They both nodded in unison, before Dominic Carrington took up the baton and moved the discussion forward.

"The next step is all a question of timing, getting Sebastian's agreement to the plan, and access to a lot of physical gold, which I'm hoping Lewis will somehow solve for us."

"He'll have to Dominic. The Bank of England can't be seen to be involved under any circumstances. The PM would have my balls if this was to leak out, and you'd be banged up in the Tower before you could count to five."

"Let's see if the boss of the Federal Reserve is on board for a spot of subterfuge and deception. Shall I call him and see if he's free this afternoon?"

"I'll clear my diary. I think I'm due at a Parliamentary select committee but I'll get one of the deputy governors to go in my place. I think the phrase *du jour* is 'bring it on'."

CHAPTER 20

US Embassy, London

Lewis Moyns was half way through a daunting stack of briefing memos, routinely sent from his office when he was travelling, when his mobile phone mercifully rang. A quick glance down towards the coffee table and he saw it was a call from Dominic Carrington. After a couple of minutes of one-way dialogue he got the opportunity to respond.

"Sure thing guys; see you at the embassy at, shall we say, three? And thanks again for the heads-up on your thinking: we are more or less in accord. It's absolutely essential however, that General Sanford and Seb are there at the meeting; for reasons which will become obvious later. I'll try and get a hold of them after this call, but assume it's OK unless you hear from me to the contrary. Plus, there are one or two things I need to get urgent security clearance on before we meet. This may go well beyond my pay grade, so I need to contact the grown-ups in the CIA and get their approval for a little refinement to your plan that I think we should employ."

Lewis knew full well that he would have to disclose yet another state secret if the complex arrangements being discussed were to work as they wished. He felt he had little choice. The various notes he was steadfastly ploughing through told him that the 'Naked Short' positions with the bullion banks were getting larger and would surely be reaching breaking point at any moment. If the dam were to burst, then, without a shadow

of a doubt, the world's banking system would be put in mortal
peril. It didn't take a genius to predict that within a matter
of days there would be demonstrations in the streets and an

He mulled over the options available to him, using jargon
an all-out attack and take the consequences on the chin: very
should he lure the enemy into a trap? He mumbled out loud,
'Damned if I do, damned if I don't'.

He reasoned that this was unquestionably Sanford's
team of Sir David, Dominic and himself, and then passed up
the chain of command for approval. It had only recently been
CIA, via a series of Joint Task Force committees. He felt sure
that this would be of enormous benefit behind the scenes: you
can always rely upon the CIA to have a trick or two up their

Sebastian's day was not exactly going well, despite the second
his spirits', as he put it to Lyn. She was about to leave for
Christ-knows-where later that evening and now he was being
enjoying the 'sins of the flesh' with his gorgeous girlfriend. Not
only that, but he had just received a text from his bank saying

that: '*As per his specific instructions, they had unwound all their gold positions at a considerable loss and could he come and explain this to the Board tomorrow'*.

He simply mumbled, "How the mighty have fallen", before texting back, '*Of course, but it's a long story and I'm not sure how much I can officially disclose'*.

"May be that will get the monkey off my back?"

★ ★ ★

Lewis was in a quandary as to how best to address the myriad issues they now faced. If he was to get the assembled dignitaries on his side, he felt he had little choice but to fully open up and hope that discretion and common purpose would prevail.

"Thanks for coming. I feel obligated to commence with an explanation and a plea for your help. Dominic and Sir David have outlined an idea they have been working on, the end game of which we need to develop and agree. I'm still waiting for security clearance from the States on several aspects of what I'm about to say, but I'm going to proceed as if I have received a positive response. The General can kill me later if I get a 'no'."

As anticipated, this produced a roar of laughter from everyone present and lightened the mood considerably.

"You've got to understand the Fed's very delicate position in all this gentlemen. Let's start with the basics. If, by any chance, my organisation somehow loses control of the dollar exchange rate, then we immediately lose control of our pre-eminent position in the world. We need people to continue buying what they perceive to be a strong dollar, in order to support the profligate spending habits of my government. I keep telling them, but they'll never learn. If the world decides to move out of the dollar and into gold then we are, not to put too fine a point on it, totally rubber-ducked. See Seb, I'm definitely getting the hang of cockney!"

The UK contingent all shook their heads in agreement.

"Our policy of staunchly defending the value of the dollar, and dissuading people from moving into gold as an alternative, has been the bedrock of our interventionist approach for years. We deliberately sell physical gold to lower the price when we think it's overheating, and have done so for decades. That's why we have bugger-all bullion left in the vaults. We cannot let people think that gold is a better bet than the dollar; otherwise our economy and banking system would collapse in a New York second."

"Amen to that Lewis!" interjected Dominic Carrington. "The last thing my colleagues need is for my association, or its members, to be brought to their knees by such a crisis. The consequences are too horrendous to contemplate, even if it is of their own making."

"To enforce this approach, the backroom boys at the Fed frequently – but very discretely – create a massive 'Naked Short' position in the gold market in order to suppress the price. We do it occasionally; the bullion banks do it perpetually. So far we believe that no one has realised it's us manipulating the gold price in this way. It certainly takes the speculators by surprise and quite a few get burnt. But we have to stop gold being considered as the ultimate safe haven at all costs. That's why China's growing accumulation of physical gold is so troubling. There will undoubtedly come a point when they can turn the tables on us, force our banks into honouring their positions for physical gold, which naturally they won't be able to do it. Default, bankruptcy, economic and political catastrophe will ensue, as surely as night follows day."

"Well Lewis," interjected Sebastian, "I'm from Head Office, what can I do to help?"

"I've briefly discussed this with Sir David and Dominic. We would like to propose that you get d'Abo's Bank to build up a significant dealing presence on COMEX in New York. We can arrange for one of the major US banks to work with you on this without too much fuss. I gather you've just liquidated your bullion positions at a thumping loss; we'll cover that, providing your board allows you to move forward as we suggest. It's fortuitous that you took this action in the light of our plan. We will be able to use your mistake, if I can put it like that, to our mutual advantage later. We'll tell the world you are doubling your bets trying to recoup your losses."

"They will be very pleased to hear that Lewis! I'm due a bollocking at tomorrow's board meeting when I'll probably be handed the proverbial 'loaded Luger' and asked to do the decent thing."

"I've no doubt you'll talk them around Seb. We'll arrange for the Financial Times to place an article saying someone at the bank make a big mistake, which is being rectified. As this all moves forward into the more critical phases of the plan, casting you are the hapless scapegoat could prove very beneficial. Hope that's not too humiliating for you: especially as there may be worse to follow I'm afraid?"

Lewis paused momentarily and looked at the assembled guests.

"General, do you think you could rustle up a bottle of cognac; Seb's looking a tad pale."

"Remy Martin and six glasses coming up Lewis! The ambassador is rather keen on the XO; we better save one for him later."

"Excellent, bottoms up everyone! Stiffen the sinews, once more unto the breach, and all that. Now Seb, once you're back in the game, and at the opportune moment, we'll arrange for a series of short sales which will drop the price of gold dramatically. We will get your American owners, SQT, to front the sales. No one will know it's us. The Chinese, or whoever the bad guys are, will be very eager to buy these contracts and at maturity insist that the bullion is delivered to them via the

COMEX exchange. Meanwhile in London, you also arrange to sell gold forward Seb and deliver it into the London vaulting system for delivery to whoever the buyers are."

"OK, I vaguely follow that Lewis. But there's got to be more to it than that surely?"

"That's the part where General Sanford tells us what utterly devious minds and conniving bastards lurk within the CIA. I've no doubt he will also reiterate that, under pain of death, this information must stays within these four walls. No exceptions. At this stage it cannot even be disclosed to the prime minister or the chancellor, if for no other reason they can later deny they knew anything whatsoever about it."

Sanford's intimidating presence filled the room as he walked to the front of the table.

"Thanks Lewis. As you revealed to our colleagues here, the CIA have been worrying about this problem for years. I mentioned at our previous meeting, we, and here I mean the intelligence agencies, have been surreptitiously accumulating gold from any source we can: on a 'no-questions asked' basis. The CIA has an enormous black budget for such purposes and it's willing to spend whatever it takes. The upshot is that we have our own stash of, how shall I put it, 'genuine gold' deep underground. These bars are all of standard 400 ounce size, correctly numbered and identifiable in accordance with the London Bullion Markets' rules. This is in stark contrast to the bars on display at the Fed's office, or Fort Knox, which for the most part are tungsten covered with gold. We never let these out of our sight for fear of disclosure."

General Sanford took a large sip of cognac.

"Some of these bars, both the real ones and the counterfeit ones, have been surreptitiously fitted with a thin-film technology which acts as an aerial. This enables the bullion to be constantly tracked by satellite. It may surprise you to know Sir David that the Bank of England has around fifty such bars in its vaults. You cannot see these minute devises with the naked eye and they are virtually impossible to detect unless you know which bars are seeded with them. Furthermore, you can't identify them with the normal ultrasound scan which we all use to distinguish gold from gold plated tungsten."

"Good God General," spluttered Sir David, "I've never heard anything so preposterous in my life!"

"As unbelievable as it may seem Sir David, it's one hundred percent true. I'll demonstrate it to you later in the situation room if you wish. I believe I can even show you exactly where they sit in your vaults. Anyway, I digress. We use this covert system to track where a seeded gold consignment ends up. Our principal concern in the past has been to track gold that goes off-the-grid to Swiss refineries to be recast into the Chinese standard 1 kilo bars. The refinery process destroys the trace of course, but no one sends good gold to a refinery unless it's to re-size it."

Dominic Carrington sat open-mouthed, "How come no one knows a bloody thing about this General?"

"For the simple reason Professor Carrington that it's so top secret, even the President doesn't know about it; or that is what he will say should he ever be asked. We have gold tracers all over the world. That's why the CIA has a pretty accurate assessment of how much under-the-counter gold is held by Russia and China. If, for one minute, these countries knew about the true level of our gold holdings, or our tracking devises, they would take draconian action immediately. Then we would all need a wheel-barrow full of dollars to buy a burger and fries."

"I presume", said Sebastian, "that we are going to use this little ruse again with the gold my bank is about to put into the system and see where it ends up. I have to say that's very neat."

"Yes, it's amazing what hundreds of millions of dollars of research budget can accomplish. So, are you all on board? I have to go to Asia later tonight, so I'll leave the detail planning to you guys. Keep me in the loop. Top up anyone?"

CHAPTER 21

Downing Street

The usual Thursday morning cabinet meeting had concluded in what could only be described as government disarray and hysteria. To say it was fractious and argumentative would be an understatement. Alarmed ministers departed muttering under their breath that the PM was losing his grip and should stop worrying about his own skin and put the party's position first. The chief whip was being besieged by cabinet colleagues to ask Charlie Sheer to go, before it was too late.

The forthcoming election was now only a few months away and the headlines were bleak in the extreme. The Sun newspaper, in what could only be described as a carefully choreographed manoeuvre, had made a dramatic intervention. Somehow they had managed to get hold of a copy of Sir John d'Abo's death certificate which differed materially from that placed into the public domain a couple of years previously.

The paper's editorial implied that there was considerably more to this affair than met the eye: 'their' certificate quite clearly stated:

"Cause of Death: multiple gunshot wounds, not consistent with suicide".

Whereas, and in stark contrast, the one circulated by the authorities at the time indicated:

"Cause of Death: Myocardial infarction".

In plain English, a heart attack. The editor, Cressida Armstrong, was scathing in her piece.

"Who then shot Sir John d'Abo? This newspaper will cower to no one in its pursuit of the truth in this matter. Did the Prime Minister deliberately cover something up here and if so, why?"

Within the inner pages of The Sun endless speculation was given over to the questions of why there were two death certificates, why they differed, which was true and which was fake? And why, pray tell, had the original coroner simply disappeared? Conspiracy theorists were having a field-day in other newspapers deprived of the scoop.

Charles Sheer had been awoken early by one of his parliamentary aides to show him the first editions of the news papers. To say he was livid would be an understatement. By eight o'clock he had called the head of the metropolitan police and the senior operatives of MI6 and MI5. As he had done on numerous other occasions when he felt threatened, or cornered, he screamed down the phone at the hapless functionaries. The PM made it abundantly clear that he wanted to know where this bogus certificate had come from, who was responsible for leaking it and most important of all, who could they could put in jail for twenty five years. No stone was to be left unturned. Their jobs were on the line unless answers were delivered in very short order.

It was only on the day after the disastrous cabinet meeting that Charlie Sheer felt he could summon up the will power to re-read the excoriating article and truly venomous editorial, that he spotted an obscure reference to Imperial College.

"It's that bastard Carrington", he said out loud, "he's behind this leak. No doubt about it. I'll have his balls for this. What did Amanda say the other day; 'watch my back'; well, he's another one going to get both barrels."

His secretary was urgently called into the private office.

"I want you to do the rounds of the police and intelligence agencies and get them to focus their attention on Professor Dominic Carrington. No, better still; let's have them keep close tabs on everyone associated with the gold meetings. Just the Brits; that way it won't look so obvious. You can always say afterwards that the possible gold crisis was so sensitive we needed to make sure the participants were not being bugged. I want detailed reports by Sunday."

With that the prime minister closed his file and decided that, tomorrow, he would go to Chequers for the weekend and plot his revenge.

★ ★ ★

The chancellor could not have been happier if she had been a cat originating from Cheshire. Part one of the plan had now been satisfactorily accomplished, with the political hand grenade exploding exactly as she had anticipated. She was positively salivating at the consequences. The next, very sweet, step would be to fulfil her promise to Cressida and organise a little 'hurly-burly on the chaise-longue' as a thank you present. Life was definitely looking up; the keys to Number 10 were now within her grasp. She felt very comfortable to let part two of the plan wait a couple of weeks, or even a couple of months. The current furore in the press would undoubtedly run and run, fuelled by endless gossip and conjecture. A myriad of hacks, digging up, or more likely making up, enough dirt to fill hundreds of column inches, would do all the work for her. It was a pity that Dominic Carrington had to be the sacrificial lamb in this drama, as she was getting quite fond of him. But 'needs must' and he was expendable; she's make it up to him later.

"Cressida darling, I have a free weekend; the sun is shining and I have a spring in my step. So gorgeous one, do you want to come out to play with me? I'd like to thank you in the time-honoured fashion. Bring your toys, the special lingerie and I'll provide the champagne."

★ ★ ★

The PM had been in a foul mood all day, reluctantly spending hours on the phone with his wavering and, in his view, utterly spineless cabinet colleagues, endeavouring to reassure them that all was well. He knew with each successive call that the mood of the party was turning against him.

As on previous occasions, when things got a little 'sticky', he instinctively knew that the only way out of the mess was to create an artificial crisis; then miraculously resolve it. He had endless real problems to deal with; it was just a question of deciding which one of them would bring him the maximum personal benefit.

Charlie Sheer was not a person prone to daydreaming in the office, especially when he had so many difficulties weighing on his mind; but he was drawn back, time and again, to the conundrum brewing in the gold market. Was the banking sector really as vulnerable to imminent collapse as his team of experts were suggesting? More importantly, where had Dominic Carrington got a hold of d'Abo's death certificate and what possible motive could he have for making it public. No, it didn't make sense. OK, he knew they both loathed and despised each other in equal measure, but Carrington faced academic isolation and corporate ridicule if he was shown to be the vindictive culprit.

All the PM had to do was utilise his boundless guile and

somehow turn the tables on his latest archenemy. What he needed was evidence, or far more importantly, someone to fabricate the evidence.

Every holder of his esteemed office knew that, when needs-must, they could call on a series of disgruntled senior police officers, rogue intelligence operatives or ex-military men, who could always be relied upon to help, no questions asked. All they sought in return was to somehow be brought back to prominence, have their prior misdemeanours repealed, or have their pensions significantly and discretely enhanced. It was time to consult what he somewhat referred to quaintly as the 'Rolodex of Revenge'.

It didn't take him long before he had selected the very man, the equivalent of a de-frocked Chief Constable, regrettably previously embroiled in falsifying his and his subordinate's submissions to an enquiry into police harassment.

He immediately went upstairs to the privacy of his suite of rooms, murmuring, 'Yes, he's perfect for the job in hand'.

By glorious coincidence he knew Robert Simons reasonably well; as his constituency was part of the area the 'bent copper' was previously responsible for. Although the PM had steered well clear of the ensuing court case, they had previously been moderately good friends, and, quite frankly, he couldn't see what all the fuss was about. If that's what you had to do to get the job done, so be it.

"Good to catch you Robert, it's been some time since we last met. It's Charles Sheer here. I need you to do something for me. Hush-hush and all that. I think it will suit your inestimable talents down to the ground...what I think you chaps refer to as a *'caught with his hand in the till'* moment. Deliver exactly what I want and I will arrange a police posting for you in some remote, highly exotic, island. Sod all to do but drink rum and ogle the local girls. I want incriminating evidence that the chairman of the London Bullion Association is taking enormous backhanders from the Chinese government. I don't care how you do it. If you need to manufacture any special documents, or plant funds – conveniently originating in Asia – into an off-shore account bearing his name, just ask. Call me in a week."

With his back covered, Charlie Sheer felt he could at last relax. All he had to do now was to have patience; wait until the weekend when the reports on the incriminating death certificate would start to roll-in from the various intelligence agencies; and then strike.

Convinced of his own brilliance, he was increasingly confident that these reports would point in Carrington's direction. With his adversaries' blood spilt all over the carpet, he could then compound the distress and reveal his own investigations into the newly revealed Chinese bribes. There would be one hell of a diplomatic row, of course, but so what.

Once more he found that he was talking out loud to himself. "That will definitely make a great story and get me off the front pages for a while. Time to pour myself a large drink and celebrate my undoubted brilliance!"

★ ★ ★

About an hour later the Number 10 switchboard put a call through to the prime minister.

"It's the chairman of the Federal Reserve, Sir. Says he needs to speak with you urgently. Shall I put him through?"

"Lewis, what can I do for you?"

"We have a looming problem Charlie; I've just heard that the Shanghai Gold Exchange has put out a press statement saying that their central bank intends to make a highly significant statement on television tonight regarding changes they are going to make in the gold market. Just putting you on notice. I'll contact Sir David and Dominic; let them know the state of play."

CHAPTER 22

Shanghai, Beijing and Brunei

For the past two hours General Xiao had been carefully and systematically reconnoitring the warehouse belonging to 'the Butler'. He had cautiously kept to the darkest shadows as he explored the unlit wharfs of Nantong, ever vigilant for danger. If he had not been there previously, the specific address would have been exceptionally difficult to identify in the dark, given the mile upon mile of similar, very poorly lit, properties. Having concluded there was nothing untoward; he warily approached the open main gates. Although Xiao was an hour later than agreed, he felt such a delay was the prudent thing to do in the circumstances; if only to ensure that there were no secret police in the vicinity.

On entering the pitch-black building he tensed immediately. Directly ahead was either his adversary, or his saviour, surrounded by half a dozen men, armed to the proverbial teeth. When they saw he was unarmed and alone, the group's anxiety immediately evaporated. They too were expecting a trap.

The Shanghai triad had enjoyed an exceptionally profitable year in the narcotics trade and just naturally presumed that Xiao was intent on extracting his personal pound of flesh. After all, as head of the army, he had been instrumental in turning his proverbial 'blind eye' to their nefarious activities. However, as they grew ever stronger and wealthier their attitude had hardened: under no circumstances would now they cede one single penny to Xiao, unless they were outflanked or vastly outnumbered.

"So, much to my surprise, you are a man of your word," said the Butler, in a deep, gravelly voice. "We were prepared for a fight. Why are you here Xiao? And what am I to make of the rumour that you, the figurehead of our once glorious military, are now little more than a pathetic fugitive on the run? How rapidly the wheels of fortune can change. Yesterday the lord of all you survey; today all I see before me is a broken man in rags. Karma, misfortune, or incompetence General?"

"Stand your thugs down; we need to talk in private."

With a wave of the hand they scattered into the darkness. Xiao was only too aware that no man, let alone a person of his stature or age, would intentionally pick a fight with the giant who stood directly ahead of him.

"I have a ship heading to this warehouse containing my family's entire fortune in gold bars: hundreds of millions of dollars worth. I need to be able to safely off-load them here and either immediately sell them, or make arrangements to store them for a few years. The question I place on the table is a simple one: can I depend on you, as you have relied on me in the past? Or do I divert the ship elsewhere?"

The Butler beckoned Xiao over to a nearby table, flamboyantly gesticulating with his gun, in a signal of supreme authority. This was his territory and now was his opportunity to extract maximum advantage. As on previous occasions when they had met, the Butler had the very disquieting habit of standing very close to his prey and staring intently into a person's soul. Most withered in the presence of such a powerful man, but not Xiao. This meeting was not about the past, or who now held the balance of power; but entirely about the bargain to be struck.

"Half the gold is yours in return for providing sanctuary for my family. If that can be agreed, then we only need an accord on how best to deal with my half? In return for your cooperation and knowing your penchant for blackmail, I am willing to supply you with something extra; something very special indeed. I hold in safekeeping a number of top secret files detailing the perversions and transgressions of senior members of the Politburo that will keep you in power for years to come."

The Butler's hand was raised to his lips to wipe away the saliva before he yet again spat onto the floor. Undaunted, Xiao continued.

"The files are secure, but you can have them when our deal is completed."

Yet again, no words issued forth from the triad leader. An intimidating stillness permeated the room for what seemed like an eternity. Detailed calculations were being silently made; and plans secretly hatched for the inevitable betrayal and theft of the entire cargo. Eventually, he chose to speak.

"When does this ship arrive?"

"I need to contact my brothers, but my best guess is three or four days hence."

"OK Xiao, we have an agreement; always providing, of course, that you are prepared to be sworn into the *Sun Yee On* triad and accept me as the Dragons Head? In return, you have my oath that I will personally buy the gold."

"If that is what is required to keep my family safe and enjoy my share of the gold during my enforced retirement then, however reluctantly, I have no choice but to accept."

"So be it. Now, let us make arrangements to contact your treasure ship and formulate plans to deal appropriately with our cargo."

★ ★ ★

Chen Liu, the *de-facto* head of China's central bank, the PBOC, was preparing for an unprecedented appearance on State television news to announce the sweeping changes he intended to make to the gold market. While deeply technical in its content – and for the overwhelming majority of the countries citizens, completely incomprehensible – what he had to say would truly rock the very foundations of the financial world.

Putting to one side the impenetrable jargon of his trade, all the ordinary man in the street really heard from the speech was that China would henceforth directly challenge the West's supremacy of the gold market. To the unalloyed delight of everyone who had even the most modest holding of gold hidden under the bed, he confidently predicted that bullion prices would increase substantially and its citizenry would be the direct beneficiaries of his brilliant master stroke for years to come.

Certain, deeply resentful, eyes within the upper echelons of the Politburo looked upon this announcement as a deliberate move into the politics of the country; which they deemed their sole preserve. Without any question, he had materially overstepped his authority and far exceeded his place in the carefully crafted pecking-order. If good news was to be given, it was their sole prerogative. Steps would need to be taken to clip the wings of Banker Chen.

By making three small, but highly significant changes, Chen would instantly and irrevocably turn the world's bullion market upside down.

Firstly, he announced that henceforth the Shanghai Gold Exchange would only undertake gold trades in renminbi, making it quite clear they would no longer peg their gold to the US dollar; secondly, they would insist that all gold bars must be re-sized to the new 1 kilogram China standard, as the SGE would no longer accept the traditional 400oz bars held in New York and London; and, finally, that from this day forward China would be willing, indeed delighted, to barter any of their exports for gold.

These steps, while totally meaningless to most of the people watching the broadcast, were deliberately calculated to destabilise the western banking system: now there would be two parallel and competing bullion markets. The upper hand now belonged to those that held the most physical gold. Pigeons would at last come home to roost.

★ ★ ★

The specially chartered plane, courtesy of the Company, left the military airfield at RAF Brize Norton, on schedule, at precisely 11pm. It had just Lyn and Sanford on board. Not long into the trip he was called to the flight deck to receive a message from Lewis Moyns. He told him of the Chinese news broadcast and asked that he stand-by when they got to Brunei so that he could participate in a secure conference call with the Director of the CIA.

"Something weird is happening Lyn. I get the feeling that the Chinese have lit the fuse in the gold market and all hell is about to break loose. Lewis said that they were working through the consequences of the proposed changes, but that we may be required to radically alter our plans."

"Situation normal then, Sir; I guess we better get some rest."

On their bleary-eyed arrival into Brunei, Sanford was handed a note by the US military attaché requesting that he immediately head to the embassy compound and contact Langley. The striking, modernist architecture of the ambassador's residence and the sheer grandeur of the gardens had been deliberately created to emulate one of the richest, and quite possibly smallest, countries in the world: just about the size of the State of Delaware. From 1888 to 1984, Brunei was a British protectorate, but it was now a constitutional sultanate and one of America's most important allies in the region. Thankfully, Sanford was on excellent terms with the local military leadership having frequently participated in countless joint exercises, more often than not covertly undertaken throughout the wider region. It was time to call in a few favours, should needs must.

"Mr. Director, its Sanford here. Major Andrews is also in the room, if that is acceptable to you?"

The head of the CIA, one Carter Meggs, had been in his post for over twenty years and was a rock-solid, jingoistic, patriot to his very core. No one came away from a meeting with him without concluding he was decidedly acerbic, downright rude and aggressively pugnacious in character. He rarely found either the time, or a plausible excuse, to be on his best behaviour; and he was guaranteed to be utterly nasty when he was at his worst. The lexicon of the phrase "military hawks" had run out of words by the time it came to describing his position on the extreme right wing of American politics.

In his view, the term 'neo-con' was for limp-wristed Republican wimps who needed more backbone in their defence of the nation against their seemingly countless adversaries. Director Meggs delighted in rattling chains whenever he was forced to appear before Congress and would take on anyone, anywhere, who ever had the temerity to threaten his beloved America. On more than one occasion however, he had to be forcibly reminded that he was not the Commander-in-Chief; even though he took it for granted that he was.

At every opportunity available to him, he would remind his audience that he was a staunch disciple of one of his more infamous predecessors, J Edgar Hoover; and that his filing system on 'the great and the good', often sat in front of him, was even more incendiary than Hoover's. The implied menace to anyone threatening his authority was as plain as a pikestaff.

"Glad the Major's in the room; saves the tedium of a second briefing. Besides which, Andrews is now a vital component of this mission. Get through this alive, I'll ensure she makes Colonel. Tell her from me she did a good job with Dark Pools."

Sanford nodded to Lyn to sit down, as the Director paused momentarily, as if for theatrical effect.

"Jim, we have a situation requiring your highly specialised skill set. I take it for granted that Major Andrews has no compunction to participate in a dirty-tricks mission? Show these commie, pinko, bastards who's boss. Do you recall Operation Skulduggery?"

"I do indeed Sir! Quite a few years since the desert sands of Libya."

Sanford let an exceptionally rare, very broad, smile cross his face. He just lived for covert operations, and that was – in his humble opinion – one hell of a humdinger. Meggs continued.

"We sure took the towel heads by surprise that day! Been the talk of the CIA for years. Anyway, we are dusting off the files and re-opening it as a current mission: one or two variations on the theme, naturally. I'm arranging for a couple of Lockheed C-5 Galaxy's, with a very precious cargo on board, to be airborne within the next day or so. One is to come to Brunei, which we'll put under the Major's command; and the other to fly into Japan for your purposes."

Sanford's eyebrows rose in delight as he wondered what on earth they were now embarked upon. The Director continued.

"I've also made arrangements for our nearest carrier, the Bataan, to haul ass for the Yellow Sea to rendezvous with you. ETA to be advised and detailed orders to follow later in the day. You should make arrangements to fly out immediately; grab some shut-eye on the journey. By the way, we've tracked down Xiao to the outskirts of Shanghai; the idiot is using his mobile phone. As far as we are concerned, he's now in play: the briefing will explain why. I want him at Langley within the week. Any resource you want, just holler. Good hunting and don't under any circumstances screw it up."

"Yes Sir; and Major Andrews?"

"Andrews will receive her instructions tomorrow when I've chatted with the Brits and confirmed my plans with the local head honchos. And one last thing General, I've put in a call to your buddy Sapphire. You'll need her special skills. She's scheduled to hook-up with you in Okinawa."

★ ★ ★

The Butler had taken Xiao to the nearest radio transmitter in order to make contact with his brothers. His family knew that any message he sent while on the run which contained the words 'stay safe', meant that they should proceed with extreme caution and, if practical, make contingency plans. They were well aware from their brother's unconventional approach to life that they must now expect the unexpected. Their conversation was short and to the point:

"Progress is very slow brother; all the family are on board as agreed, but we have repeated problems with our engines. I should also tell you that we are all very frightened and in need of your help and guidance. We are proceeding as per your instructions to the co-ordinates in Shanghai. However, we have no idea when we will get there."

"Good, be alert and stay safe. I'll be in touch again this time tomorrow."

The brothers looked at each other in wide eyed astonishment: 'stay safe'? What should they now do; what problems should they anticipate; whom should they trust?

★ ★ ★

Within no more than twenty seconds the CIA had plotted the location of the vessel and relayed its precise position to the Director.

"Good work team. Make immediate arrangements to

163

launch the Global Hawk surveillance drone and let's go kick some panda-hugging ass."

He was just about to put the phone down when another thought occurred to him. "And will one of you idle bastards bring me the 'Nitro Zeus' file. Plus, get a hold of Dr Alex Cadbury, that genius-dude from SQT. Tell him that I want to see him again, without fail tomorrow. I just love it when the fun and games begin."

CHAPTER 23

London

Sebastian entered the bank's boardroom in Berkley Square fully anticipating that he was about to be unceremoniously fired for blowing what was a king's ransom following his instruction to unwind d'Abo's position in the gold market. However, the prospect of his P45 being callously handed to him in an envelope by the human resources department was, quite frankly, not at the top of his list of worries. It fell way, way, behind his concerns for Lyn who had been whisked off to in the middle of the night to – as she eloquently put it – "do her duty for the regiment".

Instead, and much to his surprise, there to greet him was the ever avuncular, Sir David Stone.

"Seb, old chap, good to see you. Replace the frown lines with a modicum of a smile, if you could. Just had a confidential, strictly off-the-record, *tête-à-tête* with your erstwhile colleagues; I'm pleased to tell you that the board will not be taking this matter any further. It's surprising what the invisible hand of the governor can accomplish when push comes to shove. Over the years in this job I've found that I'm especially successful when I'm fortuitously carrying a file entitled, "How to Revoke a Bank Licence". I politely informed them that you were involved in something rather hush-hush for me; and that the cheque was in the post for the losses. Lots of muttering and harrumphing of course; but, as the Professor may well have said if he were here, 'bollocks to them'. He has such a lovely turn of phrase don't you think. Anyway, are you free for a spot of tiffin later; Lewis is rather keen we meet. I gather he's had a chat with that rather abrasive fellow from the CIA. Been one or two developments overnight in China apparently that demand our urgent, undivided, attention."

"It will be my pleasure to attend Governor; and thank you for your intervention today. May I humbly recommend that you don't let Lewis pick the venue unless you're partial to pork scratchings?"

"My treat it is then, old boy. I'll call you in an hour to confirm the details. Toodle-oo."

★ ★ ★

Lewis Moyns knew he had little choice but to brief the PM at some stage. However, he was increasingly convinced that Charlie Sheer had become the metaphorical 'loose cannon' in their small team; whose powerful guns could, and in all likelihood would, eventually be pointed at all and sundry to protect his own skin. Instinctively he and the good folks at the CIA felt it was a wise precaution to limit the level of disclosure to him: broad brush only, partial details, nothing he could blurt out in an interview if cornered by an impertinent journalist. To his enduring regret, given their closeness in the past, he was becoming increasingly convinced that PM was unhinged, especially after the curious disclosures regarding John d'Abo. Thankfully, divine providence intervened and he was too busy to attend. So on the spur of the moment he decided to invite the chancellor to the meeting instead.

"Amanda, I've just been told that there is an urgent meeting at the Bank this afternoon, 4pm, can you make it? Charlie is busy and my New York office tells me that it's all getting a tad fraught in the COMEX markets. Just had the opening bell and apparently there are a lot of long positions being called in. I've put my team on red alert to do whatever is necessary to stabilise the gold markets and stop any knock-on developments with the US based bullion banks. I suggest you do the same here. Dominic Carrington is having a conference call with the UK banks as we speak. He'll fill us all in later today."

"Not a problem Lewis, I will immediately put the Treasury on stand-by."

Just as he was about to leave for his appointment in the City, Lewis received an urgent phone call from CIA Director, Carter Meggs.

"Chairman; just informing you that I've taken one or two, how shall I put it delicately, rather large liberties with some of your stock. Were you ever briefed on the Skulduggery affair? Probably not I imagine: yet another of our little dark secrets here in Langley. Surprised Sanford didn't mention it to you; he got a whole row of medals for it. Anyway, I've decided that we are back in the gold business. I'll fill you in further when you get to a secure line; can't trust these damn Ruskies over the cell network."

★ ★ ★

It was far from unusual for the chancellor to have a meeting with the Bank's governor, even at very short notice. Her Friday afternoon diary had been deliberately kept free so she could fully prepare for the weekends' revelries with Cressida Armstrong. Fortuitously, the UK financial markets had closed an hour previously, with a few wobbles but no signs of undue drama, yet. If there was going to be mayhem, then it would hit the Federal Reserve first during their Friday afternoon and she would have a couple of days to plan for any untoward events on Monday. A problem in the gold markets was not going to stop a long overdue weekend of hanky-panky. In her far from humble opinion she deserved it; she had planned it meticulously; and it would be a fitting prelude to her political anointment. Just one more push and she would be elevated to the highest office in the land.

★ ★ ★

Unbeknownst to her, undercover surveillance had already been set in motion by the PM's wayward police sleuth, Robert Simons, who was well known for his unconventional, highly illegal, approach to his work. Although his prime target in the investigation was Professor Carrington, absolutely nothing and no one was out of bounds as far as he was concerned. He had no reason to suspect the governor, Sebastian, or indeed the chancellor were behind the leaked death certificate; but if only one thing was left of his tattered reputation, he was determined to impress the PM with his thoroughness. They would all be meticulously shadowed and observed.

In stark contrast, the numerous security agencies were manfully and methodically endeavouring to get to the bottom of who was responsible for the leak. Within each of these organisations, the chancellor was at the very bottom of the pile of suspects; indeed for many MI5 operatives and senior Met officers, she was not even in their top fifty suspects, such was her reputation for probity.

★ ★ ★

Sir David opened the meeting in his suit of offices, deep within the inner sanctum of the Bank, at 4pm sharp.

"Bit of a vicious bouncer overnight from the Chinese central bank, Dominic. I think we had better prepare ourselves for considerable turbulence in the banking sector on Monday."

"*Sic vos non vobis,* as the inscription at the entrance steps to your august institution so eloquently puts it, Governor."

"What in Christ's name does all that bloody mumbo-jumbo mean," interjected Lewis, "I didn't make it past the first grade in Latin class, always assuming it is Latin?"

In his usual professorial tone, Dominic continued.

"It's what you Americans would call the Bank of England's mission statement Lewis; roughly translated as: 'Thus we labour for others not ourselves'. Which in modern day parlance means we have to work our nuts off for the benefit of everyone but us! With suitable apologies to our esteemed chancellor of course! I sincerely hope your guys at 33 Liberty Street can hold their nerve this afternoon. My information from the bullion bank's here is that they are being swamped by orders to liquidate their customer's positions and exchange them for physical gold. There's no chance on God's earth that we can accommodate that, so we are going to have to either negotiate our way out of this with the Chinese, or fold our cards at the table and admit defeat; with goodness knows what consequences either way."

The governor's usual self-assurance, coolness under fire, and legendary *sangfroid* was conspicuous by its absence today. Written across his face, for all to see, was apprehension and anxiety. It had not yet developed into panic, but his experience of prior crises told him that another debacle in the banking sector could only be hours or days away. The New York Stock Exchange was already a blaze of red as bank stocks were being hammered. Gold prices were rising sharply as the punters scrambled to move out of paper and into physical; while the US dollar was being put under increasing pressure. Desperate calls were coming into the central banking system pleading for access to their supplies of gold so that the more vulnerable banks could honour their liabilities. Added to which, the speculators were now having a field day demanding physical deliveries. Dominic Carrington continued.

"I think we ought to acknowledge the fact that, barring some miracle, we are facing another meltdown here. It's our own bloody fault. Let's own-up to the problem; around this table we have had plenty of prior experience with unscrupulous bastards trying to manipulate and corner the commodities markets. Yet, somehow we have managed to bury our head in the sand and wilfully disregarding the most pernicious problem staring us squarely in the face."

The governor's normally sanguine expression, always guaranteed to induce imagery of the bright sunny uplands, gave way to dropped shoulders and utter defeat. He had drifted away into his own thoughts and was quite sure that he would be resigning before the weekend was over. Lewis Moyns felt he had little option but to try and rally the troops.

"Let's not get ahead of ourselves Dominic. We still have plenty of conventional options in the locker to stop this in its tracks. We can use the blunt instruments of the past, used by countless regulators and central bankers when times get sticky, and immediately introduce special rules to stop any more long contracts being written. That would take care of the future, but won't prevent the price of gold rising further, or the Chinese demanding still more physical gold."

Seb interjected, "I take it that means the bullion banks will continue to be very vulnerable and some may well fail soon?"

"No question about it, Seb. As we say in Texas, it'll be a cold-blooded, winner take all, turkey shoot. They are now having their gonads very tightly squeezed as a result of their own greed and folly. What's that quaint phrase you Brits use; oh yeh, we're totally stuffed!"

Dominic Carrington leaned across the table towards the ashen-faced chancellor, who probably for the first time in her illustrious career was lost for words.

"What do we do Amanda; declare *force majeure* and close the gold markets for a week? It would certainly give us some much needed breathing space, don't you agree Lewis? If we don't do anything then we will probably lose control of events, with catastrophic consequences. However, the downside will almost certainly be plummeting shares prices for the UK banks as everyone wakes up to the fact that they could go bust next week. I'm also willing to bet that we will precipitate a Northern Rock style crisis with queues around the block as everyone tried to withdraw their money? Either way we are screwed."

To the surprise of all in the room, Lewis casually and slowly took out a cigar from a container in his jacket pocket and flamboyantly rolled it between his fingers while pressing it against his ear to ascertain its quality. He then put his feet up on the table as if there wasn't the slightest hint of trouble and merely said.

"As central bankers we always have those options at our collective disposal of course. So we should certainly agree to implement some of them next week."

Much to the consternation of everyone present, he proceeded to slowly light the cigar before continuing.

"However, before we get too despondent, let's wait to see what the good old US cavalry can accomplish. I believe those conniving, scheming, don't-you-just-love-em, sons-of-bitches at the CIA have a far more devious solution in mind."

Across the table people's faces broke into half smiles or tortured grimaces: they all knew the maverick reputation of the highly volatile CIA Director.

"Fancy a night out at Annabel's tonight Seb? There's something we need to discuss. I think you should come too Sir David, brush off a few cobwebs."

CHAPTER 24

Brunei and Dorneywood

The giant Lockheed C-5 Galaxy cargo plane emerged out of the clear blue sky to land heavily on the runway with a controlled thud befitting its size and grandeur. The obligatory screech of tyres followed as the plane eventually came to a standstill at the far end of Brunei International Airport. It then slowly and menacingly taxied its way to the military hangers, situated well away from prying eyes. There to greet it was Lyn, dressed immaculately in her military uniform despite the intense tropical heat and humidity.

The US air force pilot, with his decidedly sinister companion in tow, eventually emerged into the sunlight and, after a precautionary review of their surroundings, proceeded down the steps to meet her. After the obligatory exchange of salutes, the pilot unlocked the briefcase from the wrist of the mystery man, carefully opened it and handed over an envelope marked 'Top Secret' with the logo of the CIA emblazoned across the top.

"Your orders Major Andrews: I've been instructed not to release the cargo into your care until you've read them and HMAS Darwin gets into town later tonight around 2100 hours. As you will see from the message, the Director has a rather unconventional programme for you to execute forthwith: what he calls the 'switch and bait gambit'."

"Got all that Captain, thank you. However, isn't it normally the other way around? Anyway, I'll study the briefing at the embassy this afternoon and be back here at nine tonight ready to get the mission underway."

She paused momentarily, "Did you say the Darwin? Do you know if my guys are still on board?"

"No idea Major. One further thing: General Sanford has also requested that when your duties are concluded here, you are to make your way discreetly and immediately to Beijing, in your very best civvies apparently. A room will be booked for you at the Rosewood Hotel in Chaoyang District. Wait there, incognito, until you are contacted directly by him. He'll find you. If no contact is made within five days then assume the mission is compromised and head home or anywhere your instincts tell you is safe."

★ ★ ★

The drive to Dorneywood, in rural Buckinghamshire, was normally the most welcome of pleasures for Amanda Price and a huge contrast to the constant pressures of Downing Street. The chancellor's magnificent grace-and-favour country house provided a rare opportunity to relax and put the cares of the world to one side for a few hours; and if there was a God, he – or was it she – would even let her have a couple of days' peace? Unfortunately, the problems were mounting fast with every passing moment: scattered across the back seat of the car she had half a dozen red boxes overflowing with Treasury papers on the looming crisis.

No matter which way she turned there seemed no way out of this mess. As was surely to be expected in these circumstances, the demands of high office were beginning to tell on her; and a fleeting moment of doubt crossed her mind. Without question – and with a deep sense of foreboding – sleepless nights awaited her this weekend. She would have to plumb the very depth of her undoubted intellect and systematically go through all the options which remained open to her.

If there was to be another banking calamity on her watch then, without the slightest doubt, she could kiss goodbye to occupying Number 10. The chancellor had not got this far up the greasy pole of politics without instinctively responding to such a challenge, if necessary, with a full-on fight for survival; the question upper-most in her mind was which battle to engage in first.

It would be simplicity itself to hand her favourite newspaper editor the second 'killer' document, the signed Treasury loan agreement, with the imprint of Charlie Sheer all over it. There was no way he could ever wriggle out of that bombshell. There in glorious black and white was his overly flamboyant signature on a secret government loan to Sir John d'Abo: which was illegally used to short our own bloody currency, no less. The very thing he was appointed to avoid. A few well chosen, decidedly poisonous, paragraphs on the front pages could well leave the impression that the PM had benefited financially from his traitorous actions. It would also not be beyond the wit of man to then imply that he had specifically ordered d'Abo's death to remove him permanently from any disclosure of the loan. Truth or not, no doubt about it, he would be out of office by the end of the day. But if the banks were about to go 'belly-up' because of those idiots in the gold markets, then she could not escape the flak that would automatically follow. Under those circumstances she would be obligated to leave her post and her career, without any question, would be terminally ruined.

Thank the Lord then that her co-conspirator had arrived an hour earlier and was more than willing to provide much needed succour and comfort during the lowest point in her stellar career. Cressida Armstrong was not the prettiest girl in town but she certainly was the most elegant and vivacious of companions. Quick-witted and often outrageously flirtatious, she had enough gossip to entertain even the most well informed person for days on end. As such, she was the perfect counterpoint to the chancellor who, despite her razor-sharp mind, had a tendency towards melancholy when cornered.

"I'm utterly exhausted and exasperated by this gold business Cressida. It's drained me of every ounce of energy I possess. There will be hell to pay on Monday and the bloody PM has just thrown in the towel."

"Strip off and get in; its bath time darling. Put those tedious papers through the shredder, throw your red boxes on the bonfire and let's cheer ourselves up a little drinky. No, damn it, let's have a lot! Chop-chop, where's the champagne? We require at least three bottles of chilled Crystal, then a stress relieving body-rub with my very expensive lotions and potions."

"Sounds just the ticket; the fridge is through there."

"Then, my dear, what you need is lots of fresh air and vigorous exercise. I think it's time I licked you into shape."

★ ★ ★

As part of the monotonous, routine scrutiny that was his old profession, ex-Chief Constable Robert Simons had stationed photographic teams across the country with instructions to keep a close watch on all his targets. He still had enough friends willing to, as he put it, 'go off piste', and hide in the bushes overnight if the payday merited it. Old fashioned policing was not highly prized these days, but he remained convinced that it would pay dividends in the end: it always did. So for one lucky soul, a summer weekend in the country was a prized assignment. Needless to say, the photographer could never have anticipated getting a picture of the editor of The Sun and the chancellor of the exchequer strolling romantically hand-in-hand through the grounds; nor could he ever envisage it was to prove priceless. The anonymous man in the far away bushes with his exceptionally long camera lens, would never in a million years guess what a firestorm he was about to unleash when the evidence – if evidence it was – eventually made it to Robert Simons' makeshift office.

Within a millisecond Simons realised the significance of it; Dominic Carrington was not the culprit!

If he could have slapped himself heartily on the back, he surely would have. The question now running wildly out of control in his mind was how to play it to his best monetary advantage. Two obvious options instantly presented themselves: should he embark on blackmailing the two parties involved; or should he immediately hand the photos over to the prime minister and start packing his shorts and sun cream? Blackmail would take time of course, and might be tricky; however it could be exceptionally lucrative. A broad smile crossed his face for the first time since he left prison; he knew either way that his troubles were, at long bloody last, over. It was now simple a question of deciding who had the most to lose – or indeed gain – from the incriminating photograph. A long Sunday lunch at his favourite pub beckoned when he could savour the moment before making his final choice.

★ ★ ★

Captain Graham Rogers dropped the sea anchor just before eight in the evening. They had stopped some ten miles offshore from Brunei's main naval base, for what could only be described as a hastily arranged detour. HMAS Darwin still had on board the US army detachment previously commanded by Lyn and, most importantly, the two battered containers removed from the Jin-Ton with the gold bars still inside.

It had been Captain Rogers' intention to deal with both matters, as ordered, after their tour of duty ended in a month's time. No one seemed to be in a particular hurry to have either the soldiers or the bullion back. As far as the Australian navy was concerned they were just acting as a taxi service to their final disembarkation point, when everyone and everything would be unloaded.

Until she had read her new orders, Lyn was unaware that her old team were still enjoying the Australian navy's hospitality: it would be a rare moment of joy in a hectic schedule to catch up with them. By the same token, the captured gold had never figured high in her list of concerns and was just a fortuitous side-show to her mission in Somalia.

Exactly on cue she spotted two helicopters from the warship circling overhead the international airport; both landed within twenty feet of the Galaxy cargo plane. On board were the members of her team who on rotor shutdown enthusiastically came out to greet her. Also on board were the two containers with the gold.

The captain of the Galaxy slowly lowered the tailgate of the gigantic plane, enabling his crew members to scurry back and forth to the equally colossal helicopters. Within moments, the fork-lift trucks kept for such an occasion in the aircraft's hold were in full swing. The two containers were carefully detached from the helicopters and re-opened. Within the blink of an eye their contents were removed and the precisely calibrated replacements taken from the aircraft, placed inside and re-sealed. To the casual observer the containers were exactly as they had been found on the Jin-Ton. Except this time the CIA had replaced the real gold bars with counterfeits from the Federal Reserve vaults. The switch had taken place; now for the bait.

★ ★ ★

Zucca and Oakes were anxiously awaiting the arrival of the 'top brass' onto the Jin-Ton and, however reluctantly, had tidied up their quarters and thrown at least a hundred bottles of god-knows-what overboard. Not exactly ship-shape but, in their opinion, a commendable start. They had even managed to assemble reasonably clean clothing and, after endless cajoling, persuaded the crew that a life of unending pleasure awaited them, if only they would obey the odd order. The relief was palpable when it became apparent that only Major Andrews would be joining them in around 24 hours.

The two helicopters duly arrived from the Darwin the next day and rapidly approached the Jin-Ton at what could only be described as precariously close to sea level. Lyn effortlessly abseiled down onto the deck with a couple of her colleagues from the Somalia team and began giving orders to prepare for the return of the two containers. It took over an hour of precision hovering to carefully deliver the cargo and secure it to the deck. With a salute from the pilots and a customary thumbs-up, the helicopters departed.

"Welcome aboard ma'am. Are you staying long? The quarters are abysmal and the food beyond shocking, but the company's great."

Oakes clearly had not shaven for days or weeks; it was all a grappa-induced blur.

Lyn came over and tweaked his beard.

"No showers or razors on board Oaksey? I'd have brought some perfume and soap if I'd have been told."

"Afraid not ma'am, I'm trying my level best to blend in with the motley crew of reprobates we have here. I can categorically assure you however that they are up for a fight if that's what you're planning next."

"Almost certainly is, Sergeant. The orders are to proceed to Dandong. When you get within say a hundred clicks we will extricate you and the boys: at the moment our thoughts are to swap you to another cargo ship. Always assuming of course that you're willing to stay? I get picked up from here in four hours; you can be relieved if you wish?"

"No, I'll stay if that's OK with you: to the very end if necessary!"

"Thought so, is the Captain around, I'd like to explain the revised arrangements?"

"I'll take you to his palatial suite; do mind your head on the chandelier."

Zucca was at his table studying the dog-eared charts and trying to establish how long it would take them to reach port. Three or four days he reckoned. Thankfully they had not had very much communication with Beijing and he assumed that, because they had kept their transponder on, they were simply being monitored to ensure they we're proceeding as instructed.

"Major, *ciao bella*; I'm very curious to hear why you have returned the gold; assuming that's what's inside? Been a dramatic change of plan I take it?"

"Yep, we want you to breeze in there as if nothing has happened; collect your unconscionably large pay check from your Chinese friends and then head to Europe where you'll be taken care of. What could be simpler?"

"Doesn't make a lot of sense to me Major Andrews, but frankly I am beyond caring!"

CHAPTER 25

London, Japan and Beijing

Annabel's nightclub was the last place on earth anyone would expect to find the governor of the Bank of England and the chairman of the Federal Reserve carousing on a Friday night; indeed, any night. By contrast, Sebastian's office was only across the square and he knew the venue very well indeed. He had been an active member in the 'old days', and had even taken Lyn there once or twice, but this was his first visit since his return from Asia. He doubted very much that there would be any dancing on the tables tonight, unlike on the last joyous occasion.

Lewis had been the first to arrive around eight. He politely asked one of the waiters for a discrete corner banquet and ordered a very large Bourbon and a magnum of anything red. Ever conscious of the impression such a visit would make on the outside world if the paparazzi alighted upon them, Sir David was praying no one would recognise either of them. He had made up his mind to resign next week and take the flack for the latest banking catastrophe; it was just a question of smoothly organising the succession process and writing his resignation letter.

When Seb arrived twenty minutes later they were deep in conversation.

"Ah, good to see you Seb; here, have a glass of wine. Sir David tells me that he's going to fall on his sword next week.

Do the honourable thing, and all that. I've told him that under no circumstances must he do any such thing."

"Absolutely, Lewis: we are all in this together. This is no time to divide the troops, quite the opposite. Circle the wagons and pass around the Enfield rifles; as you cowboys often say."

"It's not that easy from my seat at the B of E gentlemen. If there is even the slightest whiff of a run on a UK bank then, let's face facts, I'm finished. If, God forbid, one goes bust then it's on with the blindfold, find the nearest plank and throw myself to the circling sharks."

"I've a far better idea Sir David; why don't you instead decide to appoint our good friend Sebastian here to be your deputy. The Federal Reserve will wholeheartedly and very publically support it. He has the credentials from his time as Financial Secretary in Hong Kong, he still retains a reputation on the world stage from the Dark Pools days; and you can delegate him to go to the Chinese and negotiate on our collective behalf's. All we need to do is give him the ammo!"

Seb's brow furrowed at this suggestion as he could not immediately decide whether this was an opportunity of a lifetime, the proverbial poison chalice, or the ultimate hospital pass.

"I think I will need more than 'ammo' Lewis. You are going to have to dream up a remarkable story to get the Chinese to alter their plans. So what's the deal?"

"As Sir David may well have said, were he not too occupied in his own morbid thoughts: 'that's *sub rosa* old chap'. That is, until you get there. We'll make the announcement of your promotion tomorrow when I've cleared it with Amanda, who seems to be off the grid today for some reason. It will be all over the Sunday papers."

"Get where exactly?"

"Later Seb; first let's eat, drink and be merry, for tomorrow we…"

Before the sentence could be completed they were joined by

what could only be described as the most sultry, exotic beauty either of the Englishmen had ever seen. She effortlessly slid into the banquette besides them, replete with Monroe-esk curves, décolletage to make grown men weep, glistening shoulder length brunette hair and dazzling smile. She flirtatiously leaned across the table and kissed Lewis with an uncalled for level of passion, which had Sir David instinctively reaching for his blood pressure pills. Ravishing was the unspoken word on both their lips.

"I'd like to introduce you to someone very special in my life. This is Naylor."

★ ★ ★

General Sanford flew into the US military airfield at Okinawa, southern Japan, and immediately went to inspect the V-22 Osprey vertical take-off and landing aircraft he had requisitioned for the mission. Capable of very long range flight and enormous payloads they were the perfect complement to the Sikorsky helicopters that would accompany them on this part of Operation Skulduggery.

The two Galaxy aeroplanes landed about an hour later with over a hundred tonnes of tungsten-coated gold on board, taken directly from the Fed's vaults. With breath-taking precision, the counterfeit gold was carefully transferred, case by precious case, to the assorted fleet assembled for the operation. Each aircraft and helicopter was also in the process of boarding a full complement of Special Forces, many of which spoke a variety of Chinese dialects.

As if on cue, a military jeep – driven at what could only be described as an utterly reckless speed – came to a screeching halt less than ten feet from Sanford. Such was the piecing noise it made when stopping that virtually everyone within a hundred feet instinctively reached for their weapons expecting some form of terrorist attack. A tall, statuesque, figure emerged dressed in all-black military fatigues, demonstrably armed to the teeth, with an incongruously small backpack.

Sanford re-holstered his side-arm and roared with laughter, while pointing to the rucksack.

"Your make-up I presume Sapphire?"

"Not quite Jim, more like my precious bag of magic tricks; and a tin whistle for old times' sake."

"You've been briefed I presume?"

"Indeed, the only thing we need to discuss on the way over is the narrative. What exactly am I going to tell these guys?"

"You'll undoubtedly think of something brilliant Sapphire, you always do."

★ ★ ★

The engines of the Jin-Ton were laughably set to 'full ahead', the course to Dandong re-plotted and the horizon instinctively scanned for signs of any developing weather systems. Oaksey waved goodbye rather too enthusiastically as Lyn was winched up to the helicopter en route back to the Darwin and the next phase of her mission. He was completely unaware that the returned cargo, now safely lashed to the deck, was virtually worthless. Nor could he fully appreciate the decisive roll it would play as events moved forward. If the grasping recipients of the gold bullion acted as the Director of the CIA fully expected, then its value was beyond measure.

The inner circle of those concerned in the operation felt it was best that absolutely no one on board appreciated that a switch had taken place. As a highly trained army man, Oakes' loyalty to his country was beyond doubt, despite his lingering fondness for the 'odd drink'; but the decision had been made that he should remain in the dark about the exact nature of the cargo.

Zucca, by contrast, had already demonstrated that he would effortlessly bend with the financial wind, especially if better terms were on offer. Not a single person felt that he could be trusted with such important information: quite the contrary, the less he knew, the more likely it was that he would try and barter a last minute deal with the Chinese to up his personal return. The harder he bartered, the more plausible the cargo's value.

Zucca and Oaksey retired to the captain's cabin and resumed where they had been so rudely interrupted a couple of days ago, by deciding that it was time to try the rum.

"I gather your very cute-assed Major Andrews wants me to let those bastards in Beijing know when we are expected to arrive. I reckon Tuesday morning, assuming no problems. You happy with that *Mon Générale*?"

"Yeh, I'll go with that Cap. She has a cute front as well if you ask me!"

"OK, let's fire up the coms and tell them the good news."

★ ★ ★

Qiang Li was at the operations desk when Zucca's radio transmission was put through to him.

"Captain, I take it there is not a problem. My bosses will skin you alive if you don't make it to Dandong soon. There are a lot of very, and I do mean very, senior people here who want your cargo back in safe hands very quickly."

"Well tell those sons-of-bitches that we will be in port in three days time, max. Before we dock I want categorical assurances that our fees have been paid, otherwise I'll scuttle the ship. Neither of us want that I presume; *capisce*?"

"You'll have your blood money Zucca. But I absolutely insist that you let me know if there is even one minute's delay to your voyage. If I pass this information up the chain of command and it's wrong, I personally will remove your balls."

"I'd like to see you try."

The moment the conversation had finished Qiang picked up the phone to the Interior Minister who had been given temporary change of the army while they searched for the still missing General Xiao.

"Minister, the Jin-Ton is now scheduled to reach Dandong at first light Tuesday morning. I have made arrangements as per your instructions to have a series of unmarked vehicles ready to transport the gold to the five locations the head of the central bank has indicated. The bullion should be in the respective vaults by the end of the day. I am going there to supervise the various transfers and to complete the formalities for Zucca and crew to be paid."

"I want to make it abundantly explicit, Qiang: everyone on board is to be eliminated at the first opportunity after they have dock and no money is to be paid whatsoever. Is that clearly understood? The gold is to be relocated to the vaults as indicated and the remaining cargo and ship taken back to sea and sunk without trace."

"But Sir, they will not release the…"

"Quiet, you spineless, pathetic, fool! The entire Chinese army is at your disposal. Live up to your potential Qiang and you will avoid exile or a premature death. I suggest you say goodbye to your family and call me when the gold gets to the vaults."

★ ★ ★

Lewis placed a highly provocative hand on Naylor's knee; the squeeze resulted in a delightful giggle.

"Let me introduce you to Sebastian Fortes and Sir David Stone. You've undoubtedly read the salacious bits in their files?"

"Files?" queried Seb.

In a husky voice that could only be described as liquid

185

chocolate, Naylor turned to Lewis and above the hubbub whispered, "He's rather nice."

"Yes, Seb's far too good looking for his own good. He needs to get into a couple of bar room brawls if you ask me. A broken nose would do him the world of good. Annabel's is just the place, eh Seb?"

"No, the cute one, he's positively edible."

"Quit the act and put him down Naylor. Gentlemen, this delectable creature is my conduit into the CIA, although you would never for one moment guess it. She suggested we meet here, rather than at some more clandestine location like the embassy – for which read totally boring. She's programmed to stay away from official premises and anywhere she is likely to be spotted by the bad guys."

At that very moment all Sir David Stone could think of was how anyone could possibly miss such a delectable, jaw dropping, cleavage. Lewis had seen the effect Naylor had on men many times before and, in a moment of rare contentment, smiled inwardly. He knew that she was the perfect choice for the mission to come. Lewis continued.

"Seb, if all goes as expected, you will be off to Asia very shortly and will need as much help as you can get. Naylor here is my Bolivian *compadre* and trusted confidant. It's through her that I have a minor role to play in the CIA's complex web of intrigue. Amongst her endless list of talents she's also a cyber-security expert and, most important of all, fluent in Mandarin. Her family were part of the Chinese diaspora which settled in South America endless years ago. She's…I'm not exactly sure… let's say one tenth Chinese and without any doubt whatsoever, nine tenths wild child? Great under cover, if you get my drift."

"Very pleased to meet you," spluttered Sir David, still reeling from the very unexpected compliment, while instinctively straightening his tie. He would have done the same with his hair, except he didn't have terribly much.

"You've made my day. Is Naylor your first or last name?"

"Just Naylor, Dave; if I may call you Dave?"

The governor simply and silently mouthed 'anything', before Lewis gestured for them to gather closer.

"OK, here is as much as I can tell you tonight. Seb, assuming you still have those legendary balls of steel, you'll be going into the lion's den armed only with your ability to spin a good yarn and engage in persuasive subterfuge. We have decided to try old fashioned disinformation, delivered eloquently by a man of honour and integrity. Naturally, I'd have suggested we use Sir Dave here, but for that unfortunate incident with the tea trolley lady and the fondant fancies…"

They all roared.

"Cheers buddy, as I think is the vernacular in Dallas. Have you a plausible script I can study, or is it rather like one of your impromptu Fed news briefings?"

"It's being worked on by Hollywood's greatest minds as we speak Seb, but we need a couple of pieces of the jigsaw to be in place before we can push the button and finalise your trip details. Then your role will become pivotal to getting us out of this mess. By the way – and just in case you haven't seen the news from Wall Street at closing – we are starting to see massive liquidity strains in the major money centre banks in New York. We've started to pump squillions of cash into the system but it's going to get very tricky on Monday. I suggest you man the barricades and start singing rousing songs from '*Les Misérables*'."

CHAPTER 26

Shanghai, Brunei, London & Beijing

General Xiao had spent a second exceedingly uncomfortable night locked away in a safe house provided to him by the Butler. He had no doubt that in due course he would have to pay handsomely for such largess; but for now he clung to the thought that, at a bare minimum, it helped him stay one step ahead of the secret police. If the shoe had been on the other foot and he still commanded the army, he would have been relentless in the pursuit of any person he regarded as a dangerous fugitive. Undoubtedly there would be a substantial price on his head by now.

The Butler had negotiated a hard bargain to take the gold off Xiao's hands, eventually settling on 35 percent of its current value. But given the absence of alternative buyers, he had reluctantly agreed. The problem was: where to send the money? Moving millions and millions of dollars through the conventional banking system left a trail a mile wide which would be immediately picked-up, traced and inevitably impounded by the Americans. He figured that his only hope was to use the triad's money-smuggling routes, but this left him equally vulnerable to theft and further extortion. No, he would have to figure out some other method, when, and if, the time came. He was beginning to regret not sending the gold into North Korea and dealing with it there.

For the moment his principal concern was for his brothers

and their families in peril on the Yellow Sea. Without question he knew that his coded message to 'stay safe' would be the cause of great consternation on board ship; if for no other reason that he had not provided them with a solution, fresh instructions or escape plans. He would have to be in contact soon and rectify these problems. But solutions evaded him.

The Butler meanwhile had been exceptionally busy re-selling the much anticipated gold delivery to his equally treacherous criminal colleagues scattered around China and Hong Kong. Within twenty four hours he had on-sold over 70 tonnes; some at completely unjustifiably, highly inflated, prices to those who's arms he could easily twist; the rest at a massive discount in anticipation of favours to come from those in competing triad groups and unscrupulous politicians he wished to curry favour with. He would hold the remainder in the many warehouses he had scattered around the outskirts of Shanghai. Shrewdly, in his view, he even gave comparatively modest amounts to the endless list of local officials and the heads of the police authorities in order to deflect whatever consequences may follow, should he ever be implicated in the theft of State property.

It was also becoming clear to him that the police were getting ever closer to finding Xiao who, while in his care and protection, was gradually migrating from being an asset to a definite liability. The sooner he was off his hands the better. Perhaps he would just kill him the moment the gold arrived? With that highly agreeable thought rolling around in his head, and satisfied with his days work, he decided to pay him a visit and assess progress.

"Xiao, we must make contact with the ship tonight in order to establish when they will arrive. I have much to do before they get here. Today I have made arrangements with my bankers in the Cayman Islands to establish an account for you and make the transfer. There are some very large fees involved, naturally;

but your money will be safe, secure and accessible. On that, you have my word."

"When will I have the details?"

"You just need to tell me the name you wish the account to be set-up in and a password for withdrawals. After that is confirmed you can visit the account on-line and monitor the transfer."

All he felt inclined to reply was, "Good." He would wait at least five seconds before changing the password.

For the first time in days, Xiao experienced a rare moment of relief; tinged with an instinctive fear that he was being deliberately lulled into a false sense of security. For one fleeting moment he felt could trust this man. But in all probability he just knew that he had to be even more wary. Both men knew Xiao held a weak hand with little prospect of him being dealt an ace anytime soon.

There was still the issue of how he and his family could flee the country in a few days time, undetected, and probably at great cost; but given that there were now so many variables in play, it was almost impossible to plan anything beyond the next fifteen minutes. Xiao decided that the best course of action was to fully engage in the game, knowing he may have already lost; and hope he could somehow affect the outcome.

"Let's call the ship and find out what progress my brothers have made."

Xiao was convinced that this would be the last message he could make. There were no further code words he could send, so whatever was to be said had to be in plain language; this was not the time for any ambiguity.

"Brother, good to hear your voice, I hope all is well? We look forward to your safe passage and delivery of the cargo into the hands of our friends here in Shanghai."

The ships radio crackled with the reply: "We now expect to be with you on Tuesday, but more likely Wednesday, assuming no further mechanical issues."

"Excellent. I was reading your horoscope earlier, as we have often done together, which said: 'all will be well, but expect the unexpected'. So take care. This will probably be our last call before you arrive."

The brothers gathered round the radio in utter bewilderment to discuss what on earth was meant by 'as we have often done': none of them could ever recall a time when they had 'done' any such thing before. And just what exactly did the phrase, 'the unexpected', mean? After much discussion they all concluded that this trip was getting more and more dangerous for them all and that their difficulties may lie not behind them, but in front.

★ ★ ★

Lyn arrived back in Brunei pumping adrenalin after a textbook assignment and was immediately transferred to the ambassador's residence to collect her tickets to Beijing. All that remained was to spend the CIA's exceptionally generous budget on a new wardrobe. It would not be the first time in her career that she had set off on a mission without a clear sense of what she had to accomplish. Doing so without firearms of any sort would, however, be a first. At least the lipstick rations would suffice.

She put in a coded message to General Sanford to bring him up-to-date and let him know that she would be flying to China in a couple of days, or so, and would await his instructions at the hotel.

★ ★ ★

The second, much larger, consignment of 'gold', now on the first leg of its transfer to the USS Bataan, was a far trickier problem to address than the comparatively straightforward switch which had recently been completed at the Jin-Ton. The next leg of the programme was going to require the total co-operation of Xiao's brothers, who were an unknown quantity to the CIA team handling Operation Skulduggery, Mark 2. One mistake, one misunderstanding, and their carefully crafted plan would lie in ruins.

In a rare stroke of luck and divine intervention, the senior case officer monitoring the last communication with the ship immediately realised they had been handed a totally unexpected opportunity to address their predicament. He immediately called the Director to discuss the matter.

"Sir, do I understand we have Agent Sapphire deployed on this mission?"

"Yep, she should be on the Bataan any moment now, why?"

"It's clear to me that Xiao's family are totally bewildered about what to do next and who to trust. Most importantly they have been told by the General to expect the unexpected. I believe that he is trying to alert them to betrayal and treachery from the Butler, but if we play our hand carefully then it's quite possible that we can switch the meaning of the message to our advantage. Let's assume for one moment that we are the 'unexpected': that we are the white knights coming to their rescue. If we can persuade them that they urgently need to get off the ship and that we will look after them and their elder brother, then we have control of the vessel, its cargo and its progress."

"I'll go with that. Get Sapphire to nonchalantly drop in on the ship for a cup of chai and a friendly chat. Then get the family to leave: by force if necessary, but preferably by charm and persuasion."

"I think that can be arranged Sir. We'll immediately block all future communications from the ship to make sure they don't alert anyone. The drone surveillance is still on station tracking the ship and from the latest reports there are no Chinese vessels nearby. My best guess is that she could be helicoptered in, say, by noon tomorrow. It'll give them one hell of a fright and we are going to have to fly in at exceptionally low levels to avoid detection. All doable, but dangerous."

"She's as tough as they come; don't give it a moment's thought. Tell Sanford to go as well. Tell him I said it will be good for him. Keep the family on the Bataan until this matter is resolved; we may need hostages. Then get Sanford to Shanghai, pronto."

★ ★ ★

The business sections of the UK papers were full of speculation that the banks were once again heading for big trouble following volatile downward share price movements in New York. Those traders who were still at their desk on a late Friday afternoon were, as usual, anticipating a slow rundown into a quiet weekend. Instead they were forced into a scramble to cover their exposures and contend with plummeting banking sector stocks, which continued unabated even after the markets had closed. The more gloomy financial correspondents were gleefully anticipating a torrid day when things reopened on Monday and a rush for gold, physical gold, which they predicted could turn very nasty indeed.

There were TV interviews with Professor Dominic Carrington, in his guise as head of the London Bullion Market, who tried manfully to steady the ship armed with little more than platitudes; and a short statement from the chancellor saying she was 'on top of the situation'. She didn't make quite clear, however, which situation she was referring to; but Cressida smiled a very contented smile.

With turmoil anticipated with every turn of events – and an often repeated prediction that the economy was about to have a re-run of the crash of 2008 – the announcement that Sebastian Fortes had been appointed to be the deputy governor of the Bank of England barely merited more than the odd column inch. As far as the Bank's governor and the head of the Federal Reserve were concerned however, they had set in motion their part of the CIA's elaborate plan. The debate now raging between them was whether, and if so when, should they issue a press statement saying that they were pointing the finger of blame at the Chinese. Such an approach, they both knew, was a two-edged sword. The Chinese would simply counter that they were only speculating in the gold market, which they were entirely free to do; and the bullion banks had stupidly and greedily fallen into a trap of their own making and were now the victim of a short squeeze. Given that this had been going on for years, with no one batting the proverbial eyelid, simply made the regulators look foolish and powerless. They would have to bide their time and let China make the next move.

★ ★ ★

Within the hallowed portals of The People's Bank of China, Chen was ecstatic that his painstakingly constructed plan was now bearing fruit. He was supremely confident that the western economies, especially the hated Americans, would be forced onto their knees within the week and – at a bare minimum – his much deserved political elevation to the Politburo's exalted Standing Committee, at the very least, was now all but guaranteed. Not only that, but he would become incredibly rich virtually overnight. Gold prices would now inevitably rise very sharply indeed. His master stroke was to disgrace General Xiao and appropriate his vast stock of gold. Then, when the Jin-Ton arrives, simply give lots of it away in a magnanimous gesture of goodwill to the political elite whose support he now craved. Corruption on a grand scale was the systems weak point and he would exploit it for all it was worth. His next step would be to close out all the futures contracts his clandestine network had built up over the years and demand physical bullion, which he knew the banks did not have. An incredible victory was within his grasp.

CHAPTER 27

Downing Street

The prime minister was not known for his patience; indeed his volcanic temper and tendency to verbally castrate anyone within earshot when things were not going according to his strict dictate, was to be avoided at all costs. So the delay in receiving any information from the security agencies on his latest nemesis, Dominic Carrington, simply exacerbated the fear and apprehension of the members in his private office.

They had been calling the respective heads of the Met Police and MI6 all morning asking for their submissions and had been rebuffed on each occasion. Those closest to the PM knew that an 'empty report' – one that couldn't point the finger directly at the wayward professors' heart – would cause ructions in Downing Street. Undoubtedly therefore, those tasked with providing the evidence were not yet willing to submit an inconclusive dossier. As the clock ticked towards the self imposed midday deadline, the tension grew unbearable. Without the slightest doubt, heads would shortly roll; and yet more names would be added to the PM's list of those to receive the full force of his ire, or worse, much worse.

The day's papers were full of doom laden predictions that, once again, the government of the day had lost control of the banking sector and, in a rare moment of unison on Fleet Street, were calling for the obligatory scalps such occasions demanded. The finger had not, as yet, being pointed directly at the PM, or indeed the chancellor; but the editorials were filled with a general air of disillusionment at government incompetence, so surely it would not be long. If he could pin the blame squarely on the shoulders of Carrington he felt confident he could deflect the flack, even if he could not necessarily solve the problem.

Charlie Sheer was on the verge of getting the head of the civil service to initiate dismissal proceedings to more or less everyone in the security services when the phone went.

"Robert Simons on the line Prime Minister."

Charlie Sheer taped his fingers impatiently on the desk while waiting for his very private sleuth, the disgraced former chief constable, to be put through.

"I hope you've got some news for me. I'm on the verge of sending your old boss to the Tower for his gross ineptitude, minus his dangly bits, which I will attend to personally. I'm easily persuaded to make it a cell for two or three, so make it good."

"I'm not sure whether you will like what I have to show you, or not, Sir? Do you have anytime to meet over the weekend?"

"It better be good Simons. Tomorrow works: let me look at the diary; yes, shall we say 12.30? You have twenty minutes."

"I'll be there, it will take thirty seconds."

★ ★ ★

Amanda Price returned to Number 11 physically exhausted, but smiling contentedly: it had been quite some years since her last 'uninhibited romp in the undergrowth'. She hadn't felt as alive in goodness knows how long and, quite frankly, couldn't wait to do it again, very soon.

Sat at her desk, she reflected that times had surely changed over the past decade, even in the dog-eat-dog world of politics. Liberal attitudes were undoubtedly coming more to the fore; maybe it was time to acknowledge her predilections openly. So, there and then, she made a personal pledge to gird her loins and tell the world – and to hell with the consequences. However, her never-silent alter ego whispered a note of profound caution in her ear: perhaps it was best to postpone such an announcement until she eventually moved next door. A frisson of excitement ran down her spine at the very thought.

She also knew that a mountain of work lay ahead, as her staff made preparations for the gold and equity markets' opening to a sea of red on Monday. Her phone had not stopped ringing all day, but she had made the decision to leave it in her bag until her passions had been well and truly spent. The most persistent caller had been Lewis Moyns, who had left a stream of messages about Sebastian's new appointment and a request for her to publically support it.

Under normal circumstances she would have been consulted, fully briefed, and her prior approval sought before any such offer was made. Initially miffed, she quickly concluded that there must be a hidden purpose to this move which no one had as yet advised her of, unless the relevant memo was buried in her red boxes. With a shrug of her shoulders she simply texted Lewis to say that she had no objections and would make a formal announcement in the Commons on Monday, as part of her response to an urgent question tabled by the leader of the opposition, about her handling of the looming crisis.

On the trip back to Downing Street, Amanda had made a conscious decision not to immediately give her new paramour the second document directly linking Charlie Sheer to the dubious loan made to John d'Abo. She would save that pleasure for later, probably during next weekend's spicy rematch, and focus whatever energy she could muster on the gold market. After reading the interminable set of notes for an hour, her conclusion was stark: it would probably require a concerted effort by all the world's central banks in order to provide much needed stability and confidence. The question remained: did they have enough gold between them to cover the bullion bank's massively exposed positions? The answer was a most resounding, no! She called her PPS and asked him to schedule a meeting on Monday with the PM. They were in a hole, so she stopped digging and went to have a much needed sleep.

★ ★ ★

Sunday dawned with a flurry of activity in Westminster. It was quite clear to all the esteemed residents of Numbers 10 and 11 that trouble was only moments away; the papers once more delving into why the looming gold crisis had been spectacularly missed. Speculation was rife that there would be a series of high-profile resignations on Monday.

'Sources close to the prime minister' were quick to allocate the blame to anyone but him, with Dominic Carrington coming in for some very savage, off the record criticism, in his capacity as head of the London Bullion Market. He had been interviewed on the early morning radio bulletins and reiterated the line he had previously agreed with the governor of the Bank of England: namely, that this problem was manageable. The Bank for International Settlements, the central bank to the world's central banks, was, he reported, willing to offer every assistance and unlimited support. He refused to acknowledge that China was the culprit, and pointed the finger at international speculators and the less scrupulous hedge funds that "would follow a snowball into hell if there was money in it."

Carrington had been brusquely summoned to Number 10 for what he assumed was to be the usual haranguing and public humiliation, so beloved of the PM when in a crisis. When he got there, the meeting-room was full to over flowing with nervous Treasury officials, the chancellor, Lewis Moyns and the governor. Somewhat to his surprise the PM was already there.

He immediately sat down at the only spare seat and decided attack was the only option.

"Glad to see that you are taking my 'Naked Shorts' paper seriously at last Prime Minister."

Amanda quickly intervened to avert a full blown screaming match.

"Dominic, we are all taking it seriously. The question before us is how do we manage the anticipated melt-down on Monday. Personally, I'm in favour of closing the markets, but I think that may spectacularly backfire. Do you, or indeed anyone, have any better suggestions? Lewis?"

There was something curiously serene about Lewis Moyns as he sat at the head of the table directly opposite the prime minister, albeit twenty feet apart. His customary imperturbable demeanour was in stark contrast to virtually everyone present. Given his enormous clout, power and authority, all eyes were focused on how he would respond and what solutions he may proffer. Only those with a long relationship with the chairman of the Federal Reserve would have noticed he was wearing cowboy boots: which meant only one thing; he was up for a fight.

"Amanda, gentlemen; it would behove us all to stay calm and focused. This will all be played out over the next few days providing we don't all panic. The Fed will backstop the gold requirements of the bullion banks; if necessary we will also raise interest rates and put a temporary stop to any new gold futures trading on COMEX. I have also proposed that Sebastian Fortes go to see the Chinese central bank and other Finance Ministry officials, leaving in the next day or so. In his new capacity as Deputy Governor he will be empowered to negotiate a compromise on behalf of the Bank and the Fed."

The PM went ballistic with rage, banging the table loudly with his fist.

"What bloody compromise; and just what the hell what do you mean by 'played out'?"

He pointed his finger directly at the governor.

"Sir David, whose cock-and-bull idea is this? Where's Fortes, someone get him here immediately."

Sitting unusually upright, the governor of the Bank of England seemed at long last to have regained his composure and dignity, which had been decidedly lacking of late. If he was going to go down with the ship, then he was going down in flames.

"It's my idea Prime Minister. You know full well how much hidden gold we think China has. They have the capacity and the intention to outgun us; we have no option but to capitulate."

In his customary Texan drawl, Lewis interjected; winking conspiratorially at the governor.

"No need to take all the credit, Dave. Sorry to be a killjoy here Charlie, but the solution to this crisis is a closely guarded secret between me, the Director of the CIA and the President: eyes only, usual bullshit and certainly not for disclosure in this room. Pointless inviting Sebastian here: he hasn't been briefed, yet. I'll talk to you about it later."

The room fell into utter silence as everyone turned towards the prime minister to see how he would react to this – probably carefully calculated – slap in the face. To everyone's utter astonishment he simply closed his file, turned to his chancellor and said, "OK, let's meet again tomorrow when we know how the markets have reacted."

Lewis immediately guessed that within two minutes the PM would be on the hot line to the White House demanding that he be flayed alive for such gross impertinence. He pulled out his phone and texted the word 'DONE' to Director Meggs at the CIA, who would probably already be speaking to the president.

★ ★ ★

By the time 12.30 rolled around, the prime minister had been unceremoniously rebuffed by the president and told in very forthright language that Fortes could handle the assignment, and leave him to it. He was also politely informed that there was little immediate prospect of Lewis being brought before Congress and forced into a humiliating resignation.

When Robert Simons entered his study, the volcanic rage, for which he was rightfully famous, was at boiling point. Without the exchange of the normal pleasantries he growled.

"Twenty seconds; show me."

Simons took the photograph out of his briefcase and passed it over.

"I'm convinced Carrington's not the culprit. When the editor of The Sun and the Chancellor of the Exchequer are photographed canoodling in the bushes, you can only infer one thing. She's the source of the leak. I can't prove it yet, but one of the Downing Street drivers, Tom, is an ex-copper and he's just told me that a week ago he drove Miss Price to Imperial College very early in the morning. An unscheduled, off the grid, trip apparently. Now I know Carrington wasn't there, I checked and he was at a symposium, so who did she meet? Was the choice of venue quite deliberately chosen to incriminate the professor?"

"No, this can't possibly be true! I'm flabbergasted. She's my most trusted lieutenant; been at my side through thick and thin."

"Prime Minister, I believe the most appropriate phrase is: *Et tu Brute*. It's probably best that you give me the authority to dig a lot deeper."

"Yes, yes, whatever you want. But very, very discretely; we are in the midst of a banking crisis and, if your assessment is accurate, my reaction must be considered and timely. I don't want to lose her until I'm good and ready. And double check Carrington, I still think he's behind this no matter what you believe."

"I'll be back the moment I have more details. I'm assuming

MI5 is also looking into this so, if they are tapping phones and emails, perhaps you should get them to check if the chancellor has more than one phone. Just my suspicious mind, but I'd bet she has one hidden somewhere."

CHAPTER 28

The Yellow Sea & London.

The Chinook helicopter containing Sanford, CIA agent Sapphire and half a dozen crew members from the aircraft carrier Bataan was travelling at breathtaking speed just feet above the sea, which was mercifully calm. Their destination: the ship containing Xiao's gold and his extended family. When they arrived on station, hovering just astern of the freighter, they could immediately see that no one was on deck, the ship's progress seemed positively languid and nothing appeared untoward.

The high-altitude reconnaissance drone, which had been deployed earlier to track the precious cargo, had an accurate locational fix on the ship to within a metre. Flight controllers back on the aircraft carrier had been scanning the surrounding sky and waters for any sign of the Chinese and jamming any form of communication from the ship. The last thing any of them wanted was a desperate mayday call to the general or the Butler.

Within a matter of moments the team were suspended above the rear deck and sliding down their respective ropes to confront the occupants. The shocked faces of the family members as they entered the lower quarters were transformed when Sapphire spoke quietly to them in the local Mandarin dialect of their home town, Dandong. On the trip over she had carefully rehearsed what she was going to say; the question was: would they swallow it?

"There is no need to be afraid, we have been sent by your beloved brother, Xiao Fan, to help you escape. We are your friends: the 'unexpected' he told you about in your last call together. You are all in grave danger and must be evacuated from this ship immediately. We don't have a moment to lose. Our colleagues in Shanghai are working on a plan to rescue your brother from being captured by the State police and we expect the Chinese navy to be here at any moment. So everyone go on deck and prepare to be taken off the ship by helicopter."

A flurry of indecipherable chatter followed as the family considered their options. The eldest brother eventually turned to Sapphire and, however reluctantly, simply nodded approval. Within ten minutes they had all been winched into the helicopter, with the navy team now taking command of the vessel. A rapid assessment of the ship's cargo was undertaken and agreement reached that it could, with care and very skilful flying indeed, be extricated while at sea. It was clear that the gold had been hastily packed into a ramshackle collection of crates, boxes, anything and everything they could find in those desperate few hours they had to load the ship.

Sanford signalled the remainder of the helicopter fleet to approach in a manoeuvre they had carefully practiced only the day before and bit-by-precious-bit exchange the real bullion for that flown in earlier from the Federal Reserve vaults. It took nearly three hours to clear the holds and stow away the replacements. When the transfers were finally completed Sanford and Sapphire were winched back onto the last helicopter and flown back to the carrier.

"I have to report in Sapphire; I'll see you in the mess hall in, shall we say half an hour?"

"Sure thing Jim, I'm going to speak to the family, make sure they are being taken care of. Then I'll explain what is going to happen next."

★ ★ ★

By one of those curious twists of fate – which seem to be the very essence of covert operations – the Jin-Ton was moving determinedly, but slowly, in a north-easterly journey to Dandong, blissfully unaware that it was only a few hundred miles away from the nameless freighter now crewed by the US navy team, plodding its way southwards towards Shanghai.

Events seemed to be running in slow motion for their CIA trackers, who were painstakingly watching both radar blips make tortuous progress through the Yellow Sea. All everyone at the Agency now wanted was for both ships to get to their respective ports and commence the next phase of their mission. Detailed calculations were updated every minute as to when the vessels would arrive; with frequent reports sent to Director Meggs. It was now crucial for his entire plan that the chess pieces were in the right place at the right time.

★ ★ ★

As he awoke to a gloriously sunny Monday morning – more normally associated with optimism and hope – Sebastian Fortes was blissfully unaware of what a momentous week lay ahead. It was unclear to him what to make of an overnight text from Lyn which simply stated 'see you soon' with several kisses, but it had cheered him up considerably. Perhaps she was on the plane home from wherever she had been posted; perhaps she was home for good…. 'perhaps, perhaps, perhaps', as the song went?

His joy was short lived however. In his new capacity as deputy governor, he had been summoned to attend a mid-morning meeting at the Bank of England and, curiously, told in no uncertain terms to make sure his passport was up-to-date and a suitcase packed. There was a rather ominous post script to the email: 'be prepared to leave at a moment's notice'. His principal concern was, leave for where? Did he require Bermuda shorts or an Arctic fleece? Followed rapidly by: will he get the chance to see Lyn again before he gets on the next plane?

He rapidly flicked through the TV business channels to see what had happened to the markets in Asia overnight and what the business commentariat were predicting for London's opening. Doom and disaster were spread across the faces of the more jittery, younger correspondents who were reporting a surge in gold prices and a heavy sell-off in banking stocks. The currency and equity markets in Tokyo and Hong Kong were volatile in the extreme and reacting to any sliver of news, however tenuous, with knee jerk reactions. Price fluctuations, both up and down, were creating havoc.

A flurry of texts had also come in from Lewis asking him to keep a low profile until such time as a major press conference could be scheduled for later in the week, "probably Thursday, when we will let slip the dogs of war". All he could muster in reply was: 'Lewis, my dear friend, it would be very helpful to know if I am cast in the role of Julius Caesar or Mark Antony'?

Dominic Carrington called around nine to say he would be at the Bank meeting later that morning and suggesting Seb use the more discreet entrance on Lothbury: "a flak jacket, large brimmed hat and sunglasses may also be wise".

His colleagues at d'Abo's were also bombarding him with urgent requests for guidance as to how they should position the bank against the impending shocks. His reply of "frankly, I'm not at all sure" was met with groans.

★ ★ ★

It was becoming increasingly evident to all those present at the Bank of England meeting that one or more of the bullion banks may well fail as the week progressed. It was just proving progressively impossible to supply the speculators' requests for physical gold. Dominic Carrington stood to address the assembled officials.

"Earlier this morning I held a series of phone calls with the larger banks working in the London Bullion Market who all reported that, despite considerable strains, they were just about coping with their short positions. My concerns rest for the moment with the smaller banks and the possibility that one or more may be forced into liquidation as they try to cover their exposure as the price of gold escalated dramatically. The governor and the Fed chairman are making virtually unlimited lines of credit available, but as we all know too well, there comes a point when the market overwhelms even the promise of infinite support. The more you offer the speculators, the more is taken. There are on-going discussions to close the market and see if we can negotiate our way out of this; but no agreement has been reached with the chancellor, as yet."

Sir David Stone entered the room, having earlier left the meeting to take a conference call with Charlie Sheer and Amanda Price.

"Sorry to miss what you said just now Dominic. There is only so much 'independence' allowed to the Bank before our friends in Downing Street start to interfere. They have clearly stated that we should use every available option to stop any UK bank collapsing. I told them that this time around, we would be wise to let one fail, spectacularly if necessary. Needless to say, this piece of advice did not go down well. Indeed, just before he hung up, the PM then told me to send him an undated resignation letter."

To gasps from the assembled audience, he continued.

"I then took the opportunity to call Lewis Moyns and get his take on events. He will be going back to the States tomorrow, urgent business to attend to, and all that. His advice was to hold our nerve and irrespective of what happens, and I quote, 'slug it out till Friday'."

★ ★ ★

As had happened on a couple of occasions recently, Sebastian had no idea why he had been called to such a gathering. No one had asked him to contribute and if they had, it was unclear what exactly he could have said. Just as he was about to leave his phone rang.

"Lewis here Seb. I'm at the embassy, could you pop over for half an hour, I need to bring you up-to-date on a few highly sensitive matters and plot out your travel and meeting schedule."

"No problem, events here have just finished. Shall I come alone; Dominic and David are here?"

"Alone, if you don't mind! I'll share the details with them later in the week. This is just between you, me and the Director of the CIA."

"OK, see you in twenty or thirty minutes."

★ ★ ★

The chancellor replaced the receiver after the conference call and thought, Charlie's in a filthy mood again. Apart from the obvious, I wonder what's eating him today? He's never normally this brusk with me.

For the next hour she had to endure a non-stop series of phone calls from the chairmen or chief executives of the country's largest banks, all pleading for help. There was utter consternation in the derivatives market as the inevitable domino effect took centre stage: market after market was being simultaneously battered. It didn't take a financial wizard to appreciate that nerves were decidedly frayed. One of the smaller regional banks went so far as to say they were almost in emergency measures and desperately needed her to intervene before it was too late and they had to close down.

In the midst of all of this the Bank of England called to alert her that the pound was in free fall and they would be meeting later to raise interest rates, possibly by several hundred basis points. Faint beads of sweat were forming on her temple. She took a long hard look at the screens in front of her to see that both gold and silver prices had risen sharply in Shanghai overnight, with the upward trend continuing throughout the European markets. It looked for all the world as if everyone was dumping paper currencies and moving into anything tangible: gold and other precious metals were climbing to heights never seen before. For the first time in her career, fear almost gripped her as well. She was no longer in control of events. Carrington was being proved right.

★ ★ ★

Sebastian entered the American Embassy and was escorted to the building's SCIFF – the Sensitive Compartmented Information Facility – generally known as The Chamber and politely asked to wait for a couple of minutes. Lewis strolled in full of bonhomie and 'hail fellow well met' conviviality.

"Lewis; is this some sort of self-defence mechanism. Smiling as the fighter plane goes down in flames, that sort of thing?"

"Not exactly Seb, it's just that the good old 'US-of-A' still has one or two tricks up its sleeve which will assist our cause immeasurably. I just wanted to reassure you that all is not yet lost; so, let's crack-on. I've asked you here for several reasons. First and foremost, what I'm about to reveal is top secret, obviously. Secondly, the fewer people that know about it the better; so absolutely no disclosure to our friends in government please. And, thirdly, I think a demonstration may be called for."

"Have you joined the Magic Circle, Lewis? Can I be allowed to check the contents of your sleeve?"

"Not quite, but this is certainly from the 'how the hell did they do that' department. You will recall from our Dark Pools escapades the incredible technical expertise that your old pal, and now new colleague, Dr Alex Cadbury, brought to the table. Well he's been working on something rather extraordinary for the past couple of years. Do you recall the 'Stuxnet' affair, involving the virtual destruction of Iran's nuclear enrichment facilities with a very pernicious computer virus? And the North Korean missiles that inexplicably explode a millisecond after take off?"

Sebastian nodded.

"What was not made public at the time was that Iran initiated a revenge cyber-attack against our banking system. Technically, the computer geeks refer to this as a 'distributed denial of service' assault, where the banks computer systems are overwhelmed with gazillions of tiny instructions, such that they overload and collapsed. We fixed it pretty quickly, but it set up a train of thought at the CIA about whether we could do the same thing but, say, with much bigger fish….China and Russia being the obvious targets. Well, your chum Alex has been leading the research since 2013, and I'm pleased to say we have made considerable progress. The file I'm about to show you is a 'POTUS-only' summary of the project, code named 'Nitro Zeus'. We've recently significantly upgraded its capabilities, but its objective can be summed up in three words: disrupt, degrade and destroy'."

Seb opened the file on the desk and started to read the two page synopsis.

"Can this really be done?"

"Come over here. I'll give you the most modest of demonstrations."

Lewis sat at the bank of computer screens at the end of the desk and pointed to a live CCTV image of the Beijing underground system. He waited until the next train pulled in and the passengers, as usual, vigorously pushed and shoved past each other to get on and off. With his hand hovering over the mouse he waited until the doors were about to close, and clicked. They opened again. He clicked once more and they closed.

"Care to try Seb?"

"Well, Lewis, I'm impressed."

"That was just a bit of fun. Now, here's the interesting thing…"

CHAPTER 29

Dandong, Brunei & Shanghai

The Jin-Ton was positioned about fifty nautical miles from Dandong, in the very north-east corner of China and only a metaphorical stone's throw from North Korea, which could clearly be seen on the starboard bow. Captain Zucca and Sergeant Oakes were sat in what laughably passed for the officers' mess, having supper and running through the possible events which may unfold tomorrow. The second bottle of Chianti was the only thing between them and another fitful night's sleep. Earlier, they had radioed for a pilot to come on board, sometime around daybreak, and guide them through the last few miles of very busy shipping lanes; only to be told that a navy patrol boat would also be accompanying them into harbour.

Oaksey poured another overly generous glass for them both and with more than a slight slur in his voice added:

"I had better get a hold of my army bosses and let them know we are going to dock tomorrow, although I'm sure they know that already. I think you should also call Beijing and tell them the good news as well? Ask for a champagne reception and a few high-class strippers."

"Yeh, no rush my friend, I was thinking of getting the crew together first and making sure no one was going to do anything stupid when we arrive. On the assumption that nothing has changed, I'm guessing we just unload, get paid-up, and skedaddle to the airport?"

"Let's hope it's that simple. My personal concern is that I have no documents, for obvious reasons, so how in God's name am I going to get out of the country?"

"So much for the all seeing, all conquering, US Army! Hope you like sweating your bollocks off in the paddy fields for the rest of your miserable life. Perhaps you'd be wise to mention this to your pert-assed Major when you get through; and tell her I'd like a date, if she has the stamina."

"I've a feeling she'd rather kill you with her bare hands first; but I'll ask, if only to hear her response."

They both moved into the radio room, taking a new bottle of wine with them, to switch on the encrypted satellite radio.

"Is Major Andrews available, it's Sergeant Oakes?"

"Afraid not, Sir; I'm only at liberty to say that she is on manoeuvres."

A wry smile crossed his face. It could only mean she was, yet again, up to her armpits on some clandestine operation. A fleeting twinge of jealousy crossed his mind, followed immediately by the thought that it was going to take an eternity to get fit again, and probably a month or two of cold-turkey.

"Understood. Can you please pass the following message to General Sanford; we dock at dawn tomorrow. And is there any way he, or anyone who just happens to be close by, can find me new identity papers?"

"I'll pass those messages along Sergeant. Assuming you dock without drama, you're instructed to proceed to the Hilton hotel in Zhenxing province. Apparently it's just a few miles upriver from the port. He has arranged for someone, code name Agent Sapphire, to meet you there and escort you out of the country. He also said that under no circumstances are you to forget to throw the bloody radio overboard before you get anywhere near shore, otherwise, and I quote, 'he'll have your stripes ripped from your arm by chainsaw'."

"Glad to here he's in such a cheery, upbeat, mood. How will I recognise this agent?"

"Absolutely no idea; I suspect that you will be rather obvious to spot."

He turned to Zucca who was mockingly sharpening a knife and running it across his throat.

"I guess your promotion took a turn for the worse?"

"I'll be lucky to come out of this with my balls intact, let alone three stripes."

"Oaksey, I think it's time I addressed the crew, could you pass me that pistol and a couple of bullets. Then let's give those sons-of-whores in Beijing a call with the good news."

★ ★ ★

The six-man US navy team in charge of the ramshackled vessel containing Xiao's counterfeit gold were making detailed preparations to abandon ship when they got closer to their destination. They would steam slowly up the Yangtze River, bypassing Shanghai, and navigate towards the docks in Nantong, where his family had previously agreed to be put ashore. Once they were close they would drop anchor and make for shore in their dinghies. If all went to plan, they would be met and secretly smuggled out of the country by local CIA operatives.

Earlier it had been concluded that they could not possibly escape detection if they were to dock the ship in Nantong and would probably be faced with a fight to the death with whoever they met. The very last thing the United States wanted to have to explain away was six dead Navy Seals.

Instead they would place a call through to the Butler and let him know that, antcipating detection, the family was too scared to come ashore for fear of capture by the secret police. The navy team would take a calculated risk that – with a voice transmission full of static, made by one of the fluent crew members – they would not be recognised and could easily pass as one of the real brothers. They would tell him that they intended to make their way south without the Butler's help as they did not want to be a burden to him; throwing in the request that, as a man of honour, he must keep his oath to take care of their elder brother.

It was an empty, even futile, gesture but it had just the hint of truth, and certainly desperation. They rightly predicted that the prize of an unmanned ship, containing over a hundred tonnes of gold bullion, would surely have the Butler's man tearing down the river in minutes.

When the time came, the radio call was short and to the point.

"Could we speak to our brother Xiao Fan, we have an urgent message."

"He's not available today; I will personally pass him the details."

The Butler listened intently, smiling ever wider as they story unfolded. Greed rapidly overwhelmed caution. The thought flashed through his warped mind: 'At least I won't have to go through the trouble of killing them. Now I only have to deal with the traitor Xiao'.

He replaced the radio receiver and abruptly gave instructions for his underlings to prepare to board the vessel when he gave the signal in a few hours time and immediately bring it to his private wharf. His second in command had already made detailed plans to transport the gold to their warehouse where it would be re-packaged for distribution to a plethora of reluctant buyers amongst the triad community.

As was his wont, the Butler had reminded them all of his easily revoked patronage and, if they didn't want to lose it, they must pay through the nose for their portion of the gold bullion, or have it swiftly removed. In a more remote part of town, trucks of every size were being gradually assembled to transport the remaining bullion to a sizable contingent of appreciative, corrupt politicians, who were already salivating at the pleasure such riches could confer on them. The Butler gave a rare, concealed, smile at the thought of the long list of scum he now had in his pocket. It would simply be a matter of time before he called in the chits.

★ ★ ★

Zucca made his way to the radio room intent on calling Beijing's bluff, blissfully unaware that he too was now taking virtually worthless bullion to his Chinese masters. Earlier, he had been convinced by Oakes that he couldn't lose anything by asking for a larger slice of the cake. After all he had kept his part of the bargain by delivering the gold. He reasoned, quite justifiably in his drink fuelled state of mind, that the other drugs and arms he was also carrying must be worth more than a few million lira, so he would ask for a cut of that bounty too.

Needless to say, when Lieutenant Qiang came to the radio and heard this further demand he was inwardly furious with rage. To his credit, he managed to keep his calm sufficiently to reply:

"I will put that to my bosses. Ten percent more you say? I will get back to you with a reply as soon as possible. According to the screen in front of me here you should arrive in five or six hours. Is that your assessment Zucca?"

"Yes, providing nothing more breaks or stops completely. This heap of horse manure should be scrapped immediately we dock. Is all in place for the money transfer to my account and the cash payment of the crews' wages?"

"It is. The moment we see that all the goods have arrived safely. I will see to both matters personally."

★ ★ ★

Lyn returned to the embassy compound with a collection of the most glamorous clothes she had ever possessed in her entire life: bag-upon-designer-bag of pure extravagance, all courtesy of the largess of the CIA. Long dresses, short dresses, jackets, shoes, lingerie: you name it, she had bought it. Pangs of guilt fleetingly passed her mind as she handed over the CIA credit card and watched thousands of dollars disappear. There must be some higher reason why she was being ordered to look an absolute knockout; the question was: where's the action going to take place; and for whom and with whom?

The armed guard waved her through the barriers with the comment:

"There is someone to see you Major Andrews. Says he's from the Hong Kong consulate; their cultural attaché apparently."

"Thanks corporal."

She dropped her bags off at the reception and asked for them to be taken to her room at the back of the building. One of the secretaries then escorted her to the conference room where her guest was already waiting.

"I'll be damned, Reed how are you? It's been at least two, or is it three years? How's the gammy leg, and where's your twin Bain? And what's this bollocks about you being the cultural attaché! Have you been thrown out of the CIA because of the limp?"

"Wow, Lyn, you look spectacular, as always. Well, would you believe that's my latest cover story? Implausible I know, but I do get to see lots of the ballet."

They both laughed and warmly embraced.

"I was supposed to go scuba diving with young Mr. Bain this week, somewhere in Thailand, but it got cancelled at very short notice. I've been asked by the Director to ride shotgun on your current assignment, discreet cover, that sort of thing. I'm told that I'm more useful in the back row of the chorus than centre stage apparently."

217

"Great to have you along my dear friend; so, what's the scoop?"

"I am heading to Dandong later tonight after I have briefed you; and then I'm to head to the port area for a 'seek and extract' mission with Sanford. Beyond that limited info I'm, as per usual, clueless without Bain-the-Brain at my side. After that jaunt is completed I am to link up with you; although Christ knows how at the moment. In regard to your trip, I've been given a bunch of documents and your background cover story here. I originally received a new Irish passport for you, under the name of Miss Lingus, would you believe. Some short-trousered, raging hormoned, youth at Covert Ops must have dreamt it up."

"First name Air, I suppose?"

"No, Connie. Anyway, Sanford told the guy that he would be looking for a new set of front teeth if he didn't drop the idea. So you're back to Ms. Lyn Andrews, a highly respected director of the auction house, Sotheby's, specialising in porcelain, apparently."

"OK, I just hope no one asks me any tricky questions."

"Just keep saying it could be Ming Dynasty given the lovely glaze, even if it's from Wal-Mart."

"I'll be back to get you if this goes tits-up Reed, you do know that?"

"It'll be my pleasure. Anyway, down to the nitty-gritty, as we cultural attachés say. Your orders are to fly independently to Beijing and meet up with your old mucker Seb for a spot of high level diplomacy."

"Well, well, well, I'll be damned. At least the last bit's good news; I presume that's why I have had to get all these beautiful clothes?"

"I'm guessing that you'll be on parade amongst the social elite of Beijing? But to be absolutely truthful Lyn, I think all of us will be winging this assignment from start to finish."

"Got it. Ours not to reason why, and all that: let's go grab a couple of beer and catch up. Been shot lately?"

* * *

Sanford had arrived in Shanghai on the morning flight from Japan full of his usual vim and vigour; ready to implement the next phase of Operation Skulduggery. Within short order he was making his way surreptitiously to a rendezvous with his CIA colleagues, led by Reed, who had also flown in a couple of hours earlier. It was rare and exceptionally dangerous to have so many agents swarming all over the city, but every operative in China had recently been placed on red alert. If all went to plan then the gold shipments which were about to reach Nantong – which Sanford was tasked with monitoring – and Dandong close to the North Korean border – where Sapphire was in overall control – would occur at more or less the same time.

His immediate objective was to exit Shanghai international airport unseen and head 40 miles north up the G15 motorway to the port area of Nantong. There he was to observe the safe arrival of the vessel containing General Xiao's riches. Agents at Langley had been tracking the ship's progress for days now and more importantly, the exact location of Xiao, who was holed up in some nondescript residential apartment block to the south of the marina.

Priority number one however, was to make contact with the six man Navy Seal unit the moment they reached shore. If there was to be trouble with the Butler and his colleagues – which instinctively Sanford presumed would be the case – then he would undoubtedly need all the help he could muster. Within moments of his arrival contact had been made with the ship and a location selected to disembark the navy crew.

"Good to see you Reed, is all ready?"

"Yep, let's go kick some ass!"

CHAPTER 30

Washington & London

CIA Director, Carter Meggs, was a very difficult man to please, even when he was feeling magnanimous, which was almost never. Very few agency staff ever got beyond the grade of 'satisfactory' if he was asked to contribute to their annual appraisal. There was only one exception; and he was most definitely placed in the 'truly gifted' category, to which there were only two members: his good self and Dr. Alex Cadbury.

Like all previous incumbents of his exalted position, he could be relied upon to keep a secret: none more so than the ultra-secret 'Nitro Zeus' project. The director was especially proud of the enormous financial and human resources the agency had dedicated to it, under the impressive leadership and technical supervision of Dr. Cadbury. He had met many very clever men in his lifetime, but his was a talent beyond measure: indisputably the Alan Turing of his day.

This rarest-of-rare resource had never failed in any technical task he had asked to undertake: and Nitro Zeus was the pinnacle of his achievements. He was held in such esteem by the Director that he was the only man in the building ever to be allowed to call him Carter. In his view he had the instinctive mindset of a superlative CIA agent: devious and cunning in equal measure, especially in the context of what this project could ultimately deliver if push ever came to shove.

At his most creative, Cadbury worked alone and in

complete silence; which in Carter Meggs' opinion was no bad thing. Anyone who was happy to be squirreled away for days on end writing computer code was just the man he wanted. Despite having a full time job at the hedge fund SQT, his unique skill-set was frequently called upon in the midst of a crisis. Everyone he worked with in the Agency respected him. All openly acknowledged that had served his country with exceptional dedication and distinction. Now was the moment to put the billions of dollars and countless man hours invested in the Nitro Zeus project to their ultimate use.

"Alex, glad you could come and see us again and thanks as always for sparing the time. I need you to do something for me with the utmost urgency, then take it to Beijing and show Sebastian Fortes how it works."

"Always happy to help, Carter; especially if it involves Seb."

"Good. You probably already know that the Chinese are screwing around with the gold markets, intent once again on bringing the western banking system to its knees. I'm sure you appreciate we can't let them get away with that. Need to kick them firmly in the nuts and show them whose boss."

"Yes, I've following it with considerable interest, but I think you'll have to get someone else to do the kicking."

"Lighten up Alex, that was what we dudes in the CIA call a metaphor, or some God-damn thing. So, here is what I want. You've seen the movie 'Mission Impossible', right? Well I want you to programme an iPad, or whatever the hell they're called, with certain carefully selected components of the Nitro Zeus malware. I want Fortes to be able to casually place it on a conference table, press a single button, which then automatically triggers a sequence of events every few minutes. Hopefully when that particular party starts it should cause a few heart attacks with the guys he's going to meet. Then I want the whole thing to be wiped completely clean; not a trace of coding, or anything, is that clear? Your, 'this message will self destruct in five minutes', moment. Simple question Alex, can it be done?"

"I think we can manage that. How long do I have?"

"About six hours, so you better haul-ass. You fly to Beijing the moment it's completed. Here's a file detailing the sequence of events I want you to programme. Oh, and to spice up the trip you'll get a chance to meet the mouth-watering Naylor at long last. I'm assigning her to be your back-up on this one. Look in on me before you leave."

"Will do."

"Oh, one last thing Alex; I think it's probably sensible to prepare an identical back-up system for her. Give her the same briefing. The last time I looked in the files there wasn't any kompromat on Fortes, but its best we prepare for some retaliatory dirty-tricks and ensure we can proceed unhindered."

"Frankly, I think Lyn would be more than enough for one man: but, sure, I'll see to that."

★ ★ ★

The prime minister paced up and down his private office in a quandary about what to do if his so-called friend and chancellor had indeed been the source of all the malicious press leaks recently. True, he didn't have any definitive proof as yet. Perhaps that didn't matter? But could he, dare he, take the risk of an outright confrontation with her at this point, especially as he was armed with only the most tenuous of unsubstantiated accusations? Given the amount of security agencies now engaged in this matter, he was totally convinced that corroborative, incontrovertible, evidence would emerge soon.

Fitfully circling the room for the umpteenth time, he reminded himself that when a crisis occurred, he must stay true to his oft repeated mantra: 'Always go with your gut instincts'. Followed rapidly thereafter by, 'Always strike the first blow'.

In his increasingly paranoid state the PM was convinced that Dominic Carrington was complicit in a plot to destabilise his government before the upcoming election. It was no secret that they openly hated each other and were polar opposites politically. Which led him to reach the obvious conclusion: somehow he must be deeply implicated. The only problem was to what end, other than to force him from office. He speculated out loud if the two of them were in league together.

Either way, he was not going to let this matter rest for a single moment longer than he needed to. If the debacle unfolding in the gold market could not be contained in the next couple of days, then he would have to lay the blame squarely at their collective feet. Anyone but himself; and to hell with the consequences.

When the London bullion market had opened on Monday morning, it was immediately experiencing unprecedented demand for physical gold as speculators closed out their positions and began forcing immediate delivery from the banks. The news agencies were relentlessly piling on the political pressure; the opposition parties were demanding statements be made in the House; and even his own colleagues were pleading for decisive action to be taken in order to prevent yet another calamitous banking collapse. Blame was being liberally strewn around. Inertia at Number 10, rife.

Senior bank's executives were supplicating themselves at the feet of the chancellor, pleading for help and letting it be known that they could not withstand the speculators demands for much longer. Meanwhile, the governor of the Bank of England, Sir David Stone, had reluctantly set in motion the emergency procedures used during the 2008 crash, with a clear directive that the Bank would provide unlimited financial support to those institutions that requested it. However, when pushed on the subject by the press, he was deliberately vague as to whether this included the release of physical gold from the UK's dwindling stockpile; if for no other reason than he didn't know whether, and for how long, he could keep such a commitment.

Sir David clung desperately to the only life raft available to him: the promise by Lewis Moyns, the chairman of the Federal Reserve, that providing he could "hang tough till Friday", the United States would "fix the problem, once and for all".

Regrettably this brash and quite probably reckless bravado was not something he could share with the market, or the press. The prime minister had branded Lewis a 'bloody idiot' on more occasions than he cared to remember, so to suggest to him that this was their only salvation would be laughed at. He decided to put in a call to Amanda Price and asked if he could see her in an hour's time?

★ ★ ★

The rag-tag assortments of journalists, TV presenters and still half-sozzled hacks from the press corps had arrived especially early in Downing Street. The all-too-familiar smell of an impending financial crisis permeated the air and they wanted a sacrificial victim. As usual they were baying loudly for blood from behind the crush barriers; with unseemly questions being hurled at anyone and everyone that ventured into, or out of, Numbers 10 or 11. Under strict orders, not a single cabinet minister or government official deigned to reply or even acknowledged their presence. So when Sir David turned to the cameras at the steps of Number 11 and gave an optimistic wave, reminiscent of a man hoping to be saved from the gallows, the clicks of a thousand cameras was almost deafening.

"Amanda, good to see you as always; quite a bear pit out there today."

"If they corner you David, I don't need to tell you to choose every word with exceptional care: they want someone's head and it's not going to be mine. Now, if you'd be so kind, quickly fill me in with what's happening from your perspective."

"There's little doubt in my mind Amanda that the Chinese government, or their endless list of state-sponsored speculators, have cornered the gold market. I don't have irrefutable evidence as yet, but Dominic Carrington is in minute-by-minute contact with the bullion banks and valiantly attempting to confirm precisely where the contract holders reside. That's the smoking gun we are now searching for. I have just sent a communiqué to my counterparts at the People's Bank of China saying I've asked Seb Fortes to investigate the gold crisis and visit them to discuss a wide ranging number of issues. Much to my surprise they have agreed to a meeting on Friday."

"And what the hell is he going to say; I haven't briefed him, have you?"

"Not yet. To be quite honest I wouldn't know what to say, but apparently Lewis has been speaking to him on a fairly regular basis. He's confided in me only that he has a solution, but its top secret. He's reluctant to share it with the PM, thinks he's a security risk apparently."

"Bloody ridiculous!"

"Just repeating what he said Amanda. He seems to set great store by Sebastian's persuasive abilities; 'charm the knickers off a nun' was his somewhat indelicate phase."

"Can we survive all this till Friday, David? I'm being briefed that at least one high street bank is close to collapse and if that goes under there will be an immediate no-confidence motion in the House: which we will almost certainly lose."

"We don't seem to have any choice Chancellor. I'd better get back to the office, but before I go, here's my undated letter of resignation. You've no doubt been told that the PM asked me to place it at his disposal. Unless something dramatic occurs to save us, we may both be gone before the week is over. I'll be in the garden tending the roses or down the pub; you're welcome to visit me at either venue."

★ ★ ★

Alex Cadbury positively thrived on tight deadlines and any form of technical challenge, but this was a 'doozie' of the first order: his favourite kind. The no-brainer bit was getting a couple of secure iPads from the stores; the complex part was how to pare down the Nitro Zeus software to the specific components that had been selected by the director. Over the years Alex and his team had programmed so many options into the coding – in anticipation of an all-out retaliatory strike against every conceivable enemy of the United States – that it took much longer than he anticipated to establish the required sequence of events. However, after a couple of hours of high stakes cut-and-paste he was ready to, as he put it, 'rock and roll'.

"Carter, it's prepared and primed. I don't think it's wise to give you a demonstration; might give the game away. So, when do I leave?"

"Great job Alex. I've organised your tickets to Beijing, I'm afraid it's commercial rather than private this time. Don't want to give you access to the Company jet and have you spotted before we've got to first base. I'm assuming that you'll brief Fortes when he arrives on how to turn the damn thing on, and so forth? It's essential that he is prepared for an almighty confrontation and if necessary to let the programme run all the way."

"I don't think that will be an issue. See you in a week, God willing."

"God's got nothing to do with it. Keep on top of Naylor, you know how she likes to party."

CHAPTER 31

London & Dandong

"Prime Minister, its Lord McMullan, the Chairman of Barclays Bank on the line, says he needs to see you urgently: a matter which requires your immediate and personal attention apparently. Says he can't discuss it over the phone."

"Christ, what the hell does he want now? You give the guy a bloody peerage and he thinks he can swan in here at a moment notice...what the hell, it might be important Nadia. OK, tell him to swing on by for a very quick drink at five sharp."

★ ★ ★

Next door Amanda Price was valiantly 'wrestling alligators', as she so eloquently described it to her exasperated private secretary who was frantically charging around the chancellor's office in a state of total pandemonium. The phones had literally been glowing red hot for hours, as Amanda fielded call-after-call from distraught bankers, pleading with her to suspend the gold market and, if possible, the stock market, before the whole pack of cards collapsed.

In the last week the price of gold had shot up from $1,200 an ounce to over $3,000 and all the pundits were predicting that it would break the $10,000 mark by the end of the week if these trends continued. If you owned physical gold you were making a fortune, but if you had to buy it in the market to satisfy your clients, as the banks were scrambling to do, then it was a catastrophe. The Stock Exchange FTSE Index had fallen by nearly a 1,000 points since opening, with bank shares being especially hammered and at limit-down.

At some point in the melee she had once again contacted Dominic Carrington to seek his opinion on what action to take. Although initially he was very reluctant indeed to agree to any form of market intervention, by mid morning he had changed his mind. His principal concerns were that they would simply be handing a propaganda triumph to his counterparts in the Shanghai Gold Exchange and instantaneously ceding control of the world's bullion market to them permanently. The Chinese were totally insulated from this crisis so they had absolutely no reason to close their market, indeed quite the opposite. He had to reluctantly concede to the chancellor that such an action would simply demonstrate to the world who held the power in this market and how vulnerable the western banking system had become. Begrudgingly, but pragmatically, he concluded that it was better to halt the carnage now, while there was still time to negotiate some form of financial détente with the Chinese.

"Amanda, I'm sure at some stage – and I'm betting very soon – they are bound to reveal the true extent of their hidden gold reserves; at which point the markets will implode, if they haven't done so before then. We know how that smarmy bastard at the PBOC, Chen Liu, likes to boast of his brilliance and make theatrical gestures to the press. This will be the easiest and quickest way to let everyone know that they now control the world's financial markets. He doesn't really need to do more than that to trigger panic. Everyone will then be completely aware that the bullion banks can't fulfil their obligations and, unless we are exceptionally careful, there will be rioting in the streets and bricks being hurled through the windows of Number 10. The entire fabric of society is at risk if we don't resolve this soon."

"I've wracked my brains for an alternative solution Dominic, but I can't see one at all. I'll need to get it cleared by Charlie of course, but he's gone completely incommunicado. Silent as the grave; off the grid; quite possibly gone to ground to avoid the flack, who the hell knows? He's not taken a couple of my calls today, so he's clearly pissed-off with me."

"Well you know my views on his level of competence Amanda; its zero. You could always tell him that I said if you took this action....it would be over my dead body. Then he's bound to say yes."

"That's the first laugh I've had all day. You're right, under those circumstances he's certain to say 'go ahead'. Can you make plans for a market shut-down overnight? I'll just check I have the power to do this, but I should also speak with Lewis at the Fed before any buttons get pushed. Given the circumstances, a fully co-ordinated response with the US seems required."

"Leave the details with me Amanda. I'll try and reach Seb to let him know what we are planning before his visit to China. From memory, I think he's scheduled to leave tomorrow night. It's also probably a wise precaution that I get back to you later today with a 'pros-and-cons' paper for the official record: CYA and all that."

"Just on a personal note, Dominic: I trust you're not going to resign anytime soon. David has handed me his early retirement plan and I really don't want another one of you to quit; if you don't mind."

"Dead body it is then Amanda! Chat later."

★ ★ ★

Sebastian was in his apartment making a complete pig's ear of packing his favourite suits and shirts when Lewis' name popped up on his mobile.

"Glad you called Lewis; any idea how to fold shirts? I

presume you're calling about the markets going haywire today?"

"Yeh, we have the same problems here; markets, not shirts! There's a sea of red and blood everywhere, but it's just about containable for the time being. Putting that to one side for the moment, let's move on to more pleasant matters. I just want to let you know a couple of things for your trip which, by-the-by, I'm very disappointed to be missing. You guys get all the luck."

"Why do I get the feeling I'm being set-up here Lewis?"

"Trust me Yul Brynner, it'll be like 'The Return of the Magnificent Seven' when you get to Beijing. No, no, far better, given the amount of gold involved, it's more like 'The Fellowship of the Bling', as your favourite author, Tolkien, may well have put it."

"I don't know whether to groan, or weep, Lewis."

"Thought you'd like that; been practicing it all day! Anyway, back to the business in hand. Top of the guest list is Lyn, she's flying up from Brunei: I'd like you to make a big fuss of her; be seen everywhere, high profile, lots of mingling, that kind of thing. Second, the delectable Naylor, who you met the other evening, will be with you on Thursday. She's linking up with her new best buddy, Alex Cadbury, who's going to deliver a couple of toys for your meeting with Chen Liu the following day. You're all staying at the same hotel, so he'll explain everything in greater details when you meet. But promise me this Seb, do exactly as he says. Follow his instructions to the absolute letter and all will be fine. Fail to do so and we are well and truly buggered, if you'll excuse my French."

"How are you on suits?"

★ ★ ★

As he was prone to do in a crisis, Lewis was silently staring out of his office window at the endless stream of bankers and brokers scurrying along Liberty Street many floors below. His mind was never still under such circumstances as he tried to calculate the odds of the CIA's plan working. The director had assured him that he had completely confidence in the work Alex had undertaken; and he had given a similar assurance in return, promising that Seb could be relied upon to deliver the *coup de grâce* at the appropriate moment.

The issue troubling him, given the enormous sensitivities involved, was how much detail should they disclose to Seb or the others? He was confident that he would have no moral qualms with, say, the first three or four pre-programmed 'events'; they were just to demonstrate the awesome power and reach of Nitro Zeus. But what if matters were forced beyond that and China refused to back down? Just say the number of events ran into double figures, then how would he react?

Maybe he would have to give him a Churchillian 'never in the field of human conflict' rallying cry and, if he didn't know it already, emphasise how the world was teetering on the brink of disaster and he'd better climb aboard the Spitfire, fire up the Merlin engine, throw away the parachute and double check the guns. Or perhaps it was better for all concerned to say nothing at all?

The desk phone's incessant buzzing broke his concentration.

"Amanda, how's tricks? I gather it's getting brutal in London."

"Yes, that's what I wanted to discuss with you. We are planning to shut down the markets tomorrow before it's all too late. We have several banks that look like they are about to go under here. There are some pretty large pigeons coming home to roost I can tell you and I'm not at all confident we can last out the week. I also gather you told Sir David that you had a solution, which was going to be delivered to the PBOC by Seb? Is that correct?"

"In part. If you think it would help, I can declare a market holiday on the COMEX and the Stock Market here."

"Thanks, but what exactly do you mean by 'in part'?"

"Well just imagine Seb as Mercury, the Winged Messenger; the rest is top secret. So please don't worry Amanda; I'm confident that he won't be put in any danger. Well some, but not a lot. You never know with Seb, especially as Lyn will be with him."

"I'm tempted to say something very unladylike Lewis"

"You have my – and my Governments – complete assurance that Seb's trip to Beijing is the only way we can satisfactorily untangle this mess. Admittedly it might just get a tad bracing if he meets undue headwinds and the central bank refuses to capitulate, but I'm reasonably confident they will."

"What does Seb know that the UK government doesn't know?"

"He's absolutely in the dark Amanda, until he gets there. It's best for everyone, trust me."

"Not sure I have much choice. Shall I tell the PM?"

"No, under no circumstances! You know full well why."

"That's a rather odd statement Lewis, if you don't mind me saying so; but I'll let it pass for the time being. So we are agreed, the markets close tomorrow."

★ ★ ★

The port of Dandong, at the mouth of the Yalu River, was shrouded in mist as the Jin-Ton docked, having thankfully completed its perilous journey from Somalia.

In the pecking order of Chinese ports, Dandong was very close to the bottom, but was ideal for General Xiao's clandestine purposes: not only was it his birthplace but his private fiefdom, well away from the preying eyes in Beijing. Here he controlled everyone and everything in town. Or at least he did until a few days ago. Rumours had been circulating that he had mysteriously disappeared, with everyone conjecturing that he had been taken prisoner for somehow double-crossing his country. Any party member who broke the rules, especially someone who ran the Chinese army, would be subjected to the harshest of State disciplines: *shuanggui*, from which no one escaped the physical torture, indescribable brutality, sleep-deprived interrogation and ultimately an agonising death.

It was simply assumed that despite, or quite possibly because of, his exalted position, he had committed the cardinal sin of personal enrichment. Given the modest size of the port facilities, the frantic activity about a week ago had not gone unnoticed. Very few knew what had caused the commotion that night; only a handful witnessed the departure of the ship containing his treasure. For them it was wise to simply forget. Even fewer of his faithfully supporters or close family were left to provide any explanation. All had somehow melted into the summer haze.

So the arrival of countless secret police and armoured trucks from Beijing caused great consternation amongst some of the towns minor functionaries who were still left. All they could do was shrug their shoulders when interrogated by the army officers wanting answers to the address of any other warehouses or storage facilities used by Xiao. It was made very plain indeed that the town, and everyone in it, would be torn limb from limb if the location of so much as one speck of gold was not revealed.

Oblivious to all this, Zucca was in the wheel house bellowing instructions in a mixture of Italian, English and some incomprehensible patois known only to the more long-serving crew members. They were all well practiced at docking the ship in Dandong, having been here on more than one occasion in the past, delivering contraband of every shape, size and weight. All anyone below deck now cared about was being handsomely paid and heading off somewhere very far away and decidedly less salubrious.

Oakes was far less sanguine; fearing that, despite the newly acquired beard, clothes that more-or-less resembled rags and an odour that could down an elephant at twenty paces, he was sure to be picked upon as being distinctly out-of-place. He and Zucca had agreed upon the most flimsy of diversionary tactics should he be spotted, based around a staged fight amongst the crew, involving lots of screaming, shouting, gun shots and general commotion. They hoped that, amidst the pandemonium, he would find a moment to slip away and somehow melt into the town. If by some miracle that could be achieved, then it was agreed that he was to head to the station or airport a couple of miles inland. What would happen then was not entirely clear and should the worst come to the worst, he would have to make his own way home: head due west was the best compass bearing they could come up with.

Lieutenant Qiang had driven up from his office in Beijing and been given command of events when the Jin-Ton docked. He was to distribute the gold bullion to half-a-dozen Politburo members, each of whom had been carefully selected by the deputy governor of the central bank. They were to receive a very substantial contribution to their personal wealth in return for favours yet to be demanded. Banker Chen was intent on using the precious cargo to advance his political aspirations and, very shortly, mount a *coup d'état* against the premier himself.

The plus side to all of this for Qiang was the promise of instant promotion and a modest, but highly appreciated, payoff for himself; the downside was the order to execute Zucca and his crew. For someone who was at heart a junior mandarin, both by temperament and training, he was far from comfortable having this particular blood on his hands. He and Zucca had just finished a major argument regarding his fees which he had to reluctantly relay to his superiors. After endless haggling – and driven by their own greed – the minister had approved the funds transfer, plus the ten percent uplift that Zucca had demanded. They had also confirmed that, before the goods were offloaded, they would forward a bank confirmation to him that the money was indeed in his account.

Needless to say, this was a distinctly hollow promise: the very next instruction they would make to the tame banker running the account, was to return the funds immediately. The only thing that mattered was that Zucca was happy to proceed with the unloading. He and his crew could be discreetly killed later after the gold and contraband were ashore. It would only be weeks later, amidst the financial upheaval affecting their country, that someone realised the money had not been returned, but transferred to an account in Langley.

CHAPTER 32

Nantong

Sanford had been patiently reconnoitring the northern shores of the Yangtze River since five in the morning; his eyes intently focused on every passing ship. The thermometer had already reached 25 centigrade, with the expectation was that it would top 40 before noon. It was going to be very uncomfortable day, in more ways than one.

Moving cautiously in the shadows and flitting warily between the largely empty buildings, he held an automatic pistol in one hand and an old-fashioned torch and map in the other. As befitted his years of military discipline, he had arrived precisely on-schedule at the agreed rendezvous point: some one hundred miles upriver from Shanghai, on the outskirts of the provincial city of Nantong. There he awaited the clandestine arrival of six US Navy Seals.

Silhouetted against the dappled light of daybreak, he could see a vessel drop anchor in mid-river about a mile away and a couple of jet-black ribs quietly being slipped into the gently flowing water. The two teams silently and effortlessly paddled towards him guided by an occasional flash from his torch, leaving the ship empty and its very precious contents effectively abandoned to the Butler and his henchmen. Sometime earlier one of the Navy Seals had initiated a ship-to-shore radio message stating that Xiao's family were about to abandon the vessel and make their own arrangements to flee the country.

It surely would not be long before the Butler's men arrived to claim his prize: Xiao's hoard of gold.

From his CIA headquarters in Langley, Carter Meggs had decreed that once the Navy Seals were ashore, they should immediately be taken into hiding under the temporary command of Reed. He had already secured a safe house close by and quickly organised provisions for a couple of days enforced furlough for the troops. In accordance with the director's explicit orders (and in what was now a running joke throughout the agency, in a collective effort to stop their man in Hong Kong from being shot in the leg once again) this time he would keep his firearm out of harm's way in his shoulder holster and stay well out of trouble. His sole task on this occasion was to act as 'The Good Sheppard' to this most dangerous flock.

Reed and Sanford had met towards midnight in a decidedly down-market bar near the river to discuss how best to extricate General Xiao from under the very noses of the Butler and the State police. The next step would be considerably trickier: to safely and quickly get him to America. Their instructions were to keep the navy team on permanent stand-by; just in case anything should go wrong during the kidnap attempt and Sanford needed more firepower.

By now, Xiao was anxiously expecting the arrival of his three brothers and their extended family. He had been on the run, or in hiding, for what seemed liked weeks and was eagerly anticipating their reunion. This once invincible man now felt exhausted, broken and vulnerable. One of the Butler's flunkies had come to escort him from his squalid apartment and take him to the ship which, he told him, would be arriving in less than an hour. It was made clear, in highly threatening terms, that he was required at the wharf, at gun point if necessary. Intimidation came easily to every member of the *Sun Yee On* triad. Once there, he was to verify that all the cargo was still on board; only then would he be allowed to see his family.

The Butler had yet to explicitly confirm that payment would be made and the prior arrangements fulfilled as promised. But Xiao's room for negotiation was decidedly limited, especially if his adversary had chosen this point to renege on his agreement. In truth however, all he could focus upon was that – in a matter of moments – his family could make their escape together. He still possessed sufficient clarity of thought to appreciate that a successful getaway was going to be exceptionally tricky to pull off; especially as he had been repeatedly told that the Chinese State was dedicating limitless resources to his capture. It could only be a matter of hours before they eventually tracked him down.

True, he had plenty of associates and connections locally, but he was very unsure if he could totally rely upon any of them to help. It was only his instinctive fear of betrayal that had stopped him making contact with them, as yet. Thirty pieces of silver went a long way in Dandong. But whom should he trust? Every day he managed to evade capture he became more beholding to the Butler. He may be dependent upon him for now, but he was at the bottom of the list when it came to placing the wellbeing of his family into his money-grabbing hands.

★ ★ ★

Sanford's nascent escape plan was wholly reliant upon the profound shock about to confront Xiao when his family failed to come ashore. He had to take a calculated risk that this psychological body-blow would leave him open to the suggestion – indeed the absolute necessity – that they flee China together. He had to rapidly convince him that everyone's life was in mortal peril, including his own. Despite being on opposite sides of an ideological divide, on this occasion they were to be brothers in arms.

There was also the small matter of making sure he did not act precipitously: it was vital that he did not obstruct the all-important payment promised to Xiao for the safe delivery of the gold. Whatever was said by the Butler regarding a successfully transfer of the funds, Sanford's job was to persuade Xiao that he was being double-crossed. He had complete faith in the CIA's widely recognised ability to successfully track its movements through the complex underground banking system to be used by the Butler. Then convince Xiao that they would intercept the funds before some corrupt banker felt the need to siphon the money off into their own account.

Over several cold beers the previous evening, Reed and Sanford had painstakingly reviewed the forthcoming operation. Both readily agreed that the timing of the 'snatch' was paramount. The mission's success would be measured by Xiao simply disappearing into thin air. So the plan was to act first, explain later. If at all possible, no one – especially the Chinese security services – should ever know a third party had been involved in his disappearance. As far as the upper echelons of the CIA were concerned, their prime objective was to have the gold safely unloaded and dispersed before the day was out; the distant second was to get Xiao back to America within a couple of days.

Within ten minutes of the Navy Seals safely making it to shore, it was already apparent that smaller boats were circling the abandoned ship and dozens of men were clambering aboard. It would not take them long to get to the wharf, which was no more than a quarter of a mile away. Sanford gave the men his map and directed them to the safe house and Reed's care. He immediately set out on foot to where the ship would dock and waited, unobserved.

★ ★ ★

"Xiao, you have arrived just in time."

The Butler loomed exceedingly large next to the ever frailer and clearly desperate Xiao, who seemed to be functioning only by the indomitable strength of his will. By now the wharf was teeming with countless of his men, all scurrying to off-load the gold bars, make a rudimentary inventory and, with the assistance of numerous fork-lift trucks, transfer it to the awaiting vehicles.

"Where is my money and when do I get to see my family?"

"All in good time general, or should I now call you mister. Firstly, I need you to confirm the amount of gold we have removed was just over 5,500 bars, which is roughly 90 tonnes. I thought you had more, but no matter. The spilt is half for you and half for me. Agreed."

"Agreed."

"There is also the little matter of handing over the incriminating files you hold. It's always very rewarding in my business to be able to expose the innumerable transgressions of our glorious Politburo; blackmail is so effective, don't you concur?"

Xiao simply nodded.

"The files are at the apartment, under the bed, in my rucksack."

"Good, I'll collect those later. You are now a very rich man Xiao. Enjoy the rest of your days. Come to the office and watch me make the transfer."

★ ★ ★

From his vantage point crouched down besides one of the local fishing boats, Sanford could see and hear everything. When he realised the significance of the hidden documents he immediately sent a text to Reed to go and recover them without a moments delay. This would be a totally unexpected prize for the Skulduggery team in Langley and one that, by itself, made the mission worthwhile: even if, for whatever reason, they could not extricate Xiao.

When Xiao and the Butler emerged from the office both were beaming, but for entirely contradictory reasons. The Butler because he knew that he would soon recover the vast sum of money he had just transferred; Xiao because he mistakenly thought his troubles were over. The smiles were to evaporate almost immediately.

"So where are my family? I have done all you required, now release them into my charge and we will be gone."

"Sorry to inform you Xiao, but they have abandoned you. They jumped ship about a couple of hours ago. We have no idea where they are."

"You lying bastard, you've killed them. On the scarred oath of my brothers I'll wipe you and your entire triad from the face of the earth."

The Butler swiftly raised his hand and forcibly struck Xiao, knocking him to the ground, blood profusely pouring from a head wound.

"An empty threat Xiao; one that you are in no position to fulfil."

Turning to one of the myriad of lackeys who were frantically working nearby, tirelessly moving the gold bullion to the various trucks, he said.

"Take him to the river and throw him in. I don't want to see the snivelling wretch ever again."

Sanford knew instinctively that this turn of events was his one opportunity to rescue Xiao, who was very clearly dazed and concussed. He was now being half dragged, half carried, away from the main action. The man responsible effortless slung him over his shoulder and headed for the river front: no one gave a moments further thought to the matter, their concentration was now elsewhere. Half a dozen trucks, accompanied by escort vehicles carrying heavily armed men, were now ready to depart and deliver the gold to the chosen few. The endless bellowing of orders and flamboyant waving of hands proved just the distraction Sanford needed. It didn't take him long to catch up with Xiao and his captor.

With one well practiced blow the man was dead. Sanford immediately switched jackets between the hapless flunky and Xiao; then effortlessly threw the scumbag into the river. If they were lucky, anyone who found him would examine the clothes and form the conclusion that Xiao was dead.

Confused and decidedly befuddled, Xiao was in no fit state to resist or indeed to comprehend what had just happened. Sanford just put a finger to his lips imploring him to be silent. It took them about twenty minutes to make it back to the safe house.

Reed arrived about ten minutes later with the rucksack containing the bundle of papers, photographs and videos, and immediately started transmitting them to CIA headquarters.

"How's Xiao, General?"

"Disorientated. I've left one of the guys, you know, the one who speaks the language, to stay with him until I can explain what has happened. They probably already know, but can you make your boys aware that the funds transfer was made. I'd like to be able to tell Xiao that we have it under our control."

"Sure thing. When do we leave?"

"Let's give Xiao an hour or two. We can drive to Shanghai and then get him and the boys smuggled onto a UPS cargo plane to New York. Leaves at midnight, so we have plenty of time. We'll then hot-foot it to Beijing."

"Great, can you just make sure the official mission report says I didn't get shot?"

"Plenty of time for that Reed; tell the men to get ready to leave at 1800."

CHAPTER 33

London & Dandong

Charlie Sheer's afternoon had been extremely fraught and was about to get a lot worse. Once the Number 11 press office had released its briefing that they intended to close the markets on Tuesday, it was inevitable that he would be dragged into countless media interviews and meetings. Through gritted teeth he had little option but to defend his chancellor, knowing that at any moment he would be getting confirmation of her treachery.

It was with some relief that five o'clock was approaching and he could take his tie off and at last have a drink. His guest, if that was the correct term, was the always debonair chairman of Barclays Bank. Given the still unexplained request for an urgent appointment he felt he better be on his guard; especially against the never-ending barrage of dubious flattery that would no doubt accompany the visit. In Sheer's view, here was a man who took obsequiousness to another level.

"Lord McMullan to see you Prime Minister; he's by himself."

"Thanks Nadia, show him in. No calls for thirty minutes please; then buzz me."

"Whisky, with ice if I remember correctly?"

"Thank you Prime Minister, what a remarkable memory you have. I know you're very busy, so thank you for seeing me. With the way events are going out there I'm sure you'll be called upon at any moment to provide your 'things are totally under control' bravura piece for the six o'clock news. So if I may, I'll get straight to the point."

McMullan took the proffered drink and calmly sat down. It had been just over two years since they had briefly met for the first time, under very perplexing circumstances. He had just been appointed as deputy chairman and was still to find his feet within the organisation, having been headhunted from an American bank in rather rapid order. Although he wasn't directly involved – and indeed had been deliberately kept out of the picture – he was aware of certain very strange events within the bank that everyone involved refused to confirm or deny.

Rumours eventually reached him that Barclays had been forced by Charlie Sheer, who was then the chancellor, to unwind the late John d'Abo's shorting of the dollar and destroy the evidence that it ever took place. The cover-up had been successful and, such are the vagaries of banking, he was the only person still left in the organisation to know anything about it. It was very quickly after the two of them first meet that he was elevated to the chairmanship, as his predecessor left 'to pursue other interests'. It was time to call in the chip, although he was very unsure of its value.

"I'm sure I don't need to make you aware Prime Minister that my bank is in a very parlous state indeed and we could go under at any moment. Our bullion desk is generating stupendous losses which we cannot sustain beyond a couple more days, at best. While my board is in complete agreement with your decision to close the markets, we desperately need a significant injection of liquidity and equity capital otherwise we will be forced to close. The consequences of which will be unimaginable, horrendous."

"You'll just have to stomach the losses and take your turn in the queue like everyone else. Amanda and the Bank's governor are attending to all the technicalities."

"But we're not exactly 'everyone else' though, are we Prime Minister? There is the little matter of the rumours surrounding the d'Abo currency swap that senior parties within my bank have covered up for you. I think it's time to return the favour."

"You're not trying to blackmail me are you, McMullan? That's never a wise option; people have lost their balls for less."

"I would never dream of doing such a thing Prime Minister. In the banking profession we call it reciprocity. I continue to keep quiet; in return you help my bank. Everyone's happy."

"I think its best you leave before I really lose my temper. And McMullan, if you don't want the boys crawling all over your office, your personal life, your dubious offshore tax arrangements; then you had better forget this meeting ever happened. Is that crystal clear?"

"As you wish Prime Minister; I'll bid you good day."

★ ★ ★

Within moments of getting into his chauffer driven car, Lord McMullan had decided it was time he made a call to Amanda Price. They had a very amicable working relationship, met socially on frequent occasions when he had made numerous public references to her incisive mind, which she liked enormously. Flattery came easily to him, buttering-up gullible clients was his hall mark. However, it was clearly too late to try such an approach on the prime minister: time for a different approach.

He was remarkably unruffled despite the bad-tempered rebuff; but the future of his bank was at stake, so a little bruised ego was a small price to pay. The question was, how best to play it with the chancellor? What possible inducement could he offer her in return for giving him a helping hand?

"Chancellor, its Harvey McMullan here. Can I have ten minutes of your valuable time today? It's very important, otherwise I wouldn't have asked. An 'off-site' meeting possibly? I know there's a late night division, 10 o'clock from memory. How about supper before or a drink afterwards?"

"Harvey, you're not trying to use your legendary powers of persuasion and ask me to keep the markets open tomorrow?"

"Not at all, *au contraire* Chancellor, we desperately need a breathing space from the relentless losses we are incurring. It's just that I've had a bit of a bruising encounter with the PM which I need to discuss with you. I'm beginning to feel that he's not quite *compos mentis* if you follow my drift. You don't think it's all getting a bit too much for him, do you?"

"Fascinating. It would be extremely disloyal of me to comment on Charlie's state of mind, however bonkers he's becoming. Most unlike you to fall out with anyone Harvey: it must have been serious. OK, look, let's get together for a drink; there's someone I'd very much like you to meet and something I'd like you to do: on the QT, of course. A spot of mutual back scratching may be called for? Shall we say 10.30 tonight? I'll text you the location when I've confirmed availabilities and so forth."

★ ★ ★

After a couple of hours of unwelcome toil in stifling humidity, the crew of the Jin-Ton had at long last finished offloading the gold; all that remained in the hold were the crates of drugs, armaments and goodness knows what else they still had to remove. Oakes was endeavouring to keep a low profile on the bridge when Lieutenant Qiang and a couple of army officers approached Zucca on the quayside.

"Captain, my superiors wish to formally thank you for the tireless work you have undertaken for our country over the years. My men here will shortly distribute the crews' wages and arrange for them to be taken to the airport, or into town if they prefer. I have instructions to make the agreed transfer to you once the cargo has been safely put onto the waiting trucks. So as that is now completed, here is your record of the transfer to your personal account. You are also most welcome to attend a function in your honour this evening."

"No thanks Qiang. I'm on the first flight out to anywhere now I've been paid."

"We insist. It will be my honour to collect you at six, bring your second in command; I'd very much like to meet him."

Zucca looked up to the bridge and caught the eye of Oakes, who was listening intently: the impression on both their faces screamed, this is a trap. In very short order the trucks had evaporated into the city of Dandong and from there to the State bullion vaults, minus the various 'allocations' to the great, the good and the corruptible. Zucca bound up the gangplank and shouted that his friend should join him in his cabin.

"Oaksey, grab your gear, we're leaving. There is no doubt we are being set up. Can you use your influence to check if this transfer has actually been made; and then figure out how the hell we are going to get out of here alive?"

"Got that Cap. We can't use the radio; it's bound to be monitored by Qiang and his team. The only thing I can do is use the mobile phone they gave me which has only one number on it, for emergencies. Christ knows who I will get through to? It's a risk, but one I think we should take. It's under my bunk, shall I get it?"

"Pronto, mon ami, pronto."

Oakes dashed below and made the call. Within the space of one ring it was answered.

"What took you so long Sergeant? I think I need to get you down to the gym for a long overdue workout. I have 'eyes on' Zucca and have been tracking your progress for several days now. We have very few options available for your escape; the airport is crawling with security guys, so I'm going to take you a couple of miles north to the Freedom Bridge, linking China to North Korea. Every tourist to these parts hires a speedboat to look at the crazy guys across the river, so we should be able to blend in. So for pity's sake make sure you both wear something that's been washed in the last month."

"Bloody hell, you're a woman?"

"That's right soldier; names Sapphire, Special Ops; colleague of Jim Sanford. Get off the Jin-Ton immediately and head four or five hundred yards along the main road; red building on the left. I'll meet you both there in ten minutes."

★ ★ ★

Cressida Armstrong had become accustomed to receiving calls at all times of the day and night, more often than not at inconvenient moments. It just went with the job and required the constitution of an ox, the capacity to drink anyone and everyone under the table, live on no sleep, yet somehow remember the story whenever she got back to the newspaper's office. She was dining out with one of her more reliable 'deep throat' sources and thoroughly enjoying the salacious gossip, delicious tittle-tattle and a surprising litany of who in the cabinet was sleeping with whom, when her mobile went.

"Amanda darling, how nice to hear from you! The world's going to hell in a hand-basket and you choose me to chat to. I presume you're calling to tell me that you're heading into hiding somewhere in the South Pacific, I hear Bali Hai is terrific at this time of year?"

"Ah Cressida you rogue, you do say the most delightful things. But you're more than welcome to accompany me when this is all over. No, I wanted to meet later, say 10.30 at your house. I'd like you to meet Lord McMullan; top man at Barclays, we have some business to transact that you will be extremely interested in. Part two of the Charlie dossier."

"Now that has caught my attention. Pity I'll have to leave here early, it's all getting very juicy. Did you know that your chum Patrick was sleeping with that brazen, mini-skirted hussy from the Foreign Office, Rachel what's-her-name? ... no, neither did I, can't stand either of them...yep, it will indeed end in tears. See you later. Kisses."

★ ★ ★

"Oakes, over here! Get in the car and keep your heads down till we clear the harbour. Good to meet you Captain Zucca. We have a twenty minute drive then we hire a speed boat and go hell for leather down river to Dalu Island. I've got some very reliable friends there. We'll go into hiding till the marines come and get us in a couple of day's time. By the way Zucca, my friends at head office tell me that your money was indeed transferred. I gather by some unfathomable sleight-of-hand its now safely languishing in one of our government accounts ready for you to collect."

"Good. Any news of my crew, Sapphire?"

"Not yet, but we have spies in most of the bars, so they are bound to turn up eventually."

"Are all American agents, what do you say, such glamour-pussies; or do we get first pick?"

"It's pusses. Conserve your strength for those Tuscan signorina's Zucca or you'll be in for a fifty-click swim with rather a lot of concrete in your shoes."

CHAPTER 34

London, Beijing & Nantong

Cressida's apartment in Sloane Square was a strange mixture of styles: more mid-town Manhattan than Chelsea; more Degas than Hockney; and certainly more Absinthe than best Yorkshire bitter. She had acquired the trappings and fripperies of wealth via a mixture of inheritance and mind-bogglingly large share options in the global TV and media empire that owned her paper; while the aphrodisiac of power seemed to have oozed effortlessly from her every pore for years. Fawning at her feet was the default position adopted by every politician she met, with one exception: Charlie Sheer. The loathing was mutual. The PM had been on the receiving end of many of her poisonous headlines recently, courtesy of the constant drip-feed of salacious gossip from her secret paramour, the chancellor of the exchequer.

She had not met the highly persuasive and debonair Lord McMullan before, so was delighted to have a chance to privately quiz one of the City's most influential figures. Her interest was especially peaked, given the increasing likelihood that there could be riots in the streets at any moment. If the rumours swirling around the City were to be believed, many of the banks, especially his, were on the verge of falling like dominos. The headlines were already forming in her mind ('Silver-tongued city-slicker McMullan confirms his humiliating resignation in late night confessional with the editor') as she rapidly made plans to move her funds to Switzerland and cash-out her share options.

"Cressida, this is Harvey McMullan."

"Strange we've never been introduced before; to what do I owe this vicarious pleasure, Amanda? Always assuming it is to be a pleasure? Champagne? Or something stronger?"

"Probably both; and in the same glass! I thought we could have a very mutually beneficial conversation, away from preying eyes. I'm sure you don't need me to tell you that Harvey's bank is in desperate need of help from the Treasury. Well, as the PM won't intervene, I'm very happy to make a special concession to him, on one proviso."

McMullan's countenance switched from one of utter despair – at the ease with which the chancellor could disclose the problems at his bank – to a broad smile that indicated he may, after-all, be saved from public humiliation and shame. The unspoken question on the lips of any banker seeking assistance in the midst of this maelstrom, however, was: how much is this going to cost me; and why, of all people, am I meeting with the editor of the most notorious red-top newspaper in the world and not the far more fitting, pink-paged, Financial Times? Usually never lost for words, he almost spluttered.

"What are you proposing Amanda?"

"It's very simple really. Your perfectly reasonable pleadings for much needed help have been rejected out-of-hand by our glorious leader. Who knows, you may even feel that your honour as a distinguished peer of the realm has been traduced, if that's the correct phrase. So I'm giving you the opportunity to redress the balance."

"I wouldn't go that far, but he's certainly off the Christmas card list. What exactly do you have in mind?"

"Cressida, you recall the item certain parties have been asking you to consider publishing?"

"Yes of course; but I still haven't been able to verify whether the coroner's report on John d'Abo's death has been fabricated. It's going to be very awkward for me to run it without that?"

"Take a chance; it'll sure cause a hell of a ruckus but the story which follows will get you the Pulitzer Prize."

McMullan sat there in stunned silence before voicing his deep unease.

"Are you two in some kind of conspiracy to dethrone the Prime Minister?"

"Well Harvey, you yourself said he's lost control of his mind and by inference, the country. We just happen to wholeheartedly agree. If he'd simply gone stark raving mad, well, we could somehow deal with that: official channels and procedures, that sort of thing. It's just that we're in the midst of a major world crisis and he's bunkered down in Number 10, fiddling while Rome burns, refusing to do anything. He has to go. But you don't need me to tell you that he won't go voluntarily, so he has to be pushed, very firmly."

They all drew a collective breath and, as if as one, drank a copious slug of whatever green liquid Cressida had placed before them.

"So, to put it in bankerese, Harvey: here's the deal. I will save your beloved institution by putting unlimited resources behind it; plus I'll make immediate arrangements for my Asian contacts to commit to a major equity injection to preserve your dwindling capital ratios. Just tell me how much you need sometime tomorrow and you can announce it on Friday. Guaranteed."

"And the inevitable *quid pro quo*?"

"Easiest thing in the world old chap…"

She slid an envelope across the coffee table.

"When you've read this, and agreed to proceed, I suggest you take your pick of any number of justifications. A spot of 'blame your predecessor' always goes down well; or perhaps the more cavalier, 'nothing to do with me, Gov'; and, if all else fails, 'not on my watch, pal'. Put simply, I would just like you to leak the contents of this ticking time-bomb to your new best friend Cressida here. Naturally, it didn't come from me; you just happened to come across it at the bank while having some old files reviewed."

Harvey McMullan gingerly opened the envelope and recognised the Treasury's letterhead immediately, marked at the top 'strictly private and confidential'. It was devastating in its simplicity. He began reading as the room was swathed in complete silence. Here was Charlie Sheer, in his previous capacity as chancellor, approving an unsecured £50 million pound Treasury loan to Sir John d'Abo's bank. It was dated just before the Dark Pools crisis and only a few days before his death. His flamboyant signature was as plain as a pikestaff; undeniably and irrefutably his. The letter went on to indicate that this loan facility was a matter of national security; it was not to be disclosed to any person whatsoever."

He put the first letter down on the table with the simple statement, "Astounding".

The second document was even more damning: an original, internal memo, circulated by the previous chairman of Barclays to three of his senior colleagues. It was a formal record of a conversation between one of the managing directors in the High Net Worth department of the bank and John d'Abo. It was in respect of a transfer of £50 million pounds from his bank to, of all things, his personal account at Barclays. The document was stark in its recoding of events: the bank was being instructed to use the loan to 'short-sell' sterling, which the senior foreign exchange trader had initially queried as illogical, but as a matter of established bank protocol, he was obligated to carry out his client's request.

"I can't quite believe what I'm reading here Amanda. I think it's probably best that I don't ask how you came by these documents. They clearly imply that d'Abo used the Treasury's money for personal gain?"

The third document was another internal record of a conversation between the then chancellor and the bank's then chairman. It was explicit and unambiguous in its demand: the bank was to immediately reverse the transaction, send the money back to the Treasury and destroy all traces of its occurrence.

"I'm dumbfounded, flabbergasted, utterly – if you'll excuse the phrase – gobsmacked Amanda. I've never been made aware of any of this; and certainly never been privy to black-and-white evidence, although there were endless unsubstantiated rumours swirling around at the time. If it's correct, it's verging on treachery by d'Abo and utterly irresponsible and reckless by Sheer. No wonder he wanted this covering up."

He paused momentarily, before rapidly collecting his troubled thoughts.

"Just a minute Cressida, didn't The Sun run a piece a couple of weeks ago suggesting that d'Abo had not died of a heart attack?"

"Indeed, we surreptitiously obtained a copy of the original coroner's report, before the heavily revised version was officially issued. It clearly stated: 'death by gunshot wounds'. That's why we ran the standard story of another 'government cover-up': all this baloney about him having a heart attack, it's just nonsense."

"Ladies, are you seriously trying to tell me that Sheer was somehow directly responsible for d'Abo's death and this paper-trail proves he was trying to cover-up his misdeeds?"

Amanda looked across at Cressida, implicitly seeking her support for what she said next.

"We both believe that to be correct Harvey. You're here because I need you to be the origin of the story. I can't put my name to it, but you can simply let the world know how astounded and shocked you are to have found these documents at the back of your safe."

"But you're asking me to commit yet another misdeed on behalf of the bank."

"Quite the contrary, I'm asking you to single-handedly save the country. If we don't get a firm grip of events we will shortly have nothing to save."

"Let me collect my thoughts for a moment please."

McMullan stood up and paced the room, staring blankly at the paintings and the very expensive *objet d'art* in every corner and on every surface.

"I thought this Manet was in a French museum Cressida? Olympia isn't it? I have to say there are an awful lot of naked women on your walls."

"The chief executive of the d'Orsay lets me look after it every now and then. In return I agree not to publish the deliciously sordid details of the *ménage à quatre* he seems to be embroiled in."

His mood and demeanour visibly changed with each step as he carefully weighted the consequences of the options he now faced. Taking a deep breath, he spoke like a man about to go into battle at Agincourt.

"OK, for the good of the country, I'll do it. I just hope to Christ that I haven't triggered an avalanche here. On the other pressing matter Amanda; you'll have my numbers on the size of the equity injection needed for the bank by mid morning tomorrow. So what do we do next Cressida?"

"Excellent. I'll get everyone a top-up to celebrate. It's too late for today's edition, but we will publish and be damned on Thursday."

The three co-conspirators said a fond goodbye on the steps of the apartment block, little realising that one of ex-chief constable Robert Simpson's trusted photographers had them captured for all to see in a warm embrace. Within minutes the digital image would be with the prime minister, with a note from Simpson: 'What do you make of this?'

★ ★ ★

The recently appointed minister for the Chinese army was relaxing in his grace-and-favour house in one of the more exclusive parts of Beijing, when he received a call from Lieutenant Qiang.

"Minister, the various allocations of bullion are now in transit as instructed, with the residue en route to the nearest central bank vault."

"Qiang, just make sure you email me a precise list of the names of every beneficiary and the amount of gold each has received. I want it to be delivered to my personal inbox by tomorrow and passed to the central bank for their records."

The lieutenant deliberately chose not to disclose that Zucca and his crew were neither in custody, nor had they been 'eliminated' as instructed. To him they were inconsequential pawns in the game, even if it meant defying a direct order. It was one thing to benefit personally from his part in the corrupt events he had just witnessed; but he vowed there would be no blood on his hands. With his modest, but most welcome, gold allocation safely stored in his car boot he now had every intention to simply vanish.

★ ★ ★

Three hundred miles south in Dandong, the motley crew of Sanford, Reed, the six Navy Seals and a reinvigorated General Xiao were making their way unobserved to Shanghai airport. Their destination: the commercial air terminal run by the freight company, UPS, and the midnight departure for New York. The backroom boys in the CIA had often called upon their services to carry one or two 'precious little extras', as they delicately put it.

"OK Reed, now that Xiao is safely on his way, it's time you and I made an appearance at the big shindig in Beijing. How is the limp these days?"

CHAPTER 35

London & Beijing

It was exceptionally rare for Sebastian to feel uneasy about the outcome of a foreign business trip, for one very simple reason: they were always meticulously planned by his excellent support staff at d'Abo's Bank. It was taken for granted that he would be very well briefed on the trip's exact purpose, the client's objectives and constraints, and the precise details of the transaction he was engaged in. His journey to Beijing was due to commence later that evening and the absence of a meeting schedule was already playing on his mind as he entered the hallowed portals of the Bank of England. Over the past couple of days the personnel department had allocated him an extremely impressive office in his capacity as the new deputy governor for Special Projects and bit-by-bit he was beginning to feel more at home. A large, highly polished, desk with a delightful photograph of Lyn on it didn't decrease the queasiness in the pit of his stomach however.

Sir David Stone and Professor Dominic Carrington had asked to see him before he headed to the airport to have a last minute chit-chat. As he entered the room they were deep in conversation about the closure earlier that day of the London gold market.

"Afternoon gentlemen; I'm really hoping your respective teams have managed to prepare a briefcase full of notes for my trip and some sort of agenda? I spoke to Lewis earlier and he said that Alex Cadbury would be meeting me at the hotel, which is excellent news. He also said that he would be arriving with, and I quote, a 'super-cool, knock-em-dead, doobrey-ferker' for me to use. When I enquired what in God's name that meant, he just said, 'some very, underline very, special equipment'. In typical Lewis fashion he was decidedly vague as to what the hell would then happen. I also gather there is going to be a cast of thousands to look after my wellbeing, which tends to suggest that my liberty, and quite possibly my dangly bits, may be on the line here?"

The governor looked up from his papers, smiled nervously, raised his eyes heavenward and shrugged his shoulders.

"For Queen and country Seb; yours but to do and die; and all that. Show Johnnie-foreigner what's what, organise the community singing as the ship goes down, you know the sort of thing. You're going to love it. Just the man for the job, eh Dominic?"

"I'm not sure that even Seb's charm, audacity and bravado will cut it, Governor, but in the circumstances we are obliged to live in hope. Better fill him in with what little we know."

"Seb, the closure of the markets have stemmed the tide of losses for the bullion banks but this is just a temporary respite, by next week they may well all be bust. Added to which, in a re-run of Northern Rock, the cash machines are haemorrhaging notes as people lose faith, yet again, in the banking system. Sterling is plummeting and I've got the Royal Mint printing money like there is no tomorrow, which there may well not be. And to top it all, the Shanghai Gold Exchange is like the bloody cat that got the cream, it's still functioning and the price of physical is going through the proverbial roof. You've got to firmly, but politely, tell the Chinese to back off before this comes to blows. I'm told that the US military has been put on red alert, or whatever it is these chaps say. Other than Her Majesty sending in a clapped-out gunboat there is precious little we can do from this office. Lewis has repeatedly told me that he has something up his sleeve, but what it is; well to be perfectly frank, I have absolutely no idea. Last thing he said to me was, 'the fight's got to be won before you enter the ring'. I'm at a complete loss as to what he means."

"So, is that the full extent of the good news? Bit bleak wouldn't you say? Do we know as yet who I have the pleasure of meeting and what am I authorised to say and do?"

"For protocol's sake you are meeting with the PBOC's Chen Liu, he's the same rank as you, deputy governor. But take great heed of Henry VIII's very appropriate comments on Cromwell: 'he's as cunning as a bag of serpents'. So choose every word carefully, or it will be turned against you and splashed all over the local press within five minutes. Our diplomatic sources suggest that he is secretly vying to usurp the Chinese premiership, by fair means or foul. So in their opinion he thinks the gold crisis is his ticket to the top. It follows that Chen is not going to be easily dissuaded from whatever course of tyrannical madness he is embarked upon. Lewis probably won't be there to help apparently, but he's sending Naylor in his place."

"What a strange choice David, I thought she was a cyber-expert and computer wizard?"

"God knows what she is? MI6 were a bit sniffy when I made enquiries of her. As to what you say and do; to be perfectly candid, we are bereft of advice."

"Not much of a hand, wouldn't you say? Anything from our beloved leaders, Amanda or Charlie?"

"Between us girls Seb, I don't think the government will last out the week, and in all probability neither will Dominic or I. There is utter turmoil in Downing Street and I'm told the atmosphere between them is utterly poisonous. It goes without saying that Amanda is in constant contact, especially in respect of keeping the clearing bank system functioning. But, the prime minister is strangely absent from the fray. I've asked to see him twice today. Some Downing Street apparatchik keeps repeating that there's nothing available in his calendar apparently. And he refuses point blank to meet with Dominic to review the unfolding situation. My colleagues say that the personal animosity between the two of them – from his side – seems to be burning the PM up inside."

"In the present fraught circumstances David, a domestic squabble is the last thing any of us need. Anyway, that's a matter for you gentlemen to amicably resolve. I'll call you from the Middle Kingdom tomorrow."

His two weary colleagues simply nodded.

"All I can say chaps, by way of injecting a much needed spot of levity into the proceedings, is thank goodness we are not taking to the field against the Upper and Lower Kingdoms as well. Otherwise we'd be totally doomed."

"Hope to see you in one piece at the final whistle with the cup in hand! We need a victory Seb, by any means you can conjure up. If there are further developments here Dominic or I will be in touch straight away."

★ ★ ★

The plane carrying Sanford and Reed landed at Beijing International Airport late Wednesday evening. As they got into the waiting 'Company' limousine, looking somewhat bedraggled it must be said, Reed was handed a note from one of his local CIA colleagues.

"General, apparently the meeting between Sebastian and Banker Chen's entourage had been scheduled for Friday morning. I believe Seb gets in first thing tomorrow so the boys here have made arrangements to pick him up and bring him to the hotel. I'm also guessing that Naylor and Cadbury arrive at some ungodly hour tomorrow from New York; and I'm pretty sure Lyn is already here and Sapphire is en route. Everyone is booked into the Rosewood. I'm a little concerned that because we are all in one place, we may have a security issue on our hands. What do you think?"

"I'm not worried at the moment. I don't think it would matter where we all stayed, we will be under constant surveillance every minute we are here. Besides which, for the time being this is all politics, diplomacy and economics. The shooting only starts if, and when, it goes wrong."

★ ★ ★

The prime minister was restlessly pacing his office, very large whisky in one hand, staring intently at the incriminating photograph which he was gradually crushing in the other. If his chancellor and some scurrilous newspaper editor were in cahoots, then this could explain all the unattributable leaks over the past six month. The inclusion of McMullan merely made him further enraged, especially given that he had more or less thrown him out of his office only the other day. Perhaps the man from Barclays Bank was intent on wreaking some sort of perverse revenge?

There was no doubt about it, in his increasingly paranoid mind, his authority was at stake and his government in jeopardy: he had to decide what action to take and quickly. Over the past hour he had taken an extensive phone call from his new eyes-and-ears, Simpson, to review what else he had established, but the ex-copper had little to add. The only option he felt was available to him was to have the security services put Amanda Price under personal scrutiny, but if she somehow found out there would be justifiable outrage. He refilled his glass, stared blankly into the far distance and concluded he had no option. It could hardly make the current crisis any worse and, if true, he had a readymade culprit for the present turmoil: she had taken her eye off the ball in an act of self-aggrandisement, just at the moment the country needed her full attention. He brought the bottle over to the desk and picked up the phone.

"Nadia, get in touch with the head of MI5 and have her here within the hour."

★ ★ ★

Lyn gleefully checked into the super-swish Rosewood Hotel and, in a first for her, proceeded to supervise the placement of the newly acquired, outrageously expensive, outfits and decidedly flimsy accoutrements into the cavernous closets. The duty manager at the check-in desk had graciously informed her that her companion, 'The most honourable Mr. Fortes', was scheduled to arrive tomorrow, sometime around breakfast. He also handed her an official envelope with a US Embassy seal on it, addressed to 'Sebastian Fortes, Deputy Governor, Bank of England', which she immediately knew had been previously opened and clumsily resealed.

She patiently waited until her room was finally empty of the countless maids and bag-carriers before she decided it was appropriate to read it, despite it not being addressed to her. Lyn examined the enclosed letter in growing astonishment, delight, then disbelief.

> '*Dear Deputy Governor Fortes,*
>
> *On behalf of Mr Lewis Moyns, Chairman of the US Federal Reserve, we have great pleasure to request your presence at a formal ball to be held at the Embassy at 8pm on Thursday evening. Your companion, Major Lyn Andrews, is also requested to accompany you.*
>
> *In respect of your strategically important meeting with Chen Liu of the PBOC: this has been confirmed for 10am, Friday. There is only one item on the agenda – namely, that China immediately withdraws its wholly unwarranted assault*

on the gold market, or you are to inform them on behalf of my government that very grave consequences will immediately follow.

Yours, respectfully,

Bill Coultard, US Ambassador, China.'

Why on earth, she wondered out loud, had someone chosen to add the incendiary last sentence; knowing full well this letter would be intercepted. Was it a spectacular deception from Lewis, or possibly by General Sanford? Or an empty gesture? Or perhaps some form of opening gambit to draw the enemy out before the main event? Mystified, she shrugged her shoulders and reflected that they certainly don't teach you this stuff at West Point.

The envelope was soon re-sealed and a short note written on the back for Seb to see when he arrived:

'Darling, given where this came from, I hope you don't mind that I have opened it? I thought it may be important... and although formal balls are rarely, if ever, on my army roster, I'm game to fool around with yours anytime!'

CHAPTER 36

Dalu Island, Beijing & London

Sapphire was in no mood to slacken the relentless pace of their escape as she endeavoured to re-establish some form, any form, of military discipline amongst her distinctly motley crew of two. Apart from a particularly choppy ride, their getaway from Dandong was largely event free and hopefully undetected. They had hidden their motorboat in one of the endless, unpopulated, coves along the southern most shores of Dalu Island to consider the next phase of their return to the mission. By one of life's wonderful coincidences, it was odd, but not unusual, for a Japanese helicopter carrier to be so far north in the Yellow Sea. It had just paid a symbolic, flag-waving, visit to Beijing to yet-again dampen down tensions in the South China Sea. At 816 feet long, the Izumo was the pride of the Japanese fleet and perfect for what she had in mind. Time to call in a favour.

"OK you fat knacker, time to get fit again! We'll start with a 20k run, 100 pound pack, mid-day sun, what could possibly go wrong, eh Oakes? And Zucca, you idle bastard, sober up and get ready to leave. I've arranged for my Tokyo chums to pick us up by helicopter at 0800 tomorrow. So, let's get back in business guys: we can't have Major Andrews drumming Oakes out of the Special Forces Corps; time to sweat off a few pounds and lose that spare tyre."

"For pity's sake Sapphire, be gentle with me. I was only following the boss's explicit orders: blend in with the crew; go native; try the local delicacies. Zucca has plied me with 100% proof grappa morning, noon and night since I volunteered; it's sapped my will to live."

"Oakes, stop bloody whining. I'm certain your list of duties didn't encompass splicing the mainbrace at every opportunity. Get your fatigues on. Target time for our little jaunt: let's make it one hour fifteen. Let's go Sergeant; I'm about to show you what being on the lash really means!"

★ ★ ★

Banker Chen was staring blankly into space deliberating on how best to respond to an entirely unexpected, hand-delivered, invitation to attend a black tie ball at the US Embassy, scheduled for tomorrow evening. His mind was spinning with the question why, and more importantly, why now? The hidden motives behind such a formal request deeply worried him. This type of thing had never happened before in his thirty-odd years working at the central bank? Troublingly, such an engagement would be on the eve of what was almost certainly to be a tumultuous meeting with Sebastian Fortes? It cannot be a coincidence he reasoned. If he allowed his stupendous ego to lead the internal debate he was having, then perhaps this was, at long last, an official recognition that the Americans thought he was a man to be courted, flattered and charmed? A man of the future, a man to be reckoned with? On the other hand, it could be a cunning Yankee trick to publically compromise him, especially if no one else had been invited from within the senior echelons of the Politburo? He tried desperately to rationalise the conflicting thoughts and make a decision.

Chen regarded his palatial office as a place of Zen-like tranquillity. Here he could silently meditate, conspire with the gods and plot his inexorable progress to becoming Head of State. Over the years he had morphed into a toxic mixture of Buddha, Confucius and Machiavelli, which made him an exceptionally dangerous man when cornered. No one knew which personality would prevail at any moment in time; in all likelihood, neither did he. Such was the paucity of friends, family or colleagues – all sacrificed to the unremitting goal of attaining the Premiership – there was no one left to discuss such issues with. His ego, as was so often the case, prevailed. He would go.

★ ★ ★

Sanford and Reed checked into their rooms at the Rosewood Hotel and immediately tried to locate Lyn. They had just received notification from local intelligence sources that Chen had absolutely no intention of yielding to US or UK pressure in the ensuing discussions. Indeed, their man on the ground said Chen was hell bent on closing out China's calamitous positions in the gold market at any moment or, at the latest, on Monday next week and wreaking havoc, whatever the consequences for the western banking system.

"Lyn, Sanford here. When does Fortes get here and have you had any contact with either Cadbury or Naylor?"

"Seb arrives just after lunch today, Sir. As for the others, I've not been informed."

"Understood. OK, we're going to have a couple of hour's shut-eye and freshen-up. If there is any contact let me know immediately. We also need to talk about tonight's ball when everyone shows up."

Lyn's mood was a mixture of happiness and anticipation at seeing Seb again, counterbalanced by a deep seated, intuitive concern that something terrible was about to unfold. It had been made crystal clear by Sanford that she was not to carry a firearm at any point during her stay in China. However, the idea of being brought all this way merely to become a decorative, arm-candy trinket was completely anathema to her. The army had poured limitless resources into her Special Ops training and she was damned if she was not going to listen to her inner voice. She would talk to Reed, he could solve her problem.

★ ★ ★

About a dozen senior representatives from the London-based bullion banks had just finished a very fractious two hour meeting with their chairman, Dominic Carrington, and were now spilling out of the Royal Exchange building located in the heart of the city of London. The increasingly weary professor had made it abundantly clear that the prospects of a resolution to the crisis were remote in the extreme. Indeed, he expressed the view that, barring a miracle, it would be game-over for them all next week. By a show of hands – and to a man – they accepted his promise to resign. Drained and dejected, Carrington crossed Threadneedle Street to meet the governor.

"Hi David, fancy an early lunch? Sorry to inform you, but I've totally lost the confidence of my members and am left with little choice but to quit, go back to the university laboratories next week and play with my pipettes. Is there any possibility at all that we can get more central banks to provide physical gold from their reserves?"

"No, afraid not Dominic; absolute non-starter I'm sorry to tell you. I've been calling everyone. They are developing a siege mentality and holding tight to whatever gold they have left in what is unquestionably a futile attempt to save their own skins."

"Bugger. Better make it a liquid lunch then. Grab your coat, I'm paying. We'll go to the Shard and toss a coin for who jumps first. Changing the subject temporarily, anything new from Lewis? I just can't figure that guy out at all. He's chosen to miss the biggest and most important event of this whole unsavoury mess. I assume he's clambering to the top of the Freedom

Tower, contemplating Boot Hill and which of his Sunday-best cowboy attire to wear?"

★ ★ ★

"The Director-General of MI5 to see you Prime Minister. Oh, and the Home Secretary will be here in about twenty minutes."

"Thanks Nadia, show her in and then have Martin see me straight afterwards."

Emma Clarke was exceptionally glamorous for one of Britain's top security chiefs and a million miles away from the dowdy image of 'Control' portrayed in the spy novels. A lifetime's career in the 'Box', as MI5 was colloquially called, had not dampened her penchant for rather short skirts and risqué tops.

At her confirmation hearing before the Parliamentary committee scrutinising her appointment five years ago, she rationalised the matter thus: "I find my choice of clothing helps to put the miscreants off their stride, they quickly lose focus, then generally confess without the need for water boarding, that sort of thing". There was not one dissenting vote amongst the all-male selection board. Behind this elegant facade however, was a heart as cold as ice and a mind with the strength of tempered steel: Charlie Sheer adored her!

"Morning Emma, good to see you're still smiling in these troubling times. On second thoughts, that's probably what you folks at MI5 live for. So tell me, what's the inside scoop on my next door neighbour and that odious chap from Barclays?"

"We obviously don't have anything yet on the content of the meeting at Cressida Armstrong's house the other night. As you'll readily appreciate, we were unaware there were any issues to investigate, so couldn't get any equipment installed in time. However, and for today's formal record, I can tell you that we have undertaken a routine sweep of their phone and internet records, metadata only you understand. It's clear that the Chancellor and Miss Armstrong are in regular correspondence, but it's quite a leap from suspicion to fact. To give you the all important 'content' you require, well, I would need a formal warrant from the Home Secretary. I'm sure you are reluctant to go down that route just at the moment, until such time as something more compelling emerges? So, providing you agree that this next part of the conversation never happened today, then maybe I can enlighten you further? Can't be accused of going beyond my legal remit, eh what!"

He nodded his acquiescence.

"Good choice. First off: I'm pretty sure the Chancellor is indulging in a spot of very discreet hanky-panky, as we say in the trade."

"What, with that smooth talking bastard, McMullan?"

"Ha ha! No, no, no, Prime Minister, but very amusing. Would you believe me if I was to tell you that it's with Cressida Armstrong, your arch nemesis at The Sun newspaper? There's quite a love affair in progress."

"That scrawny-assed, two-faced, evil bitch! I'm flabbergasted, utterly speechless. Amanda, how could she? Are you completely and absolutely sure? I'll destroy them both if this is even remotely true."

"No doubt about it. They've frequently been seen having what can only be described as girly heart-to-hearts at Dorneywood in recent weeks and seem to be in regular text correspondence. Miss Price also has a very private pay-as-you-go phone with only one number on it: no guesses as to whose. I don't need to remind you that this is strictly against Cabinet Office security protocols. I asked one of my chaps who I lock away in the basement for such moments, to see if there was any correlation between their phone calls or meetings and defamatory articles in the paper. Surprise, surprise, there is always a day's gap; then bang, publication. Curious that, wouldn't you agree?"

"Emma, I'm more than a little impressed; good work. By way of a very big thank you, we'll up your department's budget and I suggest you pay close attention to the New Year's honours list. Now, I need your urgent assistance to find out what they intend to do next and when. Then I will show them how to play dirty."

"That's why you're a devious, conniving politician Charlie and I'm a dutiful spook. I gather from looking over Nadia's shoulder that you're seeing my good friend Martin next. Shall I presume I'll be getting my warrant by lunchtime, I don't want to have to go round later and duff him up?"

★ ★ ★

Seats 1A and 1B on the United Airlines flight from New York to Beijing had been reserved for the cyber-security team of Cadbury and Naylor. Despite their common interests, the fourteen hour trip would be their first opportunity to meet and, if either of them deemed it necessary, to agree any refinements to the CIA's master plan intended to thwart the gold crisis. They carried two virtually indestructible briefcases, each containing identical, ultra sophisticated, but innocuous looking iPads.

Nitro Zeus was the carefully nurtured brainchild of Dr. Alex Cadbury and a continuation of the indispensible work he engaged in during the Dark Pools saga two and a bit years previously. Given its momentous, all-embracing, capacities, the new malware had been exceptionally hard to perfect and had gone through endless, painstaking, re-writes. The newly installed software on the iPads they were carrying was version 3.12 and could best be described as toxic in the extreme. CIA Director, Carter Meggs, wanted to codename it 'Cloud Cuckoo Land', or possible 'Triple-D' to reflect its main purpose: namely,

270

to disrupt, degrade and destroy. But Naylor's proposal had eventually prevailed: it would be 'G2D': Gold to Dust.

"If we don't get this sorted, we are all toast", seemed the winning argument.

After Mackenzie Gore's retirement from GCHQ the previous year, she had often been called in to discreetly review the programmes progress and make any behind the scenes suggestions for its deployment. The rationale for her involvement was crystal clear to the head of the service:

"On this particular sports field Naylor, Alex plays for the defence, while you're in attack."

Her very highly-regarded, specialist skills were in the black arts of distraction and chaos, for which she seemed to possess an exceptional flair. These talents became evident very early on in her undercover CIA work: only the merest tell-tale smirk crossed her face when phrases such as Operation Rasputin were mentioned. She named it, she was pivotal in executing it; to this day Russia doesn't even know it's sitting there. The lists of top secret files with her name attached were legion – yet very few people in the service had ever met her. Both parties preferred it that way.

Alex made his way to his allocated seat only to see his beaming colleague had got there before him. His first impression was highly favourable: 'she's definitely as attractive as the director said she would be; and what gorgeous hair.' But was she 'mad, bad and dangerous to know'? He was already looking forward to finding out.

"Don't you think it's odd that first class is completely empty, Naylor?"

"Nothing to it my dear friend. I just hacked the airline's computer system this morning and moved everyone else to a different flight. We need privacy so that we can go over a few details, get to know each other a little better, that sort of thing."

"Very impressive. So tell me, how do you manage to get past

airport security with only one name? Any chance I can take a sneaky peek at your Bolivian passport?"

"Don't you use the back door entrance, Alex? You should try it. A smile and a very suggestive wink will get you anywhere. And don't ask me what happens when we get to Beijing. I'll temporarily disappear and see you in the limo."

"Champagne, then work, or do you prefer it the other way around?"

"What precisely are you suggesting, Dr Cadbury? By any chance are you propositioning me for the mile high club?"

"We haven't taken off yet Naylor; ask me later. It's just that I like to get down to it early on in the flight."

"I can see we are going to get on famously. Let's start with a bottle of Krug and work up a sweat from there. Tell me Alex, do you prefer to salsa or tango?"

"Most definitely the salsa for me, it's more spontaneous and sexy. The complete opposite to my day job coding G2D."

"Excellent, I'll make sure the string quartet at the embassy ball can play a couple of raucous numbers in-between the boring stuff. I've packed my favourite very sexy black salsa outfit for just such an occasion. It should focus attention away from our real purpose, don't you think?"

★ ★ ★

The Butler was in a particularly contented and relaxed frame of mind. On such fleeting occasions, he felt honour-bound to quickly counterbalance this euphoria with some heinous brutality to a rival triad boss. The pleasures of inflicting pain were never far from his thoughts. After all, he had a fearsome reputation to defend. Earlier in the day he had dispersed what amounted to a king's ransom in gold bars to his many business cronies, political pawns and newly-established allies; while making mental notes of what favours he would subsequently demand in return. Such largess was never given freely, but undertaken on a very simple business premise: for every one dollar he paid out, he would expect to receive ten in return. Western venture capitalists had a lot to learn: there was no such thing in his world as failing to pay the piper.

He made a decision to visit the most influential politicians on his list over the next few days and ensure his Shanghai fiefdom expanded significantly without interference from the authorities. With limitless wealth at his disposal, plans were quickly set in train to eliminate his enemies and triple his territorial reach towards the ultimate prize of Beijing.

★ ★ ★

The not inconsiderable contents of the Jin-Ton were also being passed around like trinkets at a children's party. Lorry load, after lorry load, of gold ingots had been dispatched to the private vaults of a long list of the most influential people in the country. The army had willingly complied with the minister's orders, who in turn had agreed how the spoils were to be divided with Banker Chen. The mood was euphoric and not one moment's thought was given to the whereabouts of the still missing head of the armed forces, General Xiao. He was yesterday's news. Every minute that passed the gold price rose ever higher. The magnanimous gesture by Chen to sprinkle millions of dollars worth of bullion, willy-nilly, amongst his cohort of new admirers was by no means altruistic. Every recipient would have a vote, all would later crown him king.

★ ★ ★

Unbeknownst to the high-flying recipients who were gratefully squirreling away their new found prosperity, the CIA was now monitoring the co-ordinates of every gold bar they had switched a few days earlier. The secret tracking devices, embedded within the fake bullion, were now yielding a treasure trove of corrupt officials and, more importantly, the location of each of their secret storage facility. It did not take them long to link a name to each address. For the intelligence community, this was nirvana. They would soon transmit the list to Cadbury and Naylor. The fun and games were about to begin.

CHAPTER 37

Beijing and London

Sebastian had slept fitfully on the journey over to Beijing and had arrived at the hotel in what could only be described as an irascible mood. It was totally out of character for him to be grumpy, but the weight of the world seemed to hang from his shoulders. Amongst a myriad of nightmares that he experienced during the previous evening's flight, he returned time and again to one overwhelming issue: was he the right man for the job? A feeling compounded by the disquieting thought that he really had no idea what the job was.

There were several messages on his phone when he landed, with one from Lewis which puzzled him.

'As we sometimes say in Texas after too many tequilas: All the world's a stage and, well, whatever it is that comes next; never quite sure to be honest. So make your entrance with your customary flair and try to exude coolness under fire Seb. We are all holding our breath here. And under no circumstances play Pepper Pig on the iPad.'

His jet-lagged mind was scrambled, for the message made no sense whatsoever. Perhaps the task that he'd been allocated in this unfolding drama was quite simply to play what New Yorker's call 'the shill'; to act the stooge while Lewis pulled the strings from his office? That had more than an element of plausibility about it. Or maybe he was to be the Federal Reserve's mountebank: his role was to ham it up and play the part of a dodgy confidence trickster with the Chinese? After all he'd only just recently managed to lose a fortune for his own bank in a gold trade gone horribly wrong. It would be effortless to set him up to take yet more blame. God knows what he had to do? He clung to the hope that his friend Alex would provide the answers, or possibly the mysterious Naylor was the trump card? Question upon question, but precious little answers. Maybe he just had to face up to the prospect that this really was game over and he was only there, cast in some bizarre ceremonial role, to perform the last rights?

If there was any consolation to be derived from his trip it was the opportunity to see the beautiful, delectable, Lyn again. But given the downcast mood he was in, he felt certain she would be quickly whisked away on yet another tour of duty and, who knows, never return. He had never felt so sombre.

"You look absolutely dreadful darling; I take it you didn't sleep too well on the flight over? We have five hours before we need to brush-up for the uber-glamorous ball tonight. I'm guessing a quickie may well kill you, so do you fancy a slowy big boy?"

"Ah Lyn, how could I possibly refuse. No handcuffs this time please, but if there's any whipped cream and honey that would be great. My energy levels are flagging somewhat."

★ ★ ★

By the time Alex and Naylor had landed in Beijing, after what could be best described as a very hands-on, bumpy ride, they had worked their way through the extensive wine list and were increasingly flirtatious. Without any doubt there was a growing admiration society developing between the two of them. Beauty, intelligence and a quick wit were the ultimate aphrodisiac. Alex felt sufficiently emboldened to move beyond the erudite discussion of computer coding that had dominated the past five hours and see if the odd risqué comment could pay any dividends.

"As I understand your position on the all important technical adjustments we need to make to the malware Naylor, you want to whip a couple of things out and I would dearly like to slip a big one in. I gave the Director my solemn pledge before I left that I would keep my end up in this joint endeavour."

Naylor leaned over and kissed his hand.

"Cheeky boy; maybe later. I preferred to describe our nascent relationship as being joined at the hip in a common cause to defeat whatever harm is put in our country's way."

Both agreed, if they were going to go down, they'd go down in flames. In that spirit, they had readily agreed to make several incendiary changes to the programme sequencing of 'G2D' which they would outline to Sebastian when he arrived. Alex could only gaze heavenward and say:

"God, you really are as devious and cunning as the Director said you were. I'm truly very impressed with your suggestions. I assume you can dance as well as you can programme?"

"About the same Alex; with slightly more wriggle. Or should I have said wiggle, or writhe; I never quite know the difference being South American. It's sometimes rather difficult to get my lips around it. You'll be pleased to know that my Mandarin is far more fluent. Maybe we can try all three as the evening progresses. As we 'masters of the dark art of tradecraft' like to say, we don't want any blowback."

"Speaking of which, I think we could both benefit immeasurably from a vigorous de-briefing? Shall we say my room in ten minutes?"

★ ★ ★

Dave and Dom – as they had now decided to call themselves from now on, (having concluded that the days of being referred to as 'the Governor' and 'the Professor' were most definitely over for good) – had somehow managed to find their way to the Gong Bar on Level 52 of The Shard, where they ordered two large G&T's in contemplative silence. They were enjoying the magnificent views on a crystal-clear day and wondering what carnage was silently unfolding, way below them, in the City of London and Canary Wharf in the far distance. The ever popular sky-bar was filling up with endless chatting, happy faces who all seemed totally oblivious to the dramatic events occurring in the banking sector only a mile or two away. Gold had now topped $5,000 in Shanghai as speculators and financial institutions scrambled to cover their short positions. It could only get worse as China put the final, death-squeeze on those foolish enough to assume the merry-go-round would last forever. Although the UK bullion market was closed they both knew that the moment it re-opened they would be presiding over the biggest crash since the Weimar Republic in the early 1920's.

"I can honestly say Dom that I've never felt more helpless in my life. My colleagues at the Bank and the Treasury just can't cope with the scope and breadth of this crisis. Amanda seems minutes away from a nervous breakdown, the PM has gone barking mad and the government seems rudderless. And we, my dear friend, are relegated to bit players who probably won't even make the final curtain."

"I just cling to my long held view that Lewis is way too clever, and far to cunning an operator, to allow Seb to go to such elaborate lengths on a whim. OK, he's without any doubt concealing something from us, but if it works then, frankly, who will care?"

★ ★ ★

Harvey McMullan was at his desk at Barclays finalising the wording to the chancellor about how many billions of emergency support the bank needed to make it through the weekend. Every line had been carefully and painstakingly crafted to ensure he didn't inadvertently incriminate himself and fall into a similar trap as his predecessors. Satisfied with the text, he pressed the send button and prayed. Earlier in the day he had agreed to speak at an urgent debate on the crisis at the House of Lords, but had been cautioned against it by Cressida Armstrong.

"You may find yourself dragged into conversations you'll later regret, once we have published the revelations on Charlie Sheer. I gather there is a big summit meeting in China on Friday involving Sebastian Fortes: much as I like a scoop, on such a delicate matter as this, timing of the story is everything. If the gold crisis is resolved then the PM revelations will get lost in the tsunami of euphoria that we are all not going to turn into rabid cannibals and be forced to eat our first born. No doubt Charlie will take all the credit and then this story will get swamped. So I'm holding it back one day. If there is a break through at the summit, well, we can then run it next week. That will wipe the smile of his face, big time!"

"As you think best Cressida."

★ ★ ★

The officials had dusted off every file they held in the cavernous vaults of the Treasury marked '*2008 Financial Crisis, Doomsday Options*' and presented them to Amanda Price. There was quite a pile on her desk when the chancellor arrived at her office sometime around 6.30am. She was a prodigious reader who, during a personal or professional crisis, always found a strange solace and inner peace in the typed word.

Her preferred tomes were obscure facts on the history of art, which could happily occupy her for hours, but she was now ploughing through papers on '*Operation Temperer: How to mobilise the Army*' and '*The Royal Mint's printing of £1,000 and £10,000 notes in the event of hyperinflation*'. There was little doubt in her mind that, come Monday, there would be a requirement to press the button on both. She had placed a call through to both Seb and Lewis, asking them to urgently contact her, but as yet neither had replied. As the morning progressed the funding request from Barclays had arrived and been immediately dealt with. She was unsure whether she had the individual authority to make such a payment, but decided to bite the bullet and at least try and resolve one problem.

By mid morning it was becoming clear that the prime minister would not return any of her calls and his secretarial team were being obstructive in the extreme about when he would be next available to meet.

"Nothing in the diary at all today or tomorrow; and his weekend is wall-to-wall meetings I'm afraid Chancellor."

"Thank you Nadia, if a slot becomes free, do let me know."

She next had a call placed through to Barclays head office.

"Harvey, just to let you know that I've now signed off the funding for you. It should be with you later in the day. Are you free for lunch by any chance? I want to discuss your availability to take on the Governorship of the Bank, which will probably become available first thing on Monday morning. Sir David seems to have thrown in the towel and will be retiring."

★ ★ ★

"Well for someone who looked dead-beat an hour ago, that was quite some performance. Shall we go for thirds, or would you like me to take a breather?"

"Just keep gently applying the Manuka to my tender bits please Lyn. So, now that I've more or less recovered, when do we meet up with General Sanford and the others?"

"As I understand it Seb, there's a council of war in his suite when the technical team arrives from the States. So I'd guess in an hour or so. I need to get a hold of Reed about something else, so you freshen-up and I'll see you in his room. Eighth floor I believe. By the way, it's black tie tonight; you're on parade at eight sharp, soldier!"

★ ★ ★

"Director Meggs, perfect time for you to call. Quick update from here: Fortes and the others have arrived and I've suggested we have a dress rehearsal of the plan in an hour's time. I gather from Alex that G2D has been sharpened-up overnight to introduce a slower start, incorporating more updated information from Xiao, then a more rapid acceleration into the military sphere. Just to be completely clear, Fortes has clearance to go beyond stage five in necessary when he formally meets with Chen in the morning?"

"Correct General, but if he is forced to six or higher, I want your team to either hunker down in the bowels of the embassy, or get out of town. I'll make sure there is a suitable plane available from midday tomorrow. The President is fully appraised and tells me nothing short of a home run from you will do."

"I won't let him down Sir."

"Oh, and one last thing: I'm getting reports across my desk that the Ruskies are trying their damndest to get in on the action. Get a seat at the party, that sort of thing. We've lots of Intel traffic to suggest they will shortly have a top man in town, if he's not there already. We don't have a fix on who it is yet, which is worrying. They know we have Nitro Zeus available to us; I'm just concerned they may have got their hands on G2D, or at the barest minimum know its capabilities. So eyes peeled and let me know the moment you suspect anything, or anyone."

CHAPTER 38

New York, Beijing and London

Lewis was staring intently at his computer screens wondering which part of the financial dam would burst first. His colleagues in the offices of the New York Federal Reserve were now in constant, or more accurately desperate, contact with every central banker in the world, cajoling them to allocate physical gold from their dwindling reserves into a contingency fund. To say they were having modest success would be an understatement. The overwhelming feedback he was getting was that the world's central banks were, in desperation, ready to switch horses and back the Chinese, who were clearly in the ascendancy. It was being made very clear to him that faith in America's ability to rescue the situation had evaporated; in which case they felt it wise and prudent to strike a deal with the inevitable winners. Flogging, and dead horses, were never far from his thoughts. Everyone, it seemed, was beating a path to the door of Banker Chen and pleading to be kept solvent as the gold crisis unfolded. Secret deals were being struck, which if implemented, would turn the world on its head. Information was streaming into the Fed that once reliable and trustworthy allies were deserting them in droves. Only the British stood firm.

Amanda Price had followed the agreed protocol in the midst of any financial crisis involving both countries and let him know that she was supporting a bail-out for Barclays; and quite possibly several more UK based banks as the day progressed. However, she also let it be known that, in her considered opinion, this was just a very inadequate sticking plaster and not a cure.

Lewis had got to know her well over the years they had worked together, but it was clear from the conversations between them that she was at breaking point.

"Amanda, are you on a secure line?"

"Yes, why?"

"I can't help feeling that it's not just the gold crisis that's keeping you up at night these days. You know you have my organisations complete confidence, but I'm not sure that this opinion is shared by your Prime Minister. Would that be correct?"

"All I can say right now is that there are some dark secrets which have been deliberately hidden for quite some time Lewis: explosive secrets. One of our red-top newspapers is getting ready to publish an exposé on Charlie which will undoubtedly end his career. Who knows, it may end mine to."

"If I were to tell you that I know exactly what's going on, would that put your mind at rest? To be quite frank Amanda, the politicos in the West Wing of the White House has been monitoring this for quite some time. You do appreciate, don't you, that you are now under personal surveillance by MI5 and some rogue cop?"

"What in God's name!"

"All true I'm sorry to say. Your country is our closest and oldest friend, which makes us honour bound to ensure we contribute to the long-term stability of the UK. But to be frank, the mood here is that we don't mind losing Charlie; he's a major liability, however we want to see the cream rise to the top. So tell Cressida to publish it immediately, today if possible, a special edition."

"How the hell do you know all this?"

"The boys get everywhere Amanda, you ought to know that. Besides which, this whole unsavoury mess will be over by the weekend. Then you can move next door."

"I just do not know what to say."

"Best you say nothing; stick to post-it notes."

★ ★ ★

Chen was having the proverbial time of his life. He was wallowing in the vicarious pleasure of receiving phone calls from a long list of unctuous politicians who were now pledging their unwavering support to his ambitions, while making plans to spend their newly acquired ill-gotten gains. His sphere of political influence – as he always planned and expected – was now growing exponentially; the mountain peak was in plain sight and very shortly would be conquered.

Simultaneously, he was having the world's financial community throwing themselves on his mercy and promising him the earth if their country could be spared from the catastrophe that lay ahead. The final three acts of the play were simple in the extreme: firstly, to squash the newly appointed deputy governor of the Bank of England beneath his feet tomorrow. He would teach the neophyte central banker a thing or two. Then he would take great pleasure in dealing a fatal blow to the Americans; and, finally, he would delight in his inevitable assent to the Premiership itself. But tonight, he would content himself with taking his newly acquired mistress to the ball and revelling in his growing influence and power.

★ ★ ★

Given the longevity of their highly charged relationship – now in its tenth or eleventh year, it was all somewhat of a blur given their hectic lives – Sanford was, as always, delighted to see Sapphire again. If they met up once a year for a discreet tryst it was regarded as a minor miracle, so to have time together in the comfort of a hotel was a rare pleasure indeed. Their first, ultra high-level, parachute jump deep into enemy territory was the source of much pride in the regiment and created an unbreakable bond between them. That they got out alive was in no small measure due to Sapphire's unbelievable ability to memorise maps, find food anywhere and yomp for miles across incredibly difficult terrain. Her astonishing fortitude and strength were in sharp contrast to her delicate figure and unassuming demeanour. Woe betide anyone who underestimated her: for she could effortlessly fell a man twice her size with one blow; and often had. Since their initial mission in northern Tibet they had joined forces on an endless stream of covert ops, but both agreed that this latest endeavour was decidedly out of the ordinary: not enough live ordnance or materiel to play with.

She had already eagerly dressed for the evening's festivities and was looking forward to a rare moment of relaxation and refinery: a fleeting commodity in her line of work. Having defected from China many years previously, she knew full well that she was running a great risk returning to the country to attend such a high visibility event. But she had been in and out of Beijing so many times in the recent past that she felt confident she would not be discovered and unmasked.

"Great work getting the guys out of Dandong, Sapphire. Everyone really appreciated your efforts. General Xiao is now in Washington and has already started being debriefed. I'm told he's being especially cooperative; not surprisingly, as he really, really, hates Chen. As for the others: Zucca will be taking up residence in Tuscany any time soon; and Sergeant Oakes is in detox, completely knackered apparently. When the tremors stop, Lyn intends to kill him with her bare hands at the first opportunity she gets. I like your new cheongsam by the way; red suits you."

"Good to see you too, Jim. What little hair you still have on display looks to have gone a shade greyer over the last couple of days. I presume we are no further forward in peacefully resolving this? So tell me, where do I fit in?"

"It's all really a matter of how they react. I'm not expecting, or even preparing, for a gun fight. So it's back to your speciality: extraction. We may well have to make an impromptu, rather rapid exit and if we do, I want you to look after Fortes. Get him off the football field, into hiding and out of the country."

"Not a problem. Where will Lyn be while all this is kicking off?"

"She'll be the diversion. I'm assuming – if it comes to this – that they will expect Fortes to escape with her. That should gives us time to use Lyn as a decoy heading in the opposite direction while you get him out of town. I'll cover Lyn's back."

"As good a plan as any I suppose. Care for a drink?"

Sapphire kissed him tenderly on the cheek and eagerly opened a couple of bottles of wine. Both were in high spirits ahead of the team's much anticipated reassembly and what they hoped would be a jolly evening to come.

★ ★ ★

Alex and Naylor were the first to arrive; the former decidedly flushed, the latter all contented smiles. On entering the room Alex pulled out some device from his pocket and put a finger to his lips, indicating silence. After a couple of taps on the gadget he spoke.

"Just being super careful General, if we are being bugged – which we almost certainly are – this little beauty will ensure we aren't overheard."

Sanford pulled an identical piece of kit from his pocket and just grinned. At the same moment Lyn arrived and greeted everyone warmly. They each took a seat on the sofas.

"OK squad. Tonight's shindig is merely the froth on the beer. The hard yards start tomorrow. Lyn I want you to schmooze Chen, gain his confidence, but make it very clear to him that you're with Fortes forever and all time. Where is he by the way?"

"He'll be here any moment now, Sir."

"Good, if he's out of my sight for more than five minutes I worry he's MIA."

"Reed assured me that he is looking after his welfare; he was busily preparing the mojitos before I left. Speaking of which, I'll have a glass of the white please Sapphire."

"The limo will be here at 1930 and given the gravity of tomorrow's events we should plan to leave no later than 2300. Ah, guys, nice to see you. I assume you know everyone?"

Reed and Sebastian had not seen each other since he left Hong Kong, about a year ago. They had frequently met on the golf course during the time that Seb was Financial Secretary and spent the day lamenting the absence of their much-loved drinking-buddy, Bain, who had decided to return back to the UK and the dreaded office job at MI6.

"Hey Alex, good to see you buddy; how's Connecticut? I gather you've brought me some sparkly new toys to play with? And what can one say Naylor, beautiful as ever; you really do rack-up the airmiles."

"Good to see you to Seb. With your permission General, can we get down to business? I would like to run through the procedure and how the iPad I have here works."

"Proceed, we have thirty minutes."

"It's not in the slightest bit complicated, even for your level of technophobia Seb. As you can see it looks identical to every model that's ever been sold, it has the standard on-off buttons and the same 'right swipe' mechanism you'll be very familiar with. We've even given you a special Bank of England embossed case: cool eh! I thought that was a nice touch. However, there are only two working apps: an innocuous version of Word and, by a million miles the most important thing on the device is identified with the G2D symbol. Look, can you see it here? All you have to do is switch the iPad on and, at the appropriate moment of your choosing, press this specific icon. It all goes onto autopilot from that point."

Seb nodded, despite his hatred of computers.

"Under no circumstances must you turn the bloody thing on before your meeting as it may inadvertently give the game away. Naylor and I have an identical piece of kit to enable us to follow your exact progress from a safe distance. The speaker on yours also transmits the discussions at the meeting, so the General here, and in all likelihood half of the CIA, will know exactly how things are going. If, for whatever reason, someone wants to inspect the iPad when you enter the central bank tomorrow, just say it contains your briefing notes; which we've conveniently placed there already. Open it for them if absolutely necessary: make a terrible fuss, but give in to their demands eventually. Don't let it out of your sight however. They'll find nothing of significance, and it will put them off the scent. We've deliberately placed the G2D app in the middle of the endless games icons, so they hopefully won't focus on it. Once the job is done, you can take it with you, or leave it. The programme will be automatically erased."

"And what exactly does G2D do?"

"General Sanford will let you into those little secrets tomorrow, just before your meeting. We can't have you having nightmares now, can we? So, Cinders, lets away to the ball, for tomorrow we…"

★ ★ ★

Just after midnight on Thursday Charlie Sheers' private secretary woke him up with a shake and handed him a copy of the first edition of The Sun newspaper.

"Sorry to wake you Prime Minister, but I thought you should see the first edition immediately."

The PM searched for his glasses and felt his chest tighten and his pulse rocket up as he read the headline.

'Prime Minister, Charles Sheer, directly implicated in a duplicitous fraud on the nations coffers. The finger of suspicion now points to his incontrovertible involvement in the suspicious death two years ago of senior banker, Sir John d'Abo.'

"Get me Emma Clarke at MI5, wake her up if necessary and get her here immediately. Then issue an urgent press statement refuting every word. Get the Attorney General and establish whether we can get an injunction to stop this being used in other newspapers and on the TV tomorrow morning. Then let it be known that I will address Parliament at midday. Someone is going to swing for this."

CHAPTER 39

Beijing & London

Within the upper reaches of the diplomatic corps, the American Ambassador to China, the Honourable William M. Coultard, was both exceptional and unique: a billionaire many times over; a distinguished Harvard scholar; and a renowned *bon vivant* with a legendary knowledge of viticulture that came from owning a hundred acres of the best grapes in the Haut-Médoc region. His much loved wife was, quite simply, a legendary hostess; an unrivalled life and soul of the party; the true definition of a sybarite. They were inseparable and – despite their seemingly carefree approach to the myriad duties and responsibilities which came with the job – they were in fact the perfect counterpoint to the occasional pomposity of their office. Formal black-tie balls at the Embassy were always the hottest ticket in town and much fought over by senior members of the Politburo. It didn't require the arrival of some young hotshot from the Bank of England for them to initiate a party. For the Coultard's this was the perfect opportunity to do what they did best: some *sotto voce* sleuthing into China's strategy for tomorrow's meeting, on which they had both been well briefed.

"General Sanford; delighted to see you again."

"You too Bill, where's Cheryl?"

"Lost in the crowd, I expect, or chatting up the new Italian ambassador. She thinks he's quite a dish apparently. Ah, you must be Mr Fortes. Good to see you have broad shoulders;

you're going to need them. I'll introduce you to Chen when he arrives. I'd stick to inconsequential topics; try soccer, I gather he's a big fan of Liverpool, or could it be Spurs?"

"I'll try my best."

"Tell me Jim, which of these charming ladies is Lyn?"

"Sorry Ambassador, may I introduce you to Major Lyn Andrews; and our secret weapon here, Naylor, who I'm sure you appreciate, works for the Company."

"It would appear that more or less all your team do Jim. Now, mingle and enjoy yourself. I recommend the 2012 Château La Lagune, should you be interested. Before you leave don't forget to say goodbye and, most importantly, if you discover anything worthwhile, let me know immediately. Tittle-tattle is the lifeblood of diplomacy; nothing like a good party for indiscretions."

It was around nine that Chen finally made his appearance, his arm adorned by some generously endowed floozy half his age. Cheryl immediately recognised her from a previous soirée as belonging, if that was the appropriate phase, to one of China's most powerful industrial magnates; renowned for his volatile temperament.

'She certainly switched horses very quickly', was her first thought, followed immediately by, 'I must drop a note to the poor cuckolded fellow saying how much we missed him at the ball, but it was good to meet up with his girlfriend again': that should light a fire in his belly and cause all hell to break loose. The delights of court intrigue and political plotting were unquestionably Cheryl's *raison d'être*.

On entering the ballroom Chen was immediately suffused in a chaotic mêlée of fawning local politicians, all of whom wanted to pay homage to what they assumed would be their next emperor. With a disdainful wave of the hand they were dismissed as he approached the host.

"We appreciate your kind invitation Ambassador. Tell me,

which of your guests is Mr Fortes, I would very much like to meet him?"

"Sebastian, may I introduce you to Deputy Governor Chen of The People's Bank of China; I'm sure you'll both have a great deal to discuss in private. I'm going to mingle, so with your permission I'll leave my two guests of honour to get to know each other. Catch my eye before you depart please Mr. Chen."

The two protagonists spent a little time sizing each other up. Sebastian was at least a foot taller, far more athletic and at least twenty years younger than the diminutive Chen. Despite these superficial disparities, few would doubt that the Chinese banker exuded the dominant presence. Seb certainly had charisma and energy, but Chen had innate authority. The issue, as always, was who held the strongest hand: twenty to thirty thousand tonnes of pure gold versus endless lines of computer mumbo-jumbo. Tomorrow would tell.

"What are you hoping to achieve on this visit, Mr Fortes? I believe in being blunt, don't you agree?"

"Well I was rather hoping you could give me your valuable opinion on who will prevail in the football on Saturday. I gather Spurs play Liverpool. My money is on an away win, much like our meeting tomorrow."

"In my experience Mr Fortes home advantage counts for a great deal, as in all aspects of life. I can see we are going to have quite a jousting contest. See you at ten sharp."

As the evening progressed and the music got into full swing, Chen casually and effortlessly mingled with an endless stream of beautiful ladies all vying for his attention. He amused himself with the irony of the situation: every gold-digger in town was now trying to get herself noticed. However, his mind was elsewhere and already focusing on tomorrow's tussles with Sebastian. Given her remarkable figure and all too obvious allure, he concluded that Lyn must be the weakest member in the UK/US delegation. She was far too good looking to be anything other than the obligatory play thing, so maybe she would accidentally reveal some important pillow-talk if pressed hard enough. When it quickly dawned on him that she was probably the strongest link in the chain, he rapidly switched his attention to Naylor.

In her deliberately provocative, 'look at me' way, she was dressed as if for an evening's frivolities on Copacabana Beach after way-to-many Caipirinhas. True to her promise, the past ten minutes had witnessed Alex Cadbury being happily hurled around the dance floor in an uncoordinated tangle of arms and legs. His first dysfunctional attempt at salsa saw him lose all his decorum and force an early retirement from the dance floor before he twisted his ankle, or worse. In the minds of virtually everyone present, who gazed in lust at this animalistic creature now joyously cavorting alone before them, it didn't matter one jot that her choice of skirt was verging on the inappropriately short.

Chen was growing accustomed to seeing his enormous wealth bestowing upon him the unchallengeable right to everything and everyone in Beijing. With every provocative turn of the hips he became even more eager to catch her eye. The feudal lords privileges implied in *le droit du seigneur* were now his to exercise.

It was not long before they were engrossed in animated conversation slightly away from the main throng of guests, who were by now thoroughly enjoying the embassy's hospitality. Bill and Cheryl certainly knew how to throw a party. It was only by the merest of coincidences that the music stopped for the briefest of seconds and the chit-chat between Chen and Naylor became momentarily clear.

"Bill darling, can you find General Sanford. I need to discuss something I've just overheard."

Sanford was tapped heartily on the shoulder.

"Mind if I cut in Jim, Cheryl wants a quick word with you

and it's my turn to dazzle the every beautiful Sapphire with my skills at the foxtrot."

"Pleasure, we need to be going anytime soon. Plus, I need to rescue Alex before he's a basket case tomorrow. Oh, hi Cheryl, what is it you need to chat about?"

"Can we go to Bill's office for five minutes please? If you just follow me. I'm assuming that Naylor doesn't appreciate that I'm as fluent in Mandarin as she quite clearly is. In here."

She closed the door and sat down on the sofa, patting it, indicating he should sit next to her.

"I'm not prone to exaggeration Jim, but I just overheard the most remarkable discussion between Naylor and Chen. Firstly, she referred to him by the very familiar, *amour*, as if they had known each other for years. OK, she's obviously very flirty, but it just struck me as odd for people who have only just met. Then she said, 'I've made the changes to', after which it didn't make any sense as it was a jumble of letters and numbers, followed by 'it will spectacularly backfire'. Then the music started again and I couldn't hear whatever was said next. A minute or so later they moved to different sides of the room as if they, well, hardly knew each other. Odd don't you think?"

"It is indeed. Can you pour a pint of your strongest coffee down the throat of Alex; I need him sober, very sober. Could you let Bill know that I'm going to the Coms Room to speak with Carter Meggs at Langley. Ask him to join me when he's free. And thank you Cheryl; I owe you one."

★ ★ ★

There was utter pandemonium in Downing Street with the local hacks jostling and pushing each other for position, screaming inane questions at anyone who passed in front of them and most definitely baying for blood. The prime minister's official car and security detail were parked immediately in front of Number

10, shielding him from the onslaught of abuse being thrown at him. He waved as he got into the car, creating even more bedlam as a thousand cameras caught the historic moment. His resignation could only be a matter of a few minutes away. Then what?

It was rare for lobby correspondents to openly boo and shriek their disdain, but the atmosphere was beyond toxic; shouts of 'for God's sake go' and 'traitor' echoed across the narrow confines of Downing Street. The crowds along Whitehall and into Parliament Square were ten or twenty deep in anticipation of the day's momentous events and were having to be controlled by a battalion of armed police as eggs and flour were hurled at the PM's car.

On arrival just before midday, he went to his private office to collect his thoughts and re-check his prepared speech before walking down the corridor into the chamber to deliver his valedictory address. The noise was simply deafening as he took his seat but stopped the moment he got to his feet. No one wanted to miss a word of what everyone fully expected would be a bloodbath. The opposition front bench was utterly delighted to at last plunge the proverbial dagger between his shoulder blades. While many in his own party, especially those who had been the subject of his wanton brutality, were as equally happy to see him go; preferably suffering as much pain as they had endured during his tenure.

What was distinctly odd however was the strange, inexplicable, absence of the chancellor, who would normally be expected to sit next to him on such occasions? There had been no reports of her being ill or travelling overseas on some, as yet, unreported matter to do with the gold crisis. Equally there was no rumour of a rift between them. With the notable exception of the editorial in The Sun, every other UK newspaper had gone into overdrive speculating how much Amanda Price had known about the shenanigans surrounding d'Abo's loan and his alleged murder. Her absence could only fuel speculation that she was somehow complicit in this unfolding drama; the ever-faithful side kick to Charlie Sheer had vanished just at the point when he needed every friend he could muster.

"Mr Speaker. With your permission I would like to make a brief statement to the House."

CHAPTER 40

Beijing & London

Sanford waited for a good ten minutes lost in thought before he decided to contact CIA headquarters. How could they have been so wrong about Naylor? He ran through every conversation he could remember that they had had together; was there anything he'd missed? He drew a blank. Admittedly he only knew her prior exploits via the operational reports that would routinely pass his desk at Strategic Air Command. From memory, every one of them was complimentary, praiseworthy and didn't raise the slightest security concerns. He pondered whether the director's reference to 'Russian attempts to become involved in the gold crisis' referred to Naylor? It would be the easiest thing in the world for the surveillance team to mistake her gender? Perhaps that was the rationale for her use of a single name; to confuse us all. There was no doubt in his mind that she was 'playing' Alex, leading him by the proverbial nose to her bed. After all, her predatory reputation preceded her and it would be well-neigh impossible to refuse. But he had to concede that Alex was no fool; indeed quite the opposite: he was an acknowledged genius. Maybe that's why Carter Meggs put the two of them together; to smoke her out? It was just on the verge of plausibility that she had surreptitiously altered the G2D coding; but to what ends? The only person who could give a yes-or-no to all this would have to sober up very rapidly indeed.

"Sanford here Director, I need to discuss Agent Naylor with you?"

"In regard to what exactly?"

"The ambassador's wife has just informed me that she clearly overheard Naylor say something quite bizarre while she was cozying up to Banker Chan earlier tonight. She is reported as saying to him that some malware, identified only by initials which Cheryl didn't hear clearly, had been secretly changed. I'm going to have Alex Cadbury immediately dig into this and establish whether it is all a misunderstanding? I'd be grateful if you could ask the 'close watch' team to go through their records and determine if this could be plausible and if she is a double or even triple agent. We'd be wise to thoroughly check her contacts with both China and Russia. I don't need to remind you that time is quickly slipping through our fingers; subject to your final sign-off we go live in about twelve hours time."

"I'd frankly be flabbergasted, Jim. Her case record is impeccable; probably the best in the service, way above anybody else. Of course, there could be a reason why she's been so consistently successful: a string of easy victories given to her by the Russians in order to lull us into a false sense of security. Yep, I can see that. And isn't she best buddies with Lewis Moyns at the Fed? I'd better check him out as well. Christ, have we all been taken in here. I'm not saying I believe it, but it's worth a serious look. I'll press the alarm bells and get back to you within the hour with a first-cut assessment."

"Thanks, the Ambassador has just arrived, so if I may, I'll sign-off?"

"Bill, good you're here. You've probably been apprised of the issue relating to Naylor. Can you get everyone but Cadbury back to the hotel? Tell Naylor that he's not well – too much to drink, feeling sick, that sort of thing – and tell her that he's staying here until he recovers. Then ask Sapphire and Lyn to be on stand-by at the hotel in one hour."

"Not a problem Jim. Where shall I put the poor fellow? I gather Cheryl is looking for a stomach pump and bags of salt?"

"When he's *compos mentis* bring him here. He's going to get the bollocking of his life shortly, unless he unlocks this mystery very quickly indeed."

★ ★ ★

"Order, Order. Would the Leader of the Opposition calm down before he keels over in excitement. Thank you Mr Hickey, we all want to hear what the Prime Minister has to say."

The opposition benches could hardly contain their glee. If ever there was a chance to get back into government after years wandering aimlessly in the wilderness, this was it. The world was going to hell in a hand basket and the prime minister was about to be defenestrated, hoisted by his own petard, put to the sword, humiliated. Life couldn't get any sweeter.

"If I may proceed Mr Speaker? I wish to address the house regarding articles in today's newspapers regarding Sir John d'Abo and myself. As many of you will be aware, Sir John has often been called upon to perform absolutely invaluable work for this country in support of our vital national interests. He was instrumental, indeed indispensible, in helping unravel the liquidation of a major Wall Street brokerage firm after the 2008 financial crash; and later performed minor miracles leading the international Dark Pools team, which prevented yet another global meltdown. This country owes him an enormous debt of gratitude. Indeed I doubt I would be here without his remarkably astute advice…"

The house erupted with raucous, hollow laughter and yells of 'go now loser', 'your time's up' and the very popular, 'throw him in jail'. Such was the hullaballoo that it was at least two further minutes before the PM could get to his feet; the Speaker by now, drained and hoarse with shouting.

"John has been a dear friend of mine since school days, so to have a series of unsubstantiated, vile rumours appear in today's newspapers fills me with despair at the depths to which our press will now sink. I would like to address each allegation in turn."

"Firstly, it is true that a temporary bridging loan of £50 million was made to d'Abo's Merchant Bank in the middle of the Dark Pools crisis. This emergency loan, along with several others made at the same time to our major banking institutions, was deliberately arranged by HM Treasury in order to provide stability to the market during a highly volatile period. In specific regard to the d'Abo loan, it is no secret that this was initiated by me personally at a critical moment for the bank, when it's Chairman and Chief Executive was working 24 hours a day for the good of his country. There was absolutely nothing exceptional about it; and indeed it was repaid in complete accordance with its terms approximately a week after it had been made."

"Secondly, today's lead story and editorial in The Sun newspaper have made the utterly outrageous statement that I was somehow an accomplice to, or quite possibly the initiator of, the death of Sir John. As many of you will no doubt appreciate, today is not the first occasion when this newspaper has hinted at my involvement in this business; indeed, it has been the primary source of speculation for many months now. I will deal with the subject of Sir John's demise momentarily. But before I do, I wish to inform the House that some weeks ago I ordered a detailed and prolonged investigation into how this whole unsavoury and deleterious matter had unfolded. The enquiry was coordinated by Emma Clarke, the head of MI5, with the added assistance of Commissioner of the Metropolitan Police, the Director of Public Prosecutions and the Attorney General. I tasked them with establishing the source of these rumours and defamatory statements aimed straight at the heart of our democracy. Their report, which I will place in the House library in due course, once it has been suitably redacted, has unambiguously identified the source of the leak. Before I elaborate upon this, I wish to inform everyone here that, just before leaving Number 10 to address the House, the police reported to me that they have formally charged Cressida Armstrong, the Editor of The Sun newspaper with Sedition."

The gasps from a packed House of Commons created a momentary silence. Sedition, as a crime, hadn't been invoked for years and years; indeed members and honourable members were seen scrambling for their mobile phone to establish what on earth it was and whether it was still on the Statute Book. Something just shy of treason seemed the consensus view. Everyone instinctively knew that the newspaper industry would act as one in defence of a free press and contest this matter to the bitter end. Charlie Sheer may well be very dangerous when cornered, but he was going to have the fight of his life to make this charge stick. What came next was even more shocking.

"Thirdly, and as previously mentioned, police investigations are also in progress to identify the precise source, or sources, of the highly inflammatory and libellous leaks which have found their way into the newspapers over recent months, and especially those reported overnight. The finger of suspicion, I regret to have to tell the House, points in one direction only; to one person in particular: the Chancellor of the Exchequer. Consequently, as of this morning, I have relieved her of her duties, effective immediately. I have taken this wholly necessary step, despite being in the middle of yet another financial emergency, because the stability of the nation is at issue here. Her replacement will be announced later today."

To say that the members of parliament who were sat directly behind the prime minister were appalled at this callous action could not be overstated. The House television cameras recorded the moment of shock on their faces for all posterity. It was as if every person on the government front bench was sat open mouthed in utter disbelief; completely speechless and in profound astonishment at the brutality of the decision they had just witnessed. If push came to shove, of the two leading figures in the government, virtually no one would have supported Charlie Sheer over Amanda Price, who was uniformly held in high esteem, unlike her boss. If anything, her colleagues would unhesitatingly have cast her in the role of a principled whistleblower, endeavouring to disclose the tantrums of her mad neighbour next door. The upper reaches of the Cabinet were unravelling before their very eyes. Yet again, the PM had to wait until the uproar subsided.

"Finally, and most importantly, I need to address head-on the allegation that I somehow initiated the death of Sir John d'Abo. On the evening in question I dined privately with him at his club in Mayfair. I don't need to remind the House that he had been under enormous, unimaginable, personal stress for nearly a month and the pressures of his onerous responsibilities were beginning to weigh heavily upon him. As the evening progressed, he confided in me that he could not find a solution to the problem he and his team were wrestling with and as a result he was deeply and profoundly depressed. Indeed he told me in private that he was on the point of contemplating suicide that very night. You may possibly recall that on the following day his colleague, Mr Fortes, and the technical geniuses from GCHQ and Wall Street, found and implemented the Dark Pools solution. He was not aware how close they were to resolving the matter; perhaps if he had been, the chain of events may have been very different."

Shouts of, 'so bloody what' and 'what on earth has this to do with it', echoed across the chamber, forcing the PM to sit down once again before order could be restored. He took to his feet yet again and straightened his tie.

"Sir John asked, or more accurately pleaded with me, for

the government's help and confidential medical support. He had convinced himself that he would be destroyed emotionally and financially because of this personal failure; and as a result his life was, as he put it to me, at an end. Out of compassion towards a dear friend, and a dedicated patriot of the United Kingdom, I agreed to help him in any way I could. On the spur of the moment we conceived a plan to remove him from the field of battle, so to speak, and place him under immediate medical supervision. He and I agreed that it would be best that he had a prolonged period of recuperation and indeed disappear totally from world view."

Disbelief and incredulity seemed to be spread across the countenance of everyone in the House. Only the PM seemed oblivious to the venom directed towards him from virtually every corner.

"To that end I made immediate arrangements from him to be flown out of the country that very evening by the RAF so that he could take a protracted period of rest on a private Caribbean island. Medical staff and police protection officers accompanied him on his departure. The Chief Constable of Buckinghamshire, the late Mr. Todd, organised the whole procedure. Most importantly, and to add plausibility to the story, Mr. Todd informed me that – by great good fortune – they had recently been scouring the County in a missing persons enquiry, for which there was an unidentified body in the morgue. Sir John specifically insisted that if he were to take this course of action, he wanted to, in his own crystal clear words, 'evaporate'. On the spur of the moment it was decided by Mr. Todd that this body could be used for the purposes of Sir John's cover story and buried it his stead."

The leader of the opposition furiously leapt to his feet to make an intervention as the chamber fell once more into complete silence.

"We, on this side of the House, have never heard such a

load of utter clap-trap in our lives. This total absurd account of events is, putting it mildly, a blatant cock-and-bull story to enable you to avoid the hangman's noose. The newspaper account was completely clear in its accusation: namely, that you, Sir, are complicit in the murder of John d'Abo."

The prime minister once more rose to his feet, crimson red with anger, slamming his prepared speech onto the table in front of him.

"Complicit in his murder you say. I think the Leader of the Opposition doth protest too much. Sir John d'Abo is, as I speak, en route back to the U.K. and will be here tomorrow morning. I think you will find he is very much alive and well."

The entire House, the packed galleries, the lobby correspondents, the parliamentary clerks, the Sergeant at arms, everyone there to witness this event, were completely flabbergasted. Instead of being dragged away in chains, Charlie Sheer, in his inimitable highly combustible style, had managed to wriggle out of the tightest spot in his career. He tidied his papers and left a stunned chamber for his private office, hell bent on taking brutal revenge to all who had stood in his path. The 'night of the long knives' had only just begun.

★ ★ ★

Under the disdainful gaze of General Sanford, Alex had sobered up quicker than the proverbial speeding bullet and was now in the process of running a series of diagnostic tests to establish if the G2D programme had indeed been tampered with.

"Yep, no doubt about it! Going by the timing of the changes shown in the log, it occurred about thirty minutes after Naylor and I had signed-off the new procedures. Look, see here: note the point when the rogue modifications were made; then the system is shut down from her computer. If memory serves me correctly, I went to sleep around that time and she must have made the alterations assuming, probably quite correctly, that I would not do any further work on the programme. We'd agreed everything, so for me the assignment was finished."

They looked at each other in despair.

"It's going to take me a while to figure out exactly what she has done as there are literally thousands upon thousands of lines of very complex code. I'll only be able to let you know if I'm able to reverse it much later into my assessment of what she's done. I'm guessing four or five hours, assuming there is nothing too nasty in here. Frankly, I'm not sure I'll have the time to make it to the end. The next question that comes to mind is: what do we now do with Naylor?"

"I'm expecting the Director to call any moment. You leave that to me. I'll pop by in say three hours to see how far you've got."

The cyber security group at Langley had formed the same first-cut opinion; not only was the programme compromised but there were some very nasty technical problems to overcome if it was to be sorted out. They concluded that it must have been very carefully and painstakingly pre-planned, as no one could have written these many alterations so quickly and accurately. The provenance of the changes would be the game changer. At the same time a large team of data analysts had been trawling through every item the CIA held on Naylor to see if anything untoward could be found. They drew a resounding blank. When the two groups compared notes in the director's office, all agreed that – if she was a double agent – then she was exceptional at covering her tracks. She had always been given considerable latitude by the agency to roam as a free agent, unconstrained by the disciplines of report writing or pre-agreeing her travel plans, with only the director himself monitoring her activities. He readily acknowledged that he had failed in his task.

"Can you fix it guys?"

"This is Alex's baby, Director, only he knows the inner

workings of G2D. If anyone can do it quickly, he can. Statement of the obvious, but we should immediately get a hold of him, have a full-on technical discussion and be guided by whatever it is he wants us to do to help."

One of the 'deep background' team at the same conference table, lap-top opened before him while he silently tapped away, had spent the last hour cross checking Naylor's file when he noticed what he considered to be the smoking gun.

"Well I'll be damned. She travelled to Saudi Arabia at exactly the same time that Chen was there. Is that a coincidence? Was she on an authentic assignment? We should ask General Xiao if he spotted her during the visit. She has also been to Beijing a hell of a lot recently. Did you know that Director?"

"Nope; I'm also pretty sure she said to me that she's never been to Saudi. I remember because I asked her at the time if she knew any of the ruling family. We've tracked Chen for years, so his trip there was rather a surprise. I just wondered if she had any useful contacts we could exploit. As for trips to Beijing, well any visits were not on my orders. Maybe she was helping Lewis Moyns on something? Let's call Sanford."

★ ★ ★

"Jim, its Carter Meggs here. We've been running a series of background checks on Naylor. I think it's fair to say that, as of this moment, the team here suspect she's up to no good. If we alert her, then we lose all tactical advantage in tomorrow's meeting. We haven't got to the bottom of what exactly she has done and were hoping that Alex Cadbury will be able to pinpoint the problem and tell us what help he needs from here. I'm assuming he's with you?"

"Yes Sir, working on it now in the other room. I'm reluctant to disturb him for, say, another hour. Give him time to get to the very bottom of what has happened. For what it's worth, I agree that we should let Naylor assume nothing is wrong and she hasn't been detected. If all of this is correct, then Chen will think he has beaten us, so his guard will be down."

"OK, back to you in one hour Jim."

★ ★ ★

Now that their time in the spotlight was over, it had become the customary practice of Professor Dominic Carrington and Sir David Stone to have a lunchtime snifter in their favourite City pub. There they would contemplate the dubious joys of retirement, share their mutual dread of the obligatory rose garden duties now opening up before them, and debate the vagaries of how to grow Jersey potatoes. Dom's contribution being limited to the helpful snippet that at least he knew how to turn them into vodka. They had only half an eye on the prime minister's Commons statement, which had just finished being broadcast on the TV in the bar, while the other eye was metaphorically focused on attracting the attention of the exceptionally pretty barmaid and a much needed refill.

They stared at each other in complete amazement at what they had just heard. Amanda Price had just been fired and the PM seemed to have taken a leaf out of the Dallas storybook where Bobby Ewing, in the guise of John d'Abo, had miraculously returned from the dead. Both events were, in every aspect of the phrase, a bombshell.

"I always told you he was a complete bastard Dave. Shafting his own Chancellor and pulling some Frankenstein trick with the late John d'Abo. We can't just sit here and do nothing. I suggest we both withdraw our resignations and square up to our responsibilities. It was OK for us to go when Amanda was in charge, but no longer. Drink up, we've work to do."

"I'll bet Lady Isobel is utterly bloody stunned by the turn of events Dom, isn't she about to get remarried?"

"Oh, Christ yes, I'd forgotten about that! She's in for the shock of her life. Some teenage Spanish football player called Sergio I gather!"

"Down your drink Prof. Let's saddle up and go see if we can rescue Amanda, then try and figure out where Seb has got to with his master plan: high noon tomorrow for us all."

CHAPTER 41

Beijing, London & New York

Chen was a creature of fastidious habits. For the past forty years he had woken before dawn for an hour of spiritual exercise in the tranquillity of his garden in order to cleanse his mind and feed his often tortured soul. He was one of the millions of Chinese who acknowledged the holistic benefits bestowed on its practitioners by the ancient exercise of *t'ai chi ch'uan*. Today, however, was to be totally unlike any other.

On most, if not all, prior occasions, he would strive to achieve the desired objectives of *t'ai chi*: which, put at their simplest, was to bestow a harmonious interplay between opposing forces. The Yin exactly counterbalancing the Yang. As he came to the end of his familiar exercise routine his focus was not on joyous harmony, but complete discord. In four hours time he would take great pleasure in crushing the upstart financier, Sebastian Fortes, beneath his feet and, in one fell swoop, initiating the collapse of the western banking system. He had passed instructions to the Singapore Gold Exchange to artificially ramp up the price of bullion overnight to the utterly destructive $10,000 an ounce mark. No bank could survive that. If physical gold delivery was not to be their downfall then the associated derivative and futures markets would ensure they were doomed. His loyal supporters would hail him for what he was: the man who created a new Chinese dynasty, overflowing with wealth and power like never before in their history. He would delight in bringing the hero of the utterly humiliating Dark Pools debacle to his knees in a brutal display of power. The changes had been made, the game was about to be turned on its head.

★ ★ ★

The first light of dawn burst brightly into the room where Alex Cadbury had been working all night with a splitting headache, causing him to shade his eyes from the sunlight. His mind was buzzing with what he had found; if for no other reason that it was so readily identifiable and not concealed at all. Obviously she didn't have sufficient time to cover her tracks effectively? During the night he had been asked point blank by his colleagues in Langley whether Naylor had tampered with G2D. He assured them that she was the only possible suspect. Thankfully however, he had managed to fix the block of coding that had been changed and, with a little tweaking, put everything back to the original settings. It had been a mammoth, exhausting task and he was only half way through checking each line of the programme. He candidly reminded his associates in Washington that he could only make these reversals to his own computer. It would not be the slightest problem to revert Seb's iPad to the original configuration, but Naylor's could not be remotely changed without her immediately detecting it.

Now that they had formally concluded that she was indeed a spy, this presented Sanford with a serious dilemma: either he immediately placed her under detention – which would surely alert all her accomplices, whoever they were – or simply let the game play out without interference. Perhaps it was time for Lyn and Sapphire to earn their corn.

Sebastian's phone pinged with a text message from Alex asking him to turn on his machine for a couple of minutes while he downloaded some vital revisions.

"Bit curious this Lyn; I was told categorically not to switch the iPad on before my meeting with Chen, yet here is Alex asking me to do that very thing. Odd, don't you think?"

"Let me call Sanford and double check before you do anything. What time is it?"

"Hell's teeth it only 6.15; but on the bright side do you think we have time for a ..."

"General, it's Andrews here; Seb has just got a request from Alex which contradicts his previous statement not to turn on his computer – if you can recall his exact quote – 'under any circumstances'. Do you know anything about it? And should he do so....ah, I see, what an astounding turn of events...yes, I understand, switch it on Seb."

"Lyn, can you phone the front desk and make sure Naylor has not decided to check-out early: if she has, call me straight back. Then wake Sapphire and ask her to come over to the embassy as soon as possible."

* * *

New Scotland Yard can be a very intimidating place indeed; especially so when you have been brought there in the full glare of a frenzied press-pack who had been tipped-off that a very prominent person was about to be interviewed under caution. Amanda Price was apoplectic with rage at the public humiliation she was now enduring. She had absolutely no intention of taking this lying down; quite the opposite. If Charlie Sheer wanted to play dirty, she could, and would, fight fire with fire.

Just down the corridor in an equally dingy interview room, Cressida Armstrong was being formally charged under the Espionage Act for unlawfully obtaining and publishing classified information. Her distinguished Queens Council was arguing vociferously that the disclosures had been published in good faith and were, without question, in the public interest. There were no government secrets involved, merely the disclosure of deeply disturbing matters that went to the very top of the political establishment. The director of public prosecutions just sneered. This too was going to be a bloody fight to the death.

The TV crews waiting on Victoria Embankment were beside themselves with excitement following the PM's Commons statement. News had also reached them that the editor of The Sun, no less, was being held in police custody pending further investigations; whereas the chancellor, now jobless and homeless, would be free to leave, providing she surrendered her passport. At his specific insistence, Sir David Stone had stood surety for her and assured the authorities that the ex-chancellor would be staying with him and Lady Fiona until further notice. He had made his way to the police headquarters with his colleague Dominic Carrington and was now running the gauntlet of a chaotic media scrum, arm-in-arm with Amanda who was stumbling to the waiting car under the obligatory police blanket more frequently used by wayward pop stars and disgraced television personalities.

"David, if it's the last thing I ever do, I'm going to get that bastard. Rest assured he's toast. Thanks for picking me up and providing me with refuge until I can sort myself out. And thank you Dominic for so publically associating yourself with me. It means a lot. I've a lot to explain to you later in private."

"Well he's tried to shaft me before Amanda, so let's say I'm well and truly on your side. Both Dave and I have withdrawn our resignations and, whether you're in-post or not, we still have the gold crisis to deal with and Sterling is about to go over the precipice. If you could drop me off at my office, I'd be most grateful. By the way, did you have any communications with Seb or Lewis before you were unceremoniously dragged kicking and screaming out of Number 11?"

"Nothing from Seb, but Lewis has been trying to reach me. My phone was taken away for police analysis, so perhaps we can call him back when we get to your house David? And do you believe this stuff about John d'Abo?"

"It's quite incredible to be honest: a bit like Lord Lucan or Amelia Earhart turning up on your doorstep. There will be hell to pay when, and if, he returns."

* * *

Sapphire arrived at the embassy within twenty minutes with the news that Naylor was still in the hotel. She had slipped the desk clerk a couple of hundred dollars and asked that he call her if she decided to leave. There was a little over three hours before the meeting with Chen.

"Jim, what on earth is going on here? If Naylor is a Russian agent there is going to be a diplomatic explosion and very senior heads may well roll at the CIA for making such a blunder. Maybe that's what they want; sacrifice a pawn to win a king? China is one thing, but China and Russia simultaneously takes the crisis into another dimension altogether."

Sanford picked up the phone.

"Alex, can you swing by my office, we need to discuss something urgently."

It was only a matter of moments before the three of them were sat around the table.

"Alex, can we deploy G2D towards the Russians? Do we have sufficient time, even if it's only to produce a warning shot across their bows?"

"Of course General. I sometimes war-game a joint assault for my own amusement. Anything we direct at China we can replicate with Russia. Please be aware however, that I haven't discussed it with anyone, it hasn't been reviewed internally, or got any sort of approval from Carter. If you want to go with my

beta version, just let me know which sequencing you want and
'Roberto is your Uncle', as we chaps in the back office have
been known to say."

"Excellent, fire it up. I'll get your approval from the Director,
who may well be mightily relieved that his judgement call on
Naylor can be rectified. The next question is: when and how to
expose her?"

"May I suggest a double bluff, if that's the right term?
We deliberately don't expose her, yet. Let's get Ambassador
Coultard to drop a non-to-subtle hint to both countries that we
have detected something rather suspicious; get him to stir up
the pot a little. Let each embassy know that we suspect the other
is intent on causing cyber mayhem later today. By the time Seb
has pressed the button the two of them will be fighting like
ferrets in a sack."

"Alex, just tell me that you've covered up the tracks and we
can't be identified as the source of this malware?"

"You have my word on that General. As regards the meeting
between Chen and Seb, it's just a question of how our friend
leads the discussion of the gold crisis. I think my time is best
spent priming the Russian version; then briefing Seb on what
to say and do when he's with Chen."

★ ★ ★

Lewis Moyns could not believe what he had just been told:
Amanda Price had been fired and was facing exceptionally
serious charges. He had tried many times to call her, without
getting any response, so he was delighted to hear her voice.

"Amanda, good to hear from you. There will be plenty of
time to discuss this unfortunate set of circumstances later;
I did tell you he was evil. Business first, if that's OK with
you? I've just got off the phone with the head of GCHQ to
alert him to what will happen in Beijing during the Chen

meeting. Both our countries will be put on the highest level of alert to counter any retaliatory cyber attack, which we are expecting will be the reaction as events unfold during the gold discussions."

"David Stone here Lewis. I'm concerned that we have run out of options at the Bank. We are unlikely to have any reserves left by the end of the day and every bank here is pleading for emergency help. The ATMs will probably cease functioning over the weekend. Whatever you have concocted with Sebastian is truly our last chance. Any advice for the condemned man?"

"Just prepare yourself for a very bumpy ride. I'll be back to you in three hours after the Beijing meeting. Oh, by the way, my team tell me that the head of the Met is about to issue a statement of direct concern to you both. The police intend to bring Lord McMullan and Professor Carrington in for questioning; helping them with their enquiries, that sort of thing. It will be on the TV in about ten minutes."

Amanda and David stared at each other, completely horror struck.

"How in God's name do you know that?"

"Amanda, just assume I know everything. There's a hell of a lot more to come, believe me."

★ ★ ★

Alex had been driven the few miles across the city to the Rosewood Hotel where Lyn and Seb were staying and where the previous day, to his now everlasting shame, he had enjoyed the sensuous delights of Naylor. He just prayed, as he entered the lobby, that she wouldn't be there to surprise him; and debated what in God's name he would say if she was?

"Hi Lyn, I presume you've heard all about the events of the last few hours. I should also say that I'm sorry to have been taken in by her. I'm paying the price this morning with the hangover from hell and my career is probably shot to pieces! Is Seb up and about?"

"Yes, he's just dressing. Can I get you some coffee?"

"Much appreciated; extremely strong, thanks. Morning Seb. We have a great deal to discuss and not a lot of time to do it in. I think it's good if we go back to the beginning of all of this. Chen is after only one thing: to consolidate ultimate power in his hands. He has chosen the gold market as the means by which he can destabilise the West and reassert what he, and others around him, believe to be China's rightful position in the world. It has been decided by the grown-ups that we need to teach them a lesson they won't forget very easily or quickly."

Alex took a very long sip of his drink before continuing.

"To that end you're going into battle armed with your wits and your iPad. Chen is not a man for small talk, so he will hit you hard believing you have nothing whatsoever in response. To him, he holds all the cards. Remember, this is not a negotiation; it's an opportunity to publically demean you. We are also led to believe that the State TV station will be broadcasting the meeting live. I think it will be just the two of you, but if it's more don't worry, it will just add to the drama. Now, here is what you say and do."

CHAPTER 42

The People's Bank of China, Beijing

Sebastian strolled nonchalantly out of the hotel and into the back of the waiting car which was to take him across town to the momentous summit meeting at the central bank. He wondered whether he could pull it off, or whether it was more likely that the fate of the world was hanging by the slenderest of threads. Judging by the previous night's encounter with Banker Chen he had little doubt that old scores were about to be settled, deep wounds reopened and the seeds of future conflicts planted. Despite the obvious tension, he was feeling remarkably chipper given the circumstances. Lyn had given him the fondest of farewell kisses and, after removing his customary crimson red pocket handkerchief with the comment, "highly inappropriate colour darling", carefully rearranged a dark blue one to her liking. A contrite and sober Alex had simply said, "It's up to you now buddy, so for Christ's sake please don't screw up, I'm in enough trouble already. Just stick to the script."

There had been a stream of emails and texts from the great and the good wishing him well, but a notable absence of anything whatsoever from the prime minister. No one had bothered to inform Seb of the unfolding dramas in London, feeling, probably quite rightly, that he had enough to worry about. It was extremely unusual for him to carry a briefcase, they were no longer *de rigueur* in the City, but an appropriate one had been found at the embassy so he felt obliged to put the precious computer in it. Earlier he had made the obvious point to Alex that Chen would presumably burst out laughing when he endeavoured to initiate the computer sequencing, assured in his belief that nothing whatsoever would happen.

Naylor, having diligently completed her task, had presented Chen with the programming tools he needed to accomplish victory. He had secretly amassed the gold; patiently laid the trap in the bullion markets; and now he had disabled the enemy's technology. As far as he was concerned the tables would now be well and truly turned in his favour.

Just before he left, Seb had been assured by Alex that she had not undertaken a last minute sweep of the programme's contents and somehow discovered that he had reversed G2D to its original settings. Given her past track record of brilliance, acknowledged by all as being almost equal to his own, he felt this was a programming dual to the death. If, God forbid, she had outwitted them at the last possible moment, then what? "Buggered if I know?" was his stark conclusion.

On arrival, Seb was escorted up the formal entrance stairs where a red carpet had been laid in his honour, then along what seemed like miles of starkly decorated corridors, their footsteps echoing as they went. No one had the temerity to ask if they could check his briefcase: perhaps everyone knew they didn't need to.

After what seemed like an eternity, he at last approached the large double-doored entrance which was flanked by two members of staff in their obligatory communist-grey uniforms. An innate feeling of British superiority surged through his veins: 'Not quite the ornate lobby of the Bank of England', he thought, 'with its pink frock-coated doormen, more a desolate mausoleum'. If his briefing notes were to be believed, this was a cesspit of venality and corruption where the normal rules of fair play stopped abruptly the moment you entered the deputy governor's office. This was going to be quite an encounter.

He was astonished by the opulence that greeted him. The grandeur was undoubtedly intended to intimidate, as were the countless camera flashes from the State-controlled press that momentarily dazzled and disorientated him. When he regained his composure he realised he was faced with a line of what he assumed were central bank and finance ministry officials whose handshakes ranged from the effete to the suspiciously strong. A great deal was said to him as he slowly progressed along the row, not a word of which was understood. When he reached the end of the formal procession the highest ranking official beckoned him to pass through yet another set of doors. There, some twenty or thirty feet into the room, sat Chen. There was a single empty seat next to him, noticeably lower than Chen's. To both left and right, the camera crews were already filming his entrance. He couldn't help feeling that the entire population of China, some one and a half billion, were about to witness his demise. Chen was beaming as he stood up to greet his counterpart.

"Welcome to my bank, Mr. Fortes. It is always a pleasure to formally meet the man who so brutally humiliated my country over the Dark Pools affair. Please, take a seat, enjoy yourself; smile for the TV cameras and posterity."

"Humiliation, Mr. Chen, surely not? I believe it is you who should be profoundly thanking me. The valiant actions of my colleagues were instrumental in stopping the more reckless elements within China from initiating a catastrophe"…he paused for dramatic effect…"those who, let us not forget, were hell bent on destroying the world economy and plunging our respective countries into chaos. If, I may add, much like you are trying to do today."

Chen was in no mood to let such an inflammatory statement go unanswered, but, sticking to the script, Seb continued his opening salvo before he could reply.

"Would I be correct in thinking that some form of vengeance

319

is on the agenda at this meeting? I'm sure your leaders have no wish for you to repeat the same mistake; after all it has taken you nearly three years to recover from your country's previous ill judged adventure."

He stared directly and defiantly at Chen who looked like he was about to explode, before brazenly adding, "Do you mind if I check my notes?"

"By all means. I would have assumed that someone in your exalted position should have managed to memorise your arguments in advance, but if you must consult your beloved computer, please do. I fear that, in the circumstances, it will not be of much help to you."

"We shall see Mr. Chen, we shall see. Now, to the matter at hand. As you are fully aware, I am here to formally express the deeply held concerns that we at the Bank of England have about China's crude attempt to corner the gold market. We are determined to stop this debacle happening before there is irreversible damage to everyone involved, especially, if I may say so, to you personally."

Chen snapped his fingers and instructed some lackey to pour tea for them both, as Seb continued.

"Ignominy, personal dishonour, public disgrace…I could go on…they are such stark words don't you think? Not at all pleasant to be on the receiving end of their implied venom."

"If I were you I would proceed with great care, Mr. Fortes."

"Mr Chen, you should know that our security agencies are fully aware of the vast quantities of gold secretly held in this country, which remain undisclosed in the official statistics. It doesn't take a genius to figure out why you have chosen to deliberately hide this from the rest of the world. We have followed your attempt to corner the physical gold market with considerable interest. It is also crystal clear to us that you personally have orchestrated a deliberate attempt to bankrupt the world's bullion banks through the malicious use of forward contracts. We cannot, and will not, allow this to happen."

"I'm not sure you are in a position to do very much about it. With one snap of a finger I can demand that all these contracts are honoured and you, what is the strange phrase you English say, will be forced to 'cough-up' the gold. I fear you may choke on the attempt. You see Mr. Fortes you have no gold to give: we have it all."

"Indeed you do. If my information is correct, much of it has been smuggled from the West and surreptitiously transported through a variety of ports in China, where it mysteriously disappears. We've often wondered where it ends up? Perhaps, before we discuss that topic in more depth, I'm sure your fellow citizens would love to hear the explanation? And while we are cleaning the stables, perhaps you could explain to those watching that the head of your army, General Xiao, has defected to America, taking with him some closely guarded secrets. Deeply embarrassing personal secrets that many of those at the very top of your government would wish not to be disclosed."

★ ★ ★

The Premier of China was instantly seething with rage. He had not authorised the TV transmission of the meeting between Chen and Sebastian and was now watching the unfolding drama with increasing concern. None of his military staff had made him aware of Xiao's defection, only very sketchily and half-heartedly relaying a report that he had been found dead in the river. He took the matter no further.

Neither had anyone briefed him on what now appeared to be vast secret hordes of gold, despite there being many people in the inner coterie of the Premier's cabinet who knew all about it. Why should his colleagues be so open with him, especially given his fervent anti-corruption campaign; it was in none of their best interests to make such disclosures? All they cared about was having their fair share of the looted gold stashed away for a rainy day.

The Premier had a track record of making highly visible and vigorous attempts to stem the tide of official corruption when it suited his political purposes, typically to have a rival unceremoniously removed, but yet again he was faced with another highly public scandal playing out on national TV. It was abundantly clear to him that unless something was done very quickly, then a typhoon of devastating disclosures was about to engulf them all.

★ ★ ★

"I have no idea what you are talking about Mr. Fortes. But we are digressing from the subject in hand. It is my intention to restore our currency to its rightful dominant position, fully supported by an unprecedented amount of gold. We now have full control the world's bullion market. America is finished Mr. Fortes, the dollar is unsustainable and you all will rot in hell as far as I am concerned."

Chen beckoned a junior colleague over and whispered something in his ear.

"For my amusement I have asked for a television to be brought into the room so that you may see the demise of your banking system in real-time as I call in all the derivative positions. And by the way, I would be extremely careful what you press on your iPad; you may find that it fails to deliver the outcome you expect."

One of the largest screens Seb had ever seen was ceremoniously rolled in and placed directly in front of him, much to Chen's delight. If he had known the Premier was watching intently, his demeanour may have been radically different.

"Ah, good, please, let us relax and watch the show as I close out all our gold contracts. The Bank of England will be in ruins within the hour."

★ ★ ★

Sanford, Lyn and Sapphire, after a rapid exchange of opinions, had taken a collective decision to break into Naylor's suite in the hope of catching her red-handed during the meeting. Through their ear-pieces they could listen to the increasingly threatening exchanges between the two protagonists and assumed that either Naylor had secretly fled, or she would be in the room controlling her version of G2D.

It was effortless for Sapphire to obtain a spare key from the housekeeper and, guns drawn, they burst in.

"Great to see you Jim, ladies, care for a glass of champagne, there are some canapés on the table? Where's Alex, the poor darling had far too much to drink last night. We put on quite a show, don't you think. I hope he's feeling OK?"

"Naylor, we know what you are about to do, so I strongly counsel you to leave the iPad well alone. I will have no hesitation in putting a bullet between your eyes if I have to."

"No need for that Jim. Get Alex, I have something I need to get off my chest."

★ ★ ★

"Mr. Chen, I advise you in the strongest possible terms to immediately discontinue the irresponsible and calamitous path you are taking. I feel obligated to make clear to you that it is not in your best interests, nor that of your country."

"I think you will find that your pathetic, bourgeois, little computer toys will not come to your aid on this occasion."

The smirk on Chen's face slowly turned to malevolence.

With his customary gesture – the dismissive, theatrical, increasingly flamboyant wave of the hand that he expected to use frequently as the country's new leader – he virtually spat the next words out.

"My people have completely disabled it; if you press the G2D icon then, whatever you intended to inflict upon us will instead be metered out to the robber barons of Wall Street and London. The supremacy of the dollar is finally at an end; a new world order beckons. So, please, do proceed; it will make the occasion all that more memorable for my countrymen watching this on television."

With his heart pounding, Seb continued.

"If you are so confident in the outcome Mr. Chen, I would be delighted if you were to press the computer just here. But be warned, I did tell you it would end in tears."

★ ★ ★

Director Carter Meggs sat listening intently, staring wide-eyed as the TV images from China which were being beamed live into his war-room deep within the CIA's headquarters. He turned to one of his colleagues and whispered, "For a Brit, this guy has balls". Everyone present was hanging on the director's every word, at any moment expecting instructions to strike back at China. If ever there was a moment in world history when you would remember where you were, and what you were doing, then this was going to be it. Probably for the first time in his life, his mouth was dry and his pulse over 150. He was seconds away from calling the Oval Office should something go disastrously wrong with G2D and military action was forced upon them. The entire might of the United States military was on stand-by; every government computer team in the country had been put on red alert to try and foil whatever mayhem was coming down the pike in response.

★ ★ ★

"It will be my last act at the bank Mr. Fortes, before my destiny takes me soaring upwards and onwards to the highest office in the land.

"I can assure you of the former Mr. Chen. Be my guest."

With a self-assured smile for the cameras he reached over and placed his forefinger on the screen and pressed. For a moment the world seemed to stand still; absolutely nothing appeared to happen. Sebastian felt the collar of his shirt tighten and, with a gigantic surge of adrenalin, the fight-or-flight trigger began inexorably to tighten his testicles. The TV went momentarily blank and then switched to a split screen. On the left were the two bankers, both looking equally baffled and nonplussed about what would happen next? Slowly scrolling down the right hand side of the screen, in Mandarin, was a detailed list of every politician and member of the criminal fraternity who had received a delivery of the counterfeit gold bars. The softly-spoken female voiceover indicated that the list would be repeated every thirty minutes along with the addresses of all concerned. She reminded everyone who could access the internet that the roll-call of thieves and swindlers would shortly be available for posterity as a warning to those who place the world's economy in mortal jeopardy. It could have been a moralistic broadcast by the premier himself, except that he knew they would quite possibly have his name on the list somewhere, probably last and in bold capitals.

Chen looked on in horror. Following Alex's instructions to the tee, Seb merely said, "Proceed". G2D automatically went to the next level.

The screen went blank again, only to be filled moments later with images of gold bars, opulent country estates, bejewelled politician's wives and girlfriends, lavish state banquets and senior members of the Politburo waving with complete disdain at the subservient proletariat, dutifully watching whatever circus they had been forcibly summoned to. The next images were those never before shown on the country's TV: abject poverty; empty supermarket shelves; slum dwellings; brutal jails where enemies of the State were incarcerated. The contrast, while crude, could not have been starker.

The melodic, almost mesmerising, voiceover continued as if the viewer was watching a documentary.

"For many years now China has imported gold from the West, sometimes perfectly legally, but more often than not it has acquired bullion from sources whose provenance is highly dubious. This gold has been meticulously tracked by satellite using the most sophisticated and undetectable thin-film, microchip technology. The recipients were too engrossed in enhancing their own wealth to notice that this counterfeit gold is valueless, completely fake and a sham made of tungsten. What follows is a listing of every private vault where these bogus gold bars are held. And for those of you who are wondering in the financial markets of the world, that includes a significant quantity of China's official reserves; all worthless, a mirage, mere dust."

The world's bullion dealers, glued inexorably to their screen monitors, went into a tailspin. The price of gold started to collapse immediately as everyone realised the enormity of what they had just heard. China was no longer capable of going through with their threat. At the bottom of the TV screen was the real-time gold price, heading rapidly south, and the mischievous words: 'Mr. Premier, call me', with an English number and a smiley face. Within literally seconds Sebastian's mobile rang.

"Good of you to call...yes, I'm afraid it does indeed get a lot worse, especially if I allow it to continue into even more murky waters and disclose some very unsavoury peccadilloes of your fellow cabinet members. Of course all this can be stopped immediately providing you unequivocally agree that we will work together to stabilise the gold market....jolly good, that's excellent news, I'm very pleased to hear you agree that it would indeed be in our mutual best interest....No, I'm afraid I'm not in a position to personally verify 'good gold' from 'bad gold' in your vaults, but I'm sure I can get our technical chaps to help should you so wish...that's correct, all the gold listed on the TV screen as being secretly owned by politicians, triad gangs, and sundry corrupt officials is one hundred percent fake. Every ounce...how did they get this gold, very good question? I suggest you ask Mr. Chen, I told him not to proceed, but as is often heard in playgrounds, he started it."

The doors to the deputy governor's office dramatically burst open and armed guards poured in. Sebastian was convinced his time had come, but instead they marched over to arrest Chen and proceeded to drag him away kicking and screaming. Seb was so shocked by the outburst that he still had the phone to his ear.

"Sorry Mr. Premier, there's quite a kerfuffle going on here....ah, you initiated it...I see...Thanks; yes I'd be delighted to pop round for drinks and a chin-wag. See you later."

★ ★ ★

Carter Meggs sat there in open mouthed, stunned silence. "What in God's name did he just say to the Premier of China.... pop round for a bloody drink? What the hell's a chin-wag? Is this guy completely bloody crazy? And who the hell gave him clearance to disclose all this classified information?"

Some underling, whose career was about to come to a very abrupt end, had the audacity to say, "You did Sir".

"Get Sanford on the phone."

★ ★ ★

At Sanford's insistence, Alex positively sprinted from his room, hoping that he hadn't abandoned Seb to the vagaries of Chinese law enforcement and yet another serious duffing up. He almost fell head-first through the half-open door with his iPad in hand, his mind racing about whether it was best to shut the whole damn thing down, or move the G2D sequencing along to the more damaging military options. What he was confronted with simply amazed him.

It was as if he had arrived at the vicar's tea-party: tranquillity and calm were very much in evidence, were it not for three very intimidating firearms being pointed straight at Naylor's forehead.

"Alex, I'm truly sorry I had to lead you astray, but I needed to get to the truth of what was going on and establish that he had no other accomplices."

Naylor had fully expected Sanford's arrival. She also presumed he would attempt to drag her away in chains. Given the gravity of the situation, and ever conscious of her image, she had carefully selected a far more demure skirt and jacket, instead of her customary flamboyant outfits. One hand resting on her lap, the other cupping a half-consumed champagne flute, she blew Alex a kiss. Completely flustered and confused, he just said:

"What do you mean, 'he' and what 'other accomplices'? I don't understand a word you are saying."

"First rule of being a top field agent Alex; always follow the clues to the bitter end. I had no choice but to take a calculated risk that you didn't have enough time to run through every line of code in G2D; and I assumed that they wouldn't either. If you look around line 100,000, plus or minus, you'll see I introduced further coding that renders the earlier changes null and void. You were sleeping so soundly on the plane; I thought I'd take my chance when it presented itself. That section completely cancels the earlier alterations. I'm a little disappointed you didn't get that far, but then again neither did your colleagues at Langley. Maybe that's a valuable lesson: the good stuff always comes at the end. Second rule of being a good sleuth: when you have a humdinger of a crisis, expect the unexpected, especially from those up the chain of command."

Sanford sat there in complete bewilderment, his brain buzzing with the ramifications of what he had just heard, as his phone went. Despite the shrill tone, no one else moved a muscle.

"Sorry Director, but I'll have to call you back. Some crazy stuff is going down here with Naylor."

CHAPTER 43

Rosewood Hotel, Beijing

"If I may be allowed to continue my explanation General? I have a rather intriguing tale to tell you and your colleagues. Alex darling, could you refill my glass? Keep the bottle handy, I'm going to need a lot more when you've heard what I have to say."

Sanford's made a perfunctory nod of the head indicating that Sapphire and Lyn should put away their guns, while he removed Naylor's iPad from the coffee table.

"Possible evidence", was all he said; she didn't resist.

"Have you ever asked yourself how many people are aware of my role as – modesty forbids, but it's important you know – what Carter Meggs calls the foremost undercover agent at the CIA? Well, I can tell you, very few indeed. My existence is classified at 'Code-Word' level – the highest security clearance there is – so by inference, the carefully selected roles I engage in are most definitely on a need-to-know basis. And up until now, you all didn't need to know. I purposely chose to be a part of this assignment for one reason only; because it was the perfect vehicle to uncover a spy at the very top of the tree."

She took a large sip of her drink and, ever conscious of her image, straightened her skirt and crossed her legs.

"I should perhaps also make you aware that, on an as-needed basis, I also cooperate extensively with British Intelligence. I've had Mackenzie Gore, who some of you know very well indeed, helping me on this case file. He's recently retired from GCHQ,

330

so I requisitioned him to look over my shoulder for the past few months to allow me to demonstrate categorically that the spy was not you Alex."

They all sat in complete stunned silence. Even Sanford was totally unaware of her links to the Brits, let alone the level of her security clearance, which was way above his. With tiredness quickly creeping up on him, Alex had begun to sink deeper into the sofa, not knowing whether to feel he had been betrayed by Mac, or to be relieved that his friend had fully exonerated him.

"The perpetrator of this series of leaks has been passing low grade information to both Russia and China over the past eighteen months. An everyday occurrence you may well think. No real heart-stoppers or alarm bells; but insufficient Intel to pinpoint exactly who it was. More recently however, and far more disturbingly, these disclosures have specifically started to reference the modifications made to Nitro Zeus as it morphed into the G2D programme. As you may well be aware, our adversaries have been trying desperately to get their hands on a copy; or, failing that, to disable it."

A growing sense of concern filled the room as Naylor drew a deep breath before continuing.

"By process of elimination and investigation, I concluded that the culprit could be narrowed down to one of four men and a couple of women. There were some bit players which were quickly eliminate of course; there always are, despite their eminence. David Stone and Dominic Carrington were quickly ruled out. I could only see a massive downside for both of them: too damaging to their respective positions and just not cricket, as I'm sure either of them would have said at some point. The third suspect was far trickier. He's been under intense scrutiny ever since he married his new and very expensive trophy wife, the exceptionally beautiful Tatiana. The blindingly obvious clue may well be in the name and where her family originate from:

Sochi, in Russia. So, using the dictum, keep your friend close and your enemies closer, I immediately recruited Lewis into the CIA and started to drip feed him carefully selected information to see where it turned up.

Alex, I decided to take a calculated risk and made him privy to the less sensitive bits of G2D. He was my prime suspect for quite some time, on the basis that he's probably been nobbled by the Russians via his wife. It's taken me a long time to categorically eliminate him from the suspect list, but he's completely clean. Despite the odd blemish on his expense account, he's a dedicated patriot. I then switched tack and spent quite some time reassuring Lewis that we would escape from underneath the gold crisis thanks to your work Alex; I needed to instil in the head of the Federal Reserve the self confidence that all would be well, eventually."

"Thank Christ for that", muttered Alex, "It's inconceivable it could have been any of them. So, it must be Sebastian?"

If looks could kill, the cobra-like death-stare from Lyn would have effortlessly completed the task.

"Hell no Alex, how could you think such a thing? You need more sleep. And for the avoidance of doubt, it's not our beloved two-star General either."

The mood momentarily relaxed as everyone in the room waiting for what they presumed was the big reveal.

"Ever since John d'Abo mysteriously disappeared two years ago, we've noticed a trickle of sensitive economic data and, more recently, cyber-security material, being transmitted from the UK to Beijing. You probably don't recall the name Anne-Sophie Moreau? At first we thought she may have resurfaced and be up to no good again; she was Sir John's lover during the Dark Pools episode. We knew that he and Sheer chatted regularly, mostly about nonsense and domestic politics according to our listening team. She's frequently visiting Guadalupe to see d'Abo, who's still besotted with her.

I gather they were intending to get secretly married. I'm sure those plans have been shelved for a while, to say the least.

I digress; back to the main event: to say the transmission of this information has been conducted surreptitiously and spasmodically would be an understatement. The person responsible for these relatively innocuous leaks has escaped detection until very recently when the level of confidential material ratcheted up considerably. Given the unambiguous hand-print of the UK Treasury in a great deal of the disclosures, we focused our attention on Amanda Price, the chancellor. But, again, it is categorically not her, despite the finger of suspicion pointing clearly towards the Treasury and her irresponsible actions with the press leaks as she tries to get herself into Number 10."

She paused, having clearly regained both the confidence and respect of those in the room. Another drink was poured as she cleared her throat.

"If any of you had been in the UK in the past twenty four hours, you would have heard that d'Abo – rather than being long dead as everyone has presumed – is, as I've just mentioned, alive and about to return to London. Lyn, can you please let me carefully explain the background of all this to Seb when we meet with him later, it will undoubtedly be quite a shock. It's both a long story and the starting point in explaining what's been happening. Needless to say, we have been tracking these messages like a hawk, especially when the phrase 'G2D' started to occur. Lewis has hinted to all of you that he had a workable solution to the gold crisis, but he didn't disclose the 'what' or the 'precisely how' to anyone other than the prime minister. We thought we had a clear responsibility to share that information with our closest allies. Then, following the interrogation of General Xiao and some injudicious disclosures to the press, care-of Amanda, the penny finally dropped."

Again, she stopped temporarily, savouring the moment. 'Surely they have guessed by now', she thought.

"I went carefully back through our files and, as we all know, there is an incontrovertible link between Charlie Sheer, the mysterious disappearance of d'Abo to the Caribbean – which the CIA knew all about but decided to disregard on the basis of his past exemplary service – and a highly unsavoury concoction of sexual favours, deceit, fraud on a grand scale and the subsequent cover-up. The latter items are critical as they found their way, via Anna-Sophie, into the hands of the Chinese who have been relentlessly blackmailing Sheer ever since: not for money, but for influence. That's why he's been putting endless obstacles in everyone's way as the experts have been trying to figure out what was going on in the gold market. Anyway, this left me with an ethical dilemma: speak up immediately and expose the Prime Minister, or try to find their 'Mr Big' by interposing myself as a double agent. It didn't take long to identify the key mover and shaker: our nemesis Chen.

I decided it was time to get close to Chen as events were becoming more urgent by the day; needless to say, this proved effortless given his predilection for the ladies. All I had to do was persuade him that, with my invaluable assistance and insider knowledge, I could help him achieve his objectives. I surreptitiously arranged to meet him in Saudi Arabia and he fell for it, hook, line and sinker. It wouldn't surprise me if, when I eventually get home, I've got hundreds of utterly useless gold bars in the post as a thank you."

They all roared with laughter.

"So a plan was hatched with Lewis. I wrote the new coding, placed it into the G2D programme while you were asleep Alex, and let Chen know he now had a winning hand. Once I had showed him the specific programming changes – which needless to say he didn't understand or bother to get someone else to double check – he was convinced that all was secure and irreversible. Lewis made the educated guess, quite rightly as it turned out, that Chen wouldn't prematurely destroy the gold market before the meeting with Seb as unquestionably he not only wanted power but more importantly, he wanted revenge: at long last we had wrestled control back. The rest was pure theatre."

"Son of a God-damned gun." Sanford shook his head in disbelief. "It's always fraud or debauchery isn't it? No wonder Sheer's behaviour has been so erratic and distinctly churlish of late." He put his gun away and walked across the room to warmly shake her hand, "I've completely misjudged you Naylor; I owe you a big apology."

Alex, who moments earlier could have easily fallen asleep, leaped to his feet utterly reinvigorated and grabbed the champagne, "Absolutely brilliant, I suggest we refill our glasses and continue the party. Anyone care to dance?" Lyn playfully waved her fist at him; partly in jest, and partly to let him know that a fat-lip was heading his way at some point.

"I think we had better round up my better half; he's going to get one humdinger of a surprise when he hears all about this. Has anyone seen Reed, I need to give him back his gun? So, General, what do we do now?"

"I've got to have a long conversation with Langley. Carter Meggs has some serious explaining to do. You guys go ahead and I'll catch you all later."

Sapphire, who had stayed quiet throughout, simply said, "Let's just thank our lucky stars that Naylor's on our side Jim. I'll come with you and keep you company. Make sure there's still some champagne left for us."

★ ★ ★

Sebastian left the central bank in the US embassy limo, now flanked by police outriders courtesy of the premier, in high spirits and headed back to the hotel; the precious iPad still clutched tightly in his hand. The ramifications for the worlds gold markets of what he had just choreographed were gradually sinking in, although he remained completely oblivious to the knock-on effects within UK political circles. The jet-lag and fading adrenaline were now taking their toll, making him question how long he'd been away from London and immersed in this crazy bubble – which he felt had now surely popped. All he wanted was a long soak in the bath, preferably with Lyn; then get the very next flight home.

They had both been invited for a ceremonial drink at the premier's official residence within the Imperial City which, frankly, he didn't really feel was deserved or especially wanted, but if he refused it would undoubtedly be interpreted as a political snub and his girlfriend would be denied the opportunity to wear her exceedingly expensive ball gown. What possible harm could an hour do?

"Hi honey, I'm home; funny how I've always wanted to say that. Be a darling and pour me a drink and get your glad-rags on for a meeting with the head honcho. And do you know where Alex is, I need a word and give him back his precious computer."

He entered the room, put down his briefcase and surveyed the scene: the room was littered in bottles and the unexpected presence of Naylor and Alex, who were entwined on the makeshift dance floor.

"Glad you're both here. Looks like the debriefing has already started? Alex, my friend, you've cut yourself shaving? Ah, no, I think I recognise the symptoms: a 'blue-on-blue' fat lip I take it? What did you say or do to upset Lyn? No matter, save it for later. I need to tell you all about the meeting with Chen: truly epic, crazy, that stunt with the phone, pure genius. Has anyone checked what's happening in the gold market? We've about an hour before we are due at the drinks do, you guys tagging along?"

Alex disentangled himself from Naylor and turned off the music, "I believe Lyn's in the shower and getting changed. If you think your day has been a blockbuster wait till you hear about ours."

★ ★ ★

General Sanford was deeply engrossed in a heated conversation with the director of the CIA about whether Naylor should have been given so much latitude and allowed to roam willy-nilly without overarching supervision. Carter Meggs could only respond that she did her job, very unconventionally it must be admitted, but she got results. As far as he was concerned that was all that mattered.

"I take it her cover is now well and truly blown?"

"She's off the active duty register if that's what you mean General. But I'm assuming she'll now team up with Alex Cadbury and they'll focus on the next version of G2D. After the bloody tomfoolery with the US election I want to be able to kick the Ruskies where it hurts."

"Fine, I just want to make it clear that I'm not amused when I could have inadvertently killed one of our best agents, simply because I hadn't been told about her."

"Point taken. I think you'd better accompany Fortes on his outing to see the Chinese Premier; then get him out of town as soon as you can. I've got a private plane en-route to pick you all up and take you back to the UK. Although the immediate crisis with this gold business seems to have passed, there is still the political mess he will probably be called upon to clear up in London. By the way, I gather Chen's life expectancy is fast approaching zero. Your chum the Butler was sliced into a thousand pieces about an hour ago and put on public display by those triad leaders who had been duped; and from what we hear, the counterfeit gold is being rounded-up by the State and disposed off along with the scumbags who received it. Ambassador Coultard has just sent through a memorandum saying that he expects the Politburo may be about half its size tomorrow: he also cautions you that there are a lot of very angry Beijingers lurking in dark recesses of the back streets today."

"Understood, I gather the drinks event is to be kept short, so let's plan to leave here in say four or five hours. Is that feasible?"

"Should be. Keep in contact. Call me from the plane."

CHAPTER 44

London & Beijing

The VIP press lounge at Terminal 5, Heathrow, was packed to the gunnels in expectation of the imminent arrival of Sir John d'Abo from his enforced sojourn in the Caribbean. As was often the case on such drama-filled, highly-charged occasions, the timing of any statement was subject to the vagaries of flight delays and the weather. Tempers had already started to fray and unseemly squabbles were slowly breaking out among the TV crews jostling for prime position as the time ticked by and deadlines were being put under severe pressure.

When d'Abo eventually arrived, some two hours late, he looked tanned, fit and, as per usual, very elegantly attired in a cream silk suit. Without a shadow of a doubt he was indeed flesh and blood and not in the slightest bit dead.

On entering the room, he deeply regretted ever having the stupidity to agree to hold a press conference; but that was the arrangement he'd been forced to strike with the prime minister before he had departed. Visibly overwhelmed, a real 'cardiac infarction' could only be a matter of moments away, as he was clearly very shaken by the unsympathetic reception being given to him by the journalists.

The flight back to the UK was consumed by his pitiful attempt to concoct a plausible explanation for his three overwhelming errors of judgement. Why had he committed a blatant fraud against his country? Why had he agreed to simply vanish and become complicit in the fabricated burial of some unnamed soul in the grounds of the family estate? What exactly was the nature of his deeply worrying relationship with Charles Sheer? The latter would surely be the first question raised, for which the answers would be equally damaging for both parties.

His draft responses, appropriately scribbled on the back of a sick-bag, were threadbare at best and utterly implausible at worst. Amidst all the journalistic pushing and shoving that accompanied his move towards the podium, he concluded that he had no choice but to throw himself on their mercy.

He would plead that, at a critical juncture towards the end of the Dark Pools investigation, the balance of his mind was disturbed; very disturbed. Unendurable stress, lack of sleep and impending financial ruin had broken him. What he did was without a shadow of doubt wrong, but in his eyes it was understandable. He would leave Charlie Sheer to answer the more stinging questions. As he approached the plinth, festooned as normal on these occasions with a hundred microphones, he paused. Out of the corner of his eye he was inexorably drawn to the back of the room where a strikingly good looking woman stood, arm tightly folded. Emma Clark, the head of MI5, was there to witness the spectacle and, no doubt, subsequently report the details of the event to the PM. Before he had the opportunity to speak, she casually nodded her head and immediately two police officers approached d'Abo. He felt reassured that they must be there to protect him but, amidst the chaos and clamour, they instead proceeded to arrest him. Such was the din that no one heard the precise nature of the specific offence being made against him. What was certain however was that a handcuffed, completely humiliated, Sir John d'Abo would be splashed all over the front pages of every newspaper and TV bulletin for days to come.

Emma casually pulled her phone from her jacket pocket and phoned the PM.

"d'Abo's arrived and, as instructed, he was arrested before anything could be said. Just so that you are aware, the Director of Public Prosecutions is having a frightful wobbly; he thinks that we are forcing him to press charges that he will find very hard to make stick. I told him to man-up, or I'd squeeze his balls till his eyes watered. I got the impression he was rather looking forward to that."

"I'll lean on him Emma. I'm guessing that the press are now sufficiently distracted with d'Abo that all my stuff will be off the front pages for a while; just get him out of the way for a couple of days and then arrange to release him without charge."

★ ★ ★

Lewis Moyns couldn't stop smiling as he watched the utterly compelling coverage on CNN of the overnight events in China. He was completely elated with the way the central bank meeting had gone between Sebastian and Chen; especially the latter's arrest which was an unexpected, but welcome, bonus. There was little doubt in his mind that the world had managed to dodge the proverbial bullet, thanks to the brilliance of the CIA's cyber team and its delivery by the ever plucky Brit.

The capricious 'Gods of Market Stability' must have also heeded his heartfelt prayers because, at long last, gold prices were approaching their pre-crisis levels. Normality, of a sort, was returning. The downside however, was having to explain to the entire world how in heaven's name thousands of counterfeit gold bars had made it undetected into China; who had manufactured them; and which other hapless countries had them squirrelled away in their vaults? Many commentators, especially those clever chaps on the Wall Street Journal, were pointedly asking whether the US Federal Reserve was the culprit and had, as a last resort, turned to alchemy to redress the economic travails of the United States. Equally troublingly, the

Senate majority leader had just issued a statement letting it be known that Congress was intending to look afresh at an audit of the country's gold reserves; "Just to check everything was kosher". On hearing this, his smile evaporated immediately.

Undaunted, and increasingly enamoured of the English phrase, 'bollocks to them all', he'd spent the last hour trying to contact Seb but was having precious little success. Lewis concluded that the best course of action was to immediately hot-foot it to London and congratulate the team in person. Carter Meggs had made him aware of the dramas surrounding his CIA liaison officer, Naylor, and the search for the perpetrator of the leaks. He was astonished to learn that they had now identified that person as none other than the British prime minister. He'd been tasked with the responsibility of making sure the PM threw himself on his sword before more draconian measures were resorted to. He was to inform Sheer that a judiciously placed leak to the UK's financial press would soon seal his fate unless he complied, leaving the door open for Amanda Price to be fully vindicated in her actions. It would only be a matter of time before she was back in government, where she had always strived to be, running it; and forever endebted to the USA.

★ ★ ★

Oblivious to all this, Charlie Sheer was revelling in the ease with which he had outwitted the House of Commons. With the financial crisis seemingly under control, he began deliberating about who to knife in the back next: the turn of events presented him with the perfect opportunity for revenge and a wholesale clear-out of every dissenter, shirker, malcontent, and bone idle cabinet minister who was not willing to tow whatever line he insisted they tow.

A reshuffle was inevitable now that he needed a new chancellor and he was delighted that the arrest of d'Abo was playing so well on the news broadcasts. As anticipated, the focus had, for the time being, shifted away from his personal travails and squarely on to the ex-City financier. More or less all the UK papers led with the similar patriotic tag-lines: 'Iconic Banking Blaggard Brought Down to Earth'; all, that is, except The Sun.

Cressida Armstrong was well acquainted with the refrain, when the story teller becomes the story then it's time to quit; but she was having none of it. Quite the reverse, this was now to be a bitter fight to the death. During a brief magistrate's hearing earlier, her barrister had little difficulty persuading the judge to release her from police custody and place her on bail. It was now time to park her tanks on Sheer's lawn.

The editor had decided that the paper must come out fighting on all fronts simultaneously: she would publish the confidential memoranda, ostensibly given to her by Harvey McMullan, in full, pointing out the inconsistencies in Charlie Sheer's story; she would put up a vigorous defence of Amanda Price's defiant role in this debacle as the only true patriot left in the government; and she would take up the cudgel and have the prime minister exposed for the scheming, conniving bastard he really was. That day's edition was eviscerating in its condemnation of Sheer, but urged a more emollient stance be taken with John d'Abo: yes, he'd done a great deal which was wrong; but the country should remind itself of the enormous burdens he was carrying at the time and cut him some slack.

As was his usual *modus operandi* when confronted with yet another slew of bad press, the PM sought to deflect attention away from himself and on to others. He lashed out at the triumvirate of the chancellor, the governor and the chairman of the London Bullion Exchange for making a total hash of the gold crisis. With utter disregard to the *actualité*, as Alan Clark once so brilliantly described as 'being economical with the truth', he briefed that only his intervention at crucial meetings prevented catastrophe.

When this blatant lie was relayed to Lewis he decided to immediately act.

"Charlie, its Lewis here. Just heard the cock-and-bull story you've released. This has got to stop right now. I have been instructed to inform you that the CIA has irrefutable evidence that you have been leaking highly sensitive information to our friend Chen. We know all about every aspect of your involvement with John d'Abo. You of all people ought to know that it's the cover up which always causes the axe to fall on the high and mighty. You have to leave office today Charlie, without fail, otherwise all this becomes public tomorrow. Am I making myself crystal clear?"

"Do your damndest. I will fight you every inch of the way and win."

"On your own head be it Prime Minister; don't subsequently say I didn't warn you. Cressida Armstrong's going to run a stake through your heart tomorrow."

★ ★ ★

Despite the pungent smell of burnt fingers, Professor Dominic Carrington was equally elated that his beloved organisation had somehow survived, at least for the time being. He vowed to bring an end to the catastrophic practise of the bullion banks being so aggressively 'naked shorts', but he was not optimistic that such a stance would last beyond a month. At least he could say that he tried.

To the vast amusement of them both, over a decidedly liquid lunch to celebrate, Sir David Stone had presented him with a newly printed £10,000 note encased in plastic.

"Bit of a souvenir old boy, not legal tender of course but something for the grandchildren and the more unbelievable chapters of your memoirs. We used to call these tombstones in the old days: quite fitting don't you think? Can you get me one of those fake gold bars in return?"

"I gather your vaults at the Bank are stuffed to the gunnels with them Dave...or at least that's what Lewis seemed to imply."

"We've only found a couple of dozen so far and have asked the American's for our money back. Speaking of which, I've just got a very cryptic messages from him about Charlie Sheer. I gather Lewis is flying over to meet up with everyone. What do you make of this text?"

Dominic put on his glasses and peered at the Governor's phone.

"I didn't realise this model was still in circulation, don't they give you new one's at the Bank?"

The message was, if nothing else, Texan in its bluntness.

'Thanks for supporting Amanda. Charlie Sheer's reign coming to an end: US Government to issue 'misfeasance in public office' charges over leaked security information. Details when we meet.'

"Seems somewhat at odds with our beloved PM's public posturing about his omnipotence wouldn't you say? I'd have thought he's firmly glued himself to his seat and become unbudgeable? I don't know about you Dave but I can't quite keep pace with all these twists and turns. Perhaps we should call it a day after all; leave the field open to someone like young Fortes?"

★ ★ ★

"Seb, its Sanford here. Just wanted to run through tonight's arrangements with the Chinese Premier and bring you up-to-date with a few things that have happened which you've possible not been made aware of?"

"Pleasure General, we should be ready to leave in say twenty minutes, if that works?"

"Perfect. The embassy has kindly laid on a couple of cars

for us. I've asked Reed to ride shotgun, or should that be gooseberry, with you and Lyn, assuming he can get his hands on a black tie outfit in time. Sapphire and I will take the second car; we've loads to catch up on before she leaves. You and I have a hell of a lot to talk about, but I doubt that a formal reception in your honour is the appropriate place to chat. So I suggest we put aside a couple of hours on the plane back to the UK. The air force pilots taking us home have filed a flight plan to depart at midnight."

"Not a problem; we are packed and ready for departure here. Any idea where Alex has got to, Lyn wants to apologise for the lip incident?"

"That's a long and convoluted two-bottle story for the homeward trip. He left a cryptic note saying, 'Let Seb know that I'll call him from the dizzy heights of La Paz', where apparently he is flying to as we speak, and I quote: 'tell him I'm going to discover the exotic delights of Cholita Wrestling with Naylor'. Not got the slightest idea what that is Seb, some Bolivian mating ritual I expect? Anyway, once again she has just evaporated into the ether, taking Alex with her. So, see you downstairs in fifteen."

Sebastian was captivated by the stunningly attractive evening dress Lyn had selected.

"You really do suit pink."

"Fuchsia darling, magenta at a push. Do you like the split skirt? Not too revealing I trust? I'm going to weep buckets when I have to hand over the CIA credit card. If we scarper, how long do you think it will be before they catch us?"

"Sapphire knows every upmarket boutique in town, so I'd give you an hours' head start before their plastic is back in safe keeping. Shall we go? I like the necklace by the way, *muy elegante, cariño.*"

The two cars were drawn up outside the Rosewood Hotel, the larger limo at the front proudly displaying the stars and stripes and the union jack on the front wings. With a mock curtsey, Reed slowly genuflected as he held the door open for them to enter and took his seat in the front next to the embassy driver, yet another courtesy of the CIA.

"An honour to be of service; sir, madam! No need to tip. I'll close the interconnecting glass so that you two love birds can amuse yourselves on the journey over. The traffic is very bad tonight apparently. Your TV debut has stirred up a hell of a lot of discontent across the whole spectrum of Beijing society. I gather that the Premier doesn't know whether to give you a large medal, counterfeit gold presumably, or run you out of town? The cocktail cabinet is fully stocked, should you wish to partake. Ah good, I can see that General Sanford and Sapphire have got into the other car. Shall we venture forth milord?"

"I think we ought to make our escape plans Lyn; head off into the sunset hand-in-hand and all that. I'll be forty in November; then it's all over. I thought thirty was bad, but hells teeth, the big four o."

The interconnecting glass window slid open once more.

"Sorry to interrupt Seb, I forgot to tell you that the ambassador suggested we go via the scenic route and show you one of the most famous Hutongs in the city; a last chance to immerse yourself in a little local culture before you go. If you've never come across them before, well they are delightful old buildings, narrow streets and alleys, mostly around Tiananmen Square. He especially wanted you to see Xijiaomin Xiang, which is world famous for being the epicentre of Beijing's financial sector and the location of the Daqing Bank, which – as I'm sure you are all too well aware – went on to become the Central Bank of China in 1912. He thought it might be a good talking point this evening if it all gets boring."

"Thanks Reed, we'll let you know by second class post if you've got the tour guide's position."

Sebastian held Lyn's hand in contemplative, contented

silence as they approached the western quadrant of the Square.

"Being serious for just a moment Lyn darling, when we get back to London would you do me the great honour of being my wi...."

The explosion hurled the car five feet in the air. Sanford screamed at his driver to stop. He leapt out and shot the man who had thrown the bomb, hurling him backwards with the ferocity of the bullets impact. Another man, not twenty feet away was rushing towards him with what was clearly a suicide vest and a pistol of some sort. Sapphire downed him before he could get one step closer. They both rushed to the upturned car in a valiant attempt to extricate their friends from the tangled wreckage. The acrid smell of leaking petrol merely adding to their frantic efforts at rescue.

★ ★ ★

The official coroner's report, when it eventually emerged some three months later, was stark in its main conclusion: it was deemed a mistake of tragic proportions to drive through the centre of Beijing on such a violently charged evening without a police escort. The coroner bluntly stated that: 'it would be blindingly obvious to anyone intent on mayhem precisely who the occupants of the car were; especially as the official ceremony had been made public knowledge'. There were more than enough people in the city, indeed the country, who had a private score to settle with Sebastian Fortes. Vast fortunes had been lost, positions of influence destroyed, and political careers left in ruins. It went on to state that, deeply regrettably, the display of UK and US flags on the official car had been the equivalent of a red rag to a bull in the circumstances that prevailed and were a major contributing factor to the loss of life. Sanford, contemplating his own mortality, left the Coroner's Court greyer, wiser and sadder.

He got into the waiting car where Sapphire put a flower in the button hole of his morning suit. His mood lifted immediately. Life did indeed begin at forty.

Dark Pools is a gripping novel revolving around the audacious attempt by China to completely annihilate the US dollar – literally in the blink of an eye, using ultra sophisticated computing power – and replace it overnight with the Chinese renminbi as the new world currency. Their provocative actions are deliberately choreographed to coincide with a riot-torn crisis in Hong Kong involving the Pro-Democracy movement, and the covert construction of a highly confrontational military airstrip in the South China Seas. The narrative rapidly criss-crosses the globe over a 22-day period in August until the plot nears its dénouement: when the Chinese intend to strike at the very heart of the foreign exchange market. Dark Pools weaves together the worlds of international banking and high finance; numerous covert intelligence agencies; computer hackers and cyber criminals; political intrigue; and the awesome firepower of a US aircraft carrier task force. If China succeeds in its ambitious scheme, they will utterly devastate the dollar and bring America, and indeed the rest of the world, to its knees. A rebel group within the Politburo are intent on making China the only superpower left standing when Armageddon strikes: can they be stopped in time?

Dark Pools is a geo-political, fast-moving, financial thriller, sweeping across London, New York, Hong Kong, Macau and Guangzhou. It will appeal to fans of speculative fiction, particularly those who are interested in contemporary issues such as cyber crime and currency wars.

A SELECTION OF COMMENTS ON 'DARK POOLS'

* A rattling good yarn, as we say in the cliché trade. Very prescient of you to choose China and the Spratley Islands as the central theme; the wily Chinese launching a cyber war on the American banking system is very much of the moment.

* Addictive from the first page -- put it down if you dare! This highly contemporary novel is fast-moving, racy and very, very thrilling. Absolutely a must-read for anyone wanting to have an insight into the edgy world of high finance and modern-day international political intrigue.

* A fantastic debut novel -- thrilling from start to finish. An amazing storyline about events in China and how they are covertly planning to wipe out the US dollar, take over the South China Sea and destroy the pro-democracy movement in Hong Kong. Very, very enjoyable.

* A really thrilling read, couldn't put it down. Great pace and excitement. The Hong Kong scenes were very well done and very true for someone who has lived and spent many years there. I even know Tung Choi Street very well – I used to buy my goldfish there!!

* Finished your book and enjoyed it very much indeed. The story rattled along and I have to confess that I stayed up far too late one night to finish it. I did enjoy the book and marvelled at how much work and research had gone into it. Well done.

* I really enjoyed your first publication Brian. Seb certainly had a fantastic time, I am surprised he had strength left to do any work!! Took me back to the times that I travelled the Far East.

* I'm not usually a thriller/espionage reader and it took me a while to 'settle' into the story. Once there I found that Brian Terry had intrigued me enough that I had to find out how the story unfolded, which of course is the aim of any storyteller.

* Just finished your book and really enjoyed it. Lovely bits in it, particularly your masterful way of executing English phrasing! Very funny.

* Really like what you have written Brian and will look forward to the next book. You did a lot of research that is for sure. I really like the way it flows. Keep up the good work and let everyone know when the next one is ready to download

* Just finished Dark Pools -- bloody brilliant

* I don't normal correspond with the author of a book. Finished Dark Pools last week and thoroughly enjoyed. What I really liked was how you wrapped up all the characters in the last chapter. Many authors seem

to cut their stories off and the characters sort of just disappear and the reader is left not knowing what happened to the personnel involved in the story. A great book, a wonderful story and a terrific author. Let me know when the next one is on the bookshelves.

★ Finally got round to reading Dark Pools and I have to tell you it was very good – indeed, great job – and just loved the solution!! Already looking forward to the next one!

★ Read your book today. Bravo!!!! Really enjoyed it. You could be the financial Wilbur Smith.

★ My husband has just read your novel! When he enjoys a book I can't get a word out of him. He read it in two days and loved it! So peace and quiet for me! Can't wait for the next one!

★ Well I am somewhat breathless after romping through Dark Pools! A gripping tale I have to say.

★ Dark Pools – what an excellent tale – I could never have put all those strings together and added the twists and turns. How did you manage all that military research?

★ The book is screaming 'I am a film' It really is fast paced and so many current elements. Such a labour of love. Hope the second book is as much fun.

★ A cracking book – could not put it down. Fabulous holiday read which moves along at a tremendous pace with lots of twists and turns.

★ It took me a little while to pick up your book, Dark Pools, but having done so it was very difficult to put it down! It is a gripping tale and just at the edge of plausibility – well researched right down to the view from the ladies' bathroom on the top of the Hong Kong Peninsula … It is indeed a splendid view!!

★ I've just finished Dark Pools. I felt like you wrote the book for me. Every other reference and/or plot twist had me recalling personal memories from Hong Kong including the Ladies Recreational Club where we were members. Fabulous read.

★ Just finishing reading your utterly compelling creation. Congrats! You demonstrated well your knowledge of inside working of the City & Wall Street, and details of Hong Kong.

★ A quick thank you writing Dark Pools – hats off Brian. Such a thrilling read. A world I knew nothing about before a few days ago but such an immersive plot: informative as well as engaging. Just what our summer holiday needed! It would make a gripping film actually.

★ Looking forward to the sequel at some point…I'm going to buy a copy for my father-in-law's Christmas present. It's exactly the kind of fiction he enjoys. Brilliant read Brian – well done!

★ If any of you lovely people are looking for an exciting new book to read –

I really recommend Dark Pools! I read it while on holiday and it had me hooked from start to finish! – This book would make such a great film. Go buy your copy now!

★ I just finished reading Dark Pools, well done! Excellent, rip-roaring read.

★ Loved it, everyone must read it. You are a genius, can't wait for the next book.

★ I've just finished reading Dark Pools and am moved to write to you about how much I have enjoyed it. It's a thrilling read and also alarmingly appropriate for our present world situation. How could you get so close to the mark? Truly astonishing! I am so impressed by the width and breath of your knowledge on the interplay of political figures with international banks, all forms of economic institutions and movements and your understanding of cyber wars and the like. My respect for international bankers now rivals my distrust of them!

★ Enjoyed the book. It's definitely a page turner; excellent first effort at a financial thriller.

★ One of the best books I've had the pleasure of reading. Can't wait to get my hands on a copy of Gold 2 Dust.